Yet Another
General

ROB MCLAREN

Yet Another General

Rob McLaren

This edition was published in 2022.
Lulu Publishing — www.lulu.com
Copyright © 2017 Dylan Trust

Robert McLaren asserts the moral right
to be identified as the author of this work.

A CiP record for this book is available from the National Library
of Australia and the State Library of Queensland.

Text and illustration copyright © 2020 Rob McLaren
Graphic design, typesetting and map illustrations by Matthew Lin
www.matthewlin.com.au

Paperback   ISBN 978-0-6484-716-8-4
E-book   ISBN 978-0-6484-716-7-7

Typeset in Bembo Semi-bold 12 pt

Not Another General
Acknowledgements

I sincerely thank the following people who generously enabled the creation of this book:

Brent Oman	Keith Rocco
Brett Reeves	Lauren Elise Daniels
Brian Robinette	Martin Boycott-Brown
Christopher Kelly	Mathieu Degryse
David Matthews	Matthew Lin
David Maxwell	Michael Hunzel
Dominic Pölt	Peter Cross
Eva Servais	Philip Koschak
Gail Cartwright	Richard Marsden
Geneve Flynn	Ross O'Dell
Graeme Hopgood	Sherry Mock
Greg Bardwell	Souella and Keith Walker
Irwing Nieto	Steven M. Smith
José de Andrade	Victor Eiser
Karl Schlobohm	

Not Another General
Maps

Not Another General
Appendices

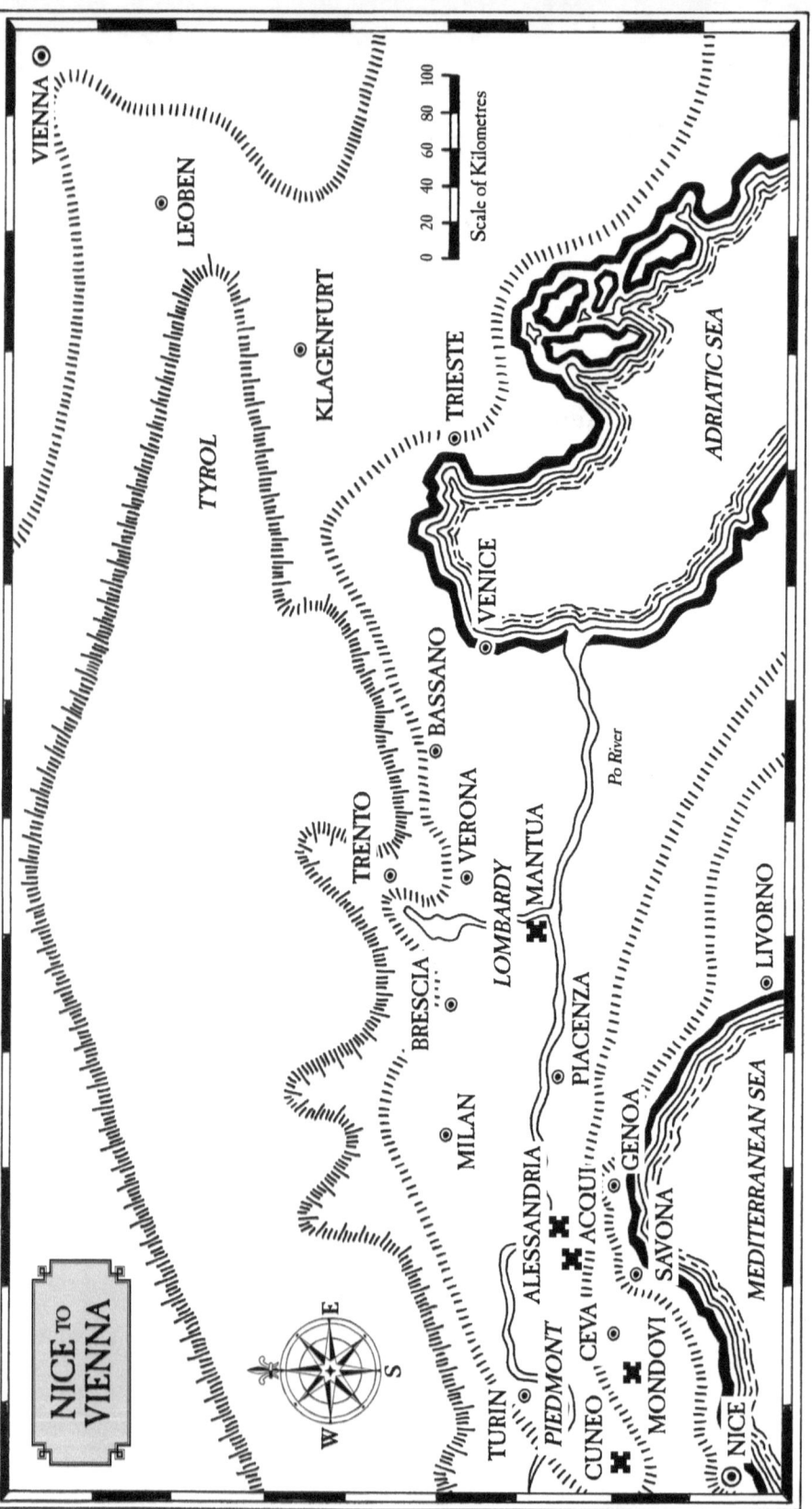

NICE TO VIENNA

VIENNA

LEOBEN

KLAGENFURT

TYROL

TRIESTE

TRENTO

BASSANO

VENICE

VERONA

ADRIATIC SEA

BRESCIA

LOMBARDY

MANTUA

MILAN

Po River

PIACENZA

ALESSANDRIA

ACQUI

GENOA

PIEDMONT

CEVA

SAVONA

LIVORNO

TURIN

CUNEO

MONDOVI

MEDITERRANEAN SEA

NICE

Scale of Kilometres

0 20 40 60 80 100

Prologue
November 1796, Caldiero, Italy

Blood poured from the wounded man's mouth, as Major André Jobert slipped in the mud to lift him. *Not you*, thought Jobert. *Not today.*

'He is too heavy,' yelled Jobert above the din of battle and the pelting rain. He staggered to raise their combined weight to his knees. 'He is waterlogged. Pull us out of here.'

Two riders pressed their horses in beside him.

Jobert put his right arm through his friend's cartridge belt and under his armpit. With his arms hugging around the wounded man's body, Jobert gripped the offside stirrup on his left. The rider reached down and grabbed Jobert's cross belts.

Jobert's left hand grasped the other rider's offered stirrup. The rider forced his gloved fingers deep within the wounded man's collar to lift his weight.

Jobert thrust his chin clear of the lolling man's neck. 'Take us away.'

The warhorses scrambled in the slippery mud. The shared weight of Jobert and his groaning burden pulled the horses together, causing the horses' shoulders to rub as they cantered. Crushed by the two heaving horses, Jobert was dragged on his knees, the wounded man limp beneath him. Jobert's splayed legs were struck hard by pounding hooves.

Through his forearms burning with the strain, Jobert could feel soggy heat oozing from the stab wound in the man's back. Despite his neck jerking at each arduous stride, the man's glazed eyes never left Jobert.

'I have you.' Jobert grunted to make himself heard above hooves thudding about him, the rhythmic growls of the labouring horses and the warning cries of their riders. 'Your wound is not deep. You will make it.'

Jobert was smacked around the head and shoulders, on his left, by one rider's musketoon, and on his right, by the other's scabbard. Jobert's grip on their stirrup leathers caused the rider's spurs to dig into Jobert's elbows. The two loose blades, his own and the wounded man's, jerking from wrists, sliced at his thighs and ribs. Jobert screamed as he willed himself to hang on.

At the top of the ridge, Jobert released the stirrups. They collapsed in the mud. The wounded man wheezed a spout of hot blood into Jobert's face. *Stay with me, brother, I need you.* In frustration, Jobert tugged to remove the slippery sword knots on his wrists and his sodden leather gloves, before flipping the wounded man over. Jobert wiped grass, mud and blood from his pale skin.

The soldier's eyes searched Jobert's face. His jaw and lips quivered as he bit at unformed words.

Chapter One
April 1796, Savona, Italy

Seven months earlier, no visible sunset marked the end of the day for the occupants of the port of Savona.

Blasts of an onshore wind whipped the rumps of thick, low clouds across the harbour before climbing the foothills of the Mediterranean Alps behind the city. Channels of yellow water coursed down the forested slopes, where the trees had been reduced to denuded stumps, the last of their branches hacked for winter's firewood.

The town cringed as sharp autumn rain lashed crumbling stone walls and broken tiled rooves. Icy drops spat through shattered windows.

In the putrid mud of the streets below, axles screeched and slab-sided horses, in either harness or under saddle, plodded. Skeletal dogs dashed amongst the hooves, intent on snatching a gulp of fresh horse manure. Wrapped in capes and coats, scarves and oilskins, columns of grey soldiers sloshed through churned slop.

As the dull light faded, bedraggled women hawked pitiful

rough-milled cakes to the hungry troops or begged alms from mounted couriers. Waifs, hoping for a small coin, scampered to either deliver messages or fetch mugs of straw-tea for men squatting in alcoves chewing on unlit pipestems. Children, with parched seaweed or dried cowpats piled high on their heads as fuel for evening fires, slipped barefoot through ruptured door-frames to relinquish their burdens and complete their efforts for the day.

It was how Raive manipulated the poker as he stoked the fire that irritated Colonel Spiccard the most. Raive caressed the hearth's base of glowing coals. Flames throbbed in response. Raive stacked the split logs with deft leverage. Embers winked sharp orange. Wafting flames slid to ignite neighbouring blocks with a puff.

Colonel Raive settled back into his upholstered armchair and brushed his moustache with the back of his finger. 'My thanks, dear sir, for the regiment assisting our friend across the frontier.'

Spiccard snorted. 'Do you trust Inoubli?'

'I value results above trust,' said Raive. 'Inoubli performed well for us prior to Savona. I look forward to the dividends from Turin.'

'Then there is confidence we will invade Piedmont?' asked Spiccard. 'Gossip is of nothing else.'

'Talk is cheap.' Raive shrugged. 'Paris must appoint our new commander before we march or stand firm.' Raive poured a rich amber liqueur into crystal tumblers. 'Here, you will enjoy this.' Raive passed across the glass. 'A toast … the 24th Chasseurs.'

'The regiment.' Spiccard raised his glass and savoured the sip. 'Another delicacy from Jobert's devious little wagons?'

'I find Jobert's family a reliable conduit of Masséna's favourite gourmet items.'

Spiccard shifted in his seat. 'How fares our illustrious Masséna?' asked Spiccard. 'Everyone is expecting him to assume command of the army. I hope your efforts on his staff these past years are rewarded with your own advancement to army headquarters?' Spiccard raised his glass.

'You are too kind, sir,' said Raive, 'but we await the arrival of the government's direction.'

'Then from your divisional perspective,' asked Spiccard, 'what are your views of the 24th Chasseurs?'

'It has certainly changed since I was with the regiment, but your second-in-command submits his reports promptly enough. Which chiefs of squadron wait in the wings? Fergnes and Jobert? I remember Fergnes as a sound company commander.'

'Fergnes is a reliable sort,' said Spiccard. 'I based him here to supervise Depot Company and our rearward escorts.'

Raive smiled. 'While establishing his household, much to Jobert's annoyance, I am sure. Damn, Fergnes' bride is a fine woman.'

'Yes, a clever match,' said Spiccard. 'Her father has done quite well in the metal trade.'

'And Jobert?' asked Raive. 'Enduring the privations of the divisional screen while Fergnes enjoys the pleasures of Nice.'

'Ah, your favourite.' Spiccard sneered. 'Did he not save your arse at Jemappes?

'Indeed, he did.' Raive's eyes twinkled. 'Does Jobert displease you?'

'He certainly makes no effort to act as would be desired of his rank.'

'However so?' Raive cocked his head. 'Is he remiss in his duties?'

'Like all … you fellows from the royal army,' said Spiccard, 'he dots his i's and crosses his t's.' Accepting the compliment, Raive bowed his head. 'It is his temperament in the field I deplore. He lacks caution. I despair at the casualties he creates.'

'Surely, if you want results,' said Raive, 'you must accept casualties. I would venture Jobert has a keen eye for opportunity and a rare sense of timing. I have the impression his men respect his judgement.'

'Who?' Spiccard scoffed. 'More sergeants like Koschak or Bredieux—'

Raive frowned. 'More?'

'—or impressionable lieutenants?' continued Spiccard. 'I am dismayed by Jobert's recklessness these last two years. Ponte di Nava, Dego and twice at Savona. I shudder to consider what calamity will come of his ill-conceived judgements should we enter Piedmont.'

'Masséna described his satisfaction with Jobert's results at those affairs.' Raive sank back into his armchair. 'Do you not concede, dear Spiccard, that Jobert obtained considerable advantage with, to be fair, negligible casualties?'

'Hah! I will concede pure luck.' Spiccard glared at the fire. 'Once we cross the Maritime Alps, Jobert's luck will dissipate to the detriment of the men and the shame of the regiment.'

'Sergeant Major, we best return for dinner,' called Major André Jobert.

Jobert watched Squadron Sergeant Major Koschak across the abandoned meadow of brown weeds. Koschak schooled the dappled grey of Moench, Jobert's trumpeter. He put the nimble-footed mare over a broken stone wall before halting, spinning and leaping back over again.

No matter the weather, Jobert schooled his new bay gelding, Jaune, every second day. The rising four-year-old, arriving with Jobert's brother's hussar regiment at the beginning of March, now joined Jobert's other veteran warhorses, Rouge and Bleu.

Jobert halted Jaune beside a packhorse tethered to a dead plum tree. One-eyed Grenzer snuffled into Jaune's flank. A few months ago, in the heat of battle, Jobert deliberately flicked the tip of his sabre into an enemy's horse's eye allowing him to dispatch the rider. Now healed, Grenzer served as Jobert's packhorse. Jobert reached down and stroked Grenzer's ears, as Koschak trotted to join him.

'This fucking mirliton!' Koschak pressed his newly issued, cylindrical leather cap, wrapped in chasseur-green and dark-orange cloth, onto his forehead. 'I have enough to think about between my horse, the ground under foot, the enemy and the state of my musketoon without being conscious that my pissing cap is going to fall off.'

Doubling over his saddle bow, Koschak erupted in a bout of throaty coughing. He groaned as he spat a glob of yellow phlegm into the mud, wiping the spittle on his lips and the sweat on his brow with the back of his glove cuff. Koschak's hands trembled as they held the reins, his eyes dull, his face flushed and sweaty in the wind.

As Jobert drank from his flask, he nodded slowly and passed across the flask.

Koschak gargled a mouthful of water and then took another deeper swallow.

'And do not start me on the loss of our dolman jackets, sir.

It is all very well for the tails of my tailcoat to fall elegantly as I promenade down the fucking *Champs-Élysées* at a leisurely trot but shifting in the saddle to complete my sabre evolutions has my tails snagging under my arse.'

Jobert and Koschak walked their horses back to their regimental billets.

The area south of Savona was allocated as an assembly area for General Masséna's division, where the division's six infantry regiments quartered in the surrounding villages. With the port's coastal road now churned to freezing mud by the endless stream of wagons, Jobert and Koschak passed infantry battalions, seven hundred fusiliers strong, marching and forming to the beat of their drums in the ruts and puddles of unploughed fields.

They stopped to allow their horses some rare green pick and watched nearby teams of an artillery battery rehearse their gunnery drills.

Bending to rub his horse's outstretched neck as it munched the meagre shoots, Koschak wheezed. 'I am tired of my horses being hungry, of my soldiers being hungry. Despite our best efforts to boil water to wash, I am angry that my soldiers are ripped with contagion from the turds in the water and the vermin on our skin. I am tired of being hungry. I am tired of wearing rags, my blankets threadbare, holes in my boots, buttons I cannot replace, my drawers rotting off my skinny arse. But ever thankful the fucking army has given me a new hat that will not stay on my fucking head.'

Jobert nodded. Every few days, some particular frustration would spark one of Jobert's squadron staff to bemoan the difficulties of their present condition.

'Only two days north of here,' said Koschak, 'those fucking Austrian bastards with their magazines crammed with blankets and soap. Larders full of sausage and jam, cheese and butter. Lambs, geese and pigs, fat for the—'

Koschak gripped his pistol holsters before being bent double with a hacking cough. He pressed a thick, gloved thumb to a nostril discharging a viscous stream of snot. 'I feel like a chained beast. I am tired of stomping these poor bastard Italians into the filth just to stay ...' Closing his eyes to settle himself, Koschak's face twitched. 'Any news of who our new army commander is, sir?'

'There may well be an announcement at the salon this evening,' said Jobert.

'If this latest general has the balls to release us into Piedmont, I am going to tear those fucking kaiserliks' throats open,' said Koschak. 'Not just for me, but for our lads. I am going to strip the bastards of every thread of clothing, every piece of equipment, their rations, their purses, their horses, their wagons. Anything we can use. Anything we can sell. I am not going to stop.'

Koschak's feverish green eyes searched Jobert's face.

A humourless half-smile twisted a grey scar on Jobert's right cheek. 'I assume you will allow the kaiserliks to retain their hats, Sergeant Major?'

'My goodness, sir! With the Republic blessing me with such a resplendent headdress, sir, how could I not?'

The Savona salon was swollen with this evening's patrons, predominantly officers of France's Army of Italy.

Jobert turned from the bustling crowd in the popular bordello to his brother. 'Bonaparte has been confirmed as the new commander, has he? My trumpeter will collect handsomely. No one put money on Bonaparte. He is our fifth army commander in three years.'

Major Didier Jobert-Chauvel appraised his glass of wine with disdain. 'That does not bode well. You know him, I believe?'

'I met him briefly,' said Jobert. 'Escorted by a company from the 24th Chasseurs, Bonaparte oversaw a transfer of powder in mid-'93. We met now and then in our Mess. The whole business was interrupted by the uprisings in Marseille and Avignon. A canny fellow, he wrote a little piece of Jacobin prose at the time. Being quite chummy with our local deputies, his essay came to the attention of Robespierre no less.'

'The dictator himself, you say?'

'When the lot of us were drawn into the affair at Toulon, I found myself on one side of the harbour, while Bonaparte was doing well for himself on the other. The deputies made him brigadier-general once the enemy abandoned the port.'

Didier winced. 'Another one?' He regained his composure by smoothing back his elegant moustache with the back of his finger.

Jobert withdrew his legs as a waiter, with his arm's full of empty bottles, navigated around the salon's babbling crush. 'In '94, the 24th Chasseurs were transferred to the Army of Italy. Bonaparte was on the staff as the Chief of Artillery. As I was a lowly company commander and he a brigadier staff officer, we did not do coffee together as much as he and I hoped we might.'

'Tsk, what a shame. He is quite young I understand.'

'My age, maybe a little younger' said Jobert. 'Last year, he departed here, only to appear in the Paris news-sheets and Michelle's letters after he slaughtered some royalist rioters with artillery.'

'He saved the Directory's hide with all of that,' said Didier. 'The government is now indebted to him.'

'Then that is how he has emerged from obscurity to become a major-general. Enough of our latest general. Bonaparte will soon float off to wherever the next bright, sparkling bauble might be.'

Anger burst from a card table nearby. The brothers looked to the card players in their pipe-smoke haze.

'How is the farm?' Jobert emptied their bottle into Didier's glass. 'How is Uncle Yann? I have not had news from Michelle in Paris since October.'

Didier sneered at the liquid in his glass. 'Uncle is busy and well. The farm continues to churn out forty colts per year to the blessed artillery. The cartage business with the senior colt herd continues to be lucrative. Who is this Raive fellow with whom we have the contract? He pays most generously.'

'Raive is a divisional staff officer for Masséna, the Army of Italy's brightest star. Raive and I were brigaded together at Jemappes before we joined the 24th Chasseurs, where he served as the regimental second-in-command.'

'Ah, how cosy. But what does he carry? Wine in and furniture out?' asked Didier.

'As any good hussar officer constantly seeks any available reflective surface,' said Jobert, 'you may not have noticed our pitiful state of supply.'

'Piss off, little brother.'

Jobert sucked on a short, brown cigar. 'Raive stocks Masséna's larder. A general is ever entertaining guests of the division.'

'Yes, more to the point Masséna, or Raive, is carting furniture out of Italy.' Didier jabbed Jobert's calf-length riding boot with his own. 'Fascinating, no?'

'Masséna has a name for organising a little something extra on the side. Either cash or flesh. Heed me, brother, stay aware of the progress of Yann's wagons to maintain a supply of necessary items. Especially coin. Paper assignats are worthless here.'

'As they are throughout the Republic.'

Jobert tilted his head to blow the blue-grey cigar smoke towards the stained ceiling. 'Perhaps Raive has a racket looting furniture from abandoned villas on Masséna's behalf and selling into Paris' latest chic set. Michelle may know its destination.' Jobert waggled the empty wine bottle at a flustered waiter. 'Michelle? What of Michelle? Her last letter spoke of evenings, parties and friends.'

Didier's eyes followed two courtesans as they glided through the leering officers. 'With the end of the Terror last year, there has been a remarkable shift in how those that can afford it play together.'

'Did you get up to Paris?' asked Jobert.

'No, unfortunately. The scandalous Parisian standards had been all the gossip in Lyon and Grenoble before the 1st Hussars departed. Not surprisingly, Michelle's letters to Uncle Yann omit the scintillating details of her social life. Although, I can now impart that the recent contract of new mirliton caps has cleared Aunt Sophie's workhouses of debt. Have you been issued yours?'

Jobert squinted into the shadows under his chair, then held up his new, tapering, tubular regimental headdress. Didier pinched the near metre long, vaguely triangular 'flame' which could either wrap around the mirliton or drape across the horseman's shoulder.

'Is this dark-orange your regimental facing?'

'Capucine,' said Jobert.

'I beg your pardon?'

'The dark-orange colour is called capucine. Why do you ask?'

'We rode into Nice with another reinforcement regiment,' said Didier, 'the 22nd *Chasseurs à Cheval*, and they wore this facing colour as well.'

'Unlike hussar regiments who may wear whatever they

please,' said Jobert, 'groups of three chasseurs à cheval regiments are allocated the same facing colour. In this case, the 22nd Chasseurs will have capucine collars and cuffs, and the 24th Chasseurs have a capucine collar and green cuffs. Somewhere in the army, the 23rd Chasseurs have a green collar and capucine cuffs.'

'How fascinating. I am so pleased I asked,' said Didier.

'My apologies, did I begin to speak of something other than how pretty hussars look on parade?' asked Jobert.

'Be careful, dearest André. Your schoolboy jibes are building the argument for the removal of my regiment from the Army of Italy's order-of-battle. With your General Bonaparte bereft of the iron fist of the 1st Hussars, not only will he be denied his glory, but the Austrians will have the five remaining divisions at their mercy for all your vaunted capucine. Now with such a reprimand, will you promise to behave?'

'I would, on my honour, if only you could afford the next bottle.'

'Why ever can I not?' Didier considered his glass with distaste. 'Indeed, upon reflection on the last bottle, why ever would I?'

'One, because your hussar waistcoat is so tight you cannot push your manicured fingers into your pockets. Two, I see you have spent your last franc trimming your hussar's pelisse jacket with the eyebrows of a Patagonian orangutan, or some such.'

'I was going to make polite enquiry into your love life,' said Didier. 'With your juvenile comments, I sense a soul burdened by unreleased frustration.'

'Again,' said Jobert, 'how distracting reflective surfaces are for hussar officers. You have ridden three hundred kilometres from Nice. Had you not noticed the condition of the country, the troops and the people? Oh, forgive me, reconnaissance is a duty beneath the hussars.'

Didier searched the crowd. 'Let me order you a pretty harlot so you might be relieved of your current humours, and we might converse like adults.'

A sullen look settled on Jobert's face, as his eyes lingered on the hips of a passing woman. 'Before your doctor of love is summoned, if they are not toothless crones, the women of this country are all whores, forced by their families so they can eat, disgraced by rape, rarely by choice. It is a formidable woman who can navigate these towns and hold a drunken soldier's desires at bay. No, any eligible society ladies have either fled east into Lombardy with their families, are companions or governesses to a general's wife's retinue, or have remained as general's or deputies' courtesans.' Jobert waved his empty wine glass at the knots of officers in the noisy room. 'And circumstances here are difficult.'

'Do tell?' asked Didier.

'The reinforcements last autumn,' said Jobert, 'from the Pyrenees and the Rhine such as your regiment, have burdened us. Weight of numbers contaminate the mountain streams with contagion. The countryside is ravaged of forage and firewood. Supply here is shocking. Our focus is bread, brandy, grain and firewood.'

'Where does the solution lie?' asked Didier.

'To take the army over the mountains and feast on the bounty of Piedmont.'

'What is precluding that from happening?'

'Our endless parade of fucking useless army commanders,' said Jobert.

'And this latest one?' asked Didier. 'Bonaparte, the golden boy. More of the same? Will this army's tattered rags tarnish his rising star?'

Jobert shrugged as he looked around the crowded, smoky salon. 'Damn you and your talk of a pretty whore.'

Chapter Two

The relentless April rain drummed against the tiled roof and dribbled through the shutters. Although the regimental clerks, *aides de camp* and couriers spoke in hushed tones as they came and went, the thud of boot-heels and spurs reverberated throughout the farmhouse.

Chiefs of squadron Jobert and Fergnes shuffled into Colonel Spiccard's office gripping their scabbards to their thighs. Spiccard, the commanding officer of the 24th Chasseurs à Cheval, slouched in his high-backed chair behind his desk and contemplated his senior officers with wary eyes.

'The new commander's arrival this week has been quite dramatic,' said Spiccard. 'On the day of his arrival, General Bonaparte reviewed a parade in Nice where he promised his "heroes in rags" food and glory. That evening, he ordered us to invade Piedmont on the 15th of April. The Directory has declared "war must pay for war" and the army must bring France gold and grain. The Republic, having forced Prussia and Spain to terms last year, must now defeat Austria. Aside from the Chouan uprising on the Atlantic coast, the entire French army's single aim is to capture Vienna.'

Jobert slid his eyes towards Fergnes. Fergnes clenched his jaw.

'Generals Jourdan and Moreau are to launch two vast armies,' said Spiccard, 'both over seventy thousand strong, over the Rhine, down the Danube to Vienna. General Bonaparte's forty-five thousand strong Army of Italy is to divert Austrian reserves by attacking into the Sardinian province of Piedmont and threatening the Austrian province of Lombardy.'

No longer a backwater, thought Jobert.

'General Bonaparte's plan is simple,' said Spiccard. 'First, separate the Austrian army of Lombardy from the Piedmontese. Second, defeat the Piedmontese and capture Turin.'

'And where are we in this grand scheme, sir?' asked Fergnes.

'Although the hussars and the dragoons are brigaded centrally, General Masséna has retained the 24th Chasseurs under his command.' Spiccard's face soured as he turned to Fergnes. 'Bonaparte has claimed our regimental second-in-command as another aide. Our dear Clemusat obviously made an impression escorting Bonaparte's powder convoy and establishing his batteries at Toulon. I have the authority to promote you to second-in-command, Fergnes, should you care to take it up.'

Fergnes blinked as he straightened his posture. 'I am at your service, sir.'

'Fergnes, your post is now here in Savona,' said Spiccard. 'No more visits to your pretty wife in Nice for the foreseeable future. Of course, if that is agreeable with Marguerite?'

Jobert dropped his eyes, his lip twitching with envy.

'My wife will be well occupied with my baby son, sir,' said Fergnes. 'I have no doubt she will furnish me with a list of purchases while we sojourn in Turin. What is your first requirement, sir?'

Spiccard scowled. 'Preparing the regiment to lead General Masséna's division into Piedmont, of course.'

'Indeed, sir,' said Fergnes. 'Over the last two years, battle and fever have reduced us to six companies of seventy sabres. Are reinforcements worth considering?'

Spiccard shook his head. 'To increase each chasseur section by one extra man would require a regimental intake of fifty recruits. Have you two been hatching schemes again?'

Fergnes looked to Jobert.

'Sir,' said Jobert, 'fifty recruits are necessary even to maintain our current strength in the face of the upcoming operations. Surely we can afford one corporal and one wagon per company, led by a lieutenant and a sergeant-major, to return to Avignon? With our former commanding officer now established within Avignon's administration, local mayors and gendarmes could assist in the raising of a small *levée*.'

'The same formula could be applied for the fifty or sixty remounts required,' said Fergnes. 'We would have these new chasseurs being brought into the line by July. We could then turn the whole circus around and bring another fifty in before next winter.'

Spiccard's humourless eyes tightened. 'Sixty horses will easily cost sixty thousand francs. The regiment can only afford half that sum.'

'I have a feeling, sir,' said Jobert, 'that General Masséna's war chest might be full at the start of the campaign season. Perhaps a reasonable argument put to our Colonel Raive, on the General's staff, might tip a handsome purse our way?'

'I will consider it.' Spiccard rocked back in his chair and stared upward at the dust-laden cobwebs in the grimy, ancient beams of the low ceiling.

'I have the authority to promote Quillet to major to join Jobert as a chief of squadron,' said Spiccard. 'His promotion will cause a change to our company commanders. I have reflected on the experience of our captains, and these are my changes. Within 1st Squadron, I will bring Geourdai across to command 1st Company and Neilage into 4th Company. As for 2nd Squadron, Chabenac will take 2nd Company. He will never be promoted if he remains as an aide de camp. As for Voreille – absolved of his sins when he claimed the honour over that hussar last year – he will be given command of 5th Company. There will be no change to 3rd Squadron. This new manning will be effective as of tomorrow morning. Your initial thoughts as second-in-command, Fergnes?'

Fergnes raised his chin from his notebook. 'Bread and grain, sir. Bread and grain.'

Spiccard coughed a mocking laugh, before his gaze evaluated Jobert. 'As for you, Jobert, in light of Quillet's inexperience ...'

Jobert lifted his chin and took in a long breath to contain himself.

Spiccard's cheek curled into a sneer, then he dismissed his thoughts with a snort. 'Perhaps against my better judgement, I will entrust you with the more wide-ranging responsibilities. In the coming days, you can expect to work predominantly with 2nd Squadron.'

Jobert released his breath. 'I am at your service, sir.'

Jobert watched the six captain company commanders complete their lists in their notebooks. Their pencils dashed off Lieutenant Colonel Fergnes' requirements for the coming inspection parades. He looked over at the new captains of 1st Squadron, his friends Geourdai and Neilage. As the commander of the regiment's senior company, 1st Company, Geourdai made his own notes yet kept a weather-eye on Neilage's list. Having already commanded a company for a year, Neilage appeared unperturbed at the preparations demanded of him with his new 4th Company.

Jobert's attention turned to the officers of 2nd Squadron, Chabenac and Voreille.

Chabenac blinked with trepidation at assuming the reins of Jobert's old 2nd Company.

Jobert reflected Chabenac had not led soldiers for over two and a half years. *Should I send Koschak to assist him?*

Voreille's face was a study in concentration.

So determined to perform well. Jobert contemplated Voreille's duel with an enemy hussar between the lines a few months previously. In the courageous act of claiming the Austrian, Voreille redeemed an issue of poor judgement and regained the esteem of his senior officers.

Fergnes flipped the pages of his notebook. 'Colonel Spiccard and I will inspect 1st and 3rd Squadrons here in Savona. 2nd Squadron will be inspected on your return to screen duties at the Col di Cadibona by Major Jobert, the assistant surgeon and one of the sergeant veterinarians. I will then have, from your company seconds-in-command by tomorrow evening, a consolidated regimental return of deficiencies that will depart with 3rd Squadron convoy for Depot Company. Major Jobert, anything to add?'

'No, sir.' Jobert gave a conspiratorial wink to Geourdai, Neilage, Chabenac and Voreille. 'But might I have a word with the commanders of 1st and 2nd Squadron once dismissed?'

'Certainly,' said Fergnes. 'Are there any questions from the captains? No? Then, gentlemen, to your duties.'

As Fergnes and the 3rd Squadron officers departed, those remaining at the table relaxed in Jobert's company.

'Lads, what are your thoughts on our invasion of Piedmont?' asked Jobert.

Relaxed postures stiffened, eyes blinked, foreheads creased and faces lowered.

Neilage raised his pointed nose, his red moustache bristling. 'Better to be out there, sir, than rot here. Here we will die of contagion—or worse. I choose Piedmont over one of our hospitals.'

Geourdai rolled his head from side to side, his mouth tight. 'Our horses come first. At least, over there will be fresh water and green pick.'

Voreille's eyes narrowed as he crossed his arms. 'Maybe we will scrounge a little something here and there for ourselves?'

'You were at Valmy and Jemappes, sir,' said Chabenac, his mask of aristocratic nonchalance firm. 'Where do the true threats on campaign lie?'

All eyes upon Jobert tightened in focus.

'We will be given impossible tasks when we are exhausted.' Jobert braced his weight, his elbows upon the table. 'The kai-serliks will surprise us when they are fresh. If they do catch us, we may be butchered.' Jobert shrugged. 'But there is a worse outcome. To catch us chasseurs napping is to catch the entire army. What is a sabre cut or a ball in the belly when we risk the loss of our good name?'

'How then do we counter being surprised when we are spent, sir?' asked Chabenac.

'Vigilance,' said Jobert. 'Look to the wellbeing of your horses. Look to your men for the correct performance of their duties. Do these few things and we will stand at the end. We have endured much together in the past three years. This will be our greatest test. I have watched you closely, my friends. Fear not, for I see that you are ready.'

A burst of laughter erupted from Didier and Fergnes across the table, each trying to outdo each other with their escapades at card evenings. As Jobert watched Didier apply his considerable charms to his friend Fergnes, he reflected on his brother's ambition.

Beside him, Raive made a polite wave. Fergnes passed them the decanter.

'Fergnes will make a sound second-in-command,' said Raive. 'Colonel Spiccard speaks well of him.'

Jobert looked at Fergnes' laughing profile. 'For a fellow in-experienced in war prior to joining the regiment, he has proven incisive. I admire the depth of consideration he gives to issues.' Jobert smiled at Raive. 'Like a good brother, he tempers my rashness.'

'Rash? Huh!' said Raive. 'Your audacity, Jobert, I would say. Do not let more wary men stifle you with their emphasis on prudence.' Jobert frowned as Raive refilled his glass. 'Your brother is a charming fellow. He remarked on General Masséna's contract with your family, particularly on the return loads into France.'

Jobert sipped at his Nardini grappa. 'I imagine Didier hoped the general was satisfied with the service of our family and the state of goods on arrival.'

'You know General Masséna exports small items of well-crafted furniture to Paris? Of course, you do. He pays a fair price to the owners, thankfully received on these desperate shores.'

'For which, I hope, he receives a fair price for such efforts in Paris?' asked Jobert.

'For which your family receives a fair price for their own services,' said Raive. 'No?'

The door opened. Candle flames shuddered. Four chasseurs crowded into the small, smoky dining room.

Jobert leant back as a young soldier removed his empty plate. 'What is your view, sir, of the Austrian and Piedmontese armies?'

'First and foremost,' said Raive, 'Austria's strength will always be focused on her provinces along the Rhine, Bavaria, Baden, Württemberg, and so forth. The emperor's ministers will be keeping a close eye on our foremost generals, Hoche, Jourdan and Moreau. Their attention always on the least distance from Paris to Vienna.

'Second, should the Austrians consider the Maritime Alps at all, what must be their views of us as a threat? We are a small, half-starved, egregiously supplied army, hamstrung by a gaggle of commanders, the latest one a complete unknown. What is the likelihood of our rag-tag force breaking through their mountain defences, advancing down the plains of the River Po, extending our lines of communication while the Austrians shorten theirs? Could they imagine us securing the Adriatic coast essential for resupply? Or us blocking the passes of the eastern Tyrolean Alps vital for any defence of our conquest? The Austrian command probably expect that eventuality extremely unlikely.'

Jobert refilled Raive's glass. He watched Raive's face for any sign of discomfort with the impending operation, but Raive maintained his good humour. *Your merriment masks many secrets.*

As a red signal flare might start with a pop to cast a giddy light, so a memory of a naval bombardment on a blood-soaked beach swung across Jobert's vision. The carnage inflicted on 2nd Company eight months ago confirmed one secret of Raive's, that twin brothers, the Inoublis, were royalist spies. This secret nearly had Jobert and Voreille shot. Raive had played a role in averting that execution.

'And will the services of our friend, or friends, Inoubli be enlisted?' asked Jobert.

'With Anissa as our pretty bait, and with the support of our influential friends in Avignon, we carefully plucked the Inoubli brothers from their web. With our twin dance masters in hand, considerable persuasive power pressed them to aid the Republic's cause.'

'They are now in our pocket?' Jobert snorted. 'And Anissa's fate?'

'She has adapted well to a domestic arrangement.'

Jobert frowned. 'Anissa was not hanged?'

'No, she was not.' Raive savoured his liqueur and responded with a tilted bob of his balding head and a grim smile. 'Their efforts contributed to our success at Loano and the recapture of Savona five months ago. The Inoublis now ply their trade into Turin, planting seeds. We will observe the harvest in the coming weeks.'

Above the port of Savona, high on the Col di Cadibona, a strategic pass across the Maritime Alps, the tavern room was small and windowless, lit only by the cooking embers and a single candle on a folding table by the hearth. The mouth-watering aroma of herbs, onions and freshly baked bread was tinged with soap and smoke. Washing lines criss-crossed the room above the hearth. Drying laundry cast shadows on the five bedrolls and saddle portmanteaus stowed in the corner.

Jobert hung his number-two tailcoat, mirliton and sword belt on a peg in the wall, before sinking onto a spare camp stool. 'My word, something smells good, Orlande. Whatever is on the menu tonight?'

Orlande, Jobert's valet, swept his red hair off his forehead and pressed his spectacles back onto his nose. 'A veritable feast, sir. As part of the regimental resupply, we have been issued rice and flour. Young Tulloc has secured us a bag of fresh mussels. Tonight, sir, mussel and olive risotto with onions and beans, with a baked garlic and fetta baguette. Bouillon, sir?'

As Orlande passed Jobert a mug of herbed broth, Jobert's mouth filled with saliva. 'Your concoctions from meagre fare continue to impress, my friend. Bonaparte's investigation of the commissariat and the supply contractors is causing all manner of supplies to reach Savona. I feel a cup of armagnac is warranted in the circumstances. What say you, Orlande?'

'Just one bottle, sir.' Orlande withdrew small, fragrant bread rolls from a camp oven. 'I am saving the other bottle for your birthday. I have paid for some decent fish for tomorrow night, sir, and Madame Quandalle has acquired flour, eggs and raisins for a pudding. We will approach the remaining armagnac with economy, if you please?'

Jobert grinned across the table at Tulloc, his groom, a muscular young man who was cleaning the locks of Jobert's pistols. 'A bag of mussels, no less, Tulloc, well done. Did you and Trumpeter Moench attend the paymaster's parade today?'

'Yes, sir,' said Tulloc. 'Thanks to General Bonaparte, sir, we are only one month in arrears now. I am grateful, of course, sir, but it is only assignats, not coin.'

'Better that than naught, lad. Speaking of pay parades and Moench, what book is he running now?'

'The date General Bonaparte will enter Turin, sir.'

'We advance on the 15th of April,' said Jobert, 'and it is a five-day ride from here to Turin without encountering any enemy. Thus, our new general will not enter the capital before the 20th of April. Do not lose your money to Moench, lad.'

Tulloc's face creased with worry.

The sound of squelching boots and the clatter of scabbards on the buttons of over-breeches came from the tavern yard beyond the door.

His vision obscured by a drying shirt hanging from a laundry line, Jobert ducked his head. The door burst open. Huin, Spiccard's aide de camp, entered with Koschak and Moench close behind.

'Orlande, we have a guest for dinner,' said Jobert.

Huin blinked the eye not covered by his eye patch, as he inhaled the fresh-baked aromas. 'Good evening, sir, Colonel Spiccard extends his compliments. An Austrian column is driving down the coast, through our outposts, south towards Savona. General Bonaparte is discussing the situation with General Masséna and seeks a report of any enemy activity here at the Col di Cadibona, sir.'

Jobert's grip on his cup tightened, slopping his bouillon on his thigh. 'The Austrians have begun their offensive before ours. That is my birthday treat. Moench, have Captains Chabenac and Voreille attend me.'

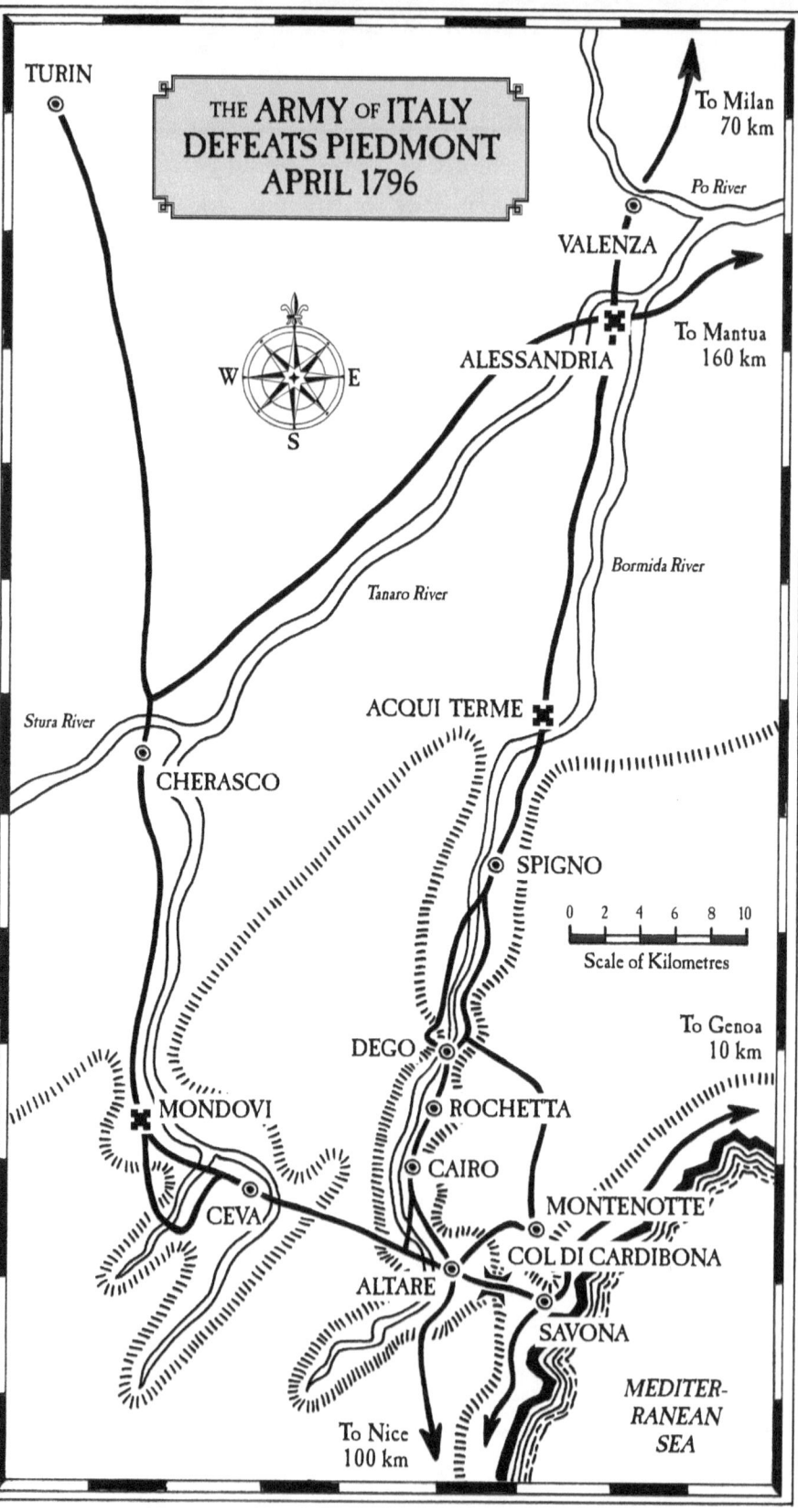

THE ARMY OF ITALY
DEFEATS PIEDMONT
APRIL 1796

TURIN

To Milan
70 km

Po River

VALENZA

ALESSANDRIA

To Mantua
160 km

Bormida River

Tanaro River

ACQUI TERME

Stura River

CHERASCO

SPIGNO

0 2 4 6 8 10
Scale of Kilometres

DEGO

To Genoa
10 km

MONDOVI

ROCHETTA

CAIRO

CEVA

MONTENOTTE

COL DI CARDIBONA

ALTARE

SAVONA

To Nice
100 km

MEDITER-
RANEAN
SEA

Chapter Three
April 1796, Battle of Montenotte, Italy

'Hussars?' Jobert peered through his telescope at the pairs of blue-clad Austrian horsemen six hundred metres away. 'Protecting the infantry? Those idle bastards are never out of bed before ten o'clock. Something is afoot.'

'Indeed, sir,' said Chabenac, commander of 2nd Company at the northern end of Jobert's squadron outpost line.

On Jobert's left, the grey snow-swollen water of the Bormida River tumbled north over its rocky bed. Although the men raised their voices to be heard over the rushing torrent, the river was obscured from the French horsemen by the dense underbrush within the forest's tree line.

Koschak looked north along the river line, across the wide flats and bright-green meadows to the smoky hamlet of Cairo, five hundred metres beyond the Austrian hussars. 'They have a troop here at the most. One platoon in skirmish order across the fields and the other platoon at rest in the village behind.'

With a spacing of one hundred metres between the six pairs

of enemy horsemen in each line, a cordon of observation was created across the dewy meadows of early spring shoots, stretching from the banks of the gurgling Bormida to the dark-forested slopes to the east.

'Where have their infantry gone?' asked Jobert.

'The village of Cairo lies a little over one kilometre from us now, sir.' Chabenac's eye was glued to his glass. 'I estimate a company or two of their fusiliers in the village, certainly not the half a battalion's worth as there was yesterday. As there has been each evening this week, wagon and torch movement during the night, but no drums. Is it me, or are these hussars in the same uniform as our own 1st Hussars?'

'Yes, the light-blue and the red facings are similar,' said Jobert. 'The immediate difference is in the headdress. The kaiserlik hussars have red shakos with pom-poms, our hussars have the mirliton with plumes and a flame. As to the mystery of missing infantry, a prisoner will tell us more. Chabenac, who do we have available to capture a prisoner?'

Chabenac snapped his face towards Jobert, his eyes alight. 'I have never taken a prisoner. I have a troop ready to skirmish into the meadow.'

Jobert slapped Chabenac's shoulder. 'Have one of your platoons form line in skirmish order here on the wood's edge. Sergeant Major, strip down the other platoon's saddles in readiness for the hunt. We will move out of the forest as six vedette pairs, to every appearance setting a counter-screen to the kaiserliks. Tulloc, fetch me Bleu.'

With an ugly grin, Koschak spun to gather the nominated platoon about him. Any extraneous equipment was stripped from the saddles to reduce the weight on the horses. Capes, horse rugs, portmanteaus, horse lines, staves, sickles, hammers, shovels, picks, nose bags, forage bags, water flasks and gourds, cartridge boxes, pistol holsters. The chasseurs would ride with just their sabres and a single charge in their musketoons.

'Chabenac,' said Jobert, 'the kaiserliks have a platoon in the screen. There will be a sergeant, perhaps a junior officer, somewhere towards the centre. They will tell us more, but with the flatter ground and the straight run to the village, they will not be easy to bag.' Jobert's tone changed as inner humours morphed prior to the delivery of violence. Jobert pointed at the Austrians high on the mountain's side. 'Those on the end of the screen will have the longer ride home. The horses coming down the slope will step short, so will not have the speed until the ground flattens. The pair of hussars at the end of their line on the upper slopes, furthest from the riverbank, is sure to have a corporal. He will be our quarry.'

'I would be obliged, sir,' said Chabenac, 'if I might be there at the "kill", so to speak. What would you require of me?'

'Moench, ride with Captain Chabenac,' said Jobert to his orange-jacketed trumpeter. 'Be the pair at the end of the line. Stay wide from each other. You may attract a shot if you appear as a single target. Do whatever you can to get higher up the slope to drive the hussars down. Yes?'

Moench, Jobert's eternal shadow, swallowed hard.

'Sergeant Major and I will be the second pair down our line,' said Jobert. 'We will mark our prey as they descend down upon us.'

'There we are, Moench.' Chabenac slapped the downcast trumpeter on the shoulder. 'A quick gallop up a gentle hill and home in time for soup. What say you?'

'Ready for my birthday sport, Sergeant Major?' Jobert called, swinging into Bleu's saddle. 'Moench, sound Skirmishers Out!'

As Moench blew the long notes of the order, the chasseurs formed in familiar pairs and rode forward to their comrades observing their enemies under the outer boughs.

The foreign trumpet call gripped the guts of the Austrian hussar from his throat to his arse. The muscular tension through the saddle had his horse jerk its ears alert, nostrils scenting the mountain breeze.

From his sentry position on the slope, with the sun just cresting the eastern mountain wall, the Austrian squinted into the shadows far below.

The hussar by his side shaded his eyes. 'There in the tree line, corporal?'

Six pairs of green-jacketed French chasseurs plodded into the meadows, the butts of their musketoons resting on their right thighs. As the line of Frenchmen advanced, a second line of paired chasseurs in skirmish order, appeared under the low boughs.

'A troop of the pricks. I can smell them from here.' The corporal shortened his reins. 'Fire! Wake the others.'

The corporal's mare flinched at the shot. 'Reload, you slug,' called the corporal. 'Forget them. Stay focused.'

The corporal swivelled in his saddle. The pair of hussars one hundred metres behind him stood in their stirrups, craning their necks unable to see the threat. The corporal raised his flat palm to halt them.

At three hundred metres, the French moustaches and hussar plaits became distinct. Their scabbards clinked on their spurs.

'How close will he let them come?' The corporal peered down the slope. 'What is the fat bastard doing?' No signal was waved from his platoon sergeant three hundred metres down the hill.

A cry from somewhere down the meadow.

'Corporal, what—?' The hussar dropped his ramrod. It clattered on his stirrup as it fell.

The corporal stared at the wooden ramrod under the horses' hooves. 'You fucking useless —'

'Corporal!'

The thunder of French hooves squeezed the corporal's heart. Six pairs of chasseurs at the gallop. Two pair flew straight up the slope towards them. They had thirty seconds.

'Fire again, corporal?'

'Yes, warn the village.'

Down the Austrian screen line, a ripple of musketry caused an instant grey cloud of gun smoke. In the village of Cairo, Austrian drummers beat To Arms.

The corporal shortened his reins. 'Retire!'

The younger soldier wrenched his remount around. With a rake of spurs, his horse leapt towards the second line of Austrian skirmishers.

The corporal attempted to predict the paths of the four closest Frenchmen. He winced at the speed of their horses.

One pair of chasseur horses bounded up the weedy rocks.

The corporal lifted his musketoon's barrel, spun his horse and urged it to race. 'Fly, Theresa!'

He glanced at the two chasseurs speeding along the slope beneath his left. Smug grins funnelled their urgent breathing. Their eyes were on the stones ahead. Their forward seats and rocking hips urged their bay horses to extend the galloping stride.

His horse slowed to the canter. His calves pulsed her ribs. She ducked her head to lean into the gallop. The corporal's eyes bulged from his skull as he sought the best path down the rutted mountain side. The weight of his rolled cape and blankets buffeted his thighs. His portmanteau behind his saddle punched his mare's loins.

The pair of enemies had split either side, the blond one on the right only five horse lengths behind.

He sought the second line of hussars. Sixty metres? Seventy? Five seconds.

On his right above him, the closest Frenchman let burst a demonic scream. He glanced back, balance shifting. Theresa adjusted her descending steps. The Frenchman's howl was framed by bared teeth in a blood-red face. Gloved fingers stretched out towards him.

One horse length.

His dropped musketoon bludgeoned his thigh. He groped for the leaping sabre hilt. The nose of the other chasseur's remount grunted with effort under his left elbow. His scabbard slapped its neck. Its chest rammed into Theresa's rump.

She dropped her head to kick out at the canter.

He lost his balance.

A tree branch, or something like it, clamped around his throat. His scream was stifled. He was wrenched by the neck from the saddle. The Frenchman roared in his ear and tugged on his own reins. Theresa leapt away with the reduction in weight towards her stablemates just ahead, yet his right stirrup snagged his boot.

Suspended in mid-air over the thunder of hooves on rocks, stale French breath blasted the hussar's ear. With the dizzying slope in his peripheral vision and his foot trapped in the stirrup of his bolting mount, vomit burnt his throat. His fingers raked for any hold on the saddlery behind him.

The second chasseur on the right snatched Theresa's trailing reins. The blond Frenchman sent a vicious snap through to the iron bit in her mouth. All three horses sunk on their haunches to a shuddering halt. The corporal's stirrup slipped free of his boot.

His captors yelled to a pair of chasseurs above them.

The Austrian's eyes implored his comrades within musketoon

range. 'Fire!' he croaked. 'You useless bastards, fire!'

The foreign trumpet screeched again. The two chasseurs spun the horses towards the tree line from which they had emerged and plunged down the slope.

Arched backwards over the saddle bow, the hussar's body jerked, his neck stretching, the Frenchman's musketoon gouging into his arched spine, his own firearm thrashing to break his knee. The blond chasseur leered at him and drove Theresa into captivity with a slash of the flat of his blade.

His vision dimmed as he choked.

Once inside the tree line, Jobert released his captive.

The blue-clad hussar collapsed on the ground with a painful thud and pawed at the earth with gloved fingers. Rough hands closed on the prisoner and threw him on his back. He curled into a caterpillar-like ball, fighting to breathe.

Jobert groaned as he dismounted, cradling his upper arm which had ensnared the Austrian. 'Tulloc, fetch Rouge and re-pack our horses.'

Jobert squatted among the feet of the inquisitive chasseurs and steaming horses. He gripped the quivering hussar. The Austrian corporal's face twitched. His eyes widened with alarm as Jobert held out a hipflask and a wicked dagger.

'Sore neck, huh?' Jobert asked in German. 'I can soothe your throat or open it. You choose.'

The corporal searched Jobert's face.

Jobert pushed the flask towards the hussar. 'Your platoon had outpost duties this morning? Yes?'

The corporal swallowed the rough grappa painfully. An ensuing coughing fit caused harsh laughter from the surrounding chasseurs. 'Yes, sir.'

'While your other platoon rests in Cairo? Yes?'

'Yes, sir.'

'It is correct, is it not, your troop has never screened south of Cairo before?' asked Jobert.

'Yes, sir.'

'Have a little more, my friend. Just a sip. But now you are in the screen because the infantry withdrew last night?'

The hussar sat up a little straighter and sipped at the biting liquid. 'Yes, sir.'

'They withdrew to Dego?'

'Yes, sir.'

'Took their wagons with them?' asked Jobert.

'Yes, sir.'

'You have a good horse, son. She did well over that rough slope. What is her name?'

'Theresa, sir.' The hussar blinked back tears as his mare was brought forward to appreciative murmurs from the crowding French troopers.

'See, my friend, she is unharmed,' said Jobert. 'Her legs are sound. We will give Theresa a little grain, yes? Your troop came forward from Dego last night, did it not?'

The hussar nodded. 'Yes, sir.'

Jobert offered the flask again. 'You would have seen other infantry arriving in Dego yesterday and last night?'

The alcohol burnt the hussar's raw throat. 'Yes, sir.'

'They were preparing to advance to Altare and the Col di Cadibona?'

'No, sir.' The hussar jerked to look Jobert directly in the eye and shook his head emphatically. 'No, sir, the infantry are advancing to Savona via Montenotte.'

'Montenotte?' asked Jobert. 'No, that cannot be.'

'Ah, no, sir, I mean …'

Your face betrays you. Jobert snatched his hip flask from the Austrian corporal. His face creased as he visualised the steep ridges around Montenotte. 'Chabenac, the kaiserliks have withdrawn their infantry to advance on Savona via the ridgelines descending from Montenotte. Do you have a messenger with a fresh horse?'

The clatter of a rider entered the camp at the trot. The chasseur peered through the low branches for the dark-orange jackets of any trumpeters, calling to his 2nd Company comrades for an officer.

'Corporal Durand! Come here, lad,' called Koschak. 'Sir, there is a 5th Company messenger.'

The young chasseur saluted. 'Sir, Captain Voreille wishes you to know of gun fire and musketry coming from Montenotte. He has sent a patrol to investigate.'

Jobert sought the sounds of the fighting. With the forested high-country shielding Montenotte eight kilometres to the east, the rumble of the river torrent and the clatter of soldiers and horses moving around the camp, the sound of gunfire eluded him.

'I need to join that patrol. Chabenac, maintain your screen. Tulloc, fetch Rouge now.'

Chapter Four
April 1796, Battle of Dego, Italy

Two days later, the cannon's fire caught everyone's attention. Then another shot cracked the cloudy April day. A further fourteen guns fired, each a second apart.

Under two thousand metres away from the two eight-gun French batteries, Jobert watched the fall of solid shot thud into the field works and skip through the wagon teams of the Austrian defence.

'What, sir,' Jobert asked Raive beside him, 'is your view of the last few days since the Austrian offensive began?'

'Early days, of course, early days,' said Raive. 'The Austrians began with a half-hearted advance along the coast which they chose to stop. Then they attack down the knife-edged ridgeline at Montenotte and were blocked by our defences. We routed that Montenotte force, who were well out of support from the coastal force. That coastal force must now march around the intervening ranges, which creates a window of opportunity for General Bonaparte. While General Masséna forces the Austrians to protect their fortress at Acqui, beyond this road to Spigno,

General Augereau is at liberty to drive the Piedmontese further to the north-west.'

From their elevated westerly observation post on the north-running Dego-Spigno-Acqui road, over two kilometres from the Austrian chain of redoubts north of Dego, Jobert, Raive and Chabenac raised their telescopes and observed the defenders' reaction to the cannonade.

All morning, as Masséna's three columns advanced from Cairo, the consistent artillery bombardment of another fierce battle ten kilometres south rent the air. Last night, Bonaparte brought up General Augereau's division from the coast and, today, was driving the Piedmontese east out of the Bormida valley.

In preparation for an assault on the Austrians tomorrow, Masséna, his staff and his commanders observed the reaction from different aspects of the field. Two French batteries fired into the Austrian defence and two infantry regiments surged forward giving every appearance of a full-frontal divisional attack. Away on the western heights of the left flank, Colonel Raive, of Masséna's staff, identified the redoubts in the depth of the Austrian defence. Around Raive sat the alert vedettes of 2nd Company, commanded by Jobert and Chabenac.

Within a minute of the French four-pound cannon balls impacting, the Austrian defence changed character. Through their glasses, Raive, Jobert and Chabenac watched Austrian guns coming into action, drums driving their infantry to put down the loads of their work parties and take up arms, wagon and their teams being urged away to the rear and couriers trotting between the small fortresses.

'What say you, Jobert?' asked Raive. 'I estimate two Austrian and two Piedmontese battalions here today.'

'We are only a day's march from Acqui, sir, they may well be reinforced through the night.'

The Austrian guns rang out in response. Since arriving on the western heights, the three officers saw the gun positions, revealed by telltale earthworks and a concentration of human activity, had been sited in ones and twos to cover each fold in the ground. As the larger Austrian six-pounders returned the French compliment in iron, flame and smoke, guns were either confirmed or new positions identified.

'What is your tally, Chabenac?' asked Raive. 'I have fourteen.'

Chabenac rechecked his notebook. 'Yes, sir, I have fourteen.'

'A heavy ratio of artillery to infantry, no?' asked Raive. 'Probably due to being committed to the Montenotte ridgelines in the last few days, the Austrian infantry would be unable to take their artillery with them.'

An open-backed fortification, or redan, on the extreme right of the Austrian line contained three guns. Watching their balls sizzle one thousand, six hundred metres to support the forward Austrian defence fascinated Jobert. As a light horseman on escort duty, Jobert knew better than to be focused on the same point of interest as the senior officer present. Jobert scanned the protective sections of 2nd Company. Content that none of the chasseurs were signalling alarm, Jobert glanced back over his shoulder down a long spur line towards the hidden village of Dego.

On the centre of the broad spur, enwrapped on three sides by the Bormida River, Jobert gazed upon a broad olive grove and contemplated a previous skirmish with Austrian cavalry over eighteen months before. On that occasion Jobert led his chasseurs in an opportunistic swarm against Austrian *chevau-léger* and dragoons.

'Will General Masséna's plan be the same as when we fought here in September '94, sir?' asked Jobert.

'Masséna has access to more infantry this time,' said Raive, 'but the ground will dictate the same approaches. General Masséna will attack along the road toward Dego. General Laharpe will command one of his brigades on the left to turn the Austrian right flank. There, toward that three-gun redan that has held your attention. I think we have seen enough. Shall we return?'

Jobert caught himself from ordering 2nd Company to assemble to return to the French lines. He waited to see how long it would take for Chabenac to cease his tutorial in tactics and become a chasseur company commander once more.

'Major Jobert, sir,' asked Moench, a horse-length behind the officers, 'shall I sound Skirmishers In, sir?'

'Forgive me, sir.' Chabenac returned from his reveries with a jolt. 'Sound Skirmishers In. 2nd Company, column of fours, walk, march!'

Once the column of chasseurs was following Raive south towards the French lines, Chabenac rode up beside Jobert. 'What does tomorrow's battle have in store for us, sir?'

'2nd Squadron is to protect the left flank of General Laharpe's attack, along this western road to Spigno and Acqui.'

'That sounds simple enough,' said Chabenac, 'but I sense … when can we expect the curtain to rise on such a spectacle?'

Jobert inspected the high cloud over the valley. 'A cold, clear night tonight will bring a thick fog in the morning. Once the fog lifts, our artillery will acquire their targets. Once our guns fire, the drums will roll and our infantry's assault will begin.'

'Go!' ordered Jobert, the next day.

In an unnecessary flourish, Voreille swept up his blade in salute. 5th Company's trumpeter sounded Skirmishers Out, the notes competing against the river torrent, the irregular thumps of cannon blasts and the thrash of drums.

Jobert's eyes followed the backs of Voreille's soldiers as their horses leapt up the banks to canter up the slope of the broad, low promontory that thrust the north flowing Bormida abruptly to the east.

Jobert's long-developed senses watched the last of Voreille's skirmishers be consumed by the gun smoke. The grey figures, a mere two hundred metres up the slope but already engulfed, checked their gait and waved to each other to redress their line, before thick clouds consumed them.

Jobert turned to Chabenac mounted beside him. 'Something is up there. A line of fusiliers ought not slow Voreille to a walk, but cavalry skirmishers might.' A blink was the only change to Chabenac's smiling mask.

The urgent beat of drums and a squadron of 22nd Chasseurs heralded General Laharpe's smoke-obscured infantry, advancing on Masséna's left flank. 'Here comes Bessières' chasseurs leading Laharpe,' said Jobert. 'Advance, Chabenac. Establish your column on Voreille's left.'

Chabenac chose to sword-salute his chief of squadron. Jobert frowned at the act. *First fight with their new companies, I suppose.* As Chabenac swept his sabre's hilt to his lips, Jobert saw his friend drive all his courage into his churning stomach, forcing icy clarity to the forefront of his mind.

'2nd Company, column of fours, walk, march!' called Chabenac. 'Sound Advance! Lieutenant Peugeot, vedettes out. Keep 5th Company on our right, if you please.'

Clumps of dark figures, French light infantry in skirmish formation, swarmed behind a band of approaching horsemen. Laharpe's brigade column was closing up to Jobert.

With his right hand gripping the waist of his musketoon's stock, and thus unable to salute, Jobert nodded a brief acknowledgement to Captain Bessières' sword salute. Jobert shrugged away his annoyance as yet another captain sought his confidence.

Bessières' sharp nod confirmed orders had not changed. Voreille's 5th Company would identify river crossing points. Bessières' chasseurs would screen Laharpe's infantry in an assault on the extreme end of the Austrian line. Jobert and Chabenac's 2nd Company would remain on the high ground left of the French attack to screen the Dego-Spigno Road.

A firm squeeze instructed Rouge to descend the banks and enter the tumbling water. Water filled Jobert's boots. Beside him, Moench's lips clenched with nerves, his stare fixed on the ridge's summit masked by smoke. Koschak and Tulloc, leading Bleu and Grenzer, followed.

On the far bank, Rouge stretched his great body to power up the slope. Sporadic musketry crackled from the right of the spur toward Dego.

On top of the promontory, Voreille trotted over to Jobert. 'I have enemy hussars to my left front, sir, and enemy infantry on our right towards Dego. Should I ... should I pass the hussars to Captain Chabenac, screen the infantry with a troop and press on down the other side of the spur to locate Bessières' next crossing points?'

'Yes, Voreille,' said Jobert, 'that is exactly what you should do. Stay close to the Bormida below us. Once 2nd Company clears these kaiserlik hussars, I will send a patrol down to link with you once Laharpe's assault goes in. Good luck.'

Rouge trotted west through the smoke haze. Jobert, Koschak and Moench passed through a section of chasseurs holding 2nd Company's packhorses, a few men with light wounds or lame horses, standing to the rear of Chabenac's battle-line. Beside Jobert, Koschak growled, with satisfaction Jobert assumed, that two four-man vedettes stood post on the flanks of the battle-line staring into the swirling, dusty fog.

On the gravelled Dego-Spigno road that ascended the ridge's spine, 2nd Company's column extended into troop battle-line. Koschak peeled away to hasten the alignment of the second rank.

Skirmishers trotted into the gloom ahead. Jobert and Moench followed them well forward of 2nd Company's battle-line. On the heights from which Raive and he observed the defences yesterday, the smoke thinned, allowing Jobert to identify the road to Spigno bending to run north.

Two hundred metres along that road stood the grey shapes of the enemy hussars, their outlines distinct with their pelisse jackets worn raffishly off their left shoulders. They too held their musketoons at the ready on their right thighs, horses on a tight rein. Jobert counted six enemy horsemen in the first line across the road. Half of a twelve-man section, the other half further back in the gloom.

Until now, a troop of hussars had been the only Austrian cavalry encountered in the Bormida valley. Jobert's mind raced to anticipate his enemy's deployment based on what the diminishing gun smoke revealed.

Jobert cantered back to Chabenac's battle-line, dropping his hips to bring Rouge into a smooth halt facing 2nd Company. His musketoon swung on its white cross-belt as he drew his sabre.

Jobert stared hard at the faces along the front rank. Scars across his chest burned. 'Five months since Savona, my lads,' Jobert called. 'Sabres!'

Musketoons slapped onto thighs. Sabres were drawn with a sizzle . Horses rocked and threw their heads. Some chasseur faces set with ugly grins. Some faces blanched, scared eyes searching Jobert.

'Shorten those fucking reins, boys,' roared Koschak. 'Get them up around their fucking ears.'

Acting on the command, the troopers filled their chests with smoke and determination.

Jobert's glare slid along the ranks ending with a sharp nod to Chabenac.

Chabenac wore a mask of confidence. '2nd Company, trot, march!'

An explosion of musketry from the skirmishers. The scream of a foreign trumpet sounded beyond the instant grey cloud.

'Moench, sound Charge!' shouted Jobert.

Amidst the thunder of shod hooves, and with the sound of Moench's trumpet piercing call over his shoulder, Jobert found himself amongst Chabenac's skirmishers. 'Clear to the flanks. Swiftly, sergeant!'

The skirmishers screamed at each other to clear the field in the face of their oncoming comrades.

Clearing the skirmishers' smoke screen, Jobert saw a full troop of hussars trotting forward with their musketoons at the shoulder.

In the centre of the Austrian line, the hussar officer held his jet-black charger in a prancing canter, his hand on his hip. A smirk completed his posture of nonchalance. *Are we not worth drawing your sabre for, you turd?*

The line of hussars was closing at the trot. Impact in ten seconds.

His twenty musketoons against our forty blades. I think not. Jobert lifted his chest and squeezed Rouge with his knees to shorten the length of Rouge's stride. Jobert rolled his extended sabre over his wrist. A warning to Moench. Options flashed though his mind.

Koschak bellowed incoherently behind him. Jobert flicked a glance to his right. Chabenac cantered front and centre of his company. The chasseurs in the charging front rank followed three strides behind him, gaps, due to avoiding the delayed skirmishers, disrupted their line as if 2nd Company had already received a volley.

Musketry exploded. The hussars were engulfed in their own smoke cloud. Beyond effective range, Jobert heard the balls skip into the gravel around Rouge's hooves.

The troop of Austrians split their line left and right, reforming column of fours and cantered away.

Jobert held his sabre aloft, as he passed into the clearer air on the far side of the hussar's gun smoke. 'Halt!'

Moench choked on the smoke as he raced to blow the urgent call of Halt.

As horses checked back into a walk and then halted, Koschak growled for the ranks to align their dressing.

Jobert scanned 2nd Company's ranks for empty saddles. None identified, he then focused on the enemy hussars' reformed troop line three hundred metres distant. Their officer still maintained a most curious pose with his hand on his hip. Jobert glared. *Why do you feel familiar? Matters not. Your strength is revealed, laughing boy, and the field is ours without loss.*

With the hussars withdrawn, Jobert looked east, across the thunderous battle in the vale beneath him, toward the three-gun Austrian redan which he observed with interest yesterday. A yellow-grey cloud, fed by gunfire or burning buildings, obscured any sense of General Laharpe's progress. *Honour enough for 2nd Company to hold the left of the battle-line.*

'Chief of squadron Jobert, sir!' called Koschak.

Jobert turned towards the glowering face of Koschak, indicating 2nd Company's relaxed state with the sweep of an open palm. Jobert saw Chabenac exchanging a hip flask with his two troop commanders, Bredieux and Peugeot.

'Captain Chabenac!' called Jobert. 'Re-establish your skirmishers, sir!'

Chabenac smiled as if, at a high tea, he was informed that his serviette had fallen to the carpet. 'Lieutenant Bredieux, skirm-ishers out, if you will.'

Jobert shuddered at the memory of the command style of the nobility.

Chapter Five

Jobert bowed his plumed mirliton beneath the canvas awning of Bonaparte's headquarters marquee.

Jobert saluted the Army of Italy's chief of staff. 'Excuse me, General Berthier, General Masséna extends his compliments, sir. He wishes you to know we have secured the field at Dego. Our enemy withdraws towards Acqui. I have his dispatches, sir.'

As Berthier blew the blotting sand from a document, he squinted to focus on Jobert in the gloom beyond the flickering candlelight, taking in Jobert's filthy uniform.

'I know Clemusat and Fergnes of the 24th Chasseurs,' said Berthier, 'but I have not met you, sir.'

One of Jobert's cheeks crimped with a brief crease. 'Major Jobert, at your service, sir.'

Berthier's eyebrows arched in enquiry. 'Something amuses you, chief of squadron?'

'No, sir.'

'I detect something does.' Berthier lounged back in his creaking chair, holding his hands out wide. 'Before I am immersed in digesting General Masséna's news and fulfilling his pressing requirements, indulge me in a momentary distraction.'

'I meant no disrespect, sir,' said Jobert. 'It is just ... you and I have met before, sir ... in America.'

A crease appeared on the senior gentleman's brow. 'I cannot place you, sir.'

'You were an aide to General de Rochambeau,' said Jobert, 'as was Colonel de Lambert. I was de Lambert's groom, sir, a mere boy chasseur in de Rochambeau's retinue.'

Berthier's eyes narrowed. 'I remember de Lambert, the chasseur colonel, of course. Forgive me, Jobert, it is good to be reunited with a fellow Virginian. I cannot recall our time together, sixteen years ago and all that, but I am sure it will come to me. Perhaps over dinner? Allow me to confirm our reacquaintance by offering you my hand, sir.'

'Scavengers,' said Jobert. 'Halt them, Bredieux.'

'Who goes?' Lieutenant Bredieux called.

In the pitch-black night, the gaggle of clattering men hissed themselves to silence.

'France,' came the response from the darkness. 'Laharpe's 75ᵗʰ *Ligne.*'

Bredieux's flint spark lit his pipe, the glow in his pipe bowl illuminating his face. 'Masséna's 24ᵗʰ Chasseurs. Approach, friend.'

A dark form stepped forward from a group, Jobert estimated, of twenty infantrymen. Far more than the usual ten-man forage parties per fusilier company.

'Any farms down this road?' asked an infantryman. Jobert heard desperate aggression in the voice.

'No, my friend,' said Bredieux. 'Keep walking and you will soon arrive at the divisional screen. The fire you see there is the inlying piquet. Beyond the chasseurs are enemy hussars. Depending how hungry you boys are, and how good your German is, they may have a feast waiting?'

Grunts emitted from the dark. The infantry foragers slouched off towards other possibilities.

Descending the road towards the fires in and around Dego, Jobert brooded at the impending thunderstorm. Despite the darkness, the meadows, groves and avenues on the plain north of Dego heaved with movement, shouts and musket shots as similar large groups sought food.

'Today, sir,' Bredieux asked Jobert beside him, 'we saw off those kaiserlik hussars, and their laughing imbecile of an officer. Do you think that hussar officer was the same fellow that Captain Voreille fought last year outside of Savona?'

'I did not take that much notice of either last year's man or today's, Lieutenant, but, yes, they are from the same regiment. Why?'

Jobert's Bleu snorted into the darkness ahead, alerting Jobert to a long column of horses lining the road. With the characteristic clink of spurs and rattle of scabbards, and the deeper clank of trace chains, Jobert guessed that dismounted horsemen were moving around a stationary column of wagon teams.

'Who goes?' called a sentry from the gloom.

'France,' said Bredieux. 'Masséna's 24th Chasseurs.'

'Bredieux, you rogue? It is me, Yinot, 5th Company.'

'Yinot?' said Bredieux. 'Surely not? We should shoot the bastard just in case it is him, sir.'

'Lieutenant Yinot, what are you doing here?' asked Jobert.

'Why are you not forward in the screen?'

'Ah, … Major Jobert, sir,' said Yinot. 'Colonel Spiccard has detached us on task, sir.'

'What task?' asked Jobert.

'My troop is to escort these half-dozen artillery teams to fetch the kaiserlik caissons from the redoubts on the heights and return to our own gun-lines.'

'How many caissons are you to fetch in?'

'I am told the Austrians fled leaving twenty-four ammunition caissons and sixteen guns,' said Yinot. 'But we have only brought in six caissons so far.'

'Sh—' Jobert clamped down on the expletive. 'Damn it, man, you will be out here all night. I accept the need to gather abandoned guns, but when this storm hits, you will be floundering in the mud in the middle of the night. What do you know of the other companies?'

'Captain Voreille asked the same, sir. Huin, who delivered the Colonel's order, reported Geourdai's 1st Company ought to be returning from screening the Austrian withdrawal north of Montenotte. Neilage's 4th Company ought to be returning from Savona following their escort of the Montenotte prisoners. 3rd Company is being held as regimental reserve at Rocchetta with the regimental trains. 6th Company has escorted the two thousand kaiserliks we captured today back to Savona.'

'Oh, give me fucking strength!' Jobert punched the *shabraque* covering his pistol holsters. 'Voreille is screening the eastern Spigno Road with only his remaining troop?'

Jobert's mind reeled at the implications. Dego was a vital defence because it blocked any movement towards the strategic Acqui fortress. From Dego, two roads ran towards Spigno and Acqui, one on either side of the Bormida. Chabenac's 2nd Company secured the route on the western heights above the Bormida, and Voreille's 5th Company observed the route in the rolling woodlands east of the Bormida.

'Bredieux, take an escort, return to 2nd Company,' said Jobert. 'Tell Captain Chabenac of the weakness in Voreille's screen. Strip a platoon out of 2nd Company and take it across to strengthen 5th Company.'

'Sir,' said Yinot, as Bredieux's escort departed, 'our escort and these gunners have orders from General Masséna's headquarters to bring in the captured caissons and guns. But with the rain threatening, the artillery officers are satisfied with simply identifying what ammunition the kaiserliks have left behind and bringing in any loaded caissons to just General Laharpe's battery tonight. They will sort the rest in the morning.'

'Why only Laharpe's guns tonight?' asked Jobert.

'The word is, sir, General Masséna is to hold Dego tomorrow and General Laharpe is to march against the Piedmontese at dawn.'

'What of you?' asked Jobert. 'Have your soldiers eaten today?'

'We had a kettle of bouillon before we marched this morning, sir. Nothing since.'

'You have already taken kaiserlik caissons from the captured redoubts? Was there any food on their dead? Do the gunners have any ammunition bread? Has Madame Quandalle brought any cantinière supplies forward from Savona?'

'I asked, sir,' said Yinot, 'and the gunners have nothing. As for corpses manning the redoubts, there was nothing there either. The kaiserlik baggage and wounded had been stripped immediately our fusiliers surged over their parapets.'

Jobert, Moench and remaining escorting chasseurs continued along the road as intermittent raindrops splattered on their chests and faces. The men adjusted themselves in their saddles as they pulled their capes tighter around themselves and their exposed musketoons. Their horses flicked their noses taking the reins from their riders' grip, extending their heads down and away from the impending deluge.

Ahead, a wavering torch flickered an orange light on the dark mirliton caps of a column of approaching horsemen. 'Who goes?

'France,' called Jobert. 'Masséna's 24th Chasseurs.'

'Laharpe's 22nd Chasseurs and 51st Ligne,' came the reply from a dark figure. 'Major Jobert, is that you, sir?'

'Captain Bessières, it is indeed, sir,' said Jobert.

'My word, is that Jobert?' asked another voice.

'Good evening, Colonel Lannes, sir,'

'There will be no supper with General Laharpe as planned, Jobert,' said Lannes. 'Tonight is an absolute shambles. Both Masséna's and Laharpe's regiments have simply ceased to exist. Including, I am ashamed to say, my own 51st Ligne. Tonight, approximately twenty battalions have dissolved into the darkness, so there are now ten or twelve thousand famished individuals dispersed in pillaging gangs seeking food. I have not seen anything like it.'

'Have I heard correct, sir,' asked Jobert, 'you are to march at dawn to support General Bonaparte's drive against the Piedmontese.'

'Indeed, sir,' said Lannes, 'General Bonaparte is satisfied we have driven a wedge between the Austrians and the Piedmontese. Now, with a thunderstorm upon us, I am to reassemble my three battalions ready to march. We are set for an utter calamity if the Austrians counterattack while we are in this state. I suggest most strongly, sir, you return to your screen.'

The incoming curtain of icy water approached Jobert and his chasseurs across the valley, sweeping branches, rooves and earth with a rattling hiss.

Hours later, Jobert drew a tin mug from his cape pocket and helped himself to the kettle's contents bubbling on Voreille's fire. 'Has Yinot returned?'

'Sir.' Voreille grunted the time-honoured word which was both the morning greeting and the question's answer.

Alpine rain had drifted down as Jobert arrived back at 5th Company's camp. With the change of the midnight piquet, heavy, soaking rain fell in earnest. Now, a chill fog seeped from the saturated mud and thickened the pre-dawn dark.

Too hot for his lips, Jobert allowed the cup to warm his fingers and the steam to warm his face. 'Why are there men sleeping in the mud around the fires?'

Voreille looked up from the coals to the sodden forms lying in the dark mud nearby. 'Lost infantrymen, sir. The rain was so heavy, they were unable to return to their regiments.'

'Their regiments no longer exist,' said Jobert. 'Every hungry one of them wandered off seeking food, love or loot. Now they are all lost. Sergeant Major Koschak?' Koschak looked up from Moench's fire. 'Have those fusiliers by the troop fires roused and set back upon the road to Dego. Or remove their muskets and have them charged with desertion.' Koschak growled with relish.

Receiving a saddled Bleu and a refilled bouillon mug from Tulloc, Jobert, with Koschak and Moench, squelched from the 5th Company's fires into the clammy, dark cloud beyond towards the outlying vedettes.

Birdsong erupted from under the thickets and groves where the fog was less thick. The outbreak of bird twitter caused the awakening of drums. Further south in the mist-blanketed valley, those insistent drums demanded Laharpe's fusiliers and grenadiers assemble and prepare to march to meet the

Piedmontese somewhere twenty kilometres to the south-east.

'The road is as quiet as a grave, sir,' said Lieutenant Yinot, commander of the outlying piquet. 'The kaiserlik hussars changed their piquet an hour ago. We heard one of their lads head off down the road when the drums summoned our boys.'

As the fog-muted light changed gradually from black to blue-grey, sporadic musket fire was heard. Jobert frowned. Due to the fog and the distance, the direction could not be determined.

Koschak pivoted in his saddle. 'That fire has an odd rhythm, sir. Not the random shot from morning hunters. Neither volley fire, nor the irregular intensity of skirmishers clashing.'

'Something is not right,' said Jobert. 'Yinot, keep a close watch on your hussars. I shall ride your outpost line, cross the Bormida and proceed up to 2nd Company.'

On the slopes above the Bormida River, the sun burnt off the fog. A cold blue day was promised. Yet irritated by the odd pattern of musketry, Jobert glanced at the first rays cresting the shrouded eastern slopes, recognising it would be hours before the fog cleared in the deeper folds around Dego.

Chabenac had been tasked with observing the western route to Spigno. Jobert, Koschak and Moench entered 2nd Company's camp in an olive grove.

Jobert took in every detail of 2nd Company's current state of preparedness. Tent flies, empty of soldier's bedding and saddlery, dried in the early sunshine. Horses stood freshly groomed, with nosebags on and saddled with loose girths. Three local farm hands raked manure. The company farrier inspected hooves. With a nod from the duty sergeant, small groups of horses were led away to be watered from farmyard wells.

Chasseurs, resting in reserve for either the inlying or outlying piquet, smoked pipes around their hazy fires, breakfasted on hotcakes baked in nearby cottages, or crooned as they cleaned their musketoons and sabres.

'Good morning, sir.' Chabenac saluted. 'Would you care for soup?'

Jobert fished in his cape's deep pocket for his cup. 'Anything to report?'

'We remain in contact with the hussars, sir. There has been no untoward movement on the road.'

Jobert observed two local women, with grimy toddlers in tow, passing out small loaves and winter vegetables to the chasseurs. 'Did any infantry foragers come into your camp last night?'

'Some sought food, sir, but were turned away,' said Chabenac. 'We are well situated here, sir. Last evening, we dined on roast chicken and received a freshly butchered goat for today and tomorrow. Breakfast, Sergeant Major?'

Chabenac passed Koschak a grubby cloth in which four boiled eggs and six onions were nestled.

Jobert and Koschak spun toward a ragged, distant blast of musketry.

'There it is again, sir.' Koschak thrust Chabenac's breakfast into Moench's chest so he could glare at the blanketed east. 'Not quite a solid volley, yet hundreds of muskets need to fire to produce such a noise. It is like skirmisher fire, but there is no reply. Look, there!'

A flock of ravens, disturbed from breakfasting on yesterday's dead, flapped through the top of the fog, indicating the musketry was in the hills east of Dego.

'Nowhere near 5th Company's outposts,' said Jobert. 'Perhaps the ill-discipline created by empty bellies has caused greater unrest? I would be obliged, Chabenac, if Bredieux might take a patrol and investigate. As it is seven o'clock, I shall inspect your outlying piquet until his return.'

Once amongst Chabenac's sentries, Jobert observed the Austrian hussars through his telescope. The huddled pairs of enemy horsemen revealed no clues as to the strange eruptions.

As the clammy valley lay in chill shadow, the unusual bouts of firing continued throughout the morning. As the fog thinned, a single cannon fired. *Why?* thought Jobert. *To clear a barrel, or*—

Bredieux's patrol cantered into the camp. 'Sir! There is a column of Austrians occupying the redoubts north of Dego.'

Jobert checked his watch. Nine o'clock. 'Why is there no fighting? No firing?'

'The roads are full of our infantry and gunners running for Dego, sir. There are officers amongst them, sir, but they are not rallying. It is a rout.'

Jobert strode towards Bleu, signalling Koschak and Moench to mount. 'Where have the Austrians come from, Bredieux? Obviously not from Spigno or Acqui.'

'The kaiserliks have come down out of the hills on the Dego-Montenotte road, sir.'

Jobert froze. All around the camp Chabenac's chasseurs stood in readiness for the expected orders. Chabenac slid a notebook and pencil from an inner tailcoat pocket.

Jobert's eyes flickered as he imagined the enemy's dispositions in his mind. 'Then there is a chance they will come in behind 5th Company's inlying piquet. Chabenac, send a message to Colonel Spiccard. It is now nine o'clock. There is no enemy movement south on the two roads from Spigno. The Austrians have arrived in the fog from the east, from the direction of Montenotte. Masséna's flank has collapsed.'

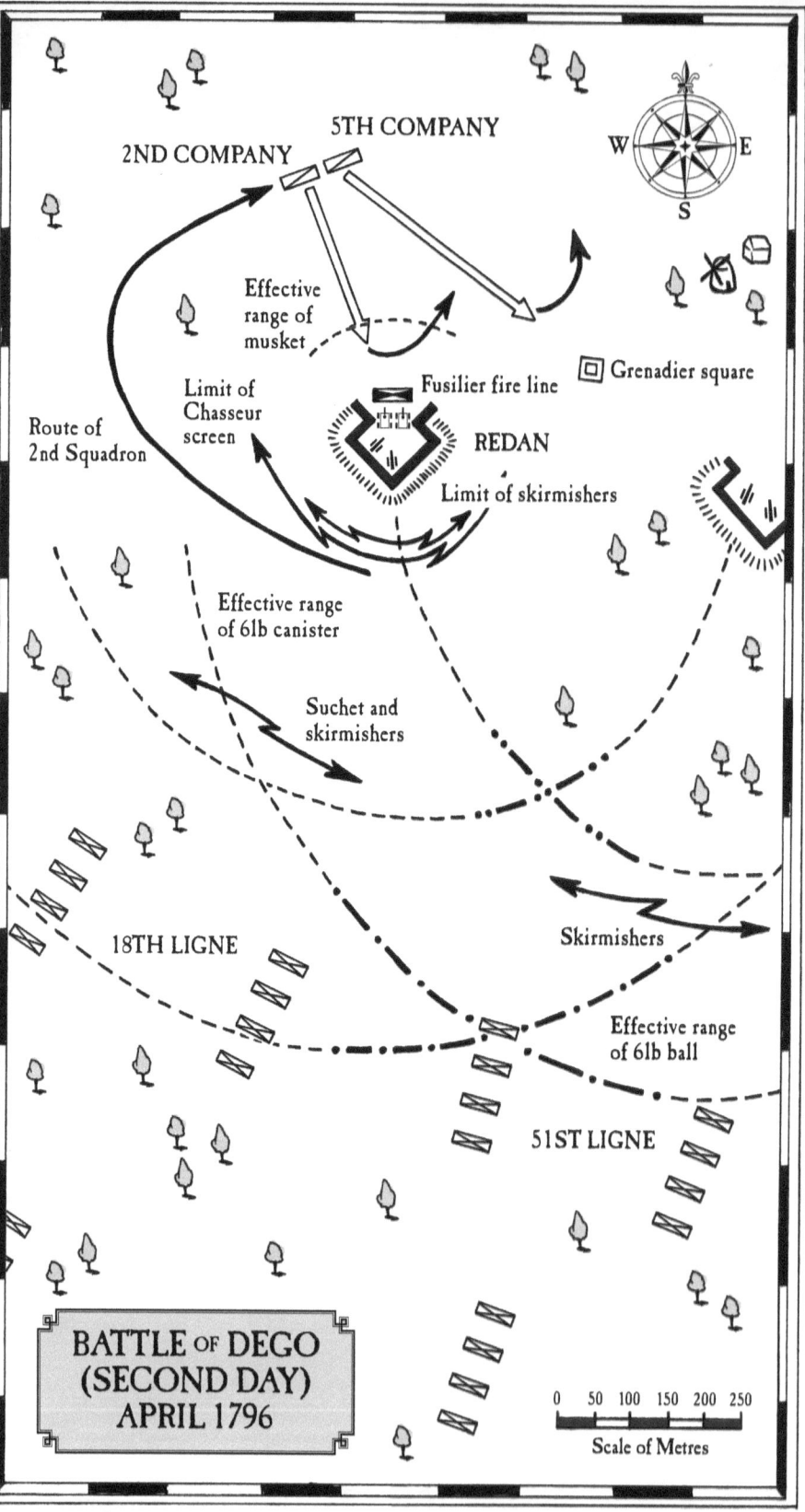

2ND COMPANY

5TH COMPANY

W · E (compass)
S

Effective
range of
musket

☐ Grenadier square

Fusilier fire line

Limit of
Chasseur
screen

REDAN

Route of
2nd Squadron

Limit of skirmishers

Effective range
of 6lb canister

Suchet and
skirmishers

Skirmishers

18TH LIGNE

Effective range
of 6lb ball

51ST LIGNE

BATTLE OF DEGO
(SECOND DAY)
APRIL 1796

0 50 100 150 200 250
Scale of Metres

Chapter Six

'What in damnation happened, Jobert?' The sinews of General Laharpe's neck strained an ugly red into his taut face.

Jobert knew Laharpe had a difficult time regathering his own wayward men in the dark and rain to march away this morning. 'My squadron maintained the divisional screen on the two routes north towards Spigno last night, sir. An Austrian brigade has approached Dego along the eastern route from Montenotte, sir. I can report no other enemy movement on the approaches from Spigno at ten o'clock when I departed my post. I can also report that the Austrian brigade has reoccupied the redoubts on the hills north of Dego.'

'I will stand witness, sir,' said Colonel Lannes, 'for Jobert's erudite attention to his duties as the screen commander last night.'

'I am not casting doubt on the honour of Jobert, Lannes.' Laharpe slapped his thighs. 'But fuck me with a twelve-pounder wormscrew, Jobert, what is happening here? Where is Masséna?'

Jobert remained straight in the saddle, jaw set. Jobert knew Masséna's division had dispersed again in the morning, as they had the previous evening, seeking food and loot. Further along the slight ridge south of Dego, Masséna's division was now re-forming from the stream of uniformed refugees pouring out of the Dego township.

'I am unaware of the location of General Masséna's head-quarters, sir,' said Jobert. 'I have, as ordered by my commanding officer, just marched from the rear of the enemy to rejoin you. I can only make reasonable comment on the enemy dispositions, not our own.'

'Then what of the enemy to my front, Jobert?' asked Laharpe.

'There are at least two battalions of grenzers, sir. The other battalions are line fusiliers. A battalion holds the promontory, a battalion occupies Dego and the remainder have re-established the redoubts north of the town.'

'Artillery?' asked Laharpe.

'I am aware that sixteen pieces of cannon remained in the redoubts last night,' said Jobert. 'At the very least they will have been recaptured.'

'Surely those guns will not be manned by trained crews?'

'Excuse me, sir,' said the captain commanding Laharpe's artillery battery. 'Their gun crews will be led by gunners from their own regimental three-pounders. The Austrians will also use their grenadier companies to complement the gun crews.'

Laharpe's nostrils flared as he glared at the Austrian activity on the promontory above him. 'Very well, gentlemen, let us fight yesterday's battle again. I will have the 4th *Légere* clear the ridgeline and re-establish our battery on the slopes above. My initial advance will again strike at the extreme right of the Austrian line. Again, at that damned three-gun redan. General Victor, will you take Suchet's 18th Ligne on the left? I shall lead Lannes' 51st Ligne on the right.'

Jobert's eyes skimmed across the assembled staff and com-manders. He was struck with unexpected delight to see General

Victor, his friend from the battles around Toulon, and then another old friend from Toulon, Major Suchet of the 18th Ligne. Victor and Suchet acknowledged Jobert's vexation with a nod and a wink.

Having confirmed his commanders understood his concept of operations, Laharpe returned his gaze to the unshaven chasseur à cheval in the faded green tailcoat. 'Major Jobert, might I request your chasseurs support the battery to the heights, then guide General Victor to the western redan and support his northern flank?'

'The 24th Chasseurs are at your service, sir.'

Having now crossed the Bormida for the fifth time since this morning's reveille, Jobert watched Moench's face sour as his sodden, numb feet dangled in iron stirrups. Despite their own discomfort of aching legs below the knees, the grumbling chasseurs in the ranks around them all watched the explosions of profound expletives as the light infantry of the 4th Légere entered the freezing, waist-high torrent of the Bormida, their musketoons and cartridge boxes held high. With ice in their shoes, backpacks and veins, Laharpe's 4th Légere Regiment surged to the summit of the spur-line and pressed the Austrian defenders back towards Dego with a violent skirmish.

From the height of the promontory west of the village of Dego, the bleak April sun shone clear on the redoubts north of the village. As the rattle of 4th Légere's musketry receded, Laharpe's commanders beheld the hurried activity in the enemy-held fortresses north of the promontory.

The thrashing of Austrian drums filled the valley with an urgent rhythm.

'My immediate aim is to capture the three-gun open-backed redan on the extreme right of the enemy's line,' said Laharpe. 'We will roll up their battle-line one redoubt at a time from there. Jobert, does the fortress still have its three guns?'

'There are only two serviceable six-pounders within the ramparts, sir. The neighbouring redoubt has only two guns to support that defence.

A sharp sense of relief hissed from Laharpe's command group at the reduction of guns available to the enemy. The Austrian six-pounders covered the lower slopes of the promontory, the river and the sloping meadows up to the redoubt. The French four-pounders would be hard pressed to make an impact on the redoubt at that range.

'Twelve hundred metres, sir,' said Laharpe's artillery captain. 'If I may prevail upon the services of the sappers of the 4th Légere, sir, we might lower our trails to gain the elevation.'

'Right now,' said Laharpe, his face a mask of forced confidence, 'the key is to advance swiftly with battalion attack columns well spread to disperse the guns' fire. Victor, with Suchet's 18th Ligne and Jobert's chasseurs, flank the left of the last redan. I will lead Lannes' 51st Ligne on their right between the now two-gun redan and the next redoubt in line which will be providing flanking fire. Our guns have their range. Then let us be about it, gentlemen. Beat the Advance.'

The valley beneath them boomed with a rolling explosion as each Austrian gun fired at the silhouetted French troops assembling on the promontory ridge. The answering crack, as Laharpe's six four-pound cannon and the two six-inch howitzers fired in response, caused horses in the command group to jump in alarm.

The warm midday air allowed the gun smoke to rise, giving both Austrian and French gunners unobstructed vision of their targets. The cannon balls from the redoubts whistled across the valley, towards the French troops descending the ridge, to thud into the thick mud of the hillside. For their part, Jobert watched the French balls slap into the sloping glacis beneath the redan's ramparts only to roll into the steep-sided ditch in front of the glacis.

'Chabenac,' said Jobert as they descended the spur line to recross the Bormida, 'stay ahead of the infantry skirmishers. We ride into the mouths of the enemy guns. For the gunners to disregard us as a target, stay in skirmish order at the trot and maintain your circling. Also, watch for canister from the neighbouring redoubt.'

Chabenac's eyes, wide with alarm, twitched toward the next Austrian fortification in the defensive line.

'Hey there, Jobert!' Jobert twisted in the saddle as Major Suchet approached down the slope. 'I know duty awaits and all that, but it is good to see you again. General Victor told me the 24th Chasseurs had been with the Army of Italy since Toulon. Yet regimental duties had not allowed me to find you.'

'Regimental duties, indeed,' said Jobert, 'Regimental commander, no less?'

'As the senior battalion commander, I am in temporary command of the regiment.'

'Suchet!' called Victor, as he drew alongside Suchet and Jobert. 'Despite Laharpe's confidence, our guns plainly do not have the range. We infantry must again assault without the luxury of supporting artillery. The 18th Ligne will attack two battalions forward and one in reserve. I shall lead the right forward battalion directly toward the face of the redoubt, on which our own guns are now firing.'

Jobert understood that Victor was using one of Suchet's seven hundred-man battalions to attract the fire of one of the Austrian cannons.

'The structure on the extreme flank, sir, is a redan, not a redoubt,' said Jobert. 'The ramparts are open at the rear. On the rear apron are artillery caissons supplying the battery as well as a casualty dressing station.'

'That is excellent,' said Victor. 'Suchet, under your command, your left forward battalion shall seek the rear of the redan.

Jobert, your chasseurs will support Suchet's left flank as he wraps around the ramparts.'

Chabenac's 2nd Company recrossed the Bormida, weary horses struggling to clamber up the stony bank before dispersing into the meadows beyond as pairs of skirmishers.

'Suchet,' yelled Victor over the cacophony of drums, 'do not let the men shelter within the confines of the banks, because—'.

Jobert's head jerked as a hollow shell from an Austrian how-itzer cracked onto the rocky shelf above the swirling grey froth, only to explode moments later in a black cloud of metal frag-ments and gravel. *The kaiserlik gunners have our range.*

The leading French fusiliers baulked at the lingering pall of smoke and rock dust. Beyond the river, any chasseurs loitering at the rear of the mounted skirmish formation hastened forward with a bellow of expletives from Koschak.

On the northern bank of the Bormida, Jobert appraised the long, twelve-hundred-metre slope to the two sets of rammed-earth forts on the crest six hundred metres apart. Each fort set at deadly canister range from each other. As an assault clambered the exposed ramparts of the first objective, victory within bayonet reach, the second fort would sweep them with a hail of vicious balls.

On the slope leading to both strongholds, Jobert's eyes fixed on the torn, twisted bodies of yesterday's unburied dead. At that moment, the dead informed the advancing French infantry, as well as the Austrian gunners, where the range bands lay for the most accurate and destructive gun fire. Jobert identified two unmistakeable areas to cross. Two distinctive patterns of corpses showed where, at eight hundred metres, the Austrian six-pound balls would skip effectively through the advancing ranks, each round sweeping away at least ten men.

Jobert's face tightened as he calculated. The Austrians would be able to fire around twenty rounds per gun in the time it would take for the French to ascend. Hence, Laharpe's orders for an advance of four columns, two from Suchet's 18th Ligne and two from Lannes' 51st Ligne. If the Austrian fire could ever be distributed evenly across the battalion columns, casualties would amount to over one hundred men, at least a full company of fusiliers, before the second area of concern was reached.

The second carpet of flayed mounds, flapping with crows, delineated the range of the canister pellets. The last four hundred metres before the ramparts and the muzzles of the guns. Even if they charged, the French fusiliers may well cross that last zone in two minutes but would still receive at least two rounds of canister per gun. The tin casing of musket balls spewing its cone of destruction from the gun's muzzle was as destructive as a volley of one hundred infantry at fifty metres and would easily mince half the front rank of the attackers in one blast.

French four-pound balls hissed far overhead to the targeted redoubt . On the crumbling bank, the blue-coated battalions sloshed forward to set their front ranks fifty men across and twelve ranks deep. Twelve hundred metres distant, the Austrians guns roared in response to the assembling, bedraggled infantry emerging from the riverbank.

'Skirmishers out!' bellowed Victor.

The dull thud of four skipping balls was greeted by a thrashing of French drums.

The four lead battalions released the one-hundred-man companies that specialised in skirmish work. Working in mutually supportive pairs, four hundred men dashed forward assured that the Austrian gunners would disregard their fleeting escapades as a low-priority target. The darting skirmishers would, at within musket range of one hundred metres of the enemy guns, pick off the enemy gunners and save their comrades in the dense columns trudging up the slopes.

The Austrians were ready for this technique.

Under the redoubt's ramparts, a sloping glacis provided the side of a steep ditch enclosing three sides of the fortification. Within the ditch and beneath the muzzles of the guns, the Austrians had a skirmish company of their own ready to hold off the French screen well out of musket range of their hard-labouring gunners. As the French skirmishers struggled to run up the slope, the Austrians set themselves in two skirmish lines out from the lip of the ditch.

Suchet leapt from his horse. 'On me, 18th Ligne, on me!' Snatching a musket from a skirmisher, Suchet raced to the lead of the French skirmisher screen and continued to run as fast as he could up the slope. The skirmishers roared with a mix of pride, terror and commitment, as they trotted to keep up with their sprinting regimental commander.

As the blue-coated infantry skirmishers entered the 2nd Company's scattered formation, Jobert dropped his musketoon onto its cross belt and drew his sabre.

Chapter Seven

At the urgent peal of Moench's trumpet, Chabenac's skirmishers surged forward into a trot. Swerving to avoid the bouncing solid shot, the mounted chasseurs soon outstripped the jogging infantry skirmishers.

As Bleu swung through his gait, Jobert knew his chasseurs would chase the Austrian skirmishers back into their stronghold, allowing the French skirmishers to close with the Austrian gunners.

But the kaiserliks have a counter for us. Jobert peered up at the looming ramparts.

A second company of white-jacketed fusiliers had formed in two ranks behind the high ramparts, between the gun embrasures and the heaving, sweating gun crews. These fusiliers would fire half-company volleys at the French cavalry as their skirmishers scampered back into the shelter of the ditch. With their muskets' longer range over the chasseur's musketoon, the French cavalry would wheel away, the Austrian skirmishers would re-emerge, and the Austrian gunners would continue their butchery undisturbed.

'Chabenac,' Jobert shouted, 'as soon as our infantry skirmishers have closed with the guns, on my signal, rally 2nd Company to the left and form line over the ridge behind the redan.'

Upon Chabenac's salutary sweep of his sabre blade, Jobert gave Bleu his head. With his knees, Jobert guided Bleu's thundering gait onward up the slope. The bay gelding stretched into his canter and, within a minute, covered the four hundred metres to the ripped bodies lying in the trampled stubble. Jobert's peripheral vision plotted Bleu's path though the blackened body parts, discarded packs, blankets and muskets. That silent outpost line informed the gunners where their hissing shot could be expected to skip more effectively.

Bleu dashed eight hundred metres from the Bormida, from the extreme range of the guns at the river's edge to within effective range of ball. Under one minute on a labouring horse. Two minutes for a stumbling skirmisher running in wet clothing and full pack. Five minutes for the grim tramp of the solid front-ranks following with empty bellies and slime-filled shoes.

The balls appeared as swift black blurs as they sped towards them. Swerving chasseurs, toiling skirmishers and those in the front ranks roared to each other as the ball bounced in the mud and leapt over their heads to plough through the infantry following behind.

Jobert approached that second line of pulped mounds, beribboned with wisps of black fabric, the sentinels of canister range, four hundred metres from the glacis. That place amongst the dead, where the Austrian battery commander would scream 'Canister, Load!' and the French battalions' commanders would scream 'Charge!'

Two horse-lengths behind him, Moench cantered grey-faced through the swollen dead and the occasional whoosh of a passing ball. Behind Moench, Chabenac's chasseurs pressed their weary horses up the slope. Koschak yelled to maintain their wide spacings and not converge on the looming earthworks.

The Austrian skirmishers knelt one hundred metres from the ditch in front of the glacis, at the extreme effective range of their fusilier mates manning the ramparts above.

Now within canister range and, at current pace, within another sixty seconds of the redan, Jobert shortened his reins, twirled his sabre over his wrist and centred his core in the expectation of cutting down infantry.

Responding to the oncoming cavalry steel, the Austrian skirmishers sprinted for the safety of the ditch.

'Moench, sound Skirmishers Out.'

Moench's trumpet screeched the command. On grass slick with black clots, the chasseurs halted their remounts amongst the twisted and peeled dead. Koschak bellowed at the chasseurs to fix the required spacing between pairs and between the two lines of horsemen.

Bleu, agitated by the explosion of the guns, the haze of gun smoke under the ramparts and the twisted bodies, thrust his jaw against the bit. Jobert urged Bleu to trot in a wide circle, allowing Jobert to observe the skirmisher's progress, deny the Austrian marksmen a stationary target and keep an eye on the discharging guns.

Scanning the gun embrasures, Jobert saw white-coated infantry sponging, loading and ramming the muzzles of the guns. Due to the angle of the slope, any brown-coated artillery ventsmen or firers working around the guns' trails were hidden. Jobert noted the Austrian fusiliers in the upper ramparts had not yet fired a volley down into the wheeling chasseurs and the darting skirmishers. *Disciplined pricks. Keeping your touchholes clean for massacring the final assault.*

Glancing back down the slope, Jobert saw that in the few minutes the chasseurs had closed from the riverbank and driven back the Austrian screen, the four hundred skirmishers from all the French battalions had raced to the outer edge of dead marking canister range. The rounds from the flanking redoubt flew behind the skirmishers' right flank, skipping heavily through the mud towards the massed infantry columns. The men from the battalions of the 51st Ligne streamed to the east into the space between the two fortifications.

Suchet and his 18th Ligne skirmishers laboured to wrap around the flanking redan's western flank. Jobert predicted that within two minutes both the infantry skirmishers would be in position to engage the redan and the assault columns would enter the effective range of the flashing six-pound balls.

Jobert's eyes flicked up to the enemy ramparts. The fusiliers behind the stone walls, and those skirmishing from the ditch, dominated the one hundred metres until the French skirmish companies arrived.

What else can be done? If only to disperse their bastard infantry. 'Moench, sound Rally.'

As the notes reverberated across the fifty-metre face of the redan, Jobert pressed a blown Bleu into a slow canter towards the ridgeline the fort dominated. Chabenac's skirmishers pushed their heaving, sweating horses into a column of fours as the growing formation passed over the crest of the ridge and trotted towards the vulnerable rear of the redan. As the lead horsemen of Chabenac's rallied column dropped into a walk and turned into line towards the redan's apron, Jobert looked down into the near three hundred Austrians toiling to defend their fortification.

The two cannon were served by both white-coat infantrymen and brown-jacketed artillerymen, now equally blackened by powder. Jobert had lost sight of any progress of the French infantry attack columns beyond the parapet. Closer to the growing line of chasseurs, three ammunition caissons, without their horse teams, and a knot of mounted officers occupied the narrow apron that emerged from the enclosing ramparts and connected the redan over the ditch to the crest.

As Jobert oriented to the scene, a half-company of Austrian fusiliers peeled away from the redan's wall. Surging through the caissons, the fusiliers formed a short line of over a dozen men in three ranks, one rank kneeling with bayonets thrust outwards and two ranks standing ready to fire.

'Sir!' shouted Peugeot. 'Enemy infantry! Left flank!'

Jobert spun Bleu to the left.

A column of immaculate, white-coated grenadiers approached on the sheltered side of the crest from the direction of the next flanking redoubt along the ridge. The grenadiers' tall bearskin caps, glossy in the midday sun, nodded in time to the steady beat of their drums.

'Chabenac, Peugeot's troop, left wheel!' called Jobert. Chabenac's face was drawn tight with apprehension. 'Cut the bastards down, Chabenac! Now!'

Chabenac wheeled Peugeot's troop to face the reinforcements. The grenadiers' drummers beat To Square, to which the grenadiers flowed into the four-faced formation with its bristling hedge of bayonets. Chabenac's 2nd Company trumpeter sounded Charge.

Jobert looked to the remaining troop of 2nd Company, Bredieux's troop, standing behind him. The two ranks of troopers appeared aghast at the scene of the seething redoubt laid out before them. Their horses' heads hung low, with red, square nostrils blowing hard. A physical jolt of fear pulsed through Bredieux's men as their sister-troop leapt with a strangled cry towards the grenadiers.

'2nd Company, sabres!' called Jobert. 'Bredieux!' Jobert's scream bared his teeth, each sinew in his neck strained. 'On me!'

'Ponte di Nava!' roared red-faced Bredieux, in memory of a previous charge against the rear of a kaiserlik gun-line.

Koschak's manic eyes rolled in his head. '2nd Company, shorten your fucking reins!'

The Austrian skirmishers scrambled up from the redoubt's ditch onto the apron. The fire-line shuffled and allowed the new fusiliers to assemble. The guns boomed again. The apron crackled in sporadic musket fire.

Exhausted, bawling French skirmishers appeared on the crest beyond the apron. Out of sight beyond the ramparts, drums hammered Charge only to be drowned out by the deep roar of one and half thousand French throats.

The Austrian fusiliers' heads snapped to their left at the vast primitive chorus. Both gun barrels belched canister. Beyond the flank of the fusiliers, Suchet and the front of his battalion surged over the crest.

Jobert shortened his reins. 'Moench, sound Charge!'

As the notes tore from Moench's trumpet, Jobert dropped his sabre forward to give point. Bleu's great power surged upward beneath Jobert's knees. Jobert locked his lower back in preparation for impact.

A dozen paces in front of the fire-line lay a solid line of yesterday's dead, French and Austrian, naked and bloated. An obstacle to any rearward interference.

Bleu sank his hips under Jobert.

Jump the corpses, my lad. Jobert surged his strength and his commitment down through his hips and thighs.

The fusiliers' front rank fired.

Bleu dug in his hind hooves in front of the grey corpses.

As balls zipped by, a blur on the left caught Jobert's eye.

In the moment of the thought, and in the moment Bleu decided to baulk, a hammer blow struck Jobert's upper chest rocking him out of the saddle to his right. Bleu staggered to compensate from the violent shift in weight. Jobert hissed a strangled scream, as he grabbed for his shabraque with his left hand. As his fingers failed to grasp the fold of sheepskin rolled back from his pistol holsters, his squeal of extreme pain was cut short by a pulse of vomit erupting up the back of his throat.

Bleu broke to a walk as Jobert wilted. Jobert's head was low as the thin, egg-and-onion bile splashed over his blade and knee.

Willing his head to turn and look at the stump where he felt his arm ought to be, Jobert could hear a wailing rant. *Who is screaming? Is it me? Take a hold of yourself, man.* The screaming persisted. 'Go! Go! Go!' *It is not me. Who?*

Jobert was wrenched to the left as Moench, the origin of the bawling, grabbed at Bleu's reins. Moench's horse's impact on Bleu created a further cry from Jobert, his vision blurring again.

Chasseurs wheeled away to Jobert's left. *Is no one pressing the charge home?* With Moench kicking into Bleu's flank behind Jobert's right heel, Bleu leapt into a canter.

The rear rank of the Austrian line fired its volley.

With an agonised shriek, Moench lurched to collide with Jobert. Jobert clung to his sabre, and moaned as his useless left arm, to his surprise still attached to his body, swung painfully away from his body.

'Fly, Moench! Fly!' Another surge of pace from Bleu as Koschak accompanied his roar with a fierce slap of the flat of his sabre across Bleu's rump.

Rocking backwards in the saddle, Jobert saw, in a nauseating haze, a wave of seven hundred roaring blue-coats rising above a wall of two hundred bawling white-coats.

'Stop!' Jobert hissed unheard. 'Please fucking stop.' Jobert could not identify blood, but the pulling action of the cross belt on his slung musketoon, pinned between himself and Moench, was intolerable.

'Rally! Sound Rally!' Jobert heard Bredieux roar.

'Moench, sound Rally!' Koschak repeated.

'I cannot,' said Moench through clenched teeth.

'Trumpeter Moench!' screamed Koschak. 'Drop Jobert's reins and sound fucking Rally!'

Moench gurgled tears and saliva as he struggled to spit out the urgent notes.

The redan descended into a cauldron of screams, grunts and musket fire. Suchet's battalion stabbed, bludgeoned and shot those defenders that evaded the gauntlet of circling chasseurs and lurking infantry skirmishers. Other battalion attack columns pressed onto the next of the redoubts in the defensive line.

With Moench's mare not pressing on Bleu, Jobert released his sabre to swing on its sword knot then lifted the cross belts off his left shoulder. With the reduction of weight from his musketoon and cartridge box, the pain in his upper chest subsided. As his vision swam in the redan's pungent mist of sulphur, burnt meat and shit, Jobert swallowed back his deep desire to vomit.

'To our first combat together, Jobert, since Mount Faron two and a half years ago,' said General Victor. Jobert choked on the burn of Victor's cognac. 'If you are finding it difficult to swallow, then drink more. Your fellows did superbly. How did they fare?'

'The squadron has four dead, sir, eight wounded and lost eleven horses.' Jobert looked towards Moench beside him. The bandage on Moench's thigh closed the slice of a musket ball that had torn his skin to shatter Moench's wooden saddle tree beneath. Moench muttered prayers of thanks for the saving of his testicles, his violin, his mare and his leg, in that order.

'The loss of your esteemed few saved many.' Victor jerked the hip flask at Jobert's arm in a sling before taking a pull on the liquor. 'And you?'

'A musket ball into my cross belts has broken my collar bone, sir. Just a bit stiff.' Jobert nodded to his thick, wide white cross belts, lying in the dirt beside him, which sported a deep musket-ball shaped gouge.

Victor raised his eyebrows. 'That was close, Jobert. I will fetch my doctor to assess the damage. Meanwhile, I have a restorative chartreuse from Suchet as— welcome, Colonel Spiccard. Your chasseurs fought bravely today, sir.'

Jobert huffed in pain to twist towards Spiccard, who had arrived behind him.

'You are too kind, sir.' Spiccard glared at Jobert. 'It was the least they could do to atone for their loss of vigilance in the screen. The regiment has much to do to recover our good name.'

'No, sir—,' said Jobert.

Victor stood straight with his hands on his hips. 'No, Colonel, you have been misinformed. Today's Austrians were a brigade that arrived late for yesterday's battle from Montenotte.' Victor pointed toward the eastern ridgelines.

'Your orders, sir,' said Jobert, 'were for my squadron screen to observe the roads to Spigno on either side of the Bormida.' Jobert thrust his stubbled chin towards the river valley to the north-west. 'And to link with the light infantry piquet on our eastern flank.'

Boyish charm melted Spiccard's face as he bowed to Victor. 'Your superior understanding, sir, brings my regiment great comfort.' Spiccard's eyes hardened as his gaze slashed across Jobert. 'Yet, such a situation of grave dereliction demands a thorough investigation and the severest punishment.'

Chapter Eight

'A litany of poor decisions resulting in unacceptable loss, Jobert.' Colonel Spiccard leant forward to Jobert, his fist pumping a rigid finger towards Jobert's slung left arm. 'Ponte di Nava. Dego. Savona ... twice. Now Dego again. Too eager to cross blades with scant regard for your men.'

'Not true, sir.' Jobert quivered with contained rage, his thoughts debating whether his sling would confound the drawing of his dagger contained within his jacket's left cuff. *Poke me and I will gut you.* 'In desperate moments, sir, I secured fleeting advantage, as the Republic would expect of any chasseur.'

Behind Fergnes, the regimental officers entered and assembled around the table.

Spiccard's menacing stance melted. 'I am not done with you, sir.' Spiccard turned to his place at the head of the table.

Fergnes directed a look of concerned enquiry towards Jobert's slung left arm.

Jobert masked his trembling to respond with an affirmative wink.

'The Austrian and Piedmontese commenced their offensive eight days ago,' said Spiccard to his assembled officers. 'In that time, it is estimated from prisoners and dead, they have lost seven thousand men, or about ten battalions.'

Soft whistles hissed from the audience.

'General Bonaparte is satisfied we have separated the Piedmontese from the Austrians. Now we have to keep them separated. As for the Piedmontese, they have established defensive lines to protect their vast magazines at Mondovi and block our advance to Turin.'

'Where are the 24th Chasseurs in this grand scheme, sir?' asked Fergnes.

'General Masséna's division is to march from Dego tomorrow to secure General Bonaparte's eastern flank. With 3rd Squadron escorting prisoners and wounded to Savona, 1st Squadron will guide the division. I will keep 2nd Squadron in reserve under Jobert's clipped wing.'

'Is there any word from General Bonaparte's headquarters of resupply, sir?' asked Jobert.

As he faced Jobert, Spiccard did not disguise his disdain.

Jobert caught Fergnes' frown at the exchange.

'General Bonaparte's strenuous demands on the commissary are having an effect,' said Spiccard. 'The next convoy is expected any day, despite the rains making the roads through the Col di Cadibona difficult for bullocks. On the bright side, the recent rains have held off the predations of the British navy to our fleet reaching Savona. General Bonaparte has shortened our lines of communication. The coastal luggers are able to resupply magazines of flour and ammunition at Oneglia, two days closer than Savona. Should we capture the supposed bountiful warehouses at Mondovi, the lines of communication will shorten further through Nice. Is there anything else, gentlemen? No? Then we are cloaked in martial glory, despite the negligence of some, and we are to receive resupply in abundance. The enemy trembles before us. We have orders to march against them at dawn. What other of our prayers need answering?'

Koschak had warned Jobert against riding, with one hand, an inexperienced Jaune up mountain paths. Jobert had reasoned, with little expectation of action, the ride would be an opportunity to school Jaune.

They had both been right.

Jaune's youthful energies, released from the constraints of Orlande's cart's traces and excited to be moving amongst a column of remounts, bounded up the rocky path, his body swerving and his head sweeping from side to side as he took in every new circumstance. The six-hour jolting of Jaune's impetuous footfalls had undone any healing of Jobert's broken bone.

Now Jobert's bruised chest, shoulders and back ached as he perched above the fire on a folding camp stool. The small fire swayed, flared and crackled with each wild gust. The eddies of wind in the gully caused resinous pine smoke and gritty ash to assail the eyes of those clustered around its intermittent heat.

In the still morning, the view of the distant dawn-touched Swiss Alps to the north or the vast, soft grey Mediterranean horizon to the south, was truly heart lifting. Apart from that dawn respite, the rest of the day on the heights of the lower Maritime Alps, and all through the night, the wind never abated. Exposed in their ridgeline outposts, the chasseurs cringed in their capes against the relentless wind. The camp of the inlying piquet found scant shelter amongst the stands of pine in the crags and gullies under the ranges' crest.

Moench played a mournful tune on his violin. The huddled chasseurs droned the ballad of misery.

Jobert stared into the whipped flames, his breathing humming Moench's dirge, his upper body pulsing with dull pain. Beyond the flames, in his mind, he walked the ranks of his dead. A purple scar across his right cheekbone spasmed. *Damn you, Spiccard, I can look them in the eye still.*

A cough broke his reveries. Catching Jobert's red-rimmed gaze, Orlande nodded towards the hissing kettle, the wash basin and the bar of soap. Jobert winced at the thought of removing his shirt in the biting wind. 'Orlande, I believe I will fall asleep well enough tonight. Place my evening draught under my saddle's pommel, so when I wake from rolling onto my injury, I might take my medicine and sleep until reveille.'

Orlande swept back his red forelock to reveal a forehead creased with concern. Orlande was most strict in his allowance of two drops of the dangerous hashish oil in Jobert's evening bouillon to assuage the pain and induce sleep between Jobert's blankets amongst the rocks.

'3rd Squadron has returned from Savona, sir,' said Moench, cradling his fiddle. 'The boys spoke of passing resupply convoys coming up the mountain. How far are we from Turin, sir?'

'Eighty kilometres, or three days march, I suppose.'

'Am I correct, sir,' asked Moench, 'if we break them tomorrow, we ought to dine in Turin on the evening of the 27th of April?'

'Is turnip gruel no longer to your liking, Moench?' asked Jobert.

Moench ducked his face to avoid the whipping smoke. 'Not at all, sir.'

'Why is today any different?' asked Jobert. 'We have been plagued by lack of supply for two years. Corrupted supply contracts, lines of communication interrupted by cities in open revolt, an uncaring commissary, wholesale theft by the carters and interdiction by the British navy. Why should we care about bogged bullock drays?'

Moench sank into his cape a little more.

Jobert rubbed his eyes to repress his pain-induced pessimism. *He did not deserve that.*

'Give thanks, lads,' said Koschak, 'for our post on the army's flanks where our horses can graze, rabbits be hunted, and local peasants be relieved of excessive goats and eggs. Be grateful we do not trudge the wasteland of the divisional columns, where the infantry, artillery and dragoons bicker for scraps.'

Jobert winced as the fire smoke blew embers into his face. 'The generals have the eternal choice from any campaign in history. Either feed the men or hang them when they steal.'

On this gloomy 25th of April, Masséna's screen maintained its pursuit of the broken Piedmontese army for a fifth day. The saturated columns of blue-coated Piedmontese evacuated the town of Cherasco across a series of bridges, stone and pontoon, spanning the rocky bed of the tumbling Stura River.

From their vantage point high on the steep riverside escarpment, Jobert and Chabenac's 2nd Squadron remained as regimental reserve, watching Colonel Spiccard and 3rd Squadron, in skirmish order, push back a troop of Piedmontese chevau-léger towards their retreating infantry columns.

Chabenac and Voreille, mounted beside Jobert, tucked their heads into the drizzle.

Jobert arranged the folds of his cape and covered his thighs over his sodden over-breeches. With his single good hand, he tugged the cape's collar against the bitter rain stinging his neck. As Jobert's right hand was busy with his cape, he pinched his reins in the fingertips emerging from his sling.

Rouge took a gust of rain as a reasonable excuse to wrench the reins from Jobert's hand and lower his head and nibble. Rouge's unkind movement yanked on Jobert's tender shoulder, at which Jobert moaned, hunching in an effort to control the pain. Rouge's reins slipped to the back of his ears, which presented an immediate danger of the horse stepping through his own reins and entangling himself. Once entangled, a horse might slip, fall or buck against his entrapment.

Chabenac dropped his sabre tip and retrieved the loose reins.

Jobert coughed his thanks as he reached with his dripping gloved hand to recover his reins.

'Sir,' asked Chabenac, once Jobert had controlled his breathing and resumed an erect posture, 'is it true the Piedmontese are seeking peace?' Chabenac's enthusiasm, despite the dreary weather, derived from a spirit that had enlivened all the chasseurs of the regiment.

'I believe so.' Jobert quivered with nausea. 'Colonel Murat, Bonaparte's senior aide, met with the Piedmontese yesterday.'

'Fifteen days, six victories, twenty-one colours, fifty-five guns, fifteen thousand prisoners, ten thousand dead.' Voreille recited the Army of Italy's recent proclamation to the troops with boyish pride.

'I would caution against declaring such a supreme victory too loudly, Voreille,' said Jobert. 'We have only pushed back a few defensive lines. We have not yet met the might of the kaiserliks in open battle.'

'Surely, sir, it is news well received,' said Chabenac, 'Moreover, glad tidings only a day after the trains distributed bread, beef, salt, brandy, vinegar, horseshoes and a quarter ration of grain.'

'Did news from your family arrive with the resupply?' asked Jobert. A calm smile spread across Chabenac's lips. *Your mask, my friend, when all is not well.*

'I am in no doubt mail from Paris will arrive soon,' said Chabenac. 'It gives me great comfort, sir, to know my mother and sister are safe with your family.'

Jobert grinned. 'Your mother maybe. I cannot imagine that schemes hatched by Michelle and Valmai may be considered safe.'

A 3rd Squadron trumpet screamed Charge.

Jobert, Chabenac and Voreille watched as 3rd Squadron, led by Spiccard, trotted forward in the slippery riverside meadows, sabres drawn. The rain ensured no chevau-léger discharged their musketoons, so the Piedmontese turned their horses and trotted towards the river.

Despite neither side retaining the ability to fire sodden weapons, a stand-off had occurred as a battalion of Piedmontese infantry had formed square on the far bank of a bridging pontoon. Spiccard held 3rd Squadron back from clattering onto the bridge. Away from Spiccard's command group, a rider, aide de camp Lieutenant Huin, cantered towards the drenched 2nd Squadron.

'Major Jobert, sir.' Huin saluted as he halted. 'Colonel Spiccard sends his compliments, and requests that 2nd Squadron maintain contact with the enemy cavalry across the Stura. With the Piedmontese infantry and chevau-léger established on the far bank, enemy sappers are preparing to cut the ties between the pontoon floats with their axes.' The four hunched their shoulders into the rain to appraise the bridge in question. 'Colonel Spiccard,' Huin continued, 'desires that 2nd Squadron's presence on the far bank causes the enemy to quit their destruction and resume their progress toward Turin.'

Chabenac's and Voreille's shoulders slumped as they looked to the white froth in the Stura's racing torrent beneath them.

Jobert's face sunk in despondency as he recognised fording the river, with Rouge slipping on the river rocks, would aggravate his injuries. 'Bath time, gentlemen. Let us be about it. Voreille, have 5th Company secure the near bank. Once 2nd Company has secured the far bank, I will signal you to cross. Moench, sound Advance. 2nd Squadron, column of fours, trot, march!'

Jobert was mesmerised. Sharp stars shone in the wide, indigo sky above the vast plains of the great River Po. The northern horizon was brushed by a dull glow of Turin fifty kilometres distant. *What delicacies lie within?*

'Here comes His Majesty's delegation now,' said Koschak.

Since sunset, mid-way between the opposing French and Piedmontese vedettes, a post had been established to coordinate the movement of delegates between the armies. Now, over a dozen mounted officers, French, Piedmontese and Austrian, peered towards a column of jogging torches moving south along the dim Turin road towards the 24th Chasseur picquets.

'Sergeant Major Koschak,' said Jobert, 'inform Captain Geourdai that the Piedmontese delegation is approaching.'

Didier leant toward Jobert – Didier's hussars were the French escort for the Piedmontese.

'Brother,' whispered Didier, 'I urge you to consider serving elsewhere before you are tarnished. Masséna, with his scandal at Dego now repeated at Cherasco, is an army-wide embarrassment. You risk too much. How is your shoulder?'

'It mends slowly,' said Jobert. 'Days in the saddle do not aid the healing process. I still cannot bear any weight on my left shoulder. No cross belts, musketoon or cartridge box.'

'Why, as a chief of squadron, do you persist in carrying a musketoon?' asked Didier.

Jobert shrugged with his right shoulder.

Raive, beside them, gave a derisive snort. 'You can take the man out of the battle-line, but ... say, my lads.' Turning his horse so as not to be overheard by the Piedmontese, Raive leant in. 'Bonaparte had three men shot today for looting.'

'Bonaparte's proclamation yesterday did not mention shooting.' Didier passed Raive a hip flask. 'I read those men found looting are to be sent in chains to the road gangs. But, I suppose, the proclamation was in response to Masséna's division's outrageous pillaging of Cherasco.'

Raive coughed on his sip of local rosolio.

'Gentlemen,' said Didier, loud enough for the Piedmontese officers to hear, 'France has striven for four years to remove the Piedmontese threat to our frontier and here we have achieved it in fifteen days. We ought to savour the moment.' Didier lifted his hipflask in a toast towards the Piedmontese officers.

The Piedmontese officers spun in their saddles and glared at Didier.

'Is it correct, sir,' Didier continued, 'that General Bonaparte's brother, Joseph, Deputy Saliceti and our friend Colonel Murat departed for Paris today with over twenty captured colours? With the armistice declared for tomorrow, we will enter Turin and enjoy all that it has to offer.'

A Piedmontese chevau-léger officer tugged his horse to face Didier, fumbling to reach for his sabre. 'If you wish to cast dishonour on my homeland, sir, then I am at your service.'

Didier pressed his horse forward and, with an innocent smile, raised his hand in mock surprise at the chevau-léger's reaction.

Didier's humourless eyes dared the man to draw his blade.

Raive squeezed his horse between them. 'Gentlemen, enough! Compose yourselves this instant. Here you are, sir, goading us with your comments of ill-discipline. What do you call this? We shall not impede His Sardinian Majesty's delegation of peace between our two great nations with our petty squabbles.'

'Didier, stop it this instant,' said Jobert. 'I was hoping to send Koschak and Orlande into Turin with a shopping list. Do not upset my scheme.'

Didier bowed to Raive and the Piedmontese officers and, withdrawing from any potential affair, backed his horse away a few steps.

'Ah, there will be no entry into Turin under the negotiated arrangement,' said Raive, loud enough for the seething Piedmontese. 'The Army of Italy will remain south of the Stura and Tanaro rivers. His Majesty will retain his army, but we have been granted the honour of garrisoning key fortresses. No, we will not be entering Turin.'

Jobert twisted his face. *Damn! There goes our new stockings and Orlande's box of pepper.*

In the last light of the day, an enclosed coach, drawn by a team of four-in-hand, carried the Piedmontese plenipotentiaries. Flanking the coach's lacquered sides were four aides followed by an escort of blue-jacketed, torch-carrying Piedmontese dragoons. Jobert inspected the gleaming black horses of the dragoon escort. The Piedmontese dragoons raised their chins with disdain after running their eyes over Jobert's scruffy, slab-sided Rouge.

'Good evening, gentlemen.' Didier farewelled Raive and Jobert with a mischievous smile and joined his hussar escort in front of the carriage. With that, the delegation pressed on into the dusk for the twinkling lights of Cherasco on the escarpment above the Stura.

'Good evening, sir.' The Piedmontese chevau-léger officer addressed Raive, with a bitter look towards Didier's receding escort. With their evening duties complete, the chevau-léger returned to their outposts.

'Ah, here is my man,' said Raive.

As the coach and its attendees clattered into the evening, Jobert watched one of the Piedmontese aides move his horse to the roadside. The carriage continued and the Piedmontese dragoons trotted past him. The Piedmontese aide removed his feathered bicorne with a flourish and bowed his head plastered with powdered curls.

In the last light of the dull western sky and the receding torchlight of the delegation, Jobert recognised the sharp face and steady eyes of Inoubli.

Inoubli, once an Avignon dance master, now revealed to be one of a pair of identical twins.

Inoubli, a spy able to be in two locations at once.

Poor consolation for no pepper.

Chapter Nine
May 1796, Cherasco, Italy

The vine-enclosed cloister under which Jobert and Raive sat, high on the northern Cherasco escarpment, ought to have provided them with a commanding view north of the Stura River. Yet this afternoon, any vista of wide, green plains, or the snow-capped majesty of the Alps, had been shrouded by the shifting drizzle.

Having found a slouched position on his folding camp chair in which his bruised shoulder throbbed the least, Jobert's mind drifted with the curtains of soft rain that wafted around him.

'How is the shoulder?' asked Raive.

'I am to keep it slung for a further two weeks, sir. I still cannot take the weight of my cross belts, even without my musketoon or cartridge box attached.'

Raive arched his eyebrows. 'When might you consider conducting yourself less like a sergeant and relinquish your musketoon?'

Jobert shrugged.

'My goodness, Jobert,' said Raive, 'what downcast lumps we are. What weighs on your mind?'

Jobert's mouth curled with bitterness as he twisted his sling's fraying edge. 'Being the object of mistrust. Spiccard persists in blaming me for the Austrians return at Dego.'

Raive nodded slowly. 'His ill humours will pass, my lad. The basis for my own melancholy is the supply crisis, the origin of the division's shame. Our infantry has now devolved into a pillaging mob twice, at Dego and again on our entry here. The 24th Chasseurs received their resupply, have they not?'

'Yes, sir,' said Jobert, 'we received a load of bread, grain and horseshoes in the last few days. As for local sources, our horses have plenty of forage, but the farms and villages were stripped of food by the retreating Piedmontese.'

'If there was only a means to guarantee supply,' said Raive. 'Speaking of which, your family's carts have arrived.' Reaching into his tailcoat's pockets, Raive handed Jobert a hefty purse and an envelope.

Jobert enclosed the purse within his own waistcoat, then turned the envelope over in his fingers. 'My cousin in Paris, sir.'

'There we are! A bright note on a dreary day. I have two items of news that might add to the merriment. While on his trip to Paris to present the captured enemy colours to the Directory, Deputy Saliceti has had his official seal stolen.'

'Indeed, sir?' Jobert smirked. 'Used swiftly, that seal could provide a passport to great comfort.'

'Perhaps.' Raive shrugged. 'On an unrelated topic, our division will soon be receiving a full ration of salt, candles, weapon oil, axle grease and stationery.'

'Hah!' Jobert's eyes narrowed. 'What of leather, sir. Harness and saddlery repairs and soles for boots. And grain. If we are to match the Austrian cavalry on the open plain, we must return to at least a daily half-ration—'

A quiet cough from Moench. Jobert and Raive turned to steaming cups of coffee.

'How heals the thigh, Moench?' asked Raive.

Moench grimaced towards the bandages evident through his unbuttoned over-breeches. 'It has closed well enough, thank you, sir. I have not been in the saddle these last two weeks to avoid the sutures splitting open. It remains stiff and tender.'

'No fever?' asked Raive.

'No, thanks to the Blessed Virgin.' Moench crossed himself.

'Virgin?' Raive turned to Jobert. 'I have heard you referred to at headquarters as a Virginian. Why ever so?'

'A curiosity, sir, invented by ...' Jobert noted Moench lingering. 'Is there something else, Moench?'

'May I ask a question, sir, while you are both together?' Moench winced. 'Now that we will not be entering Turin, sir, I am unsure how to close my book.'

'The armistice with Piedmont was signed on the 28th of April,' said Jobert. 'That agreement included the provision that the Army of Italy would not enter the capital. Pay all wagers placed for the 28th of April.'

'Pay the winnings in coin, young Moench,' said Raive. 'That will encourage more punters for your next round.'

Moench's eyes darted above his thick, curling moustache to calculate the financial impact. 'What do you feel the next wager might be, sir?'

'The number of days from General Masséna's orders until entry into Milan,' said Jobert into his steaming tea.

'Milan, sir?'

'Milan, Moench,' said Jobert. 'The Austrians gather behind their river-line defences in their province of Lombardy. To secure our gains in Piedmont, the Army of Italy now needs to press into Lombardy. That requires the capture of the capital, Milan.'

'May I ask how far it is to Milan?' asked Moench.

'One hundred and eighty kilometres. Six days march,' said Jobert.

'More than just Milan, gentlemen,' said Raive. 'Milan is certainly the rich prize Paris seeks. But, for an army to hold Lombardy, a great fortress must be captured. The fortress city of Mantua.'

Paris
11ᵗʰ April 1796

Happy birthday, darling André,

I hope the Mediterranean weather provides a delightful day for a birthday picnic on the seashore. Thirty-one years. How time flies. Has Didier joined you on the Mediterranean coast with his regiment? How much fun it must be for you both to be together again.

Aunt Sophie is very well and sends her love. Our workhouses continue to fulfil the government contracts. Have you received your mirliton cap? That particular contract has been a great boon to our situation.

Life continues to be both challenging and exhilarating. The extreme inflation of prices continues to plague the city in the aftermath of the Terror. Cooking oil, eggs, meat, wine and flour are outrageously expensive. The hunger of the mob continues to affect the stability of the government. We are ever thankful for every arrival of the carts from the farm. The provender they bring is heaven sent.

We see Duque often. He is preparing for his end-of-year exams. He is nervous and morose, yet he applies himself to his studies.

For Valmai and I, our evenings and Sundays are spent in a whirl of engagements. Balls, garden parties, card evenings, recitals and meeting friends at the flush of new restaurants. Have you and your friends tried dining at a restaurant yet? Everyone meets with everyone. Liaison is easy. Aunt and Madame de C. are scandalised. I am unsure if the fashion has reached the south, but evening gowns here in Paris are nearly transparent. Valmai and I create quite a stir when we step out. We must hide our gowns from our despairing matrons under heavy coats.

Valmai and I have met three gorgeous brothers. Édouard, Alphonse and Auguste Colbert. Of noble birth, the family having lost their property and fortune, the boys demonstrated their loyalty to the Republic by joining the National Guard. All three have paid us the most respectful and courteous visits at home.

Valmai is quite taken by young Auguste. He is a second lieutenant in the infantry. Although the middle boy, Alphonse, is quite a dear, I am enjoying the attentions of elder brother Édouard. Édouard was a second lieutenant in the 11th Hussars but was recently denounced based on his former nobility and suspended from the Army of the West. It is all blatantly unfair. There he is serving against the wicked royalist Chouannerie on the Atlantic coast, is not that proof enough of his loyalty? I thought the Terror was over.

Nevertheless, I am very fond of Édouard, and he is very attentive towards me. I want you and Didier to meet the three brothers Colbert. I know for sure that all you boys will be firm friends immediately.

I suspect Aunt Sophie has summoned father from the farm. I am terrified as to his reaction. But I am assured of Édouard's fondness for me, and that father will find him a most erudite fellow.

More news soon,
Write to me this minute,
We love you very much,
Your loving cousin,
Michelle

'Welcome to great River Po, brother,' said Jobert, 'and beyond, behold Lombardy, a province soon to be taken from the Holy Roman Empire.'

Didier whistled at the immense width of rippling grey-brown water, the setting sun daubing a pink hue to the white-capped waves which surged onto the long, dark islands that wallowed mid-stream. The current gurgled and insects hummed while water birds flapped and squawked to their evening roosts.

'Then prior to us receiving more beneficence from His Imperial Majesty in the coming weeks,' said Didier, 'I come bearing gifts already bestowed from his Italian, Austrian and Hungarian domains. General Bonaparte is distributing the spoils of the great fortress of Alessandria.'

Returning to the glowing coals of Orlande's cooking fire, Didier conjured wondrous gifts from his packhorse's panniers. Moench and Tulloc gasped in delight at each novelty produced. Didier held up a solid haunch wrapped in muslin, then hefted a heavy sack. 'Smoked ham, flour, a fromagio Raschea, and a salsiccia di Bra.' Didier held up a spiral sausage. 'And for you, Orlande, old friend, pepper.'

Orlande opened the tin canister, inhaled its exotic scent, then passed the canister to Moench and Tulloc.

Didier passed a bottle to his brother. 'And for our good cheer this evening, Hungarian unicum.'

Jobert pulled the cork with his teeth and savoured a mouthful of the contents. The smooth liquor glided over his tongue to warm his belly. 'Didier, I have a letter from Michelle. Have you had news from Paris?'

'I have not.'

Jobert fished about in his waistcoat pocket and passed an envelope to his brother. He sipped on his wine as Didier read.

With a sardonic smile, Didier folded the letter back into the envelope. 'Beautiful young men meeting with beautiful young women. Is there anything finer in life? There was talk of transparent dresses as the 1st Hussars passed through Grenoble and Lyons. Possibly a reaction to having survived the Terror, Paris is daring to breathe again. How stunning our beautiful cousin must look in a sheer shift?'

Jobert scowled into the campfire's flames.

'Why ever would we not be happy for her?' asked Didier. 'For so long our gorgeous cousin has held out against suitors. Would you rather be here on campaign, or cutting a fine figure, in your well-cut uniform highlighting your broad shoulders, your dress boots flashing as you dance with an attractive girl at a Parisian party?'

Jobert drained his unicum, avoiding Didier's eye. 'Do not patronise, Didier. The attractive distraction of there can never be an alternative for the gravity of here.'

'Hah! You acknowledge the delight of young women in sheer gowns. Then what disturbs you so? You eschewed both braids and queue, preferring to be clean shaven and wear your hair cut short in the Roman style. How very fashionable you are, dear brother.'

'Your point, dear brother?' asked Jobert.

'You adopt the latest fashion but resent your cousin the same.'

'I feel protective,' said Jobert. 'A twenty-three-year-old woman of comfortable means, with no immediate male protector, should we not feel concern?'

'We are not her father, André,' said Didier. 'Neither are we there beside her to know of these three brothers, and whoever else is influencing her. We love her and support her, do we not? Until she chose to wear the latest fashion, did we not trust her implicitly?'

Jobert turned his cup around in his hands. 'What allows you to be so open-minded?'

For a moment Didier dropped his eyes, tightened his lips, a sadness passing across his face. With a laughing snort, he dispelled the sentiment. 'We must trust her judgement. If she is lost to love, then so be it. Have we not all been swept away by its violent currents?'

Jobert's mouth soured as he refilled his cup.

Didier raked some errant twigs into the fire. 'What absorbs your regiment here on the Po?'

'Deception.' Jobert looked to the northern banks where twinkled a multitude of Austrian campfires extending far along the bank in both directions only to fade into the gloom of dusk. 'The army would take up to five days to cross at one place. Five days in which the Austrians can concentrate and drive us back into the river. We provide deception for Bonaparte's actual crossing point. We intercept Austrian reconnaissance patrols. We gather boats and put on a show as if we are to build a bridge. I masquerade in a bicorne with extra feathers to appear as a senior officer conducting reconnaissance of the far bank. We huff and puff, point and strut in front of the Austrian vedettes. Is your regiment not part of this deception?'

'No.' Didier stared hard across the expanse of dark water. 'Because we are part of the strike to the far side. Are you aware of Bonaparte's new advance guard?'

'Is that so?' Jobert sat upright on his camp stool. 'I have heard that Bonaparte has stripped the grenadier companies out of the line battalions and the carbineer companies out of the light battalions to form a composite brigade. I know one of the advance guard's new commanders, Colonel Lannes.'

'Indeed, a formidable six-battalion force,' said Didier. 'As for me, the hussars and the dragoons have been added to this advance guard. My regiment has received orders to advance south of the Po, behind your screen to an easterly crossing point.'

Jobert arched his eyebrows in enquiry.

Didier leant conspiratorially towards him. 'Piacenza.'

'What? That would put us one hundred kilometres behind the Austrians ...' Jobert's eyes glinted in the firelight. '... and amongst the bounty of Milan. When do you march?'

'In three days,' said Didier. 'Sixth of May.'

Chapter Ten
May 1796, Battle of Lodi, Italy

'Welcome to Piacenza, sir,' said Jobert.

Spiccard flopped in a folding camp chair, his stockinged feet stretched out toward the fire. Spiccard looked as they all felt – haggard from three long days and two long nights in the saddle from Valenza to Piacenza. Despite numerous camp stools around the headquarters' fire, Spiccard gave Jobert no inclination he was invited to sit. Jobert rolled his hips to set his aching lower back in a less uncomfortable position.

'Jobert, is 2nd Squadron in camp on the north bank of the Po this evening?' asked Spiccard.

'Yes, sir. General Bonaparte's advance guard crossed here yesterday. General Laharpe's division crossed here today. May I ask the progress of General Masséna's division?'

'The last elements of General Masséna's division will have closed up by this evening,' said Spiccard. 'The division's infantry and artillery will cross the Po tomorrow morning. Are the pontoniers still operating the barges after dark?'

'Yes, sir,' said Jobert. 'What is your intent for 2nd Squadron, sir?'

Spiccard's eyes narrowed as he considered Jobert's slung arm. 'With us having secured the Po at Piacenza, the Austrians have lost Milan. They now race to Mantua to retain their failing grip on Lombardy. To facilitate a swift onward advance, General Bonaparte's intent is to capture key river towns, and their bridges, across the first of the Po's northern tributaries, the River Adda. General Masséna has been ordered to secure the bridge over the Adda at the town of Lodi. The 24th Chasseurs à Cheval are to ensure the division moves swiftly across the Po tomorrow and strikes out for Lodi the day after. Is there anyone on the road to Lodi?'

'Lodi is thirty kilometres from the Piacenza crossing points, sir,' said Jobert. 'The new advance guard man the bridgehead. Their northern outposts are halfway to Lodi.'

'Throughout tomorrow's crossing,' said Spiccard, 'and the advance north the day after, it is of pivotal interest to General Masséna whether the Austrians have destroyed the bridge. So, at four o'clock tomorrow morning, Jobert, march 2nd Squadron for Lodi.'

'Very good, sir. If that is all, sir, would you excuse me?' Jobert turned his aching frame towards the horse lines.

'Jobert ...' said Spiccard, the tone menacing. Jobert turned back. Spiccard directed a sour stare at the fire. 'Jobert, there is too much at stake for you to act impetuously. General Bonaparte has divisions here, there and everywhere. My focus on General Masséna's requirements need not be diverted by some fiasco of your manufacture. Do you hear me? In the coming days, you are to make no decision without reference to me. Send me the choices that you face. I shall send a response that accords with General Bonaparte's desires. Is that understood?'

Jobert saluted and responded through clenched teeth, 'Yes, sir.'

The elite advance guard battalions secured the town of Lodi at midday. An Austrian rear guard defended the far bank of the Adda River, especially the eastern end of the vital Lodi bridge. Clouds of ravens rose from their rooks in the town disturbed by the cannons' thunder as the French gunners established their ranging shots across the Adda. Beyond the town, a vast haze of dust identified the approaching columns of Masséna's infantry.

Jobert withdrew his pocket watch. Two o'clock. He watched dusty columns of blue, brown and red hussars with their jaunty mirlitons, followed by further columns of green-jacketed dragoons, with their brass-helmets set with sweeping long manes, assemble for a flanking manoeuvre.

Didier and a small hussar escort trotted to a halt beside Jobert's retinue. 'Good morning, brother,' said Didier, 'General Bonaparte has ordered the cavalry to seek fords upriver of Lodi, then outflank the Austrian defences from the north.'

'My patrols have found a possible site,' said Jobert.

'You have found a crossing?' asked Didier. 'Where? Why have you not sent your squadron across?'

'I cannot as the crossing is unproven.'

'Then prove the crossing,' said Didier.

'No,' said Jobert.

'Why not?'

Jobert lowered his face to inspect his gloves. 'I have sent a request to my commanding officer seeking approval.'

Didier stared at Jobert with incredulity. 'Since when have you ever sought approval?'

'You know how Spiccard is disposed to me,' said Jobert.

'He will be none the wiser if Murat, or some such, has ordered you.'

'Leave me alone, brother.' Jobert bunched the reins in his fists. 'You just want the glory of appearing on the far bank. If you want the crossing, you find it.'

'Leave me alone, big brother? Are you five?' Didier lunged forward in his saddle towards Jobert. 'We all want that crossing, you idiot, especially the infantry about to assault across the bridge into the kaiserliks' gun muzzles. With the Lodi bridge still standing, time is critical. If this bridge is destroyed and our advance on Mantua delayed, a delay caused because a chasseur officer waited for orders ... André, you have a squadron. Send a troop across. Please. Spiccard need never know. Go on. Let me know what you find.'

Jobert gritted his teeth and glowered at Didier. 'Corporal Duval, take us to this possible crossing.'

Following the patrol to the site, Jobert dismounted to force his way through muddy gullies, sticks and branches, boulders hidden by a carpet of ferns and pools of dead murk that shielded the riverbanks.

Once perched on the two-metre banks, Jobert and the 2nd Squadron commanders assessed the Adda River. The shallow shoals stretched away to deeper, swifter current before sloshing against the far banks some two hundred metres distant.

'The far bank is close here, sir,' said Voreille.

'Or it is an island,' said Koschak.

Jobert assessed, from the debris hanging in nearby branches and banked up against rock ledges, how far the water had receded from the snow-melt flood peak. 'The effort required to cut a path is far from ideal and the depth of the river unknown, yet the gunfire at the bridge demands we press on.' Jobert turned to the concerned faces around him. 'Voreille, have 5th Company stand to horse. Parade your best swimmers ready to cross, stripped down to their drawers and sword belts.

'Sergeant Major, have 2nd Squadron's trains parade with 5th Company. Collect and connect all horse- and tent-lines so that a rope can be tethered across the river. Gather the squadron's shovels, axes and bush-saws.

'Moench, pass to all trumpeters, no calls to alert the kaiserliks. Keep your wound out of the water. Stay with the horses. Tulloc, dismount and bring your rifle. Fetch Corporal Duval and his rifle.

'Chabenac, if a ford is possible, 2nd Company will cross and secure a bridgehead on the far bank. Until then, post vedettes behind us onto the road and to our north and cut a better laneway from the road to this point.'

'And where might you be, sir?' asked Chabenac.

Jobert grimaced as he withdrew his arm clear of the sling. 'I will go with Voreille.'

Chabenac set his eyes hard on Jobert. 'I must state my concern at your participation in this endeavour, sir.' Chabenac lowered his voice. 'We are less, sir, when you are injured.'

Jobert snorted with frustration. 'I am thankful for your concern, truly, but my arm is fine. It has been over three weeks.'

Chabenac looked to Koschak. Koschak shook his head without unpinning his disapproving glare from Jobert,

'Sir,' said Chabenac, his face determined, 'I beg you only cross when the line is established.'

Jobert gave a single nod of compliance. 'I acknowledge that I am not required to confirm a ford, especially as I recover from injury. Yet, I need to know what lies beyond before committing my chasseurs.'

Naked, except for their underdrawers, four chasseurs waded across the muddy shoals for twenty metres, before bobbing and paddling through the next one hundred and fifty metres of current. Jobert tempered his excitement when he saw the men standing mid-stream with the current slapping their chests. Jobert then knew mounted men could ford the river, without their horses needing to swim and their firearms safe from immersion.

Initiated by a wave from the far bank, ten more chasseurs entered the brown thrashing current, wearing underdrawers, boots and sword-belts and feeding out lengths of rope usually held for hitching horses and suspending tents in camp. With an exultant cheer from the horsemen watching their mates, the line was secured to stout trees on either bank.

'Voreille, Yinot, Sergeant Major,' called Jobert, stripping out of his tailcoat and over-breeches, 'on me.'

After trudging across the boot-sucking mud, Jobert led Yinot's troop into the deeper water.

The weight of men clinging to the sagging line bowed to an alarming degree in the surging current. The rope was to guide the men, not act as a firm banister upon which to take their mass. Jobert gritted his teeth in effort and discomfort as he paddled his tender left arm to remain upright in the deep water, dragged down into the current by the shifting rope and tripping over the rocks lining the riverbed.

Having trudged across the shoals and ascending the banks of the eastern side of the Adda River, Jobert sank to his knees, breathing heavily, surprised at the exertion required. 'Voreille, send a message back to the hussars that we have confirmed a ford. Yinot and Koschak, vedettes out. Find the edge of the river's tree line.'

Jobert watched Voreille supervise the crossing of men with their musketoons, cartridge belts, shovels, axes and bush-saws floating on make-shift rafts of staves, paillasses and water casks. The long line of men, slipping on the unseen river rocks below, gripped the unsteady line with one hand and struggled to direct the rafts bobbing on the current with the other.

As Jobert hailed the squadron's marksmen, Duval and Tulloc, to join him, Koschak came scrambling over the rocks in heavy, mud-slimed boots.

Koschak shook his head, wiping the sweat from his forehead with a muddy shirtsleeve. 'It is a mid-stream island, and a channel of bog lies on the other side. The best path is to keep to the island's banks towards its upstream tip then cross to the far bank.'

Jobert turned to the bedraggled men around him. 'Voreille, I will take Yinot's troop and seek the best way across to the edge of the tree line. Yinot, take one of your platoons, Koschak, take the other. The marksmen and I will mark the centre of the line.

'Voreille, with your remaining troop, form a line of guides starting from the far bank. Dressing the head of your line off me in the centre of Yinot's screen, re-tether the rope spanning the river. Have some of your men stand in the stream marking the shallowest water and the best footing should 2nd Company need to cross. Have others clear routes around the island's banks and dig out the banks to allow horses to ascend.'

Following quick directions to the 5th Company soldiers, Jobert and Voreille moved forward, off the island and into the slime-capped ooze which separated the island from the true eastern bank, then patrolled further through a thirty-metre belt of stunted trees and thick scrub separating the riverbank from the open meadows to the east.

As Jobert observed the alignment of the patrols as the shadowy vegetation allowed, Yinot came flailing through the branches towards himself and Voreille, his thick, black queue still sodden with river-water but his drooping moustache slick with sweat.

'We have found the edge of the tree line, gentlemen,' said Yinot. 'Kaiserlik hussars are patrolling along the road beyond.'

'Have we been seen?' asked Jobert.

A pistol shot, then shouting, sounded from beyond the edge of the trees.

Jobert exhaled a disappointed sigh. 'If Bonaparte wants this crossing, we need to fight to hold it. Voreille, send a runner to Chabenac. Have him send a troop across. Leave a troop in reserve on the west bank.'

The three officers pushed through the branches to kneel beside Koschak. Duval and Tulloc, cradling their prized rifles, crouched nearby. Squatting in the concealing grass and bushes, they observed in the meadow beyond a troop of blue-clad Austrian hussars, formidable in their cylindrical, peaked shakos, forming a battle-line. As the Austrian trumpets screamed a repetitive call, other fainter trumpet calls from the north responded.

'Kaiserlik reinforcements will soon be here,' said Koschak.

'Captain Voreille, sir,' asked Yinot, 'is that the hussar officer you struck down last year?'

Everyone glanced at the tall, thick-set Austrian. Astride a glistening, impatient black charger, the man was clean-shaven and sat with his hand on his hip, flaunting his contempt for the French by not drawing his sabre.

'They all look the same with powdered wigs,' said Jobert at the distraction, more intent at assessing the vegetation's disruptive effect on mounted troops transitioning from column in the river to line before departing the tree line.

'No, that is not my man, but a similar build though,' said Voreille studying the enemy officer with his own glass. 'My fellow had a badly crushed nose and cheekbones.'

'I recognise him as the commander of the hussars we pushed back on the first day at Dego,' said Koschak. 'Bredieux also felt that this prick was your man at Savona, sir.'

'Stop being distracted by this idiot,' said Jobert. 'Tulloc and Duval, kill the hussar officer.'

Duval and Tulloc fired.

The legs of the glistening black charger folded, the horse sinking with a long groan to its knees. A soldier in the line behind the now alarmed officer was punched from the saddle.

'The wind, sir,' grunted the flash-scarred Duval.

'Piss off, you idle bastards,' said Koschak. 'Try again. Load!'

'Stay focused, lads,' said Jobert. 'Chabenac is now moving forward and will become trapped in this wood line. Voreille, have your guides bring their shovels, axes and bush-saws to clear access forward to these enemy hussars.'

Jobert and Voreille returned to the riverside to see the progress of the 5th Company guides and the assembly of Chabenac's leading troop.

Jobert, Chabenac and Voreille glanced across in alarm when the reserve troop of 2nd Company, led by Lieutenant Peugeot, splashed into view at the tip of the island.

Voreille looked at the glutinous morass at the base of the banks and determined where his men might cut more egress slopes. 'The mud will suck their horseshoes off.'

'Lieutenant Peugeot, no one ordered you forward,' yelled Chabenac. 'There is no room within the tree line. The horses will become stuck in the shallows.'

'I was told by the 1st Hussars to push across, sir,' called Peugeot. 'The hussars are just behind me.'

Jobert watched Didier leading a column of 1st Hussars around the end of the low island, weaving a torturous route around Chabenac's waving guides who marked out the firmest, submerged passage. Jobert's mind raced as he foresaw hundreds of bogged horses with nowhere to turn, and hundreds of horsemen making independent decisions as to where the best path lay.

'Didier!' Jobert yelled above the pandemonium of Peugeot's chasseurs, cursing as they urged their remounts to clamber the bank and Didier's splashing, swearing hussars. 'A squadron of enemy hussars is forming beyond the tree line.'

A concentrated cannonade erupted from the direction of the Lodi bridge causing every head to spin towards the powerful roar, although nothing could be seen within the restrictions of the low, dark canopy.

Didier contemplated the slope of slurry he urged his horse to ascend. 'They are assaulting across the Lodi bridge,' called Didier. 'My regiment is behind me and the 15th Dragoons follow them. Clear the way. I need to set a battle-line.'

Jobert stumbled across the rocks towards the seventy horseman clumped amongst the trees, chasseurs bent over their horses' necks to avoid the low branches. '2nd Company, skirmishers out on the northern flank of the enemy hussars. Go, Chabenac, go!'

The 2nd Company trumpeter's call of Skirmishers Out was muffled due to both the intervening foliage and the invective of the non-commissioned officers urging the chasseurs, blocked by stumps, rocks and boughs, to press forward.

Jobert heard a ragged volley fire on the far side of the stumbling horsemen followed by a muted roar of voices.

Didier's hussars crammed into the spaces left by the Chabenac's chasseurs, the low vegetation knocking their mirliton caps and catching on their musketoons and sky-blue, fur-trimmed pelisse jackets.

Jobert stood on a rock, his arms wide with sabre in hand, encrusted with filth, sodden hair plastered to his forehead, face pale and trembling with cold, squelching boots, muddy shirt sleeves and sword belt, with neither hat, coat nor horse.

What will Spiccard make of this?

'On me, brother! Form the 1st Hussars on me!'

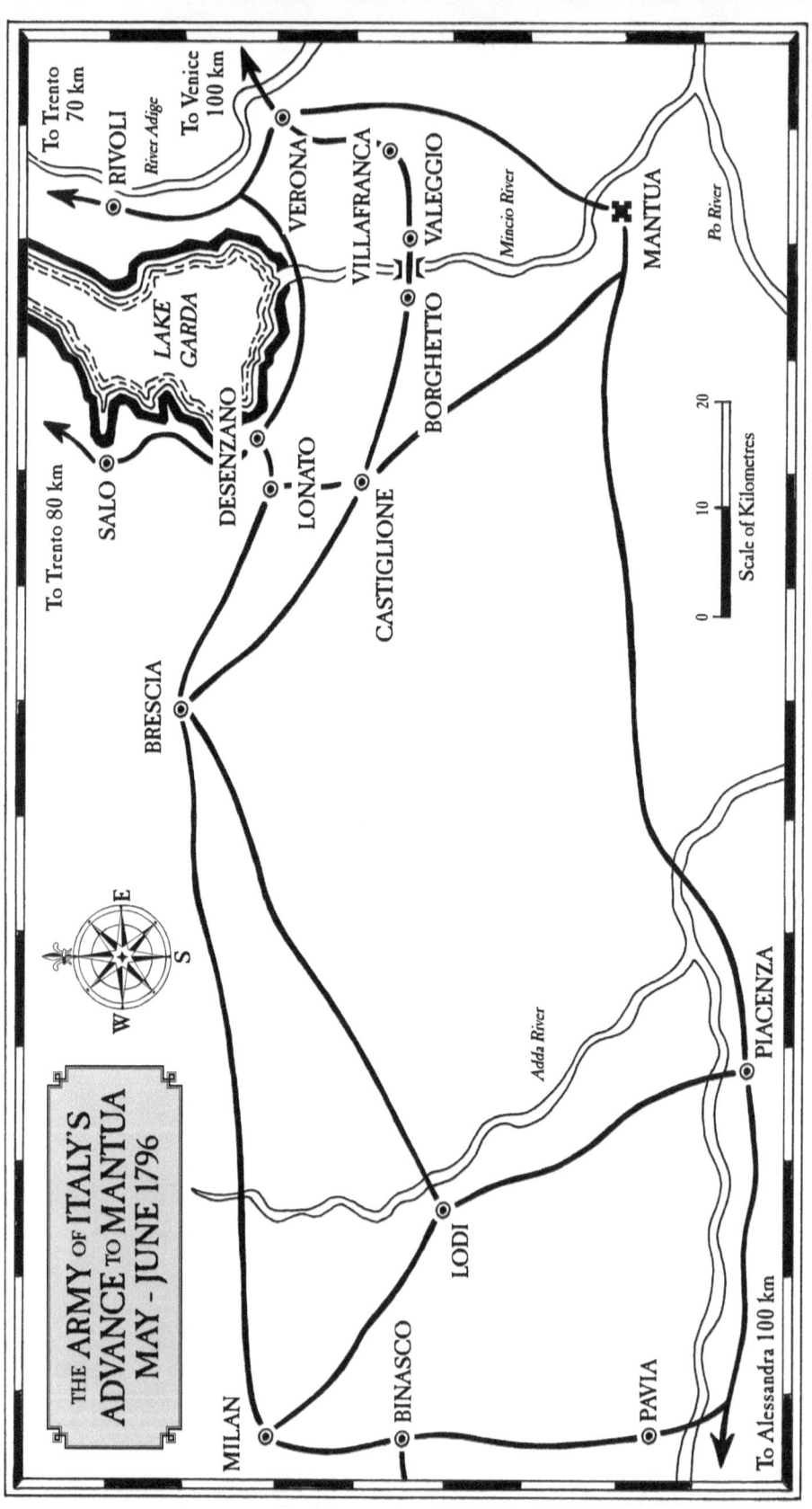

THE ARMY OF ITALY'S
ADVANCE TO MANTUA
MAY - JUNE 1796

N
W E
S

To Trento 70 km

RIVOLI   River Adige

To Trento
80 km

SALO

LAKE
GARDA

DESENZANO

LONATO

To Venice
100 km

VERONA

VILLAFRANCA

VALEGGIO

BORGHETTO   Mincio River

MANTUA

Po River

CASTIGLIONE

BRESCIA

Scale of Kilometres
0   10   20

Adda River

PIACENZA

LODI

BINASCO

MILAN

PAVIA

To Alessandra 100 km

Chapter Eleven
May 1796, Milan, Italy

Four afternoons later, Jobert stretched out his legs on his washed woollen shabraque overlaid with his scrubbed blankets. He wriggled his bare toes as he bit into a large strawberry.

Leaning on a warm stone wall in the late afternoon sun, Jobert watched the darting dragonflies zip in and out of the shadows of the leafy boughs covering the nearby stream. Troopers from 2nd Company were singing and laughing as they watered their horses in the cool, fresh water.

Picking another strawberry from the punnet, Jobert looked to where his horses grazed in a sheep fold. The grass was so long he could not see the tops of their ears while they ate. Bleu groaned with both effort and pleasure as he rolled on his back amongst the sweet leaves. Overcome with emotion, Jobert's eyes watered at the sight of his precious horses so much at ease.

Before he replaced his clean stockings and polished boots, Jobert stretched his left arm wide in an arc around his body, testing his range of movement, delighted in the freedom from the sling. As he moved his arm in the golden light, Jobert's freshly bathed skin tingled with the contact with his clean drawers and shirt – Jobert's first bath in a tub since he departed Savona some five weeks before. Jobert had even engaged the village barber to attend to matters of appearance above the collar.

Jobert entered the enclosed farmyard to stride across the gravel towards Tulloc holding Koschak's horse and the packhorse, as Orlande unpacked paper-wrapped parcels from the cart.

Koschak paused in his unbuckling of the packsaddles. 'You have done fucking what? Oh, Tulloc, you dumb bastard.'

Tulloc trembled.

Koschak gripped bulging panniers to steady himself. 'Our pay is four months in arrears. We are paid two months in coin. This is the first pay in coin since we left Avignon in over two years. I cannot believe you have spent twenty francs in less than forty-eight hours. I cannot fucking believe it, son.'

Tulloc cringed. 'I still have two francs left, Sergeant Major.'

Jobert held up his hands and let Orlande fill his arms with parcels.

Standing in the cart above both Koschak and Tulloc, Orlande sank onto one of the trunks he was sorting. 'Tulloc, on what did you spend it?'

Tulloc glanced up to Orlande, his face creased with anguish. 'Moench's wager and repaying my tally to you,'

'You are an utter fool to bet on Moench's wagers,' said Koschak. 'But you should still have over a month's pay remaining, man. What did you spend eight or nine francs on?'

Tulloc dropped his eyes and searched the pebbles under the cart for answers.

'Is it this girl?' Orlande asked.

'What fucking girl?' asked Koschak. 'Not those little tramps in the market. Moench is leading you astray, my lad. I will kick his arse when I find the little bastard.'

'No, Sergeant Major,' said Tulloc, 'she is not a whore, she is ...'

Orlande gave Koschak a hard stare. 'She is special, yes?'

'Yes,' said Tulloc.

'And you bought her something nice?' asked Orlande.

'Yes,' said Tulloc.

'And that was?' asked Orlande.

'Ribbon and a brush from Madame Quandalle.'

'For shit's sake, boy,' said Koschak. 'Even the cantinière's prices should not cost you eight francs. A couple of sous, a franc at the most.'

Tulloc bit his lip. 'I also bought a bottle of wine.'

'Are you a fucking imbecile?' Koschak slashed a surcingle into the gravel. 'You bought wine in cash? In a city occupied by an army, you bought a one-franc bottle for eight times its price.'

'You bought the wine to share with the girl?' asked Orlande, pressing his glasses up his nose. 'Yes, you should have sought Madame Quandalle first, nevertheless, did you have a pleasant picnic?'

Tulloc allowed himself a slight grin.

'You could have had a harlot for a franc and be done with it,' said Koschak. 'Oh, get out of my sight, lad. Wash all the horses in the stream before turning them out.'

As Jobert followed Koschak and the panniers into the small, dirt-floor cottage of their billet, Jobert smelt the alcohol on Koschak's breath.

Koschak let his anger subside by dumping the panniers on-to the kitchen table. 'Paying us in cash. What was Bonaparte thinking?'

Orlande pressed his spectacles back onto the bridge of his nose as he sorted the parcels causing fragrant odours to fill the room. 'That we would toast his health, I am sure.'

'From where did he conjure the money?' asked Koschak.

'I have heard he has collected twenty million francs. A fair price for Milan to pay for liberty from the Austrians.'

'The sum is equivalent to Milan's annual taxation for four years,' said Orlande. 'The Duke of Modena has been forced to pay over seven million francs so French troops will not enter his lands. This is creating deep aggravation amongst the people.'

'You think so? Koschak considered Orlande with a scowl. 'Surely Lombardy seeks to become a republic? More so than Piedmont, anyway.'

Orlande stared hard at Koschak. 'Planting trees of liberty in each town we pass through may not be enough to appease the people we steal from. Our convoys depart the city loaded with artwork. I have heard a troop of dragoons has taken one hundred of the finest carriage horses to Paris. No doubt a reminder to Parisian officials to think kindly of the Army of Italy.'

'And its commander,' said Jobert.

Orlande laid out a series of parcels wrapped in wax paper and tied with string, smaller bundles, metal canisters and small bags. 'I have satisfied most of our needs, sir. Three sets of underwear, two toothbrushes, a comb and one new blanket each. Toothpowder, bars of soap, tobacco, chocolate powder, sugar, herbs and spices. I will return to the city tomorrow. It will take another day to have boots resoled and our over-breeches and gloves repaired. And I found these for you, sir.'

Jobert unwrapped the paper to find a small matchwood box containing eight slim cigars. 'Thank you, Orlande,' said Jobert, inhaling the scent of rolled tobacco. 'What news of Milan, gentlemen?'

'Masséna entered Milan today, sir,' said Koschak. 'Bonaparte will enter tomorrow. The Austrians still occupy a citadel in the centre of the city, but no one seems to care. The city turned out to gawp at the parade and the markets continued to trade.'

'Any more news concerning the death of Laharpe?' asked Jobert.

Koschak breathed deeply and straightened his shoulders, cleared his throat and spat forcefully into the fire. 'The word is that when General Laharpe was killed last week, it was probably by his own men. An unintentional mistake in an Austrian night attack, they say. The division is devastated.'

Jobert stopped wrapping the ham with a rag and lowered his head.

'Lodi is required to supply forty thousand loaves per day,' said Orlande, 'from a population of ten thousand.'

Jobert winced. 'Then we had best enjoy our moment in paradise.'

'The hussars attached to the new advance guard have disgraced themselves,' said Koschak.

'The 1st Hussars?' asked Jobert

'I am unsure, sir. The hussars in question hold the outpost line to the east. They have looted a village. The hussars have stripped the church and stolen from the women sheltering within.'

Jobert uncorked a bottle of amaretto. 'I wonder if Bonaparte will shoot a hussar?'

Koschak held a glowing twig to his pipe bowl. 'They have nicknamed him the "little corporal". At Lodi last week, he confirmed the lay of individual gun barrels, as would a corporal, prior to the assault across the bridge.'

Jobert shrugged. 'He is an artilleryman, I suppose.'

'Soon all these divisions will cease resting and become restless,' said Orlande. 'We will devour the countryside, as we did on the Mediterranean coast, and we will soon be in the midst of a disgruntled population. Like a plague of locusts, we need to keep moving. What would be your views on what is to come, sir?'

'As Tulloc has shown us, we are gorging on the bounty we have so long sought.' Jobert bent forward into the flames for a twig to light his cigar. 'May well Bonaparte and Masséna play at conquering heroes in the capital of their enemies, to strut in the halls of Milan as they were unable to in Turin, but we still have not defeated the Austrians. We have orders to march east to capture Mantua. Five days march east, Mantua is tucked tight, like a tick on a dog, between the Mincio and the Po. The might of the kaiserlik army still holds the Po valley between here and Venice.' Jobert's face soured. 'To enhance that triumph, Colonel Spiccard has relegated 2nd Squadron to guiding Masséna's divisional trains onto the march route.'

'But what of Venice, sir?' asked Orlande. 'What pleasantries might that city hold?'

'Hah! You can have Venice.' Jobert blew a long, blue stream of cigar smoke though a wicked grin. 'I want Vienna.'

'Jobert, what task occupies you presently?' asked Lieutenant Colonel Clemusat, as they met beyond the walls of Milan.

Jobert saluted the former regimental second-in-command, now aide to General Bonaparte. 'General Masséna's division assembles to march for Brescia, sir. I have a squadron assembling the divisional train before escorting them forward.'

'A squadron is with you now?' asked Clemusat. 'Excellent! You are at this moment at the disposal of General Bonaparte.'

'I am at the general's service, sir.'

'News has just been received that a public uprising has erupted in Pavia yesterday,' said Clemusat. 'There is currently an uprising in Milan. General Bonaparte and Colonel Murat have just departed for Milan where they will take immediate measures to ensure security.'

Jobert was aware of Bonaparte's measures. Last October in Paris, Bonaparte had fired artillery canister into royalist crowds.

'Colonel Lannes is marching his grenadier battalions,' said Clemusat, 'with dragoons and a battery of eight-pounders, for the town of Binasco on the Milan-Pavia road. You and your squadron are to report to Lannes immediately. Which squadron do you currently command?'

'2nd Squadron, sir. Company commanders Chabenac and Voreille. Moench, sound Commanders In. Forgive me, sir. Colonel Spiccard would want to know of my reassignment in writing. If I take down your orders, sir, would you countersign, please?'

'Good gracious, you are the man's chief of squadron. Surely, your word is good enough, Jobert?'

'Ah … new requirements from General Masséna's headquarters, sir,' said Jobert. 'What is known of the situation in Pavia?'

'The newly planted Tree of Liberty was cut down in response to the town's Jacobin Club tearing down a bronze Roman statue. I would say, of both Milan and Pavia, the local people are much aggrieved at our treatment of them. Both the official removal of enforced contributions as well as the widespread thievery of our troops.'

'Is there not a town garrison ensuring our lines of communication?' asked Jobert.

'Our garrison has surrendered, and their arms taken up by the fugitives. General Bonaparte is furious and is determined to quell such dissatisfaction.'

Chabenac, Voreille and Koschak halted their trotting horses and saluted.

'Gentlemen,' said Jobert, 'I have orders from General Bonaparte to march at his discretion. Chabenac, 2nd Company and Yinot's troop shall accompany myself and Lieutenant Colonel Clemusat forward to join Colonel Lannes' column on the road to Binasco. Voreille, the remainder of your company shall escort the trains. Have a courier take these orders to Colonel Spiccard. 2nd Squadron is being utilised by General Bonaparte to suppress an uprising.'

Chapter Twelve
May 1796, Binasco, Italy

Two hundred metres from the outer walls of the town of Binasco, Jobert watched Bonaparte sweep his telescope slowly left to right, ignoring the milling movement of Bredieux's skirmishing chasseurs. Within ripening crops and groves, the tiled rooves of Binasco shimmered in the summer heat. Astride the Milan-Pavia road, not more than two hours march from the walls of Milan, the town of Binasco had become enflamed with the popular spirit of insubordination.

Lowering the glass, Bonaparte handed it backwards to no one in particular. 'A harsh lesson will be meted out to those who impede our progress.'

Clemusat closed his watch cover before taking the offered telescope and collapsing it. 'Ten o'clock, sir.'

Bonaparte summoned the artillery officer commanding the four eight-pound cannon. 'Captain, set your gun-line at eight hundred metres from the gate house and commence your fire upon the town.'

Is eight hundred metres the effective range of eight-pound shot?

Jobert wobbled his head in calculation. *As a gunner, I suppose he would know.*

'Battery, action!' called the artillery battery commander. 'Form gun-line, trot, march!' Gun-teams' drivers roared with curses to start their drowsy horses forward. Limbers and caissons wheels screeched on their axles.

As the guns were brought into action, Binasco's bells clanged with alarm, causing a cloud of doves to flee their rooftop havens. Chabenac's troop of skirmishers might obscure the deployment of the guns from surveillance at the barricaded gates, but not observers high in the church spires.

'Murat,' said Bonaparte, 'to the east of Binasco, a tree-lined road appears to cross a dike or irrigation channel. Take the dragoon squadron and secure that easterly approach. The dragoons, either mounted with swords or dismounted with their dragoon muskets, will be more suitable in the face of such an obstacle.'

Murat bobbed his head, his numerous feathers fluttering on his bicorne.

'Lannes,' continued Bonaparte, 'the tree-lined road to the west indicates yet another approach to the town. Take one of your battalions and enter at that point. I shall lead your other two battalions directly forward along this Milan road. When the guns cease fire, it will signal that my assault has begun. Enter the town at that time. Cut down or detain anyone with a weapon. Those detained will be shot. Be prepared to raze the town once the assault is complete.'

Lannes saluted. 'Yes, sir.'

'Jobert,' said Bonaparte, 'you may retire your skirmishers from screening the guns. Clemusat, moving to the west with Jobert's chasseurs, cover Lannes' approach from the west and secure the southern road to Pavia. Thank you, gentlemen.'

Passing between the lumbering gun and caissons teams and their gunners trotting alongside, Clemusat and Jobert rejoined

Yinot and Peugeot, commanding the remaining untasked troops of 2nd Squadron.

'Moench,' said Jobert, 'sound Skirmishers In. Lieutenant Yinot, follow Lieutenant Colonel Clemusat to the town's southern gates.'

'Aubagne, eh, sir?' said Yinot.

Jobert snorted a half-smile at the memory.

Moench's trumpet call caused Bredieux's troop in the screen to fire a ragged volley, which formed a lingering smoke screen through which the mounted skirmishers retired away from the walls.

'Lieutenant Peugeot,' said Jobert, 'you and I shall secure the western tree line for the grenadiers. We shall wait there for Captain Chabenac to join us with Bredieux's troop.'

As Jobert led Peugeot's troop of chasseurs along the dusty paths towards the western tree line, the eight-pounders roared. The thrashing of infantry drums signalled the stepping-off of the grenadier column. The tolling of Binasco's bells muffled the sound of eight-pound balls impacting into Binasco's stone gatehouse .

Once inside the shade of the tree-lined road, Jobert dropped Jaune's reins and scanned the western entrance to the town through his glass. At the village end of the road, townsfolk rushed, yelled and gestured to erect a hasty barricade of carts, barrels, crates and tables.

A barricade! Now is not the time to idle. Jobert swivelled in his saddle and estimated the arrival of Lannes' grenadiers and Chabenac with Bredieux's troop. *Another five minutes.*

Jobert slipped his telescope back into its pocket within his tailcoat and groped for his absent musketoon. Realising his recent injury had amended his old habit, Jobert pulled back his shabraque drawing one of his silver inlaid pistols. 'Peugeot, form column of platoon at the halt.'

As the 2nd Company soldiers responded to their old commander, Peugeot's face twitched with agitation.

'Are you with us, Peugeot,' asked Jobert, 'or will you stand aside today?'

Peugeot blinked, his stare jerking between Jobert and the barricade. 'I am with you, sir. I am here.'

Jobert pivoted Jaune to face the four ranks of chasseurs stretched from gutter to gutter across the road. 'Ready!' Jobert cocked his pistol, to which the thirty horsemen behind him cocked their musketoons.

'2nd Company,' called Jobert, 'do you remember me?'

'Sir!' The chasseurs roared in response, pumping their musketoons in their gloved fists.

'2nd Company, do you remember Sergeant Major Koschak?'

'Sir!' The chorus screamed. Their remounts jostled and pawed at the growing excitement.

'2nd Company, do you remember the brothers we lost at Aubagne and Marseille?'

Jobert brought back memories of 2nd Company's first casualties three long summers ago. 'Yes, sir!'

'2nd Company, trot, march! Moench, sound Charge! On me, 2nd Company, on me!'

The citizens of Binasco paused in the carriage of tables and barrels into the street and watched the wall of horsemen streaming between the tree-lined verges. The thunder of hooves, the piercing scream of the trumpet and the bloodthirsty roars were magnified to a terrifying degree by the enclosing walls and hedges.

Within ten metres of the overturned carts, Jobert thrust his pistol into the air. 'Moench, sound Halt, then Stand To Horse.' Moench's new calls rebounded from the outer walls of the town.

The townsfolk, many carrying firearms, backed slowly away from the protection of their half-formed barricade.

Jaune shuffled sideways with agitation. 'Moench, take Jaune.' Jobert swung down from the saddle. 'On me, 2nd Company. On me!'

One stout citizen raised a musket towards the jumble of men and horses beyond the hastily erected obstacle. Jobert raised his long-barrelled cavalry pistol and fired. At ten metres, the pistol ball hit the man in the upper chest with the ferocity of a giant swinging a sledgehammer.

As firing erupted all around him, Jobert sped through the rote process of loading his pistol. He then grabbed the leg of an upended kitchen table with his left hand and dragged the table forward, creating a gap in the barricade.

Someone screamed. A lad ran forward with a pitchfork levelled at Jobert's chest.

A musketoon exploded above Jobert.

The youth was crushed into an immediate squat.

Jobert glanced back. With a stern look at Jobert, Koschak reloaded his weapon. 'Moench!' called Koschak. 'Stay close to me!'

With chasseurs tearing at the furniture and barrels within the barricade, a breach was soon made, through which Jobert stepped.

The firing on both sides of the barricade became less. Screamed commands were issued within the yellow-grey gun smoke choking the street.

A bonneted woman emerged from the smoky gloom, aiming an ancient fowling piece. Jobert raised his pistol and fired. The woman's head whipped away, her body toppling as her firearm sprayed stinging pellets into the legs of the horses pressing through the gap.

Firing erupted behind the barricade from the horsemen who had entered the tight streets.

The thrash of infantry drums announced Lannes' approaching grenadiers beyond the bitter cloud of smoke.

No time to reload. Jobert thrust the hot pistol barrel into his waistcoat before throwing his shoulder against the tray of an overturned wagon. 'Tear the barricade down, lads. Help me clear this bastard.'

As the wagon crashed back onto its wheels, a scream beside him caused Jobert to spin. A chasseur collapsed beside him, his hands clutching a jagged slice to his neck, blood pumping through his fingers.

A man from the town, his face contorted into a vicious rictus, swung a hay sickle at Jobert's chest. Jobert threw himself backwards, moaning in pain as he collided with the iron tread of the wagon wheel. The sickle swept down his belly, leaving an arc of gore across his chest, glancing off the pistol emerging from Jobert's waistcoat. The attacker reversed the swing of his blade, aiming for Jobert's abdomen.

Jobert drew his sabre. Before his blade could clear the scabbard, Jobert punched the hilt into the oncoming iron edge. Having blocked the strike, the sabre cleared the scabbard, and with a flick of his wrist, Jobert brought the tip of the sweeping edge down onto the man's neck, just beneath the jaw. The man hissed a gurgling cry as he collapsed. Jobert focused on maintaining the sabre's momentum, dragging the blade free, stepping over the wounded man and coming *en garde.*

With the firing lessening, the smoke either cleared on the day's warm air or slunk down tight alleys. Jobert advanced further into the street, conscious of the grunts of the murderous chasseurs, the screams of the terrified citizens, the weapons discharging, the tolling of the bells, the cracking cacophony of iron-shod hooves on cobblestone, the sound amplified by the enclosing stone walls.

'The town is ours, sir!' cried Peugeot, red-faced, eyes bulging, waving his sabre.

Jobert noticed Peugeot's sabre shine blood-free.

Lannes cantered past, eyes wide, teeth bared. 'Well done, Jobert, well done. Leave the rest to us.'

Lannes' grenadiers ran through the street, following the trail of wounded, knocking down anyone still on their knees with the butts of their muskets, thrusting their bayonets into the chests of the prostrate.

Lannes spun his horse to point his sword at the glowing coals in a blacksmith's forge. 'Raze Binasco to the ground.'

Jobert and Peugeot entered the room. In the light of the hearth's fire and a candelabra on the table, chairs scraped as Chabenac, Bredieux and Koschak stood rigid. Peugeot also halted by the door and braced to attention.

Jobert had eyes only for the bottle of chiavennasca on the table. 'I need a drink.' Jobert uncorked the bottle and gulped down two glasses in quick succession.

'I came as I received the first report, sir,' said Chabenac. 'Is there anything you require of me?'

'Are you aware of all the details of this evening's calamity?' Jobert drank another glass.

'Not everything, sir, no.'

Jobert trembled as he placed his palms down on the table, his shoulders slumping. 'Having razed Binasco to the ground and executed over one hundred rebels yesterday, we approached Pavia this morning. The news of our punishment of Binasco and the Archbishop's proclamation arrived in Pavia before us. Lannes' grenadiers assaulted the gates and Pavia's insurrection evaporated. While the grenadiers secured the city and the dragoons shot the guilty, all that was required of 2nd Company was to patrol the environs beyond the walls. Not an onerous task, would you agree, Captain Chabenac?'

Chabenac raised his chin and smiled. 'Sir.'

'So where does Bredieux lead his patrol?' asked Jobert. *I cannot look at that little prick or I will kill him.*

Bredieux wobbled against his strict pose, blinking hard to focus on the shadows opposite.

'To a tavern on the Piacenza road,' said Jobert, 'where, in dereliction of his duty, his patrol gets drunk and starts a fight. Two local labourers are stabbed and a third shot in the calf. Which leads to the tavern being set ablaze and a riot erupting in the village square.'

Jobert drained his glass and refilled it.

'The alarm is sounded,' continued Jobert. 'Surely, the tolling of the village bell will bring respite. Instead, it brings Peugeot's patrol.' Peugeot's face flickers as he stiffens his posture further. 'Having baulked at Binasco, Peugeot now, in the middle of the night without any reconnaissance, forms line, draws sabres and charges the village. A child is trampled to death. Peugeot's Chasseur Billiez is sabred by Bredieux's Chasseur Docuse, who is in turn ...' Jobert's jaw clenched as he searched the smoke-blackened ceiling. '... shot dead by Peugeot's Chasseur Saint-Henri. A dead girl and a dead chasseur. Well done, Lieutenant Peugeot.'

Jobert drained his glass.

'In his wisdom, Peugeot thinks fit to truss the child's father, an upstanding local citizen as he wails his loss. The crowd is outraged. A priest attempts to intervene, whereupon Peugeot escorts the entire circus to Pavia to arrive at the door of Colonel Lannes.'

Jobert picked up the bottle to repour.

'The only redeeming feature of this fiasco is Lannes' delight at the arrest of the priest, a wanted Austrian informant. The eldest son of the grieving father was secured as a hostage to the city's ongoing good behaviour. Our esteemed local citizen is unbound to receive the limp body of one child and watch another being escorted away in chains. Thank you, yet again, Lieutenant Peugeot.'

Jobert toasted Peugeot with the bottle, before upending it over the glass to find the bottle empty. 'I have returned from a prolonged and unpleasant conversation with Colonel Lannes. I was marched in to explain to General Bonaparte, where I looked my commanding general in the eye and lied to him.' *Thanks to Lannes.* 'I reported that two fugitives were captured, and a riot was suppressed with three locals wounded and the death of a child for the loss of one chasseur.' Koschak stiffened. 'I now dread my detailed report to Colonel Spiccard, which upon receipt will result in my head being mounted on a stake.'

Jobert threw the bottle, with enormous force, into the fireplace. 'Fuck!' The bottle exploded. The fire flared. 'I have never before lied to a superior officer. I am so ashamed. I am so ...' *Disappointed in them.* '... fucking angry.'

The room was silent as Jobert's breathing subsided. 'In my absence, has anything else eventuated?'

Koschak raised his chin from his rigid position even further. 'Permission to speak, sir?'

'Yes, Sergeant Major.' Jobert glowered.

'The parade state at the end of the village riot revealed two horses, from Lieutenant Bredieux's troop, missing, complete with saddlery, three pistols and two musketoon, and ...'

Jobert's face of cold menace swivelled towards Bredieux. Bredieux swallowed hard, his efforts to remain upright caused him to rock. *He is still pissed, the little bastard.* Jobert's eyes narrowed to slits, his nostrils flared, his teeth bared, his knuckles whitened as he gripped his glass. 'And?'

'And ... Chasseur Billiez has died of his wounds,' said Koschak.

Jobert's fist was a blur. It struck Bredieux before the dropped wine glass shattered on the floor. It was remarked later that it was well that Bredieux was so relaxed due to his inebriation as his injuries would have been much worse.

Chapter Thirteen
May 1796, Battle of Borghetto, Italy

As Colonel Spiccard entered the regimental command marquee, he turned to Jobert and leant close. 'I have spoken to Colonel Lannes. General Bonaparte is satisfied with ... what has been reported to him. Jobert, your dereliction has placed me in great debt to Lannes. What punishments have you inflicted on Bredieux?'

'I had him dig both graves, sir,' said Jobert, 'and I have arranged with the paymaster to dock his pay to recover the cost of the remounts.'

Spiccard considered the brown scar on Jobert's cheek. Jobert thought Spiccard's face on the verge of smiling.

'Are you inclined to being demoted to second lieutenant and assuming the position of latrines officer for the rest of your military career, Jobert?' asked Spiccard.

Jobert stiffened. 'No, sir.'

Spiccard gaze pinned Jobert. 'You no longer hold my trust. Make a decision without my direct approval, and that situation will eventuate. Do you understand me, Jobert?'

Jobert held his commanding officer's eye. 'Yes, sir.'

Spiccard moved to the centre of the marquee and addressed his commanders. 'Gentlemen, this chart shows how Lake Garda empties into the River Po via another north-south flowing tributary, the Mincio. We are to cross the Mincio River at Borghetto. Beyond the Borghetto bridge there is an ancient riverbank, an escarpment. On the escarpment is the town of Valeggio. Beyond Valeggio is another north-south tributary, the Adige River, on which the city of Verona lies. Between Valeggio and Verona lies the town of Villafranca.'

Spiccard raised his face from the map to glare at Jobert. Jobert remained impassive, eyes glued to the map.

'The Austrians must secure the Mincio to hold the fortress of Mantua,' said Spiccard. 'The Austrian defence is stretched thin and will only succeed by concentrating their reserves at our chosen crossing point. Those reserves will be assembled somewhere beyond Valeggio, between the Mincio and the Adige rivers. A light cavalry role unchanged since antiquity, it is the task of the 24th Chasseurs to find those enemy reserves.'

Spiccard looked about the gathering. 'General Bonaparte has aimed Lannes' grenadier battalions directly at Borghetto. The 24th Chasseurs and the 1st Hussars, with a battery of horse artillery, will lead the advance guard. It is now two o'clock. With twenty kilometres to Borghetto, we should arrive at the bridge by dawn. Questions? No? Then 24th Chasseurs, column of fours, walk, march.'

The white gravel road ran straight towards the vibrant orange fringe of a late-spring dawn, anointing the far purple horizon.

The air on the road was still and cool, the vast cloud of dust created by hundreds of hooves wafting sluggishly around the crunching columns. Above the dark green gloom of the Mincio floodplain, kites and hawks spiralled on the morning thermals.

A distant musket shot, followed by an unknown trumpet call, caused crows to caw and flap. Dark clad outriders morphed from the shadows in the undulations and trotted into deeper shadows. 'Kaiserlik hussars!'

'24th Chasseurs,' ordered Spiccard, 'prepare to break the enemy outposts. Dressing by the centre, form squadron battle-line. 1st Squadron to the right of the road, 3rd Squadron to the left. Jobert, 2nd Squadron, skirmishers out. Huin, inform the 1st Hussars the ground lends itself to forming on our right.'

'2nd Squadron,' called Jobert, 'form squadron skirmish line. 2nd Company, to the right of the road, 5th Company, to the left. Trot, march! Moench, sound Skirmishers Out.'

Now reduced to sixty sabres a company, thirty pairs of skirmishers trotted to the southern side of the road and another thirty pairs trotted to the north. Forming two distinct bands one hundred metres apart, Jobert remained on the road level with the lead line of skirmishers.

Jobert twisted in the saddle and looked back to the French cavalry forming on the ridge. A rare but impressive sight, two green-clad squadrons stretched for one hundred and fifty metres along the low ridge.

On the last high ground before the river flats, stood a long skirmish line, a company of Austrian hussars, the leading hussars a mere one hundred metres from Jobert. Beyond them lay the village of Borghetto, the smoke of morning fires deepening the shadow under the river's escarpment. Beyond the dark smudge of the escarpment, the rooves and trees of Valeggio were dimly discernible. As the sun's rays sprang into the morning sky, the Austrian hussars expanded their battle-line to two companies.

'They have two companies in line and a company in skirmish order,' said Jobert to Chabenac and Voreille. 'There will be more on the reverse of the ridge. Any sign of guns or infantry?'

'No, sir,' said Voreille, squinting into his glass, 'but the Austrian officer at the centre of their battle-line is my man from Savona. I recognise the broken nose.'

'You can see an uncanny resemblance to the other big fellow we met at Dego and Lodi,' said Chabenac.

'Remain attentive to your duties, gentlemen,' said Jobert. 'You are as obsessed with these hussar officers as maidens at a ball.' Jobert looked to the enemy's flank. *Remember, latrines officer, no decisions.* 'Lieutenant Peugeot, take a message to Colonel Spiccard. Would he approve a patrol to determine any other enemy to our south?'

In the time Peugeot delivered Jobert's request and returned, the 1st Hussars formed their squadrons with a long line of blue uniforms alongside the chasseur-green line.

'Colonel Spiccard has denied your request for a patrol, sir,' said Peugeot. 'Furthermore, Colonel Spiccard wishes to know from Captain Voreille if the Austrian officer is his man from Savona.'

'Oh, give me strength!' cried Jobert. 'Are we here to slaughter the bastards or invite them to tea?'

French trumpets screamed from the ridge. At a roar of eight hundred throats, Jobert twisted and looked back to the French line. The solid line of the 24th Chasseurs and the 1st Hussars advanced at the walk, sabres twinkling in the morning's low beams.

Jobert glanced up the slope towards the centre of the Austrian line. A blue-jacketed hussar, his pelisse jacket flapping off his left shoulder, cantered away from the Austrian command group to the end of the mounted ranks then disappeared over the crest of the ridge. A foreign trumpet call sounded beyond the ridgeline. The warming air lifted a cloud of dust clear of the crest.

As Chabenac's and Voreille's skirmishers rallied to clear the ground for the impending charge, a one-hundred-sabre Austrian hussar company drew up in battle-line.

In the centre of the reserve company, the enemy officer encountered at Dego and Lodi sparked a dull sense of recognition in Jobert's memory.

A short trumpet call rang out. The Austrian hussars glided about at the trot, flowed into column, and rode toward the bridge.

With 2nd Squadron reformed within the regimental march column, Jobert continued in the dust of the hussars towards the village of Borghetto and its bridge.

The Mincio river was forty metres wide with banks so steep Jobert could not see the stream. Despite the plastered walls of Borghetto shielding the bridge from prying eyes, the bridge's location was clear from the road leading away from its eastern abutment, ascending across the face of the towering escarpment.

The three companies of Austrian hussars had formed in line just out from the most external garden walls of the village. Behind the hussars and within the gardens, two companies of fusiliers raced to take up fire positions. A stream of wagons proceeded through the town, across the bridge and up the escarpment on the far bank.

'Huin!' called Colonel Spiccard. 'It is time for Colonel Lannes' grenadiers. Inform the commander of the advance guard that we hold the near bank.'

The senior officers of the 24th Chasseurs all took out their telescopes from within their tailcoats and scanned the far bank. Three Austrian guns were soon detected, one sited to fire down the bridge and two flanking it by four hundred metres. All three guns sited to converge their fire on the end of the bridge.

'Make way for the guns! Make way for the guns!' Two batteries of eight-pounders, twelve guns total, rattled and puffed up the road, determined to come into action where the chasseurs stood. Within a minute of limbers and caissons wheeling from road column into gun-line, both batteries spat iron, flame, smoke and roar.

'24th Chasseurs, stand to horse,' ordered Spiccard. 'Seven hours in the saddle. Time for soup.'

As the ridgeline above Borghetto was consumed with choking gun smoke, Jobert watched the Austrian hussars withdrawing along the side of the village's orchards and olive groves, then descend into the bed of the Mincio. *There must be a ford.*

The advance guard marched hard behind the guns. With a swift glance at the scene before him, Colonel Lannes ordered his drum corps shake the lead battalion into a wide attack formation. Lannes dismounted and led his grenadiers straight into the musket fire behind the garden walls of Borghetto.

Jobert walked away from the chasseurs' soup-kettle fires and observed the progress of the infantry. As the first battalion of grenadiers jostled and weaved in the blinding smoke for any scrap of advantage over the well-protected Austrian fusiliers, Lannes returned to the ridge overlooking Borghetto for another battalion.

'Enjoying the theatre, Jobert?' asked Lannes. 'Their bloody sappers are cutting the bridges' arches.'

Jobert scanned the vicinity for Spiccard. 'Are you aware of the ford, sir?'

'No. Show me.'

By ten o'clock, Lannes sent his second battalion across the Mincio up to their armpits in cold water.

Jobert threw the dregs from his mug onto the crumbling embers. 'It is now one o'clock. The bridge is repaired. We will cross the ford and allow our horses to drink. 1st and 3rd Squadrons are to observe the north of Valeggio. We are to observe the south of the town.'

Once bellies and water gourds were refilled from the Mincio, the chasseurs climbed the farm tracks weaving up the escarpment from the bridge. As they ascended, Jobert and Koschak observed wounded Austrian infantry sitting amongst damaged artillery caissons and abandoned guns.

'Permission, sir, for a section to strip the caisson and the wounded?' asked Koschak. 'Before the 1st Hussars get their dirty hands on them.'

'Any other time, yes,' said Jobert. 'But since I neither understand what lies beyond Valeggio nor know where the kaiserlik hussars have withdrawn to, I am loathe to send out forage parties this early in the battle.'

2nd and 5th Companies spent a warm hour on the gentle farmland on the outskirts of Valeggio as dust filled the sky, tinting the sun a vivid orange and its corona a bruised pink. Masséna brigades fought alongside the advance guard's grenadiers to secure the town. Valeggio was wreathed in the smoke of cannon fire and musketry.

When Spiccard and his escort entered the camp of 2nd Squadron's inlying piquet, the squadron's officers were scanning the flat horizon, observing the exodus of Austrian trains from Valeggio towards the thin, blue-smudged line of enemy hussars on the Villafranca road.

'Your report, Jobert?' asked Spiccard, reaching into his tail-coat for his glass.

Jobert performed a crisp salute without looking Spiccard in the eye. '5th Company observes a column of infantry, guns and dragoons approaching from Villafranca,' said Jobert. 'I have sent a messenger into Valeggio to warn of potential counterattack.'

A sharp crack of artillery sounded from the far tree-lined roads initiating the Austrian bombardment. Deep thuds sounded as great iron balls skipped once or twice before shattering the outer homes of Valeggio in which the exhausted French fusiliers, having secured the town, now sheltered.

'May I direct your attention south, sir?' said Jobert. '2nd Company observes an approaching Austrian infantry brigade with a battery of guns.'

Spiccard extended his telescope and peered south towards the road leading to Mantua. 'Aha! The enemy's reserves arrive. Cavalry?'

'None seen yet, sir.'

The group turned as Lieutenant Colonel Clemusat, aide to General Bonaparte, and a pair of chasseurs galloped into the camp.

'Ah, Colonel Spiccard, sir.' Clemusat saluted. 'Austrian hussars have entered Valeggio from the north and attacked General Bonaparte's headquarters. The bulk of Masséna's division is still west of the Mincio and must be urged forward. I seek an escort to Masséna's headquarters as the roads are blocked leading back to the bridge at Borghetto.'

Jobert raised his chin and looked to Spiccard.

'A section will suffice,' said Spiccard. 'Jobert, dispatch a section at once. I am satisfied with your dispositions. Valeggio will soon be ours. Now, await my orders to advance to Villafranca.'

'Thank you, sir.' Jobert saluted the senior gentlemen's departure.

With a clatter of scabbards on spurs and hooves on gravel, Spiccard and Clemusat departed with their escorts.

Jobert dipped his face away from the cloud of fine dust engulfing him and spat noisily.

'Valeggio, Villafranca and now Verona. What next, Huin? Venice?' asked Jobert.

Eighteen hours later, the next morning, and thirty kilometres further east, Lieutenant Huin drooped exhausted on Jobert's camp stool and received a mug of bouillon from Orlande.

'The Austrians have withdrawn north, sir,' said Huin. 'General Bonaparte has secured Verona. The Army of Italy has broken the enemy's defence of Lombardy in less than thirty days, advancing over three hundred kilometres from Cherasco. General Sérurier's division is now investing Mantua. To create an outer cordon around the siege, General Masséna has been ordered to send a brigade north along the Adige to Rivoli. Colonel Spiccard is to cover the infantry with 1st and 3rd Squadron.'

'And 2nd Squadron?' *How much further?* Rubbing aching eyes, Jobert steeled himself for Huin's response.

'Colonel Spiccard desires 2nd Squadron maintain this divisional screen on the road to Venice.'

Jobert exhaled with relief. 'So ends the battle of Borghetto. More broth? How far to the other side of the Italian peninsula?' Jobert poured the hissing kettle.

'Thank you, sir. Eighty kilometres, I believe.'

Jobert looked to the eastern horizon and rubbed his unshaven jowl as he considered the three-day journey to the Adriatic. 'We have succeeded, Huin, and they have not. Bonaparte has won another battle, but not the campaign. Our lines of communication are over-extended. To our south, the impregnable fortress of Mantua contains twelve thousand troops and three hundred guns. To our north, the Tyrolean Alps into which the Austrians have withdrawn, where they will rebuild their strength only to re-emerge. It is now our turn to be spread thin in defence, Huin. Very soon, the kaiserliks will come hunting us.'

Chapter Fourteen
June-July 1796, Verona, Italy

'How goes our transition from invaders to besiegers?' asked Jobert.

'Activity abounds in all directions.' Lieutenant Colonel Fergnes' lips tightened as he straightened patrol reports with his fingertips, eyes narrowing as he regarded Jobert across from him. 'Artillery from the Piedmontese fortresses has now reached the siege of the Milanese citadel. Sérurier's division has invested the fortress of Mantua. While Bonaparte waits for his siege train to arrive at Mantua from Milan, he is departing on a foray towards Rome with Augereau's division.'

Jobert poured another coffee. 'A grab at further gold?'

'Is that not why the Directory has sent us here?' asked Fergnes. 'An armistice with Naples is the opportunity to put the Pope in his proper place. And yes, the Holy Father will pay handsomely in gratitude of the Army of Italy not entering Rome.'

'Our new armistice with Naples now impacts on the Rhine, does it not?'

'Quite so,' said Fergnes. 'Generals Jourdan and Moreau and

their armies of seventy thousand each will soon march down the Danube to Vienna. I have heard Bonaparte has sent Moreau one million francs as an inducement to march a little faster.'

'And the 24th Chasseurs?' asked Jobert.

Fergnes shifted a stack of portfolios and revealed a map. 'Masséna's division has been reinforced to hold the siege's outer cordon. We watch the northern Alpine passes, east and west of Lake Garda, alert for any Austrian attempt to raise the siege. Rivoli, east of the lake, is where Bonaparte and Masséna are most focused. That is where the bulk of the regiment lies. Spiccard wants you with 2nd Squadron west of Lake Garda, based out of Salò.'

Summer on the shores of Lake Garda. Jobert smiled.

Fergnes leant forward on the desktop. 'It pains me, Jobert, to openly state the need for you to keep your chasseurs' excesses in check. Spiccard has not …'

Any pleasure derived from the possibilities at Lake Garda slid from Jobert's face. 'Pissed soldiers do dumb things, sir. Young officers' judgement is reliably poor. I can no longer participate in—'

Fergnes held up a palm. 'The caveat to your assignment required stating. Enough said.' Fergnes relaxed with a smug grin. 'Colonel Spiccard has permitted my household to move forward to Milan, in order to provide a pavilion of respite for the regiment's officers. Marguerite would be delighted to welcome you. Indeed, it would bring me great comfort, my friend, knowing my household was within your reach.'

Jobert's cheeks attempted a weak smile. 'I am at your service, sir.'

'What is more,' said Fergnes, 'Depot Company, having received our fifty recruits and bales of leather, is to move forward from Oneglia to Milan.'

Jobert sat straight and searched Fergnes' face. 'Those fifty men will replace our losses since Savona?'

Fergnes' face drooped with disappointment. 'Even with this draft of men and horses, our strength state hovers at three hundred and fifty sabres. One new man to reinforce each section in the regiment. But have you heard of the recent depletion of our ranks?'

Jobert frowned. 'No.'

'Do you remember Bonaparte's headquarters being overrun by Austrian hussars at Valeggio?' asked Fergnes. 'With Lannes' grenadiers at Bonaparte's immediate disposal, Bonaparte has decided to add a company of cavalry guides to his retinue.'

Jobert winced. 'Guides?'

'A chasseur company of fifty sabres is being raised to protect Bonaparte's headquarters. Bonaparte's senior aide, Colonel Murat, has selected his friend Bessières to command these guides. The four chasseur regiments of the Army of Italy are to provide one platoon each of our best eleven men. One sergeant, two corporals and two sections of four chasseurs. All dressed in the best number-one tailcoats, over-breeches and bicornes. All mounted on our best black horses.'

Jobert slumped in his seat. 'Shit!'

'Your resolve to control outbursts of barrack-room invective no longer in vogue, Jobert?' asked Fergnes. 'Moreover, we are to lose Huin.'

'Oh, no. Why? To where?'

'Huin and Murat were chasseurs together before the Revolution. Murat has recommended his old comrade-in-arms as second-in-command of Bessières' Guides. Yinot will replace Huin as aide de camp.'

'Huin is a fine officer.' Jobert rested on his knees with his elbows. Three years of memories of their service together paraded through his mind. 'He would have made an outstanding company commander. Huin's departure, plus the loss of our dozen best soldiers, is devastating. If Bonaparte can steal what he desires from the Holy Father, what stops him plundering his regiments?'

'Fucking … babies!' Jobert crushed the note in his fist, then threw it across the room. The crumpled paper fluttered beyond his fingertips before twirling to the floor.

Michelle's latest letter drooped in Didier's fingers, his face creased in confusion. 'I beg your pardon, "babies" plural?'

'After we captured Milan in mid-May,' said Jobert, 'my groom, Tulloc, courted a local girl. He has just received a note from her sister. She is pregnant. Orlande found him wandering in the dark, bawling in distress. The idiot is intent on marrying her and establishing her as a company cantiniere.'

'Perhaps one child at a time, eh?' Didier waved the letter in his fingers. 'Michelle's child is due in mid-December. Her letter is dated 7th of June. Have you written to her?'

'Not yet.' Jobert rubbed his face with his hands.

'Michelle needs our love, André,' said Didier. 'We shall compose a letter this evening before I depart. Do you share the moral high ground of righteous indignation with our great aunt Sophie?'

Jobert's chest deflated. 'No.'

Didier's raised eyebrows expressed his doubt.

Jobert threw up his hands. 'I have reflected on how I feel about our cousin since we last spoke. I trust her judgement.'

Didier scanned the letter once more. 'Michelle identifies this Édouard Colbert as the father. She speaks of Colbert but does not indicate if he has proposed marriage between them. It has an operatic air, does it not. The love between the wealthy spinster and the destitute nobleman.'

'And the destitute nobleman's two destitute brothers prowling in the wings,' said Jobert. 'When will Yann appear on stage?'

'Perhaps a letter this evening to our uncle as well?'

'I cannot help feeling that marriage is a greater threat to our family than not,' said Jobert.

'Whatever do you mean?' asked Didier.

'What impact does a husband have on our shareholdings in the family business?'

Didier scowled. 'I do not understand.'

'Unable to legally represent herself,' said Jobert, 'Aunt Sophie's uniform contracts and her burgeoning workhouses have always sat under grandfather's horse-breeding enterprise. Does the company Yann raised upon grandfather's death, which now presides over the horse contracts, also encompass the garment contracts?'

Didier blinked. 'Yes, it does. Indeed, I am sure it does. We will seek confirmation in our letter. Orlande, would you be so kind as to bring me the writing box?'

Both men stretched back on their wooden kitchen chairs as they waited, stretching their booted legs towards the cool air whispering through the gate's ornate iron railings and along the painted tiles.

'Bonaparte's expedition south of Mantua has bagged him an armistice with Rome,' said Didier. 'The haul of art, sculpture and bejewelled ornaments is beyond all expectations, I am told.'

'Hah! Raive subcontracted our cartage fleet to carry part of it,' said Jobert. 'I have no doubt a little treasure will fall Masséna's way. Bonaparte has also captured the port of Livorno, forcing the British navy to island ports well out into the Mediterranean.'

'Thank you, Orlande,' said Didier, as he received the small wooden box. 'Having forced the Pope to kneel before him, whatever will Bonaparte do next?'

Jobert watched Didier's wavering quill swirl across a yellow piece of parchment. 'The siege train for Mantua is the greater concern. The citadel within Milan has now fallen. The captured Piedmontese guns are rolling forward to the siege works around Mantua.'

Didier reread his draft. 'I have heard the British have captured a coastal fleet carrying our heavy mortars bound for Genoa.'

'Then let us give thanks that the bastards have lost access to Livorno,' said Jobert.

'You should not swear, André, it is unbecoming for an officer,' said Didier. Jobert rolled his eyes. Didier passed the letter across the table. 'I have written to Yann before I write to Michelle. I am unsure of how much he knows of Michelle's situation. Will it suffice?'

Jobert nodded his approval. 'Speaking of Milan, our depot company is to move forward from Oneglia to Milan, as well as—'

'As well as Bonaparte's new wife from Nice,' said Didier, dabbing the quill point into the ink well.

'Ah, yes, that, but there is more. A confidante in Madame Bonaparte's coterie is one Madame Marguerite Fergnes, wife of the 24th Chasseur's second-in-command.'

Didier looked up from his letter. 'I remember Fergnes' wife from the wedding breakfast in Avignon eighteen months ago. Absolutely gorgeous.'

'Colonel Spiccard is subsidising an apartment in Milan for both Fergnes' household and a place of respite for regimental officers on leave. A roster is now in place for a week's leave in Milan.' A broad smile creased Jobert's scarred cheek. 'I have secured a room in the coming week.'

Didier blew on the ink before passing the letter across.

'Excellent! You must arrange an invitation for me. How does this missive to Michelle read?'

Just as the stirring score, on piano and violin, ended with a flourish, Jobert crept into the salon and collapsed on the settee beside Raive. The room erupted with feminine exclamations of praise and gloved clapping.

'Haydn?' asked Jobert.

'Tsk, Mozart.' Raive clapped the tiny hands of Fergnes' baby son wobbling at his knees. 'We sense good news, do we not? Yes, we do.' Jobert grimaced at Raive's baby talk.

Marguerite, Fergnes' wife, raised a discrete finger signalling Orlande and a female maid to serve cordial to the assembled ladies. Orlande offered Jobert and Raive aperitifs of rosolio di Torino.

Jobert drained the dainty crystal cup. 'My good news is an alarm confirmed false. Young Tulloc was informed he had fathered a local child when the regiment was last in Milan. I arranged for a discrete doctor to confirm the girl's condition. A flush of maidenly exuberance is the diagnosis. All now flows as it should. I am spared a laundress in my retinue.'

Raive beamed in an avuncular fashion at the dark-haired little boy. 'That is good, little man, is it not? Yes, it is. Oh, yes, it is. What a clever fellow?'

The baby shuffled sideways to grip Jobert's knee. Jobert stiffened in alarm. The little boy's face, framed with dark curls escaping the embroidery of his white bonnet, reflected the concern of the tanned face above him.

Raive leant back from his young charge. 'You know you have not replaced Spiccard as our officer in residence. Our erudite colonel has taken to his bed.'

Jobert glared at the baby staring up at him and waggled his empty glass at Orlande.

'I feel he has taken in the contagion of Mantua's swamps,' said Raive. 'The locals call it "mal-aria", or sick air. The humours from the swamps are quite vile. Sérurier's division, holding the inner lines of the siege, is losing fifty men per day to the illness.'

'And Fergnes is in temporary command of the regiment?' asked Jobert.

'Indeed. Once Spiccard is bled, as the fevers last only a few days, he will be back with the regiment soon enough.'

Jobert dared not to move his legs and unbalance Fergnes junior. 'How does the siege progress?'

'Bonaparte has now returned from his foray into the Papal States,' said Raive. 'The siege works are nearly complete. The siege train is assembling. The bombardment ought to begin in the next ten days.'

'After we crossed the Mincio,' said Jobert, 'the Austrians withdrew into the Tyrol. It has been over a month. What delays their return?'

Reclaiming the child's pudgy hands within his own gloved fingers, Raive addressed the baby. 'You remember Bonaparte's proclamation, do you not? Oh, yes, you do. The Austrians have lost twenty thousand dead, wounded, and captured, and lost fifty guns. Have they not, the silly fellows? They need to find reinforcements while Jordan and Moreau's armies threaten Vienna across the Rhine. Do they not? Oh, yes, they do.'

Jobert looked aghast at Raive's infantile turn of speech. Searching for distraction, Jobert noticed Marguerite laughing with the attractive Madame Bonaparte, while a petulant, smooth faced young man sat beside her cradling a small white dog. 'Bonaparte's new wife? The fellow with her? The stepson?'

Raive glanced across the parlour. 'Ah, yes, and no. The son is about fifteen, an aide on his stepfather's headquarters. No, that is Madame Josephine's ... special friend.'

A rustle of silk gown caught Jobert's attention. 'Young Fergnes seems quite taken with you, Major Jobert.'

Jobert bowed his head to acknowledge Camille, companion to her cousin Marguerite. *A smile which never quite extends to your eyes.* Camille wore her bodice cut alarmingly low. With Camille seated beside him, Jobert struggled to banish the thought of Camille in the new transparent gowns now all the fashion in Paris.

'When can we expect a Master Jobert being bounced on Uncle Raive's knee?' asked Camille.

Jobert's imagination froze at the suggestion. The diminutive, plump version of his friend Fergnes apprised him with his father's dark eyes. Jobert returned an anxious smile.

Camille clapped her hands. 'Hah! Major Jobert, it would appear you have been vanquished. Come, sweetheart, pay your respects to papa's brave friend.'

With that, Camille bent low, brushing Jobert's thigh with her breasts, to scoop up the child and seat him on Jobert's lap.

Despite the momentary relish at the touch of her bodice against him, Jobert blanched and shrank back from the unsteady infant.

'Good gracious, man, hold him,' said Camille.

Jobert gripped the tiny, soft body through the cotton gown embroidered with pale green and violet flowers. *Is this my first? Foals, calves and lambs, certainly, but never a baby.*

The boy's face became redder and redder. A piercing wail sprang from the child's throat. Such a note of alarm sounded with such volume that a brigade of fusiliers would stand to arms.

Here in the drawing room, the scream initiated nothing more than a murmur of matronly cooing and gentle laughter.

Raive chuckled, removing the bawling youngster from the rigid Jobert. The howl calmed upon young Fergnes being jiggled upon Raive's knee. The yowl replaced by a tiny, white fist in a toothless mouth. The child's interrogative stare at Jobert continued unabated.

'How good you are with children, Jobert,' said Camille. 'Fatherhood would suit you.'

'I will be sure to seek guidance in the paternal arts from our mutual friend Geourdai,' said Jobert. 'That happiness should be approaching you both soon, should it not?'

The smile broadened on Camille's lips, but delight faded from her dark, hooded eyes. 'Then I wish Captain Geourdai and his intended bride every success in that undertaking. Anissa, take young master to the nursery.'

Anissa? Jobert's mind reeled. An Avignon prostitute who, with the shadowy Inoubli, had contributed to 2nd Squadron being ambushed twelve months previously. *How could Fergnes accept her within his household?* Jobert sensed the intrigues of Raive at play.

'Stand to arms!' cried Raive, recoiling from the baby in Anissa's grasp.

The child bent forward and vomited on Jobert's thigh.

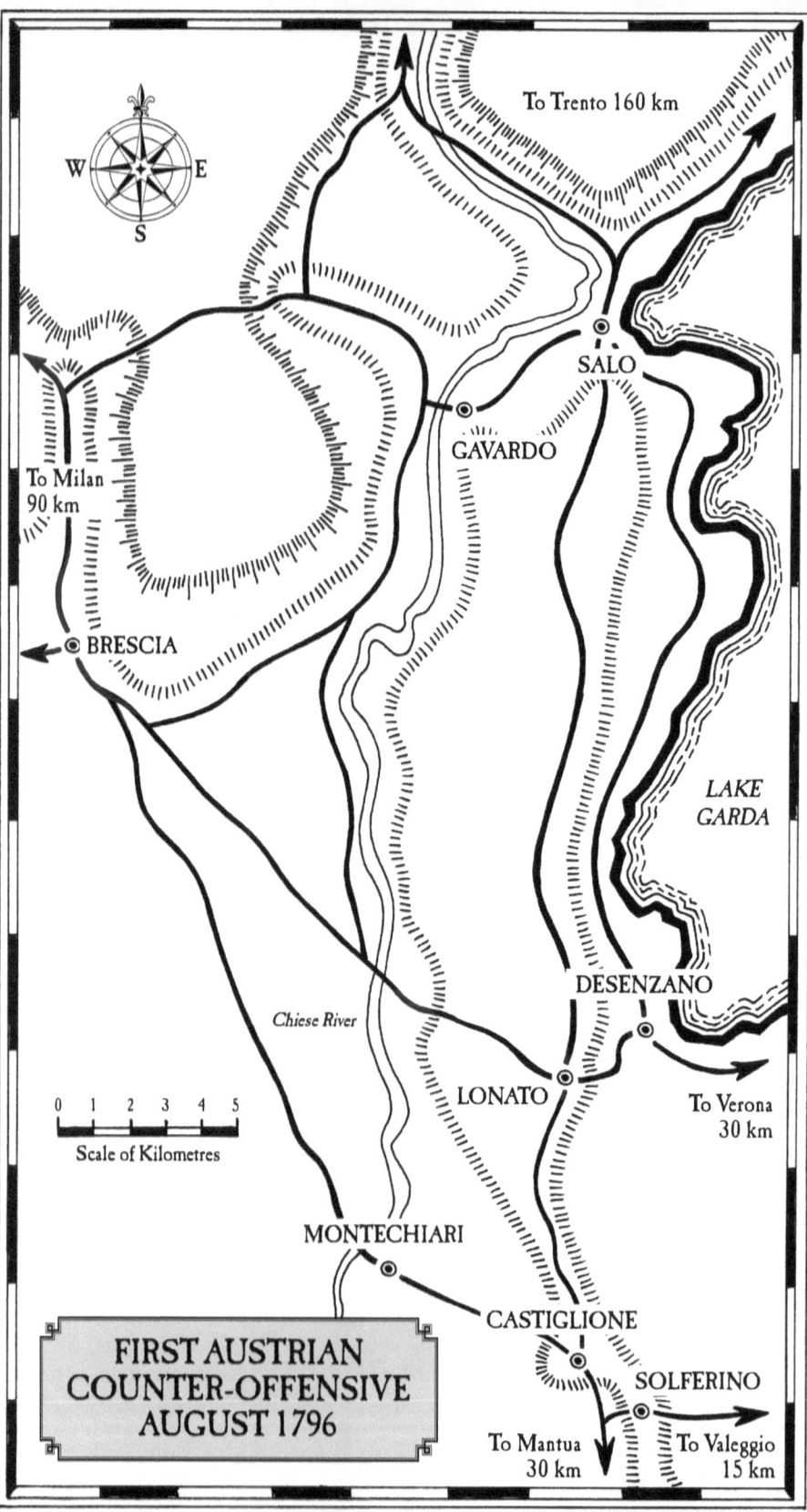

To Trento 160 km

SALO

GAVARDO

To Milan
90 km

BRESCIA

LAKE
GARDA

DESENZANO

Chiese River

LONATO

To Verona
30 km

0 1 2 3 4 5
Scale of Kilometres

MONTECHIARI

CASTIGLIONE

SOLFERINO

FIRST AUSTRIAN
COUNTER-OFFENSIVE
AUGUST 1796

To Mantua
30 km

To Valeggio
15 km

Chapter Fifteen
August 1796, Salò, Italy

The hubbub in the dining hall was raucous. The vast refectory of the Convento Cappuccini guild hall was one of the few buildings in Villafranca where General Masséna could host tonight's guests, their former Neapolitan enemies. Jobert estimated around one hundred and fifty souls crushed around the tables. The French chasseur green full-dress tailcoats highlighted the white tailcoats, with sky-blue lapels and collars, of the Neapolitan dragoons.

The Republic had concluded an armistice, removing Naples from the coalition with Austria. The Neapolitan cavalry were withdrawing overland to their home beyond the Papal States, while their infantry travelled by sea. As an intelligence gathering exercise, Masséna hosted the Neapolitan officers only to subject them to directed banter by the officers of the 24th Chasseurs.

Chasseurs, hands full of empty platters and sloshing bottles, scurried the length of the long trestle tables stretching into the candlelit gloom. Jobert raised a finger to a passing chasseur. 'Corporal Durand, have the barrels of ale for the troops in the kitchen been broached?'

'Flowing quite freely, sir, and thank you for that. Hot work this evening.'

A young captain of dragoons, heavily in his cups, lamented that the Austrians had held the Neapolitans too far back in reserve for his regiment to put to flight the raggedy French dragoons.

Jobert reclined back in his dining chair and blew a long stream of blue-grey cigar smoke to the rafters above him. 'And there I must correct your opinion, sir.'

An uneasy silence fell on both the French and Neapolitan diners around Jobert.

'Our dragoons play a vital role within our army,' said Jobert, 'albeit they are dressed in rags and mounted on wasted nags.' Jobert gave a wicked smile. The Neapolitans sensed a challenge. 'Our dragoons hold the rear of our army's column to care for us chasseurs. Their ceaseless duties ensure no grain for our horses comes forward to founder our horses, no brandy comes forward to inebriate our soldiers, no bread nor meat comes forward to make us too fat, and no mail burdens us with unnecessary sentiment for home.'

Smirks crept under noses and moustaches.

'No, sir,' said Jobert, 'our dragoons play too vital a role to cross swords with the foe. How do I know? My brother joined the dragoons, sir, and I have never spoken to him since.'

Diners coughed with reprieved laughter and filled each other's glasses.

Jobert appreciated this rare occasion where he could drink from a glass vessel. He relished the strong botanicals in the wine – camomile, lavender and lemon.

A Neapolitan face caught Jobert's attention, but he did not pursue eye contact.

It was Inoubli.

The Neapolitan's eyes were restless, gauging the faces around him. The fellow sported a large drooping moustache with an encouraging smile beneath. Nodding. Listening. Not contributing. Watching. Waiting.

Unlike the well-cut tailcoats of the dragoon officers, trimmed with sky-blue of the regimental facing, Inoubli, if it was him, wore a darker coat, less well cut. In the shimmering candlelight Jobert could not discern the colour. *Arriving with the dragoons from the Tyrol? Or joining the dragoons to enter Naples?*

'Valhalla,' said Chabenac across the table, raising his glass towards Jobert.

'I beg your pardon?' asked Jobert.

'Valhalla!'

'The liqueur?' asked Jobert.

Chabenac glanced at his raised glass. 'No, this is rosolio di Torino. Valhalla is a hall of pagan gods, where dead warriors, enemies' side by side, feast, fight and whore for eternity.'

'How wonderful? Valhalla, then.'

A cavalry trumpet blew two long notes from somewhere near the head of the table. All the cavalrymen in the refectory stopped speaking and peered towards the head table raised on platforms.

General Masséna, seated beside the Neapolitan commanding officer, rose to speak. 'Gentlemen, the great fortress of Mantua has been under siege for some seven weeks now, but now silence, if you will ...'

The sound of constant low thuds was distinct beyond the open doors of the hall. The bombardment of Mantua had begun.

Originating in the high Alpine passes, a cool breeze rippled the choppy waves of Lake Garda down its twenty-kilometre length. The moisture gathered the dust of roads and fallow fields, the pollen of elm, willows and spruce, the fragrances of lilac, lavender and jasmine from the shoreline gardens of Salò. The exotic tang wafted through the Salò courtyard where Jobert shared a soft local cheese and a jug of bardolino with Chabenac.

'And your leave in Milan?' asked Chabenac. 'Were you able to complete your shopping?'

Jobert watched the play of sunset caress the flanks of Monte Baldo squatting beyond the eastern lakeshore. 'Ah, yes, I suppose.'

'No Verona revisited?' asked Chabenac. Jobert looked askance. 'In fair Verona, where we lay our scene? Romeo and Juliet?' Chabenac waved his hand. 'An obscure play of no concern. Did you enjoy the delights of Fergnes' apartments?'

'Sisterly remonstrances from Marguerite. Terrorised by a baby. Taunted with fatherhood by Camille.'

'He returns from Milan without gossip.' Chabenac pouted. 'What occupies you, sir?'

'The expected Austrian counter-offensive,' said Jobert. 'Locals report an Austrian force earmarked to strike west of Lake Garda to cut Bonaparte's lines of communication with Milan and Genoa. Fifteen thousand infantry with twenty-four guns, supported by twenty-four companies of cavalry.'

Chabenac whistled. 'What does Masséna have on this western flank?'

Jobert shook his head and exhaled. 'A brigade of five thousand. The enemy's advance will press upon our squadron screen. We will be stretched thin, driven to think and act fast to survive the evolving offensive.'

'Under your hand, sir,' said Chabenac, 'I am in no doubt both 2nd and 5th Companies will succeed.'

Jobert glanced at the door as boots and spurs cracked down the cool, tiled corridor outside. 'But I am burdened with the need to keep Spiccard informed, and he situated on the far side of Lake Garda.'

Chabenac leant towards Jobert. 'My family and I are in your debt, sir. I give thanks for ... forgive my impropriety, our brotherly connection.' Jobert smiled. 'In this coming storm, tell me what is to be done, and I shall obey without hesitation. If questioned for rashness by Spiccard, I shall assume all—'

A soft rap on the door. Jobert gripped Chabenac's shoulder. 'Enter.'

Koschak's bulk projected a broad shadow. 'Captain Voreille presents his compliments, sir, and wishes you know the kaiserliks are on the move. We have just had a local priest present himself to the 5th Company outposts. He declares the Austrians are marching south tonight, sir.' Koschak stepped aside and revealed a bent figure in a ragged cassock. 'Our friend, sir.'

Jobert sat erect. *Inoubli!* 'Sergeant Major, may I rely on your immediate discreet arrangements to personally deliver whatever it is to wherever it must go.'

Early in the morning on the first day of the Austrian offensive to raise the French siege of Mantua, Jobert and Koschak sat in the steep, gloomy valleys of the Tyrolean Alps, north of Salò. Still hours before the sun burnt off the mist clinging to the valley floor, the dark pines squatted heavily on shadowy skirts.

French light infantry had maintained a steady fusillade against the advancing Austrian skirmishers leading their battalion columns. The smoke from their exchanged musketry entwined with the murkiness of shadow and mist.

'Since joining the Army of Italy,' said Koschak, 'we have consistently advanced against the Austrian defence. With the situation now reversed, I can appreciate how the Austrian cavalry felt in the outpost line. Stretched and vulnerable.'

'We are a thin outer curtain seventy kilometres from the siege,' said Jobert. 'The kaiserliks feel with their fingers to find a hole through which they can tear. We chasseurs must find those fingers so Masséna's infantry and artillery can cut them off.' Jobert tucked his telescope within his tailcoat. 'If the Austrians have a column heading for Brescia, they will cut our lines of communication with Milan. Warning must reach Brescia.'

Jobert turned Jaune towards Moench, Koschak and Tulloc. He ran his eye over Rouge, Bleu and Grenzer standing beside Tulloc's remount. 'Men, this will be the first of many long days in the saddle. The information we carry allows commanders like Masséna to delay the enemy, giving General Bonaparte the time to rearrange the Army of Italy to defeat this Austrian offensive. If we do not gain that time in the next day or so, the kaiserliks will bundle us back to Nice.'

Nine hours later, Jobert stood in Colonel Lannes' headquarters in Brescia.

Lannes and Bonaparte's aides de camp, Murat and Clemusat, pored over a chart on a wide table. Lannes traced his fingers along the map. 'Two enemy columns west of Lake Garda. One to cut our lines of communication to Milan here at Brescia, one to block us south of Lake Garda at ...'

'Possibly Lonato, sir,' said Jobert.

Murat grimaced as he looked up from the map. 'You know

this country, Virginian. If the enemy cuts our connection to Milan, where would they concentrate?'

Jobert masked his irritation at his headquarters' nickname by frowning at the map. 'Along the Chiese River, sir.'

Lannes' fingers traced the river line. 'Jobert, my grenadiers will watch the vales from the north. Take your 2nd Company and watch the Chiese River south of Gavardo.'

'It is a six-hour march to Gavardo, sir,' said Jobert. 'The 24th Chasseurs will be in location before dawn.'

Murat stood up from his study of the terrain, sweeping his thick, brown curls from his face, and turning to Clemusat. 'Clemusat, ride now to General Bonaparte and inform him that the army's line of communication with Nice is about to be cut.'

At midday on the second day, four hundred metres out from Brescia's walls, sat a patrol of Austrian hussars, distinct in their tall red shakos, their blue pelisse jackets swinging from their left shoulders and their musketoons resting on the right thighs.

Early morning gunfire had recalled Jobert towards Brescia. Jobert now observed Brescia beyond the enemy hussars. Under a sullen yellow cloud of smoke and dust, the town emitted the occasional sound of dull musketry.

A small group of French horsemen reined in beside Jobert. Lieutenant Colonel Clemusat evaluated the town through his telescope. Bonaparte's aide de camp was protected by an escort of Bonaparte's Guides.

Jobert did not recognise any of the grim-faced Guides, under their jaunty bicornes, as chasseurs recently transferred from the 24th Chasseurs. 'The Austrians have taken Brescia from the northern passes, sir,' said Jobert. 'Any news from General Bonaparte?'

'Two Austrian jaws are closing upon us,' said Clemusat. 'By capturing Brescia and threatening Lonato, the western jaw, which we face, has trapped the Army of Italy. An eastern jaw now races to relieve Mantua's garrison of fifteen thousand. Then the two jaws will close somewhere on the Mincio to crush us.'

Clemusat took his eye from his glass to consider Jobert. Jobert's features remained impassive.

'To concentrate our strength to break this blocking force behind us,' said Clemusat, 'General Bonaparte has ordered the siege of Mantua to be abandoned.'

'Have my reports been received, sir,' asked Jobert, 'detailing how the Austrian columns poke like outstretched fingers from the lake's shoreline toward Brescia, each column too far away to support the next?'

'They have,' said Clemusat. 'General Bonaparte senses an opportunity to reclaim Brescia, then deal with the enemy approaching Lonato. General Masséna has orders to recapture Brescia. Jobert, maintain your observation of the slower column along the Chiese and Lake Garda's shoreline.'

Jobert saluted as Clemusat, and his escort, turned south once more.

'Pull in our vedettes, Sergeant Major.' Jobert brought out his notebook and pencil. 'We have a four-hour ride back to 2nd Company. Task a courier with my report to Colonel Spiccard.'

Koschak hawked the dust from his throat and spat towards the Austrian hussar patrol. 'Mark my words, sir, those kaiserlik pricks will be seeking any opportunity to repay our compliments from Dego, Lodi and Borghetto.'

At noon on the fourth day, glaring heat wilted the apple branches under which Jobert crouched. In the crisp, dry grass, Jobert devoured the burnt drumstick of a recently liberated chicken.

Newly promoted Lieutenant Yinot saluted him. Since Huin's posting to Bonaparte's Guides, Yinot had been posted as a new regimental aide de camp. In front of his former company colleagues, Yinot appeared awkward in his officiousness.

'How is Colonel Spiccard's health?' asked Jobert.

'The regimental surgeon bled him yesterday evening, sir,' said Yinot, 'and he has woken well this morning.'

Jobert nodded. 'No gunfire to the west. Masséna must have retaken Brescia.'

'Yes, sir, the lines of communication to Milan and beyond have been re-established.' Yinot swallowed hard to lubricate a parched throat. 'But we have lost Mantua. Having relieved the fortress, the advance guard of the Austrian eastern jaw approaches. With Brescia ours, General Bonaparte's intent is to attack the enemy column threatening Lonato before the eastern jaw is upon us. General Masséna is to return from Brescia and secure Lonato.'

Jobert passed Yinot a gourd of watered bardolino wine. 'And where is the rest of the regiment?'

Yinot's face creased in concern. 'We are spread wide, sir. 1st Squadron stands east with the division's rear guard on the Mincio. Here in the north, your 2nd Squadron watches Salò and the Chiese. 3rd Squadron remains in reserve to the south. My horse and I are spent.'

'Piss on being spent, Yinot. Gather your courage, and what apples and bread you can.' Jobert chewed the gristle on the end of the bone. 'This may be our last decent meal before the kaiserliks return us to Nice.'

On the morning of the fifth day, Jobert's 2nd Squadron rejoined Masséna's divisional assembly area west of Lonato. At Spiccard's headquarters, Jobert observed with concern how grey Chabenac and Voreille appeared, haggard from four days of marching and countermarching.

'The enemy's Salò column has captured Lonato,' said Spiccard, hands shaking from ill-humours as he unrolled a map. 'Lonato is the anvil upon which the enemy's eastern jaw will hammer us. Bonaparte would have Masséna retake Lonato.'

As Spiccard bent to prod the map, Jobert noticed rivulets of sweat seep beneath Spiccard's woollen collar.

'And the regiment, sir?' asked Jobert.

'The 24th Chasseurs are dispersed to the four winds. 1st Squadron, as part of Masséna's divisional rear guard, has been cut off east of the Mincio. To the south, 3rd Squadron watches the approaching eastern jaw from Mantua.' Spiccard winced as a convulsion gripped him. 'Jobert, you and 2nd Squadron are all that is available to support the effort to re-secure Lonato.' Spiccard's fevered eyes blinked at Jobert. 'I demand your prudence in the coming clash.'

Chapter Sixteen
August 1796, Battle of Lonato, Italy

Jobert was aware of at least four separate battles being fought this day, the sixth day of the Austrian offensive.

To the south at Castiglione less than five kilometres away, General Augereau fought with the Austrian advance guard approaching from Mantua. For his part, Masséna had one brigade attacking Gavardo, while a second brigade, guided by Voreille's 5th Company, was attacking Salò.

Here, under Bonaparte's direction, raged the battle for Lonato.

The south-western corner of Lake Garda was a pall of dust churned by the tens of thousands of boots and hooves. Smoke from gun powder and grass fires thickened the haze. Despite being mounted high on the Lonato escarpment, Jobert was unable to discern Garda's shoreline, let alone observe the heights of Mount Baldo on the lake's eastern rim.

With Chabenac's 2nd Company screening the north of the town, Jobert had a good view of the thick swarm of French infantry skirmishers maintaining a thunderous roar of musketry into the walls of an old castle that protected Lonato. As another battalion assault column assembled, individual cannons were manhandled forward by Masséna's gunners and fired at short range at individual buildings.

From Jobert's perspective, the spurts of gun smoke puffing from Lonato's defenders within the homes and barns seemed to be lessening. His observations were supported by the stream of foot and wagon traffic descending the eastern escarpment road for the shoreline town of Desenzano.

Jobert turned to assess 2nd Company's dispositions. Bredieux's troop of thirty sabres stood ready in battle-line. Peugeot's troop was split as a platoon of chasseurs forward in skirmish order, and two half-sections posted as flanking vedettes. A section remained at the rear of the battle-line with the packhorses, with those chasseurs running water flasks from the packhorses' kegs to the chasseurs in the ranks. Prowling the rear rank, Koschak gave a satisfied nod to Jobert's enquiring eye.

Jobert's focus returned to the immediate threat of over one hundred and fifty Austrian hussars four hundred metres away. Yet again the sixty chasseurs of 2nd Company faced the same blue-jacketed hussars they had first encountered at Dego four months ago. Today, two hussar companies protected the flank and denied any movement toward the rear of the town. One troop in skirmish line, two troops in battle-line and the final troop in reserve.

'Do they know it is us again?' asked Chabenac, mounted beside Jobert. 'These fellows have withdrawn every time we have met. The prisoner at Cairo. Their troop screen at Dego. The patrol at Lodi. They had three companies in front of Borghetto. Do they know they continually yield to the 24th Chasseurs?'

'A hussar's uniform,' said Jobert, 'either theirs or ours, is clearly identifiable. In our chasseur-green, we are as indistinguishable as an infantry regiment might be in a line of fusilier blue. As to them withdrawing, that would have more to do with compliance with orders than our fearsome reputation.'

'Major Jobert, sir,' called Koschak, identifying a rumble of horsemen approaching from the rear. 'A senior officer with Bonaparte's Guides.'

Jobert identified Captain Bessières, of the Guides, and a senior officer with a befeathered bicorne. 'Colonel Junot,' said Jobert to Chabenac. 'One of Bonaparte's Toulon crowd.'

Chabenac winced as Junot swayed in the saddle.

Jobert shrugged. 'A lawyer before joining the artillery.'

As Jobert trotted to the rear to attend Colonel Junot, Bessières halted his column in a shallow fold to the rear of 2nd Company.

Jobert ran his eye across the Guides. Tough, steady men on gleaming black remounts. *Good to know grain is received as far forward as Bonaparte's headquarters.* Jobert exchanged a curt nod with a grim face in the ranks, his old marksman now Guide, Corporal Duval.

Good natured jibes, swapped between the rear rank of 2nd Company and those Guides who had served in the 24th Chasseurs, were silenced by a snapped command from Lieutenant Huin at the head of the Guides' column.

Jobert saluted Colonel Junot. Junot halted heavily, acknowledged Jobert with a nod and extended his telescope towards the Austrian wounded and chattels departing Lonato down the escarpment.

'Good day, sir,' said Bessières, his dark eyes appraising the enemy hussars. 'General Bonaparte has received your report that the Austrians are withdrawing from Lonato down the escarpment to Desenzano. General Bonaparte directs us to encircle the withdrawing enemy, causing their rout and capturing their trains. I suggested to Colonel Junot we might seek your views before engaging the foe.'

'I commend your choice, sir, in shielding your Guides in the low ground,' said Jobert. 'I would suggest an immediate charge by us before their skirmishers can reassemble in their lines. I would aim my line of charge to the right, giving the appearance of attempting to separate the hussars from the town. In so doing, my intent is to draw the commitment of their depth troop and expose our left flank to their envelopment. In the time the affair develops, sir, your Guides might form on our left and launch into the flank of the hussars' envelopment and their reserve.'

'Are you Berthier's Virginian?' asked Junot. 'Your scheme is too complex, man.'

Bessières glanced at Jobert. 'Forgive me, sir, may I suggest Major Jobert's proposal has merit. Jobert's moves to the right. Unaware of our presence, the hussars swing to envelop him. We attack their flank.'

Junot flapped his reins against his pistol holsters. 'Very well. At them, Virginian.'

Jobert saluted before cantering back to 2nd Company's line.

'We are to go straight at them,' called Jobert to Koschak as he passed the rear rank.

'Sabres!' roared Jobert, shortening his reins and looking to Chabenac. 'Take our line to the right, Chabenac. Aim for the end of their line.'

Chabenac blinked to comprehend the sudden change. 'And the Guides will support my exposed flank?'

'Quite so,' said Jobert. 'Moench, sound Charge!'

Moench's trumpet startled the drowsy horses. Jobert accepted the urgency of catching the enemy snoozing in the midday sun, but it also caught the chasseurs unawares. Yet they drew sabres and pressed their remounts to the canter. With only thirty to forty seconds until impact, and taking their dressing from Chabenac, the frontage of fifteen men skewed to the right. Koschak galloped towards the left flank screaming for the trailing troopers on the left to ride faster and maintain a solid front.

Forward in the screen and alerted by the trumpets' insistent call, the front rank of chasseur skirmishers fired. Jobert signalled with his outstretched sabre indicating to which flank the French skirmishers must flee. Then the second rank of skirmishers trotted forward and fired, adding to the dense wall of smoke that obscured the troop battle-line.

The ruse began well. The hussar skirmishers were caught, either by returning fire at individual chasseurs darting in the smoke or as they raced to their own ranks as their trumpets recalled them.

Bursting free of the acrid cloud, Jobert's mind raced in the twenty seconds before impact. Chabenac led Bredieux's troop towards the flank of the enemy.

The Austrians drew sabres at the walk before their forty horsemen in their front rank broke into a trot. Cavalry racing towards moving cavalry halved the time available. Ten seconds.

Picking a hussar skirmisher as fleeting cover, Jobert sank his right hip, skipped Bleu onto a left lead and pounded towards the now familiar broken-nosed hussar commander. The Austrian was looking away from Jobert, roaring for his right flank to wrap around the small French attack.

Jobert aimed Bleu for the rump of the officer's black charger, bringing his sabre back for a nearside cut at his opponent's rein arm.

The fleeing skirmisher screamed a warning.

The Austrian officer sank his weight into his left spur, spun his cantering horse's rump to the right, and dropped the tip of his blade along his left side for the parry. The two steels clanged with the force of Bleu's rush. Although the Austrian's instinctive skill saved his left arm, Jobert's firm hold allowed his slice to drag across the fellow's left triceps and shoulder blade as Bleu passed.

Jobert pounded past the officer's trumpeter, checked Bleu's pace with a hard pressure through knees and bit before skipping Bleu back onto a right lead as he collided with the soldiers of the front rank.

Everyone around him was yelling.

Taking the front-rank hussars on their oblique left, Jobert thrust Bleu's face into a defensive sweep from one man. Standing high in his stirrups from Bleu's rapid deceleration, Jobert blocked the closer man's strike with his sabre hilt, rolled his wrist to create tip-speed to slice through the hussar's face. Jobert did not look at the impact of his cut. That his arm felt the solid change during the follow-through was sufficient.

Jobert looked forward to the hussar that had Bleu's head stretched across the rear of his saddle, his blade trapped by Bleu's neck, his own remount staggering from Bleu's charge into its ribs. Jobert reversed his wrist, twirled his blade now coming free of its previous cut, and brought a back hand cut across the throat of the overwhelmed hussar.

With Bleu moving into the space behind the front rank, and blade arcing away from the now reeling hussar, Jobert looked for the expected attack against him from the rear rank. Again, seeking the slim gap between the two nearest oncoming Austrians, Jobert launched a collected Bleu at the left-most man and gave point at the right-most.

Jobert caught the enemy soldier's blade with his tip, feeling its firm strength sizzle towards his hilt-guard. Sensing the hussar had the advantage, Jobert forced the attacking blade wide of his kidneys and Bleu's loins. As the blades squealed in passing, Bleu sprang into the space beyond the rear rank.

Along the front of the depth troop, away to Jobert's right, the other Austrian commander roared to bring his hussars into action against Chabenac.

Struck by a sense of *déjà vu*, yet confronted by the oncoming hussars, Jobert fought the distraction and urged Bleu onto a left-lead canter. Knowing the hussars would be locked into maintaining their relative position within the formation, Jobert aimed his sabre at the hussar sergeant at the end of the line. The hussar slashed to parry Jobert's blade as Bleu galloped past.

Wheeling around the second rank of the depth troop and observing the backs of his enemy moving away from him, Jobert checked Bleu's racing before glancing around for Moench. With his dark-orange jacket identifiable in the midst of Austrian blue, and his white mare highlighted by surrounding black remounts, Moench, clutching his trumpet and reins, eyes wide with terror, pounded into view.

'To Mess, Moench! To Mess!' Jobert screamed for 2nd Company's signature tune hoarsely, urging Bleu to leap forward once more.

Despite the cacophony of hooves, blades, trumpets and throats, Moench's call elicited a distinct bellow from behind Jobert. Jobert twisted to discern the source. Chasseur-green tailcoats, plumed bicornes and racing black horses, led by Junot and Bessières, the Guides had arrived on the flank of the enemy's reserve, howling in their desire to join the kill.

'Stay with Bleu, Moench!' Jobert gave point and urged Bleu forward.

The hussars in the rear rank of the depth troop were checking their horses, yielding to the left due to the colliding ranks to their front. Aware of Jobert galloping towards their backs, hussars screamed at the threat pounding along their rear rank. The Austrian formation dissolved.

Riding along their rumps, Jobert's blade tip caught one man under the jaw, then floated to the next hussar catching him under the ear. Jobert's blade sliced though the man's left cheek, entangling Jobert's sabre in the hussar's chin strap. Bleu swept both the sabre and the shako forward.

The next hussar along the line glanced back in fright and leant away from Jobert's gliding sabre and its adorning red helmet. The shako's chinstrap now fouling Jobert's cut, Jobert dropped his sabre onto his sword knot and lunged at the leaning man. Jobert caught hold of the hussar's collar. Wheeling Bleu clear of the pack of the Guides, Jobert pulled the hussar clear of his saddle, before releasing him under the hooves.

Jobert watched a horse race stream towards the retreating Austrian columns. *The Guides can charge on. Leave the pickings for us. Bredieux's debt repaid.* 'Rally, Moench! Sound Rally!'

At midday on the seventh day of the Austrian offensive, Jobert inspected the inlying piquet's horses.

Having fought at Lonato yesterday, Jobert and 2nd Squadron were ordered to pursue the withdrawing Austrian column thirty kilometres to Salò. Now, as he moved down the line of remounts and packhorses, stepping over puddles of thick, pungent urine and scattered, hard balls of manure, Jobert took in the horses' sunken sides and prominent ribs, their eyes half shut, ears flopping outwards and sagging lips. All signs of extreme fatigue.

Later, Jobert addressed the knot of 2nd Squadron's officers. 'Gentlemen, we have marched two hundred kilometres in seven days. This afternoon, we will follow the kaiserlik withdrawal and re-establish our piquet north of Salò. Before we sleep tonight, horses and men will bathe in Lake Garda.'

'The squadron has no food, sir,' said Koschak. 'The Austrians have depleted their own supplies and have drained the local villagers most thoroughly. Upon reaching Salò, we might consider harvesting fish from the lake.'

As his weary mind digested the implications of resupply, Jobert considered a scene across the village square. Hunched against a stone wall in an air of malevolence, one hundred and fifty captured Austrian infantry stragglers watched the chasseurs rummage through their satchels.

'Beware, sir,' said Koschak. 'A harbinger of doom approaches.'

Hard stares from 2nd Squadron's officers greeted Yinot's salute.

'General Bonaparte is satisfied that we have defeated the western jaw of the Austrian vice, sir,' said Yinot. 'The eastern jaw that raised our siege, now lies to our south between us and Mantua. General Augereau holds the enemy advance guard. General Masséna is to march south and join General Augereau at Castiglione.'

Moans and soft expletives from the squadron's young commanders were directed at each other's booted feet.

Jobert narrowed his eyes and ground his teeth. 'Castiglione lies forty kilometres from here. A twelve-hour march. When does Colonel Spiccard require us to step off?'

Yinot grimaced. 'Tonight, sir. To arrive before dawn.'

Chapter Seventeen
August 1796, Battle of Castiglione, Italy

South of the town of Castiglione, an ancient north-south ripple in the Lombardy plain had a steep eastern face and a gradual descent to the west. The village of Solferino and its prominent castle surmounted the undulation along a series of knolls.

A dawn westerly pulsed cool, fragrant air from the meadows, vineyards and orchards well out across the Po's plain up the slope on which two opposing armies stood. Jobert inhaled the morning's breeze.

Facing the village and tower, Masséna's division held the eastern high ground on the left of Bonaparte's line. From the 24th Chasseurs' reserve position behind Masséna's left flank, Jobert and Chabenac had an uninterrupted view down the steep gradient to the Mincio River and the Borghetto bridge ten kilometres to the east.

Across the battlefield, Jobert identified that the Austrians had anchored their eastern flank on the high village and the sharp slope to the east. Their line then extended west down the slope to a small hill, on which a solid redoubt was established, which dominated the road south to Mantua.

'We appear even, sir, at around twenty thousand each.' Chabenac assumed his relaxed smile which Jobert knew masked his anxiety. 'This is the first opportunity to appreciate such a spectacle.'

'I have not attended an affair of such size since Jemappes.' Jobert slapped Chabenac's shoulder. 'Take heart, dear sir, for today will be a clash of cannon and bayonet. What I hear from courier gossip, two of our divisions march to join us. One division from Brescia behind us, the other from the south behind the enemy's line.' Chabenac raised an eyebrow in surprise. 'I wager we chasseurs will be called upon late in the day.'

Jobert stood in his stirrups and craned his neck to peer westward. Four kilometres away, on the right of the French line, the sabres of the dragoons and the hussars glinted.

'Developments on that flank, sir? asked Chabenac.

'Just Didier's hussars.' Jobert's jaw clenched with a brief prayer.

'Major Jobert,' called Colonel Spiccard, 'attend me.'

Under the flapping regimental standard close by, Colonel Spiccard trembled as he signed an acknowledgement on the order he had just received. 'General Bonaparte desires the enemy to relinquish their heights and follow us into the lower ground. Generals Masséna and Augereau are ordered to retire our line as a feint, a manoeuvre fraught with risk. Masséna requires the 24th Chasseurs and a regiment of light infantry to screen the withdrawal. With 1st Squadron screening the division's eastern flank, I shall maintain 3rd Squadron in reserve.' Despite the twitch of his fevers, Spiccard stared at Jobert. 'Jobert, take 2nd Squadron forward. Perhaps being in full view of the entire army, you might contain your impulsive designs.'

Jobert resolved to remain impassive at both this slight and recent rebukes in the wake of Lonato two days ago. '2nd Squadron,' called Jobert, 'skirmish line, trot, march! Moench, sound Skirmishers Out.'

Trumpets blared. 2nd and 5th Companies dissolved into fifty pairs of skirmishers.

As Jaune trotted forward, Jobert flexed his right hand, uncomfortable in the absence of his musketoon. His eyes dropped to his pistol holsters. He cocked both pistols before drawing his sabre.

Battalions of French light infantry swarmed towards the companies of Austrian fusiliers earmarked for the work. The chasseurs fell in behind the blue jackets. Within thirty minutes, musketry rippled all along the skirmish line.

On the northern rise, drums signalled the French fusiliers to turn about and march away.

With his skirmish line set, Jobert's thoughts wandered. *What is Spiccard's game? The prick knew I was under Junot at Lonato. Must I subdue all reason?*

Jobert watched a surge all along the twenty-thousand-man Austrian front.

Solid attack columns of Austrians tramped toward Masséna's left. Driven by bugles and whistles, pairs of flitting light infantrymen conceded ground in front of the marching ranks.

Jobert glanced from the spectacle of the enemy advance towards Chabenac's and Voreille's officers coordinating the movement of the chasseurs. Koschak fumed at the chasseur pairs, dull from eight days of marching, and demanded individual alertness.

Drums thrashed all along the French line. Light infantry skirmishers ceased firing to appraise the ridge behind them. The retiring French line had halted and now refaced their advancing enemy.

Jobert's head jerked at a trumpet call from the rise behind him. 'Moench, repeat the call. Sound Skirmishers In.'

Content that the companies' skirmish lines were falling back in good order, Jobert rocked Jaune into a trot towards the solid line of Masséna's bluecoats.

Two eight-pound foot batteries had brought their twelve guns into action side by side. One battery marked the flank of Masséna's division, and one battery held the left of Augereau's division. Jobert selected the batteries as the space through which 2nd Squadron could re-enter the lines.

Waiting for the skirmishers to clear the battlefield, gunners raced to resupply their trail-boxes from the waiting ammunition caissons. Satisfied that the chasseurs had cleared his muzzles, an artillery officer bellowed his fire orders. The twelve guns spat flame one after another. Punching out five rounds in three minutes at the advancing Austrian ranks, the field erupted in a cannonade of nearly sixty guns. Thick smoke soon masked all.

The French drums beat Advance. As the infantry assault moved forward, the gunners swabbed their guns. Only the two howitzers belched their fused shells high over the heads of the infantry.

Sapped by the acrid smoke, the ranks of light horsemen rested behind the reserve battalions, where clots of wounded infantrymen either limped or were carried past . Sinking to a halt near the wafting *tri-couleur* standard of the 24th Chasseurs, Jobert saluted Fergnes as the senior officer present.

'Spiccard's fevers confound him,' said Fergnes, his eyes emotionless. 'He can no longer maintain his seat in the saddle and has retired to the rear to be bled. Masséna has conferred command of the 24th Chasseurs upon me. The regiment is to rest in the rear line of the reserves as the infantry advance. Might you supervise the rotation of ranks standing to horse, Jobert?'

Jobert scanned the ranks. 3rd Squadron sat ready to march. Chabenac formed 2nd Squadron in column of companies behind them. Rotating through levels of readiness, the first company sat in the saddle, musketoon charges tamped. The second company stood by their horses, relieving the pressure from their remounts' backs, rubbing their ears under their bridle straps. The third company took the opportunity to loosen girths, refasten straps and piss. The final company had a kettle brewing and purchased apricots and mugs of grappa from Madame Quandalle's keg.

For three hours, as the chasseurs and their remounts rested, the explosive discord thundered.

Jobert was sharing a cup of thin wine with Fergnes when Yinot approached.

'Excuse me, sir,' said Yinot to Fergnes, 'General Masséna presents his compliments. The day is nearly ours. The enemy are breaking south-east toward the Mincio's crossing at Borghetto and Valeggio. All along our line our attacks are moving forward. The castle of Solferino at the left of our line has been captured. General Masséna has directed two reserve battalions of the 32nd Ligne to descend the escarpment to our east then re-ascend the escarpment to attack the exposed flank of the Austrian line. General Masséna requires the 24th Chasseurs to support the infantry's flank.'

The 32nd Ligne's drum corps paradiddled the one thousand resting infantrymen to attention.

'Moench, sound To Arms,' called Jobert. 'Tulloc, fetch Rouge.'

Once freshly mounted, Jobert turned Rouge towards the four companies of 2nd and 3rd Squadron set one behind the other in the twenty-five-metre-long company line. Due to the supervised rotation, 2nd Company sat ready in the saddle. 5th Company mounted at Moench's call. 3rd Company tightened girths before swinging into the saddle. Leaving kettles to be stowed by the packhorse sections, 6th Company regirthed and mounted.

'Jobert,' said Fergnes, 'I shall attend the 32nd Ligne's commanding officer to understand his intent. These two battalions are to turn to the left then march to a point below the escarpment, where they then about-face and ascend once more to assault the enemy line. Such manoeuvres from the infantry invariably produce a pig's breakfast. Take the 2nd and 3rd Squadrons clear of them. Once they have sorted their muddle and are prepared to attack, set our line on their left, or southern, flank.'

Jobert evaluated the amount of space required to complete the task. '24th Chasseurs, form column of troops to the left, walk, march!'

As Chabenac lead Bredieux's troop in a wheel to the left, followed by the other eight troops, Jobert kept an eye on the infantry's progress. He was surprised by what he observed.

The infantry's attack columns wheeled to the left, or east, each sliding into columns of half companies. When both the foot and horse columns descended the Solferino escarpment, the fusiliers maintained their tight formation by wheeling about. Now facing west towards the rising slope, the infantry expanded once more into attack columns, each a frontage of two companies, before halting. The achievement of the man-oeuvre caused a ripple of hearty congratulations throughout their ranks.

'Impressive,' said Chabenac. 'Well done, the 32nd Ligne.'

'Our volunteers are maturing,' said Jobert. 'I have not seen such infantry precision since before the Bastille. Now we will dress off their left.' Jobert twisted in the saddle to call over his shoulder to the ranks of horsemen behind him. '24th Chasseurs, form column of squadron at the halt.'

The sixteen ranks of horsemen twelve-wide morphed to a halt, in four ranks fifty-men wide, 2nd Squadron in front of 3rd Squadron.

The infantry drummed Skirmishers Out as Fergnes returned at the trot. 'Jobert, escort the colonel of the 32nd to the top of the escarpment so he can view the ground before setting his line.'

'Bredieux,' called Jobert, 'troop skirmish line, trot, march! Moench, sound Skirmishers Out.'

Once more upon the escarpment's crest, the cool westerly breeze refreshed the heaving horses. As Bredieux set a skirmish line, Jobert and the colonel of the 32nd Ligne observed the eastern edge of the battle.

The ancient tower of Solferino stood four hundred metres to Jobert's right. Beyond the tower, two duelling lines of musketry, battalion after battalion, stretched away into the dense smoke. As a French battalion or two surged behind their skirmishers on the closer face of the tower, the last few Austrian battalions shrank back under the canopy of farmhouse groves beyond musket range.

'That is where we will strike,' said the commander of the 32nd Ligne to his chiefs of battalion. He pointed at the end of the curving white-jacketed battle-line three hundred metres distant, its flank covered only by darting skirmishers. 'Bring up the 32nd. Dress the right of the regiment from here, then beat To Line.'

On the slope behind and below, Jobert heard drums thrash the two battalions' attack columns forward. Yet he remained focused on the flank of the enemy.

Alerted to the French cavalry by its skirmish screen, the drum corps of the last Austrian battalion of the line beat its fire-line into square.

'Bredieux, clear the escarpment edge for our infantry,' called Jobert. 'Reset your screen two hundred metres south of the kaiserlik square.'

As the front of the two French attack columns crested, 2nd Squadron's trumpets sounded Advance. 2nd Squadron galloped up the slope to halt beside the infantry, whose battalions had extended into a two hundred metre fire-line.

A cheer erupted from the Austrian ranks. Steady drumming approached through the trees.

'Major Jobert,' called Bredieux. 'The kaiserliks are reinforcing this flank. A battalion of grenzers is marching up.'

'Moench, sound To Arms,' said Jobert. He begrudged the discipline of the two enemy battalions exchanging flanking roles. The square of fusiliers extended into fire-line once more, as the reinforcing grenzers slid their march column into square.

Skirmishers of the 32nd Ligne sniped at the battalion coming out of square. The drum corps ordered the French infantry to advance. Jobert held up his palm to Chabenac, so that 2nd Squadron stood firm, and did not advance into the infantry firefight.

'Sir, more bastard grenzers.' Bredieux pointed beyond the existing Austrian flank. 'And a troop of mongrel dragoons.'

Again, the flanking battalions conducted a smooth transition to extend the flank, the grenzer square unravelling into line and the reinforcements squeezing into square. Forty-odd black-bicorned dragoons halted in line beside the square, sabres drawn.

'The 32nd are exposed to a flanking charge,' said Jobert. 'Moench, sound Advance.' 2nd and 5th Companies duly responded to Moench's call. 'Halt them alongside the infantry.'

Jobert winced when a red-trousered Austrian general appeared between the two battalions of grenzers, one in line, one in square with its dragoon escort. 'Bredieux, watch out for more infantry,' called Jobert. 'See the kaiserlik general. They have sent up a brigade. The 32nd Ligne may be in trouble.'

In the time the Austrian line had extended, the 32nd Ligne had advanced to within two hundred metres of the enemy, re-absorbing its skirmishers into its ranks. The Austrian fire-line, including the square, was now the equivalent length of the 32nd Ligne's frontage.

Jobert looked to the stationary line of blue coats. He watched the regimental commander evaluate the growing threat to his own flank by the Austrian reinforcements.

'German fusiliers, sir,' called Bredieux.

A third reinforcing battalion of white-legged, black-gaitered fusiliers, tramped into square, as the grenzers extended the line further. The dragoons again formed beyond the new square.

'Moench, sound Skirmishers In,' called Jobert. 'Bredieux, reform in the squadron line.'

Jobert lifted Rouge into a fast canter back to Chabenac and Fergnes. 'Chabenac, wheel left,' called Jobert, as he cantered past. 'Face the dragoons.'

Jobert sank Rouge to a halt beside Fergnes.

'The 32nd Ligne will engage the Austrians, as ordered, with their rightmost battalion,' said Fergnes. 'The second battalion is to swing left to this growing threat. Why have their dragoons not charged? They are bred for such a moment. I will not receive their charge at the halt. After your antics at Lonato, I dread to ask if you spy opportunity.'

Jobert scowled. 'Forgive me, sir, is this a reprimand, idle banter or are you seeking my opinion?'

'Yes, Jobert,' said Fergnes, 'I seek your thoughts.'

'Are not our orders to protect the flank of the 32nd Ligne, sir?' asked Jobert. 'I would hesitate to commit until our infantry are in direct peril of being crushed. The Austrians play for time. They succeed by standing solid as a rear guard and allowing their army to depart the field in good order. It is the infantry who will destroy us by fire, not their dragoons by blade.'

'But these reinforcements arrived as we arrived. How so?'

Jobert shrugged. 'More than likely Masséna's opposing commander saw the same ... look! More German fusiliers. A fourth battalion has joined us. Masséna's moment to turn their flank may have passed.'

As one end of the enemy battle-line extended yet again, the first battalion of the 32nd Ligne exploded in smoke at the other end.

The colonel of the 32nd Ligne reined in beside Fergnes and Jobert. 'My two battalions are now faced by four of theirs in line and one in square,' said the regimental colonel. 'I am forced to refuse my left to handle their expected ... look here they come.'

At the pace of the shuffling square, the Austrian drums hinged their line, swinging to smother the French.

'Quickly, gentlemen, your views?' asked the colonel. 'Can your chasseurs match their heavier dragoons?'

'Yes, sir,' said Fergnes, 'without doubt.'

Fergnes and Jobert exchanged affirming glances to reinforce the lie.

'May I suggest, sir,' said Jobert, 'their dragoons are to counter-attack any move we chasseurs take against their infantry. I wager the dragoon ace will be played last.'

'They have twice the number of muskets than we,' said the colonel, 'and our back is to the escarpment. I will send word to General Masséna and prepare to retire my line. Can you see any way out, gentlemen? I am open to any reasonable proposal.'

Chapter Eighteen

In the final moments of the battle, Fergnes blinked through the gun smoke at the approaching wall of Austrian white. The commanding officer of the 32nd Ligne Regiment stared at Fergnes.

Spent musket balls whizzed past Jobert. He winced as he calculated the enemy would be in musket range in two dozen paces.

Fergnes frowned then slid his eyes to Jobert.

'What of your previous idea, sir? asked Jobert.

Fergnes raised his brows in enquiry.

'Lieutenant Colonel Fergnes had mentioned, sir,' said Jobert to the infantry colonel, 'should we stop the square, we stop the swinging line. As you arrived, sir, we were preparing to charge.'

'Good idea, Fergnes,' said the colonel. 'I approve. Continue with any act you feel appropriate. Our casualties increase from the weight of fire. I must attend to my battalions.'

As the colonel departed, Fergnes shook his head slowly, his impassive eyes locked onto Jobert's. 'Sabres!' cried Fergnes.

'3rd Squadron, stand fast. 2nd Squadron, forward march ten paces, walk, march. Sound Advance!'

The chasseur's feint surged forward. Koschak and the company sergeant majors behind the rear rank bellowed last moment reminders.

The dragoon trumpets screamed over three hundred metres away.

The fusilier square's drums thrashed Halt.

The two swinging battalions, one fusilier and one grenzer, shuffled to a stop.

2nd Squadron's one hundred chasseurs shook their sabres in a jeering roar.

'There, Jobert, we have played our bluff,' said Fergnes. 'We have no low cards left. We can now play for the dragoons' blades, the fusiliers' balls or flee in dishonour.'

Ten minutes passed as the Austrians redressed their line, all the while the firefight spat and tore at the opposing battalions on the right of the line. Then drums commanded the enemy fusiliers and grenzers march once more. The square's infantry roared at the chasseurs with mockery of their own. The dragoons remained standing, remounts on a tight rein, poised to launch. As the line advanced, the square obscured Jobert's vision of the dragoons.

'They are nearly in musket range, Jobert,' said Fergnes. 'I am forced to charge that square. If we continue to stand, they will eventually anchor their line to the escarpment edge and shoot us off the crest.'

'You wish to charge a square supported by dragoons?' asked Jobert. 'If we go, sir, we will wrap around the square, where the dragoons will counter-charge our disorder on the far side.'

'You surprise me, Jobert. A reckless charge not your style?'

'Not if my men are massacred to visit a mild inconvenience upon the enemy, sir.'

'It is not my desire to slaughter us, Jobert.' Fergnes punched his saddlebow. 'And I will not flee. What reasonable action is available?'

'The 32nd Ligne are about to be destroyed,' said Jobert. 'We need to provide a diversion to get them off the ridge.' Jobert squinted through the smoke haze at the dragoons. 'We need to attack their flank. As we did before, sir, descend off the escarpment and re-ascend behind the square.'

Drums beat for the French infantry to retire their line.

The musketry coughed to a stop.

The Austrian line cheered. Their drums rattled for their line to advance.

'Yes!' Fergnes twisted in his saddle. 'Yinot, inform the commanding officer of the 32nd Ligne of our intention to reappear behind the enemy line, and request his approval. Jobert, take a troop and set guides in anticipation of my move.'

'With your permission, sir,' asked Jobert, 'can I recall Geourdai's 1st Company into our line. Having won the field, Masséna will still have 4th Company in his flanking screen.'

'Yes. Go now.'

'Bredieux, troop form column of fours to the rear, trot, march!' cried Jobert. 'Moench, sound To Mess.'

Jobert and Bredieux's troop descended the escarpment.

'Bredieux, there are Geourdai's skirmishers,' called Jobert. 'Inform Geourdai that 1st Company is to canter march to me. I shall set guides. 4th Company is to remain in the screen.'

As Bredieux cantered towards 1st Squadron's outlying piquet, Jobert and the column of chasseurs ascended the escarpment once more.

Through the dark groves, Jobert identified the white jackets of both fusilier square and dragoon line, although no firing was heard. South of the crumbling Austrian defence, Jobert watched columns of enemy infantry and guns, wagons of wounded and swarms of stragglers jostling along the road towards Valeggio to cross the Mincio River to safety.

Where is Fergnes? A thunder of hooves caused Jobert to look to his rear.

Over the crest cantered Chabenac leading Peugeot's troop. 'The day is ours, sir,' said Chabenac. 'Although Masséna has been obliged to withdraw his flanking manoeuvre with the 32nd Ligne.'

'Where is Geourdai and 1st Company?' asked Jobert.

'All companies have been recalled. Lieutenant Colonel Fergnes requests you attend him for further orders. We are to prepare for the pursuit.'

Three hours later, with the sun low on the western horizon behind them, 24th Chasseurs formed regimental battle-line.

Following eight days of extreme effort, and pursuit from Castiglione, the now three hundred chasseurs pressed their wasted, listless remounts into two ranks. The horses moaned as they urinated, pawing and tugging at their reins as they smelt the gurgling waters of the Mincio River beyond.

As dust lingered on the cooler air closer to the banks of the Mincio, Jobert peered through the haze.

Behind a thick band of their skirmishers, two companies of sky-blue hussars faced the regiment. The bridge was clear of retreating Austrian infantry and trains, the cloud of their passage mottling the evening's deep purple tinge, as the road disappeared into the rolling hills to the east. Only this hussar rear-guard remained on the western side of the Mincio.

'We need water, Jobert,' said Fergnes. 'I want that bridge.'

A jerk of Jobert's head returned Fergnes' attention to the enemy.

Three hussars cantered forward. Two of the three were the near-identical officers who had fascinated the chasseurs for months. The third was an attendant trumpeter. The hussar skirmishers parted around the officers as their prancing black chargers approached the French line.

A frisson of energy rippled through the chasseur ranks. A bark from Koschak behind the rear rank restored silence.

Illuminated by the last rays of the day, Jobert scrutinised the senior officer. As Jobert noted his height and powerful build, his crushed nose and cheekbones, a shadow of *déjà vu* shivered through him. Jobert blinked away the irritation. The hussar's left-arm was in a sling resulting from Jobert's near-side slice yesterday. The hussar's mouth twisted into an ugly snarl. His face glowed with fever. *Either Mantua's poor air or contagion in your wound.*

The other tall, deep-chested officer attended him. Again, he rode with his gloved fist on his hip, not caring to draw his sabre. At close range it was obvious they were related. The man with the broken nose in his late-twenties, the other in his late-teens or early-twenties.

As Fergnes stood the furthest forward of any French officer from the front rank, the older hussar rode towards him then swept up his sabre in salute. 'Colonel?'

Fergnes gave a curt nod as he saluted in response.

'I am Graf Valentin von Maefeld,' said the broken-faced, older hussar. 'Am I correct that I crossed blades with a young officer of your regiment outside Savona last year?'

Fergnes, betraying no emotion, looked to his left and stared at Voreille.

Von Maefeld followed the direction of Fergnes' gaze until his eyes locked with Voreille's. 'Colonel, a matter exists between that gentleman and me. A matter that has not been resolved to my satisfaction. I call that gentleman out. I demand he attend me at this hour.'

Voreille's eyes darted between Fergnes and Jobert.

Fergnes looked again over his left shoulder at Voreille. 'Captain Voreille, last year this gentleman extended a challenge. You accepted it. This gentleman claims the affair is unfinished. Is there any reason you are unable to oblige?'

Voreille squeezed his bay mare forward. 'I am at your service, sir.'

'I will stand as his second.' Jobert pressed Jaune behind Voreille, his eyes locked on von Maefeld. *Before your fevers take you, you must redeem your drubbing at Savona.*

Von Maefeld's face convulsed with anger as he recognised Jobert. Von Maefeld's eyes returned to Voreille. 'My injuries restrict my ability to face you on horse. Will you do me the courtesy of meeting me on foot?'

Voreille nodded.

Followed by the other hussar officer and the trumpeter, Von Maefeld cantered to the empty space in front of the skirmishers. The hussar trumpeter sounded a call at which the hussar skirmishers returned to the ranks and the hussar line advanced to within three hundred metres.

There was excited muttering along the ranks from the French chasseurs.

The Austrian hussars stood still and silent.

Voreille dismounted and passed his reins to Jobert without looking up. As he took the reins, Jobert checked that his shabraque was rolled back exposing both of his cocked pistols in their holsters.

Valentin von Maefeld clicked the heels of his boots together and swept his sabre up to his lips in salute. Voreille returned the compliment.

'Valentin, he does not deserve such,' said the younger von Maefeld. 'He is not a gentleman.'

'That is obvious, Wolff,' said the older man, 'but I am.'

Von Maefeld then took an odd stance. He flopped his blade over his right shoulder, his right fist raised high within the sabre's hilt guard. Now free of its sling, his left hand hooked into his belt in contrived nonchalance.

The hatred in Von Maefeld's eyes flashed between Voreille and Jobert, the Austrian's nostrils flaring as he breathed.

Jobert considered the options of such an unprepared pose. *You gamble on an all-or-nothing strike.*

Voreille wavered before von Maefeld.

'Observe, Wolff,' said the elder von Maefeld. 'As at Savona, he quails, waiting to leap away. He will not strike. He will attempt something cowardly.' Von Maefeld's malicious eyes slid to Jobert. 'They all do.'

Voreille advanced a step, his blade tip raised in expectation of von Maefeld cutting from his right shoulder down onto Voreille's left.

Jobert expected the same. Jobert foresaw, should Voreille step his left backwards, von Maefeld could reverse the downwards cut into a slash onto Voreille's right thigh.

Voreille advanced another step.

Von Maefeld raised his chin, exposing his neck.

Voreille hesitated at the invitation.

Von Maefeld sneered and, with an imperceptible nod of encouragement, dared Voreille to try.

The audience hissed as Voreille lunged, the tip of his blade aimed at the Austrian's throat.

Von Maefeld exhaled a screech, his left-hand flashing from his sword belt to coil around Voreille's sabre and catching Voreille's jacket at the elbow.

Voreille tugged at his trapped blade.

Von Maefeld punched his hilt guard into Voreille's face. An audible crunch from Voreille's nose caused a low 'ooh' from the mounted audience. As Voreille's ensnared blade sliced along his opponent's ribcage, von Maefeld drove three more powerful blows into Voreille's unprotected face. Von Maefeld released the caught arm.

Voreille staggered a half-circle until he collapsed on his back.

'That is what the French understand, do they not, sir?' Von Maefeld gasped from his exertions, leaning heavily on his sabre's point. 'To brawl like a stevedore, not strike cleanly like a sabreur.'

Voreille moaned and gurgled at von Maefeld's feet, his spurred heels gouging the earth.

Von Maefeld regained his balance, and with teeth bared and blade tip raised, stepped towards Voreille with every outward intention of impaling the writhing Voreille.

'Valentin, no!' called the younger von Maefeld.

'Stop!' Jobert drew a pistol and aimed at von Maefeld. 'You stand on the field of honour, sir. Withdraw and allow your man to stand or state your satisfaction with the affair.'

While keeping his blade tip hovering over Voreille's heaving chest, Von Maefeld's manic eyes rolled to consider Jobert. As his gaze focused on Jobert's pistol, von Maefeld's eyes widened with alarm. Von Maefeld blinked at the outstretched barrel, its silver inlay glinting in the setting sun. 'Show me that pistol.'

Jobert frowned in confusion.

As von Maefeld's broken face coalesced in anger at Jobert, Voreille thrust his sabre awkwardly upwards. The blade slid beneath von Maefeld's right ribcage.

Von Maefeld bellowed and recoiled, dropping his sabre to clutch at his side.

'No, uncle!' The younger von Maefeld swung down from his horse.

Despite his wound, von Maefeld's fevered eyes never left Jobert. 'Show me that pistol. Now! Wolff, fetch me that pistol.'

Jobert's mind raced between the pistol and the Austrian. Jobert gritted his teeth, raised the pistol and fired into the air. Jaune flinched at the explosion. Jobert reversed the pistol and handed it butt first to Wolff von Maefeld. He then drew the second pistol and held it low by his thigh.

Valentin Von Maefeld ogled the pistol's silverwork. 'Wolff, these are your father's weapons. Look. The boar's head insignia. His name inscribed. A gift from your grandfather.'

Wolff looked aghast as he examined the pistols engravings.

The elder Von Maefeld blinked up at Jobert. 'Did you take these pistols from an Austrian officer on the field at Jemappes?'

Jobert's memory of Jemappes flooded back. *Duque. Blanc. Three hussar officers. Brothers? I ran two through and bludgeoned to death the third.* Jobert blinked at von Maefeld in confusion. *Obviously not.*

'I demand to know,' said van Maefeld, 'did you kill my brother and take his weapons?'

'I did,' said Jobert.

Anger contorted Wolff's face, mottling his cheeks.

Valentin gasped and collapsed to his knees. 'You had a moustache and braids.'

'At Jemappes, yes,' said Jobert.

'You broke my face, you bastard.'

Jobert tickled Jaune's cropped mane at the memory of shooting Blanc. 'I did.' Jobert raised the barrel of the second pistol. 'I remember Jemappes. I remember you, von Maefeld, and your brothers. Now return my pistol.'

Valentin steadied himself with his injured left arm, only to moan with pain. He collapsed heavily to the earth.

'Return my pistol, sir,' said Jobert to Wolff. 'Who is he to you?'

Wolff quivered with rage. 'I am Wolff von Maefeld. This is my uncle. You killed his two brothers at Jemappes, one of whom was my father. You broke my uncle's face with my father's pistol butts, then took them as your grisly prize. The family von Maefeld has a debt of honour that must be repaid.'

Valentin vomited a clot of blood, collapsing face down as the retching subsided. Wolff took his uncle in his arms. Despite his mouth trickling blood, Valentin's face was grey and his lips blue.

'I shall return my uncle to our family,' said Wolff, his young face twisted with malice. 'Then I will hunt you down and claim satisfaction. What is your name, sir?'

'Jobert, sir, André Jobert. I am at your service, sir. Send word and I shall attend you.'

Wolff von Maefeld allowed the name to form on his lips. Then he spat in disgust.

'My pistol?' asked Jobert.

'I shall keep my father's pistol until we meet again. You have my word, sir.'

'And there I shall reclaim it, sir. You have my word.'

5th of August 1796
Castiglione, Italy

André,

A time of great sorrow for the 1st Hussars. Despite our triumphant feat of arms in the action this day, we have lost our commanding officer on the field of honour. I have been promoted in the field to lieutenant colonel and posted as the regimental second-in-command.

Despite our loss, there is always honour,
Didier

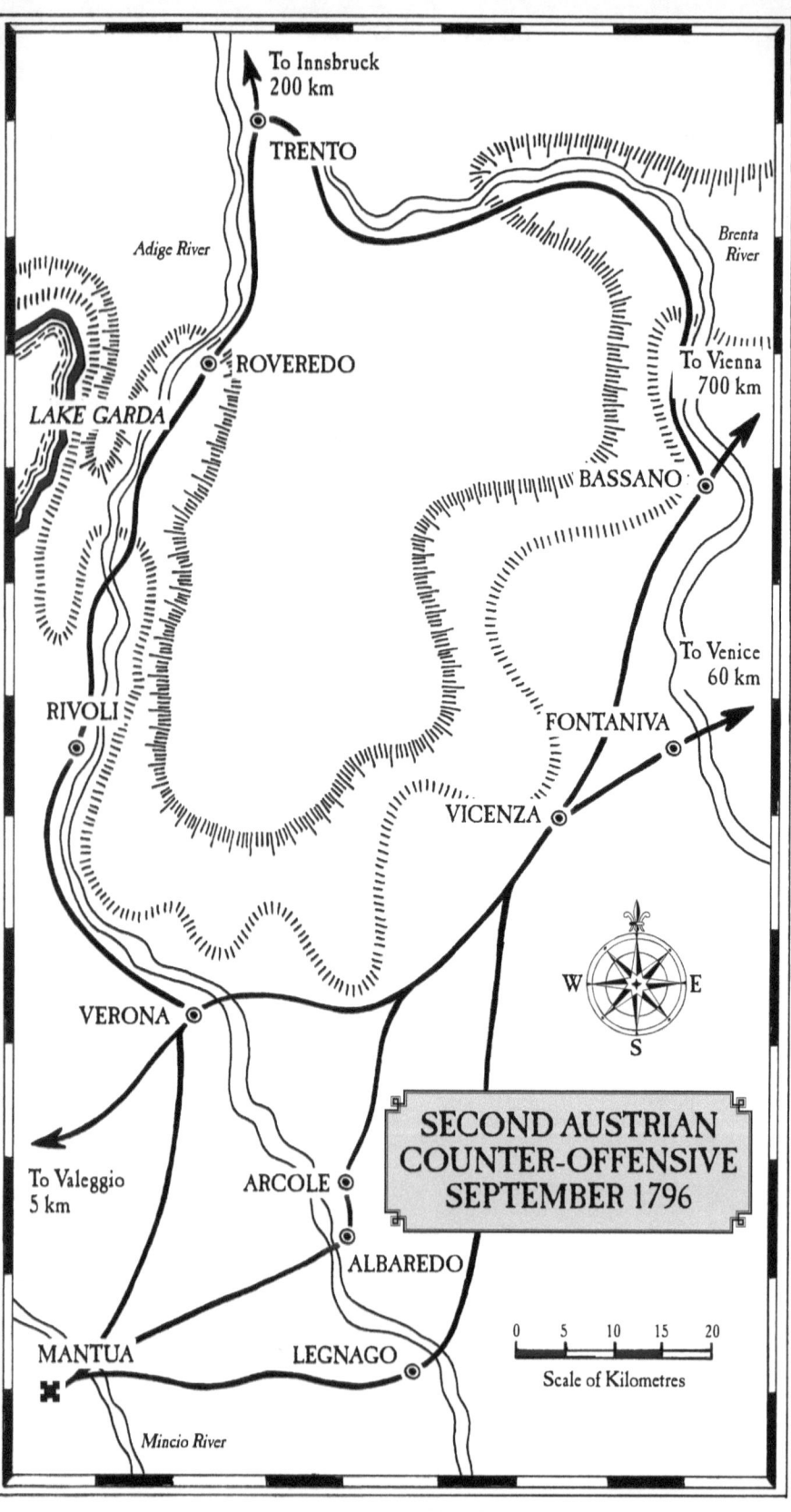

To Innsbruck
200 km

TRENTO

Adige River

Brenta River

ROVEREDO

To Vienna
700 km

LAKE GARDA

BASSANO

RIVOLI

To Venice
60 km

FONTANIVA

VICENZA

VERONA

W · E
S

SECOND AUSTRIAN
COUNTER-OFFENSIVE
SEPTEMBER 1796

To Valeggio
5 km

ARCOLE

ALBAREDO

MANTUA

LEGNAGO

0   5   10   15   20
Scale of Kilometres

Mincio River

Chapter Nineteen
August-September 1796, Rivoli, Italy

'I have just received the latest bulletin from army head-quarters,' said Spiccard, addressing Jobert and the other senior officers of the 24th Chasseurs. 'In their attempt to relieve Mantua three weeks ago, the Austrians lost twenty guns, one hundred and twenty ammunition caissons, one thousand prisoners and two thousand casualties. Our attacks have driven the Mantua garrison back inside their walls. The blockade has been resumed. Despite their losses, the Austrians are now massing in the Tyrol.'

'Will the Army of Italy be in any shape to meet them when they come, sir?' asked Fergnes. 'The local towns are unable to provide bread. With no firewood nor forage, pillaging increases as does the rise in armed insurrection. The bounty of Lombardy is no more. We are desecrating the banks of the Po as we did the Mediterranean coast.'

'With our observation around Mantua re-established, Bonaparte intends to strike first.' Spiccard lounged back in his chair as he surveyed Fergnes, Jobert and the others. 'At long last, the

German campaign has opened.' The audience snorted with disgust. 'Generals Moreau and Jourdan are advancing with two armies of seventy thousand each from the Rhine down the Danube. With Moreau approaching the northern Tyrol, Bonaparte intends to drive north crushing the enemy between himself and Moreau. Masséna is to lead the advance north from Rivoli to Trento on the 2nd of September.'

Jobert watched Fergnes clench his jaw and inhale his seated posture erect.

'What is our current strength state, Fergnes?' asked Spiccard.

'Three hundred sabres, sir, including the summer draft of recruits,' said Fergnes. 'Each company can now boast a strength of fifty sabres. My concern is these recruits are mounted on cart horses. These fifty horses require significant schooling if the chasseurs are to take their place in the battle-line. Without grain in their diet, these new horses will be unable to develop to the standard required.'

'Sir, may I suggest ...' said Jobert.

Spiccard's eyes dropped to scan his desk. His fingers wiggled approval for Jobert's contribution.

'May I suggest ... not integrating fifty recruits across all six companies,' said Jobert. 'If we did so, we would have one new man and his ill prepared horse within each section of the regiment. I predict we will lose them all to sickness and exhaustion within two weeks of stepping off. I have an alternate suggestion, sir.'

His face showed boredom and doubt, yet Spiccard raised an eyebrow at Jobert to continue.

'I have an intimate knowledge of the men and horses of 2nd Company and 5th Company,' said Jobert. 'I suggest 2nd Company reinforces 1st Squadron with sixteen men and 5th Company provide sixteen reinforcements to 3rd Squadron. That would bring the other four companies up to a strength of fifty sabres each, reinforced by veterans on sound horses ready to march.

'That reinforcement would result in fifty men remaining in 2nd and 5th Companies. I would advocate exchanging their sound remounts for the recruits' horses. This would result in 2nd Company having fifty veterans schooling green remounts and 5th Company comprised of recruits on experienced horses overseen by a cadre of experienced non-commissioned officers. Furthermore, I would propose those two companies be tasked with rear duties, escorting trains, wounded and prisoners, until their effectiveness increases.'

Spiccard's scowl considered Jobert. 'Your thoughts, Fergnes?'

Fergnes slid a look of confidence towards Jobert.

'My views on expected casualties amongst the recruits are not dissimilar to Jobert's, sir,' said Fergnes. 'I am uncomfortable that we may repeat the mistake raising a second draft of doomed recruits before year's end. Jobert's suggestion certainly protects our investment in horses. Eight veterans reinforcing each company is attractive. Yet 2nd and 5th Companies will swallow a bitter draught when they are to lose comrades as well as their own horses.'

'I will manage the transition, sir,' said Jobert.

Spiccard snorted. 'Then make it so.'

'What has happened?' asked Jobert, as he entered the billet's kitchen.

Koschak leant on the table with both hands, his head hanging low over an opened letter. The others waited for Koschak's next move. Orlande pressed his glasses onto the bridge of his nose. Tulloc wiped away his tears with his jacket cuff. Moench sat frozen in a corner.

Koschak straightened and jabbed the letter with a thick finger. 'Tulloc has fathered a child, sir.'

'Not the same Milanese girl he slept with in May?' Jobert glowered at Tulloc. Tulloc hung his head. 'Did we not resolve this in July? She believed herself with child, yet a doctor identified her nerves had conjured the misrepresentation. Was his diagnosis incorrect?'

'No, sir, the doctor determined correctly,' said Koschak. 'It would appear, in elated relief, Tulloc and the girl fell once more into each other's arms. We have just received news that, due to their mutual stupidity, the imbeciles have conceived successfully.'

'The girl has been cast out by her family, sir,' said Orlande. 'She is only sixteen. Tulloc … is determined to marry her.'

'Your stupidity, Tulloc,' said Jobert, 'and your belated decision to uphold the maiden's honour does not mean I am to be burdened with a laundress in my retinue. No, I am not entering the field with a pregnant girl on my staff.'

All eyes lowered under Jobert's glare.

'We could spend an age discussing the wisdom of your choices, Tulloc,' said Jobert, 'but what is done is done. I shall arrange, at my expense, employment for your fiancée within Fergnes' household as a scullery maid. When is your child due, Tulloc?'

'I do not know, sir,' said Tulloc.

'April, sir,' said Orlande.

'You will repay me, Tulloc, every sou,' said Jobert. 'I now hold a lien over your pay. Enough. Of other matters, Sergeant Major.'

With a jerk of Koschak's head, Tulloc stumbled from the room.

'I am tasked with integrating the recruits into the regiment,' said Jobert, 'but not one man per section as might be expected.'

'How then, sir?' asked Koschak.

'2nd and 5th Companies reinforce the other companies to the tune of sixteen chasseurs each. The remaining fifty men become a new 2nd Company on green remounts. The fifty recruits become 5th Company on 2nd Company horses.' Koschak stared at Jobert with incredulity. 'I am well aware of how unpalatable the men will find this assignment.'

Blowing out his cheeks, Koschak rocked back on his chair, his head wobbling in consideration. 'I see the value of reinforcing the other companies with a section of veterans, sir. I see the value in exchanging horses. May I suggest a small amendment to your plan?'

'Of course,' said Jobert.

'Once reinforcements have been stripped out of the two companies,' said Koschak, 'create sections of half veterans on green horses and half recruits on solid horses. Then the half-section of veterans can school the remounts, maintain a close eye on the horses they have just given up, and support the development of the recruits' skills.'

'Yes, eminently sound,' said Jobert. 'Moench, gather the officers and sergeants of 2nd Squadron. Together we shall create a list of who is going where before I address the men.'

Bitter faces and crossed arms of 2nd Squadron greeted Jobert as he stood in the centre of the barn floor. *Regimental scuttlebutt has arrived before me.*

'Men, 2nd Squadron is to be tasked with a heavy responsibility,' said Jobert. 'The Holy Roman Emperor forced war on our families and our homes four years ago. This war is about to end. One hundred and forty thousand men under our proven generals Moreau and Jourdan have crossed the Rhine and are advancing down the Danube to the Emperor's courts in Vienna.

'The Army of Italy has a role to play in that victory. General Bonaparte has ordered Masséna's and Augereau's divisions to strike north over the Alps and crush the kaiserliks blocking Moreau's advance. What better mountain horsemen could General Masséna have to lead his division over the Alps than the 24th Chasseurs?'

Sullen, unimpressed faces met Jobert's roving gaze.

'Another challenge has arisen,' said Jobert. 'Integrating fifty fresh remounts into the regiment. Colonel Spiccard knows 2nd Squadron are his premier horsemen and the most reliable means of delivering green horses over the Alps and into the lush valleys of the Danube. Yet 1st and 3rd Squadron need reinforcement. Two sections of seven men will be formed from each of 2nd and 5th Companies to join the other four companies.'

Discontent rumbled from the audience.

Jobert held up his hand. 'I have been assured by Colonel Spiccard, these sections shall remain together as 2nd Company or 5th Company mates. For those of you not tasked with improving the combat skills of 1st and 3rd Squadrons, you will exchange your current remounts for new remounts.'

Murmured expletives bordered on insubordinate.

'Men!' Jobert turned on his dusty stage and locked eyes with each man. 'Colonel Spiccard relies on the regiment's best horsemen to school these green horses, all the while supervising the care of your own beloved remounts in the hands of the new men. These recruits are from our homes around Avignon, men well known to us. Who better than us to guide their handling of blade and rein? As for living off the land, what better tutors in the art of scrounging than you brigands?'

Jobert glared at the soldiers he had lived with for three and a half years as they wriggled. 'I can see from your demeanour, Corporal Durand, you feel this is all a steaming pile of absolute fucking horse shit. Am I correct?'

The men laughed.

A calculating smile split Jobert's face. 'Do you trust me, Durand, when I promise the reward of fucking and feasting in the palaces of Vienna?'

'Stop it, sir,' said Durand, 'now you are just tickling my balls with a feather. I understand why we are being fucked over, sir. Yes ... we can do all that you ask, but ... when we lead the division, we eat well. If we escort trains, wounded and prisoners in the wake of the infantry, those locust pricks, we will starve into the bargain.'

Jobert winked at Koschak. 'Then, Corporal Durand, you agree the toughest bastards in the 24th Chasseurs have been selected for the most difficult task?'

The tattered audience sagged with acceptance.

'Squadron, attention!' called Koschak. Every man in the barn stood braced as Koschak saluted. 'Colonel Spiccard's orders are most clear, sir. The officers have other pressing duties. The sergeants and I shall carry on.'

'What news, sir?' asked Koschak, six days into the advance.

'Our screen has been set on the Trento road, north of Rovereto,' said Jobert. 'The Austrians continue to withdraw north. Having advanced only four days at a leisurely twenty kilometres per day, the squadron's parade state remains unchanged. With no losses in either men or remounts, all bodes well. How have 5th Company's escorts progressed?'

'With the heavy fighting ahead of us at Rovereto, Calliano and Trento,' said Koschak, 'escorting wounded convoys has opened the eyes of the new men. There have been no prisoner escorts, as most prisoners are wounded and have already been stripped, so slim pickings for our lads in that regard. How is it with you and 2nd Company?'

'Divisional trains are slow through the tight mountain passes and the interminable river crossings. The new lads are learning to forage in the wake of the infantry and savouring the culinary delight that is ammunition biscuit. Madame Quandalle does what she can to supplement our rations with tobacco, eggs and wine.'

'Is it true what I hear, sir? Your brother, Didier, now commands the 1st Hussars?' asked Koschak. 'This is welcome news, is it not?'

A broad smile split Jobert's face, as he shifted in his saddle and rearranged his reins. 'Yes, I received a brief note from him. Unfortunately, his commanding officer, newly promoted at Castiglione, was killed at Calliano. I look forward to catching up with Didier this evening in Trento.'

'Excuse me, sir.' Yinot saluted. 'Colonel Spiccard presents his compliments and wishes you to know he has just received news from Germany. General Jourdan and his army of seventy thousand have been defeated.'

Jobert's face melted in disbelief. Stifling his desire to swear, Jobert set his teeth at the news.

'With his flank unsecured,' said Yinot, 'General Moreau has been compelled to withdraw from the Danube.'

'Surely not?' Jobert sagged. 'Moreau, too, has seventy thousand men. Look at the economy forced on the Army of Italy. Thirty-five thousand of us maintain a siege of a major fortress, secure our lines of communication to Nice, maintain an outer-cordon that defeats repeated Austrian attempts to raise the siege, and these ... these ...' Jobert shook off his disappointment. 'With these reverses beyond the Alps coupled with Mantua holding firm, the Austrians will now double their determination to break the siege. Have orders changed due to Jourdan's defeat, Yinot?'

'Yes, sir,' said Yinot. 'Before the Austrians can redirect their reserves against us, General Bonaparte has issued new orders. He has directed a small column will hold the tight passes of the Adige River north of Trento. Our main effort will now swing south-east down the Brenta valley towards Bassano. Bonaparte's intent is to cause the Austrian's eastern force to withdraw further away from Mantua, hastening the fortress' winter capitulation.'

Bitterness lingered on Jobert's face as he sought a solution. 'If we catch them at Bassano, we can expect a pursuit east to Trieste or even north-east to Austria. Anything more, Yinot?'

'Yes, sir.' The aide de camp rummaged in his sabretache. 'I have a letter for you.'

Chapter Twenty
September 1796, Bassano, Italy

7th of September
Rovereto, Italy

Greetings André,

Did you receive my note dated the 4th of September? My commanding officer was shot in an ambush at Calliano on that day and died of wounds. He was a decent man. His loss is felt deeply amongst our ranks. My note carried the good news that General Bonaparte promoted me to command the 1st Hussars.

My delight lasted less than forty-eight hours. Sadly, I have had my right foot amputated and am now on my way to Milan with the wounded.

'Oh, shit!' Jobert reread the paragraph. 'Oh, shit!'

Late yesterday, north of Trento, Colonel Murat rode up to the regiment and declared, 'Colonel Jobert-Chauvel, General Bonaparte desires you take your 1st Hussars and drive the enemy from the town.' Can you imagine my rapturous feelings at the kindness shown to me by our commanding general in declaring the 1st Hussars mine?

In support of an infantry assault into the town, I led the regiment in a flanking movement through a ford. The flanks of the enemy were screened by an Austrian hussar regiment. Indeed, it was the same hussars we had forced back at the crossing of the Adda River on the flank of Lodi in May. The hussars whose sky-blue uniforms are remarkably similar to our own.

Upon my order we were soon amongst them. I was challenged by a red-faced bull of an Austrian officer, screaming 'Jobert! Jobert! Are you Jobert?' Someone must have called out my name in the melee for this fellow to identify me. Then most oddly, he screams at me, 'Who is André Jobert to you?'

A claw crushed Jobert's chest. *Von Maefeld!*

I was astounded at the comment and the blaggard took the advantage. When I responded, 'André Jobert is my brother', he charged me.

Due to the undulating ground and the press of troops, my horse was struck down. My right leg was broken in the fall, and I was unable to stand. My hysterical assailant continued to slash and roar. My hussars pressed close to protect me. I did all I could to parry his blows, but his horse stepped on me breaking my right ankle. My faithful sergeant standard-bearer stood over me and was cut down by this curious scoundrel. My glorious hussars saw them off.

What slight of yours has offended the fellow so? No matter. My military career ends cloaked in glory. A colonel of hussars wounded on the field of honour. My wound is well tended so the pain is bearable.

Oddly, my right toes are itchy, but I can no longer scratch them. Send all your news to Uncle Yann. Should I survive the trip to Milan, I will arrange travel home to recuperate.

Yours in glory ...

Jobert's throat burnt with acid as his mind swirled with emotion. *Wolff von Maefeld!*

Three days later, an ominous cloud hung over Jobert as he approached. Chabenac and Voreille straightened in anticipation. Koschak rocked his remount into a trot toward Jobert.

Koschak wheeled his horse in beside Jobert. 'Did you not receive leave to attend your brother, sir?'

Jobert's lip curled in sourness, as he avoided Koschak's eye. 'No, my duty is here.' *Piss on Spiccard. There is nothing I am doing that any captain cannot.*

As Jobert and Koschak joined Chabenac and Voreille, Jobert sank his hips and dropped his heels to halt Rouge. 'Gentlemen, the day is ours,' said Jobert. 'Bonaparte has secured Bassano.'

'And now the pursuit into Austria, sir?' asked Voreille.

'No, not quite.' Jobert rubbed his dust-encrusted eyes. 'The enemy has declined to conform to our plan. With us blocking their lines of communication north and east, the Austrians are now racing south-west to Mantua.'

'Where? Mantua?' asked Chabenac. 'They are behind us?'

'And we behind them,' said Jobert. 'They have abandoned their bridging train and have chosen the longer road to

Mantua. Their intent is to secure the established crossing points at Legnago. Augereau's division is to follow them. Masséna's division is to take the shorter route and cut them off.'

Chabenac's urbane smile spread across his face. 'A task for 24th Chasseurs, no doubt.'

'With 1st and 3rd Squadron exhausted from today's fighting,' said Jobert, 'Our 2nd Squadron recruits now have the honour of leading the division. I know our new men have done well since the advance increased its pace to ninety kilometres in the last three days, but we now have ourselves a horse race. Our immediate objectives are possible crossing points at the villages of Arcole and Albaredo some eighty kilometres hence. And we have forty-eight hours to get there.'

Jobert watched the three lift their chins and maintain their composure, their eyes flickering in consideration of the difficult march ahead.

Jobert thanked their resilience with a nod. 'Sergeant Major Koschak,' said Jobert, 'have the company stores transferred to packhorses. We march in one hour.'

Two days later, Jobert welcomed Spiccard to the village of Albaredo.

'Having marched forty kilometres a day for two days,' asked Spiccard, 'what is the state of my investment in your recruiting scheme?'

Jobert tickled Jaune's shorn mane. 'We have maintained our pace due to the ease with which the country is able to keep our horses watered. Not surprisingly, the new remounts are our weakness. We have lost one quarter of 2nd Squadron in the two days since Bassano. I am inspecting horses at each two-hour mark. To avoid a dribble of stragglers littering the landscape, I am detaching lame horses under guard to be brought forward after twelve hours rest. Brigaded under Koschak, the dismounted chasseurs, with portmanteaus slung, march behind our column.'

'Yes, I have encountered your casualty posts during our march here,' said Spiccard. 'What of the enemy?'

'One hour south, Chabenac's outlying piquet maintains contact with uhlans screening a body of hussars. Twenty kilometres to our south, the bulk of the Austrian column is crossing the Adige at Legnago. Mantua is forty kilometres distant for them and us.'

'A day's forced march for us both.' Spiccard stared with contempt at the western horizon. 'Then there is little chance of inserting Masséna's infantry between the enemy and the prize. The best we can hope for is to stay on their heels, give them neither respite nor the opportunity to victual themselves from the surrounding country. Then snap them shut in their foetid prison.'

'I sense the Italian people are assisting their passage, sir,' said Jobert. 'Our rapacity has engendered their hatred, be it our soldiers stealing food from households, or the wholesale stripping of valuables by the agents of the Republic. The Austrians never conducted themselves so poorly.'

Spiccard swivelled in his saddle to face Jobert with a harsh stare. 'Cease your diatribe, sir. Your fatigue fails to contain your emotions. Perhaps our experiment in Italian nationalism is failing, but do you disagree with the Republic collecting a debt long owed? Does your family not benefit from the arrangement, Jobert?'

Jobert lowered his eyes. 'My apologies, sir.'

'Be that as it may,' said Spiccard, '2nd Squadron must now close the forty kilometres to Mantua. March, Jobert.'

The autumn afternoon light was muted by smoke from guns, muskets and burning stubble. The domes and terracotta roofs of Mantua were glimpsed behind the drifting curtains. Opposing batteries coughed and spat, as the remnants of the Austrian column withdrew into the city's fortifications.

Along the lanes radiating out from the citadel's bridges, the trees still held their leaves. Beneath the canopy of red and gold, 2nd Squadron escorted an artillery convoy of six ammunition caissons and two spare four-pounder cannons. Limbers and caissons creaked while men and horses shuffled.

Within the lines of exhausted men and beasts, the occasional weary croak urged the reinforcements, the prisoners, the wounded and the stragglers. Jobert glared at the branches around him. *Sixty remain from the one hundred that set out.*

'With the enemy's successful arrival at Mantua,' asked Chabenac, 'what are your views on this dramatic increase in the fortress' garrison, sir? Does it bode good or ill?'

'Being trapped in a siege is a sacrifice for a greater good,' said Jobert. 'Although a larger garrison consumes more and sickens faster, the Austrians have three months to capitalise on the reinforced garrison, rebuild their army and break our siege before winter.'

'But they have done so twice now. In so doing they have claimed our siege train and levelled our siege works on both occasions. With Moreau's and Jourdan's failure on the Danube, will not Austrian reinforcements be rushed from Bavaria?'

'That is indeed our threat in the coming months,' said Jobert. 'I cannot believe that Jourdan's and Moreau's armies are now back behind the Rhine. I hesitate to express "military wisdom would dictate" but a French force of one hundred and forty thousand on the Rhine ought to be sufficient to fix Austria's focus on Bavaria.'

'How long do you believe we have before they come on again?' asked Chabenac.

'Perhaps six weeks, mid to late October before the rains dissolve the roads.'

'Then six weeks to build on the admirable achievement of the men.'

'How so?' asked Jobert.

'2nd Squadron is in high spirits, sir,' said Chabenac. 'Since setting out from Rivoli, marching through Rovereto, Trento and Bassano and then conducting a pursuit from Bassano to Mantua, we have ridden three hundred kilometres in ten days. Admittedly we lost one-third of the squadron in the last three days' march from Bassano. With the stragglers re-joining the ranks, I admit to a modicum of pride at our resilience.'

'Savour that sensation of pride in your soldiers as I have unpleasant news in that regard,' said Jobert. 'I am informed that Bonaparte's Guides are to triple their strength.'

Chabenac's mask of composure disappeared. 'Oh, say it is not so.'

'Each chasseur à cheval regiment in the Army of Italy is to provide their best two corporals, twenty-five of their best chasseurs and twenty-seven horses. The horses will be traded with dragoon remounts for the best black horses available. Despite our recent good husbandry of our recruits, our regimental strength will return to two hundred and fifty sabres once more.'

Chabenac's body folded with despair. 'That is devastating.'

From his flank guard position, Corporal Durand approached at the trot. 'Sir, there are grenzers in that hamlet. They appear cut off as the rest of the kaiserliks scurry for Mantua.'

Jobert's face soured at the mention of Austria's tough frontiersmen.

'Was it just over a year ago that grenzers ambushed us on the beach?' asked Chabenac. 'It seems an age.'

'Moreover,' said Jobert, 'it was less than a year ago, last November, we broke two of their battalions at Savona.'

'Just like Savona, sir,' said Durand, 'there are dragoons with them.'

'Moench, sound Commanders In.' Jobert twisted in the saddle to the ammunition convoy's commander, an artillery sergeant. 'Stand the guns two hundred metres from the hamlet's walls. Then make a show of bringing the guns into action.'

'But the guns' ready boxes are empty, sir,' said the gunner. 'I cannot break open the ammunition from the caissons without a direct order from the battery commander.'

Jobert punched the front of his saddle. 'Just make a show of it, sergeant. Chabenac, form a single rank behind the guns and sound trumpets in readiness to charge. Do you have a handkerchief?'

With a flourish, Chabenac drew a grubby handkerchief from an inner pocket. 'Always.'

'Durand,' said Jobert, 'attach Captain Chabenac's handkerchief to your musketoon. Then take me to them.'

Jobert, Moench and the four chasseurs of Durand's vedette approached the leafy walls in the afternoon sun. A small party emerged from the hamlet's gardens, led by a brown-jacketed, blue-trousered grenzer captain and a dragoon lieutenant in a white-jacket, tall boots and a black bicorne.

Beyond the walls bordering the groves, Jobert estimated the

rump of a grenzer battalion and the remains of a dragoon troop. For the grenzer soldiers, distributing water from the pump stand seemed more urgent than manning the walls from imminent attack. Those dragoons moving with any sense of military purpose were all dismounted.

A grim half-smile creased Jobert's cheek. *Forced marches have crippled your horses.* 'Gentlemen,' said Jobert, in German, 'You are unable to rejoin your own army. Nor are you able to secure access to Mantua. I demand your surrender.'

The weathered grenzer appeared resigned. The young dragoon was defiant and looked to his senior to dismiss the request.

Bellowed commands from the guns coming into action caught everyone's attention.

Jobert held up his hand. 'I acknowledge your bravery by expressing your intent to hold your position. But allow me to warn you of the implications of not offering me your swords. Your esteemed dragoons have a reputation amongst French infantry as being manned by foppish noblemen and the sons of wealthy merchants. A myth exists in our army that an Austrian dragoon's holsters are crammed full of gold coin and spicy sausage.'

The grenzer scoffed a laugh.

The dragoon inflated. 'That is not true, sir—'

'Establishing the truth is not the issue, sir,' said Jobert. 'Your generals have led us all a merry dance from Bassano. Our battalions arriving late to the field are jealous that no spoils remain. One hint that this hamlet holds a handful of dragoons will be sufficient to send the closest French battalion berserk.'

Chabenac's trumpets screamed To Mess.

Jobert looked at the grenzer. 'It will be a massacre.'

The dragoon lieutenant blinked. 'No ... no, we ...'

The grenzer captain drew his sword and offered it to Jobert hilt first. 'Sir, would you accept our surrender?'

'Just the grenzers, sir, or your entire garrison?' asked Jobert. The dragoon officer sagged as he drew his sword.

Chapter Twenty-One
October 1796, Bassano, Italy

Colonel Spiccard vomited into a bucket between his feet.

'Jobert, assist the colonel to his bed,' said Fergnes. 'I shall summon his valet.'

As orderlies carried hot water and towels to Spiccard's bedside, Fergnes and Jobert moved to the end of the cramped passageway.

'How many times have the Austrians returned?' asked Fergnes, resuming the thread of Spiccard's orders. 'This would be their third attempt at Mantua, would it not? How are we disposed? What needs to be done? How are the men?'

Jobert glanced at his friend. Fergnes' stance, his cultured tone and his eyes spoke only of confidence, but Jobert knew better.

'Having stood piquet in the cold rain for over a week,' said Jobert, 'our chasseurs appear wet and miserable. They are quick to inform anyone who will listen of the injustice.'

Fergnes' jaw clenched.

'The fact is, sir, our soldiers are in good shape,' said Jobert.

'They rotate onto piquet for not more than three hours day or night. They have warm billets and stables in the surrounding villages. Troops on rest are drying clothing, boots and saddlery. I have had pig's lard purchased to keep capes and horse rugs waterproof. There is so much water, the men have bathed twice last week. We are the first French troops along the Tagliamento River, so the country has not been pillaged. Villages have food, firewood, forage and grain. Men and horses have not eaten so well since Milan.'

Orderlies squeezed by with buckets of rancid bile.

'And we are doing better than the Austrians,' Jobert continued. 'Just as Bonaparte predicted the rains have come, the roads have dissolved, the rivers are in spate. The Piave River is so swollen the Austrian bridging train sits idle on the far bank. Their supply system is bogged to the axles. Their advance guard achieves barely twelve kilometres per day.'

'But the rains will stop,' said Fergnes. 'The Austrians will press again. Their other column is moving south toward Trento, despite the snows in the northern passes. They still have six weeks before winter sets in to relieve Mantua.'

'What is Bonaparte doing?' asked Jobert.

'He appears content to let the Austrians battle the elements. Until then he keeps Masséna and Augereau's divisions ready for either east or north.'

'At their current march speed, the Austrians will arrive at Bassano in three to four days,' said Jobert. 'Is Masséna ready to defend the Brenta River?'

'Masséna will contest their crossing at both Bassano and Fontaniva,' said Fergnes. 'Bassano is their link between eastern and northern columns. Fontaniva is the direct route to Vicenza, Verona and Mantua.'

'What does Masséna desire of the 24th Chasseurs?' asked Jobert.

'The same. Everything,' said Fergnes. 'We call ourselves a regiment. He expects a regiment of work. But we have three squadrons with the strength of three companies.'

'No matter our strength,' said Jobert, 'we have watched the kaiserliks so far and we shall continue to watch them as they advance further, with Masséna appraised soon after. Has Spiccard considered the option of disbanding 3rd Squadron?'

'He has,' said Fergnes. 'He is adamant that he will not. He is determined to maintain our current organisation. Since joining the regiment as a chief of squadron, he has always had a long association with 3rd Squadron.'

'We have discussed this, sir,' said Jobert. 'You agreed it was folly to make demands of a company of forty sabres as if it were fully manned with one hundred.'

'Yes, we have discussed it, Jobert,' said Fergnes. 'Yes, we are both agreed. Our commanding officer has heard our counsel and has made his decision. Now we will abide by his orders.'

Jobert considered the dark circles under Fergnes' eyes. Jobert braced his shoulders. 'Yes, sir.'

Jobert watched Spiccard approach his vedette position overlooking the Brenta River.

Spiccard's horse ambled and slumped to a halt. Spiccard wobbled in the saddle and clutched at his pommel. His eyes blinked as if he could not see his horse's ears. His lips trembled between each panted breath. His feet twitched in the stirrups.

Fergnes and Yinot stood downcast two horse lengths away.

Jobert sidestepped Bleu closer to Spiccard. Bleu and Spiccard's horse dropped their heads towards each other. Their nostrils touched.

Jobert leant on his saddle bow. 'Sir, may I relay what I hear around the troop fires.'

Spiccard faced jerked as he searched his toe caps.

'Sir,' said Jobert, 'the men stand in deep admiration of your fortitude. Burdened by an illness that has removed the strongest from our ranks, your determination to sit tall in the saddle inspires us all.'

Spiccard blinked away and struggled to straighten his spine. 'If that is indeed so, Jobert, I demand that you see to your men. Direct their vision at the enemy to their front, not gawp rearward to a swaddled invalid who can barely maintain his seat at the walk.'

Spiccard reached out and gripped Jobert's forearm tight, wheezing as he came closer. Jobert dropped his face away lest he breathe in Spiccard's 'mal-aria'.

Spiccard wiped his nose on his sleeve adding to the crusted smears on the fabric. 'I can see, Jobert, but I ache. The discomfort pushes all else from my mind. Describe the scene below.'

'The Brenta River lies to our front, sir. We are south of Bassano, at Fontaniva, where the road runs straight towards Vicenza.'

'Yes, I know it. Am I losing my sight? I cannot see the town.'

'We are not across the river from Fontaniva, sir. The Austrians have thrown a pontoon bridge over the Brenta. It rests on an island mid stream.'

'Who watches the Fontaniva bridge?' asked Spiccard.

'1ˢᵗ Squadron, sir.'

'I see lances . Do we have uhlans to our front? How are the kaiserliks disposed?'

'Two infantry battalions hold the bridge, said Jobert. 'Four companies of hussars hold the far bank. Four companies of uhlans hold the near bank.'

'The same hussars as the fellow Voreille took on last year.'

Jobert stifled his irritation. 'No, sir, a different regiment.' Jobert expelled von Maefeld's face from his mind. 'I am most attentive to which enemy hussar regiment presents itself, sir.'

'Have you found the uhlans pushing hard in their screen?' asked Spiccard.

'No, sir, they stay close to their bridge.'

'Lost their nerve, eh?' asked Spiccard.

'I do not doubt the bravery of these Croatian lancers,' said Jobert. 'I expect their generals keep them on a tight leash. Having shadowed their columns for nearly two weeks now, they are the only cavalry this eastern column has available. They remain one hundred and twenty kilometres from Mantua. There is much that lies ahead for them.'

Fergnes squeezed his charger forward to Spiccard's side. 'Sir, as Jobert says, much lies ahead for us all. Sir, we need you rested. Might you consider—'

A rasping cough bent Spiccard across his saddle bow. 'No, Fergnes. Only catching a musket ball would give me cause to dismount before nightfall. Now, what is our situation, Jobert?'

Jobert looked across the swollen grey river, choosing not to exchange glances with Fergnes. '1st Squadron watches Fontaniva, sir. 2nd Squadron watches this pontoon bridge. I see you have brought 3rd Squadron from Bassano.'

'We ... we, ah ... Fergnes, why have we marched from Bassano?' asked Spiccard.

'The Austrian press their advance hard on our northern defences, despite the weather souring,' said Fergnes. 'Their pincers tighten, albeit slowly. Masséna has withdrawn from Bassano and marches for these pontoons. General Bonaparte has sent Augereau to block any exit from Bassano.'

'What opportunity exists here for us, Jobert?' asked Spiccard.

'We have two squadrons at our disposal, sir,' said Fergnes, before Jobert could reply. 'The enemy have no artillery on the far bank and only a single battalion on the near bank. A swift attack onto the bridgehead will bundle the uhlans back onto their infantry.'

'No, Fergnes,' said Spiccard.

'You would forego the opportunity to damage the uhlans, sir?'

'I said "no".'

'What can you predict, sir, that I am unable?' asked Fergnes.

'No,' said Spiccard.

'Jobert, are there crossing points over the Brenta?' asked Fergnes.

'No,' repeated Spiccard.

'Sir, a raid on their bridging train,' said Fergnes, 'resulting in its destruction or capture will impede their advance markedly beyond this point.'

'No, Fergnes, no,' said Spiccard. 'Jobert?'

Jobert looked across the bowed Spiccard to Fergnes. 'I can discern no opportunity here today, sir.'

Spiccard nodded his approval. 'A prudent conclusion. Then we shall watch and wait for General Masséna's arrival.'

'I am at a loss,' said Fergnes. 'I do not know what to do.'

Jobert frowned as his stomach growled. 'What do you feel requires resolution?'

'This. Everything.'

'I have spent a long cold day in the saddle, sir,' said Jobert.

'I have not taken more than two cups of coffee in twenty-four hours.' *The price of leaving Orlande in the safety of Milan.* 'Perhaps I might provide clearer insight to your ... this dilemma tomorrow morning?'

'We may not last until then, Jobert,' said Fergnes.

Jobert ran his fingers across his grimy scalp. 'Are you referring to the Austrian advance?'

'Of course. What else occupies us?' With a look of mild inconvenience, Fergnes wiped sweat from his flushed brow with a handkerchief.

Jobert noted the rapid pulse above Fergnes' jacket collar. 'Fergnes, do you feel well? You have not contracted the colonel's contagion?'

'I am quite well, thank you.'

Jobert's eyes narrowed. 'Then, should I offer my views, will they be respected or are you determined—'

'I am determined in nothing, sir. And yes, of course, I seek your ... otherwise I would not ...'

Jobert softened his shoulders and inclined his face towards the floor. 'Sir, Mantua is weeks away from falling, and in so doing France wins Lombardy. With us holding northern Italy, we can feed the Republic. The Austrians are desperate to relieve Mantua. They are losing this war. After a seven-month struggle, they are mere weeks before an Alpine winter snuffs out their hope. Their advance is crippled by the weather. Snow in the northern passes. Rain-swollen rivers to the east. This eastern column has advanced a pitiful two hundred and forty kilometres in twenty days.'

'But advance they continue to do,' said Fergnes. 'Their pincers close.'

'And is not that to our advantage?' asked Jobert. 'That is certainly Bonaparte's opinion. For Bonaparte, the moment of decision has not arrived.'

'Yet his army is divided north and east, each wing too weak to keep the pincers either open or at bay.'

'As it is for their army against us,' said Jobert. 'You have seen the reports from their prisoners. They have been issued muskets yet given no instruction in drill. They have battalions of over one thousand recruits yet have fewer than three officers to command them. Let alone no issue of tentage to shelter from the endless rain. They are a shambles. We are not.'

'A shambles, are they?' asked Fergnes. 'Today at Fontaniva's pontoons, one infantry regiment held against each of Masséna's ten attacks by six regiments over an eleven-hour period. A shambles? I think not.'

'Two regiments, sir,' said Jobert. 'Both well-disciplined line regiments. Standing beyond reach across the flood-swollen Brenta. And on our withdrawal this evening, the cost of their determination, paid for in their casualties, was plain for all to see.'

Fergnes fussed with his jacket's straightness, before curling his moustache with the back of a finger.

'We are both tired, my friend,' said Jobert. 'We must not argue. Bonaparte's strategy of careful withdrawal has a way to play out. Every day we watch the Austrians advance, the Mantua garrison eats the last of her rats. Masséna's attacks today at Fontaniva caused them to withdraw their pontoons. That action alone snatches three precious days from their eastern force. Our soldiers are weary from screening a tedious withdrawal, I will admit, but they are ready for whatever is asked of them.'

'Our soldiers are nothing—'

'You go too far, my friend,' said Jobert, lifted a warning finger. 'Our soldiers are everything.'

Fergnes raised his open palms. 'I mean our regiment is nothing. Two hundred and fifty sabres do not a regiment make.'

'If Masséna had six full-strength companies he would use six full-strength companies. Masséna reads his regimental strength returns. He is well aware that we have the strength of three companies. Whatever he asks, you and I will do our best with the very fine men we have the honour of commanding.'

'And there lies our predicament.' said Fergnes.

'What now?'

'That we will do our best.'

'Will we not?' asked Jobert.

'That you and I ... and our chasseurs will do our best is not in doubt. It is ...'

'Spiccard?' asked Jobert.

Fergnes twitched.

'Despite being a miserable prick, Spiccard is brave,' said Jobert. 'He remains in the saddle.'

'But today we were frozen, figuratively and literally, by his "no, no, no". An enemy pontoon bridge was there for the taking and he said "no, no, no".'

Jobert's face tightened. 'That pontoon was held by two infantry battalions and eight companies of cavalry. We would never have taken that bridge. Even supporting an infantry attack, we could not have crossed the Brenta. If the Brenta denies passage to our enemies, why would she grant passage to us? The bridge was dismantled and withdrawn. Its use denied to the enemy for three days to re-establish it and recross. Surely, Spiccard's caution was reasonable in the circumstances.'

Fergnes searched the mantlepiece above the hearth. 'But what about next time?'

'Next time?' Jobert's stomach moaned. 'Really? You wish to debate a combat we have not yet fought?'

'Bonaparte's moment of decision ... of crisis draws near. In all likelihood, Bonaparte will have to meet them towards Caldiero. Masséna will be tasked to rout the Austrians as he was at Castiglione in August. The opportunity for victory or defeat will present itself. The 24th Chasseurs will be called upon. Spiccard will mumble "no, no, no" before toppling from the saddle. And there we will be.'

Jobert searched Fergnes' face. 'Where?'

'Bonaparte, Masséna, our chasseurs, all looking at the moment of opportunity closing, and I am the one ... the one who must ... it will all be up to me.'

'Stop. Stand up.' Jobert lifted Fergnes by gripping the front of his tailcoat. Jobert crushed Fergnes to his chest in a bear hug.

'Brother,' Jobert whispered, 'I have stood beside you these four years. In each crisis we have faced, your careful consideration has given me strength. How you navigate the difficulties of regimental command has earned my respect. You have never failed. Not once. Whatever Caldiero brings, you will not fail. Go to bed. Now!'

Chapter Twenty-Two
November 1796, Battle of Caldiero, Italy

Just east of the town of Caldiero, two armies met along the crest of two ridges. The day's weather delivered a deluge in which only the artillery could fire. On the western ridge, on the northern end of Masséna's battle-line, 2nd and 3rd Squadrons of the 24th Chasseurs cringed in their capes. Their horses' heads lowered against the stinging shower.

Gossip, dribbling along the line, reached Jobert. The opposing enemy infantry were Bavarians, fresh from the Rhine. Masséna's infantry squelched across the intervening basin into driving rain to push the Austrians back with the bayonet. The French fusiliers, many without shoes, slipped and fell on the muddy slopes, causing the attack columns, unable to maintain their dressing, to fail in their assaults.

Yinot's remount squelched towards Jobert and Spiccard's command group. 'Sir, General Masséna has ordered the division retire to Verona,' said Yinot. 'General Masséna requires the 24th Chasseurs to act as rear guard.'

Spiccard, swaddled in blankets and leaning on the regimental guidon's staff, said nothing.

Fergnes looked hard at Jobert before addressing Spiccard. 'Sir, to comply with General Masséna's orders, might I suggest 1st Squadron forms line to our rear. As you have the better eye, sir, might you choose the ground? It will raise the hearts of 2nd and 3rd Squadrons to rally on your standard.'

Jobert smiled that Spiccard still had the energy to sneer before departing.

'Sound Skirmishers In,' ordered Fergnes.

Geourdai's 1st Squadron, having spent the day observing the enemy's flank, withdrew their screen at the walk across the sodden low ground between the crests.

'Lieutenant Colonel Fergnes, sir,' said Geourdai, 'the enemy are bringing up reserves on their northern flank. At least two regiments, possibly a brigade, escorted by cavalry.'

'Possibly a brigade, Captain Geourdai? Possibly?' asked Fergnes. 'Did you identify artillery? And what manner of cavalry?'

'My apologies, sir, the rain is too heavy to make out. My glass cannot see anything in this downpour.'

Over Fergnes' shoulder, Jobert gave Geourdai a wink before dismissing him with a sharp nod.

On the opposing crest, the reinforcing Austrian infantry halted. Mounted commanders, clutching their bicornes to their powdered curls, contemplated the scene developing on the French ridge.

The exhausted French guns limbered and retired. The saturated French infantry slunk away.

Fergnes glanced at Jobert. 'Our moment has come, sir.'

Jobert raised his chin. 'And we are found ready, sir.'

'Sabres!' called Fergnes. 'The 24th Chasseurs alone hold the field. Commanders in.'

Koschak surged along the rear ranks. 'Wake up, my lads. Stow capes.'

Chabenac and Voreille, hunched in their sodden capes, plodded forward to attend Fergnes.

'We have outfoxed them, Chabenac,' said Fergnes. 'Their infantry cannot cross while we hold ... wait, our uhlans from Fontaniva have joined us.'

Jobert peered through the curtains of rain toward the enemy-held crest. Two companies of two hundred horsemen formed line in two ranks. The commander of the uhlans surveyed the 24th Chasseurs in turn.

Jobert noted the uhlans seemed unaffected by the rain. Their erect outlines were rounded by capes and sheepskin hats, except for the upright three-metre lances resting on their stirrupped toes. Thick laces from their shoes entwined their lower legs.

Chabenac's nonchalant smile crept beyond his cape's collar. 'Have you had the honour of attending lancers, Major Jobert?'

'No,' said Jobert. 'I imagine on level ground, a well-dressed line at speed would present a concern. But today, on slimy slopes within a bog, I would be happy to match them.'

Chabenac's smile remained plastered. Voreille scowled.

Jobert watched an aide trot from the group of enemy commanders towards the uhlans. The uhlans shifted from line into column.

'Look there, Jobert,' said Fergnes. 'The uhlans have received the order to shift us. Our uhlan captain has decided to maintain height by following the contours around to our ridge.' Fergnes considered the saturated ground between the two bodies of cavalry. 'There is no space to hold them on the sharp crest. I shall lure them into the mire. Jobert, hold 2nd Squadron in support. 3rd Squadron, in line, left wheel, walk, march.'

Jobert scowled as his mind calculated the angles to rob the uhlans of the advantage of the lance and the inevitable disastrous outcome.

Voreille inclined toward Jobert. 'Sir, I fail to see the advantage generated by Lieutenant Colonel Fergnes' manoeuvre.'

Jobert knew well the impact of sloping terrain on a horse's stride. Horses race up a slope, yet slow to choose their steps coming down, not unlike a man descending a ladder hands-first. The lengthened ascending stride of the horse allows the rider to reach forward with his weapon. The shorter descending steps of the horse become more pronounced as the forward-reaching rider overbalances his steed even further.

'Beneath the lancers,' said Jobert, '3rd squadron have the advantage charging uphill. But if the infantry advances down while 3rd Squadron is stuck in the mud, I hesitate to consider.'

As the French cavalry moved on the slope beneath the uhlan flank, the uhlans reformed line. On the blast of a horn, the second rank of uhlans pushed forward, lances slung across their backs, sabres drawn.

'Had Fergnes expected to face sabres?' asked Chabenac.

With a sharp toot, the uhlans who had remained on the crest couched their lances against their ribs, tips forward, soggy pennants flapping, before advancing in support.

'Shit!' Jobert gathered his rain-slicked reins. 'Their "sabres" are to blunt 3rd Squadron. They will meet at the walk. Should 3rd Squadron flee, the lancers in the second rank will be released to tear our boys' backs open. I must engage those lancers, yet the ground is too tight, too uneven.'

Jobert drew his sabre. 'Chabenac, have an eye for the enemy "sabres". Follow them into 3rd Squadron's melee if you must. Voreille, work to flank their lancers. 2nd Squadron, form column of troops, walk, march. Moench, sound Advance.'

3rd Squadron churned the mud to meet the uhlans at the walk. Both groups had difficulty urging their horses onto solid enough footing to strike at each other. Leaders on both sides bellowed to their men to join battle.

The following uhlan lancers halted at 2nd Squadron's advance.

Horns blasted from the ridge. The uhlans peeled away and cantered to the crest.

Jobert leant back in his saddle as Bleu plodded down the slope. *Good! Someone recognises the stupidity of a mud bath.*

Jobert saw Fergnes just ahead of the front rank, white plume nodding on his mirliton, as he slashed at those of his enemies extracting themselves from the mud.

Fergnes surged through the bogged uhlans' sabres towards a pocket of remaining lancers.

'Fergnes, stop!' shouted Jobert.

Rally sounded. 3rd Squadron halted and turned.

Too early! Jobert's eyes widened in alarm as he reeled to identify who ordered the call.

Fergnes looked back at the retiring ranks of chasseurs. As he did so, two uhlans thrust forward their lances and pierced Fergnes' horse in the neck. The horse screamed as it toppled sideways down the hill. Fergnes threw himself aside to avoid being crushed.

'No!' Jobert urged Bleu onwards.

Slapping the shaft of his lance into his frightened horse's flanks, one uhlan forced his mount forward before thrusting his weapon deep into Fergnes' back. Fergnes raised himself to his hands and knees, vomiting blood.

The remaining uhlans sought the opportunity to finish Fergnes off. Fergnes' trumpeter slashed at their extended lance tips. Fergnes' horse staggered to its feet between them all.

Jobert rolled his sabre-wrist to warm his forearm for the intended strikes at the prowling uhlans. 'Stand clear, you miserable pricks,' he bellowed.

The uhlans looked up to the new threat splashing towards them. One uhlan thrust his lance and pinned Fergnes in the mud. Once the lance jerked free of Fergnes' body, the uhlans spun their horses away to rejoin their mates on the crest.

'Chabenac, halt in line. Moench, take Bleu.' Jobert held out his reins as he dismounted.

'The uhlans have reformed on their crest,' said Chabenac.

Koschak stood guard uphill of wounded Fergnes. Infantry drums thrashed out above them. 'Quickly, sir, their infantry will be upon us.'

Blood poured from Fergnes' mouth, as Jobert slipped in the mud to lift him.

'He is too heavy,' yelled Jobert above the din of battle and the pelting rain. He staggered to raise their combined weight to his knees. 'He is waterlogged. Pull us out of here.'

Koschak and Moench pressed their horses in beside him.

With his arms wrapped around Fergnes and grasping a stirrup of both Koschak's and Moench's, Jobert thrust his chin clear of the lolling man's neck. 'Take us away.'

At the top of the ridge, Jobert released the stirrups. They collapsed in the mud. Fergnes wheezed a spout of hot blood into Jobert's face. *Stay with me, brother, I need you.* In frustration, Jobert tugged to remove the slippery sword knots on his wrists and his sodden leather gloves, before flipping the wounded man over. Jobert wiped grass, mud and blood from his pale skin.

Fergnes' eyes searched Jobert's face. His jaw and lips quivered as he bit at unformed words.

'Your brave actions ... have saved Masséna's division,' said Jobert. '3rd Squadron has reformed ... the 24th Chasseurs stand proud yet. Can you hear me, Fergnes? In the moment that you were called upon, you were not found wanting.'

Fergnes' eyes took on a note of alarm. Rapid gasps puffed from his slack cheeks.

'Marguerite?' asked Jobert. 'Your boy?'

Fergnes' eyes welled with tears.

A cold vice gripped Jobert's heart. 'I give you my word, my

brother, I shall care for Marguerite and your son. I swear no harm will come to them. I will raise your boy—'

Clawing at Jobert's cheek, Fergnes spasmed, hissed and went still.

The last of the season's swallows darted in the settling dusk. A farm dog howled. Lowered heads along the horse lines rippled as the burial detail hunched past. Subdued embers fizzed. Caped silhouettes mumbled over their soup kettles.

Another regimental grave in a corner of another meadow. Another naked, blue-grey honour guard aligned in a horizontal rank. The half-opened eyes of Fergnes and the other fallen chasseurs were fixed upon the mist-shrouded stars before earthen gates entombed them to their eternal duty.

Jobert lifted his heavy head as the company commanders shuffled around the farmhouse's kitchen table. Numb faces blinked in the act of taking notebooks from waistcoats.

Colonel Spiccard was rigid, his eyes fixed on the map spread in front of him. 'Until I have received correspondence from General Masséna, Major Jobert will act as second-in-command of the regiment.'

Jobert gave a curt nod of acknowledgement.

The assembled heads neither turned in congratulations nor calculation of the next captain to be promoted to chief of squadron.

'The Austrian advance has stalled following the affair at Caldiero,' said Spiccard. 'General Bonaparte has ordered Masséna and Augereau to outflank the enemy via Arcole. Jobert, you passed through that country during the pursuit from Bassano in September. Remind us of the terrain.'

Jobert drew his dagger from his cuff as a pointer and held a candelabra above Spiccard's map.

'Gentlemen, the Adige River and the Alpone canal form a letter Y. Between the arms of the Y is a marsh. Beside the arms of the Y run dikes to channel the water. On top of the dikes lie the small villages of, west to east, Belfiore, Bionde, Ronco, Arcole and Albaredo. The villages are linked by causeways along the tops of the dikes. There is a bridge across the Alpone at Arcole. There is a ferry across the Adige at Albaredo. Do our infantry still guard a pontoon bridge at Ronco, sir?'

'Yes, they do,' said Spiccard. 'Exact enemy dispositions are unknown. Following a three-week advance, the Austrians are one day's march away from connecting their eastern and northern pincers at Verona. As we did at Piacenza and Lodi in May, Bonaparte will have us outflank them and attack the rear area of their eastern force, with the intent of forcing that column to withdraw away from the northern force. Augereau's division will lead the advance to Ronco and secure the bridge at Arcole. Masséna's division will cross the Adige and secure the western flank at Bionde and Belfiore.

'Due to the restricted access along the tops of the dikes, this is a predominantly infantry affair. The Arcole bridge should be secure by this time tomorrow. With cavalry and artillery in reserve, the 24th Chasseurs are to act as rear guard on the road back to Verona. This will allow us to rest before we are released on the far side of Arcole. To that end, outlying piquet 1st Squadron, inlying piquet 2nd Squadron and 3rd Squadron to guard the divisional trains. We march in two hours. Second-in-command?'

Jobert jerked when he realised all faces were on him. He blinked at the sudden responsibility. 'Ah … company parade and ammunition states to me within the hour … and …'

Gloomy eyes peeled off their scribbled pages to regard Jobert.

'Gentlemen, I have listed Lieutenant Colonel Fergnes' effects. I have kept his sabre for his son.' Jobert coughed to clear the emotion tightening his throat. 'His valet is willing to be engaged by either an individual or a mess of younger officers. The rest of his effects and his horses are now for sale. All officers are to put their name to at least two items.'

Jobert lowered his face over his notebook to hide his trembling jaw.

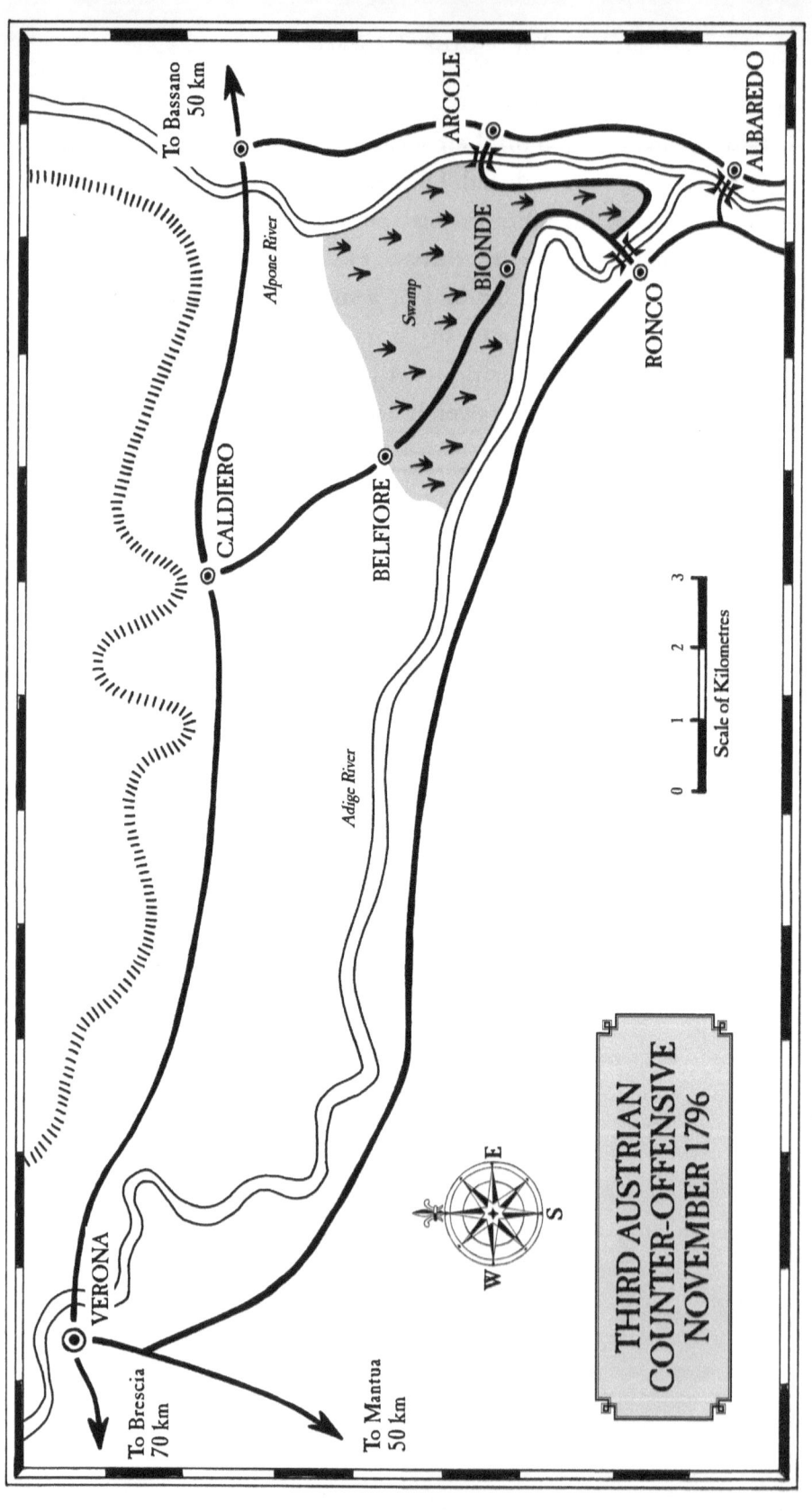

THIRD AUSTRIAN
COUNTER-OFFENSIVE
NOVEMBER 1796

Chapter Twenty-Three
November 1796, Battle of Arcole, Italy

Stars sparked a bitter blue the next evening. The captains gathered about Jobert's campfire on the eastern banks of the Adige, capes bundled snug, bonnets-de-police wrapped under scarves.

'My apologies, gentlemen, for rousing you at midnight,' said Jobert. 'Colonel Spiccard sleeps. I have his permission to convey his orders. You will be aware Augereau's infantry secured Arcole at dusk after a long day of heavy fighting. General Bonaparte has now decided to withdraw from Arcole.'

The gathering mumbled. 'Why do that?' and 'Slaughtered for no purpose.'

'Silence!' Jobert's eyes blazed. 'I have served with General Bonaparte three years since Toulon. Whether his plans were enacted either as a staff officer or as a commander, his evaluation of the situation has been consistently sound. On this occasion perhaps he knows something we do not. General Masséna, Colonel Spiccard and I trust his judgement. Is that sufficient, gentlemen?'

The company commanders rocked backwards from the campfire's flaring heat.

'General Masséna's regiments are being fed into the fight,' said Jobert, 'which weakens his flank guard at Bionde. General Masséna requires the 24th Chasseurs to step forward.

'Geourdai, you will attend Colonel Raive on General Masséna's headquarters. 1st Company will act as couriers and escorts for aides. Neilage, traffic is a crush around the Ronco pontoon bridge. 4th Company is to escort the wounded convoys from Arcole to the hospitals at Ronco and then guide the empty wagons back to the divisional casualty stations.

'2nd Company and 5th Company, you are to provide dismounted screens along the marsh paths that extend from the dike causeways. Maintain a platoon here in the trains to secure your companies' remounts.

'3rd Company, place yourself at the disposal of the divisional battery commander and escort the artillery wherever it is called. 6th Company, piquet the divisional trains. Escort the trains to wherever on General Masséna's command.

'Colonel Spiccard shall maintain his headquarters here with the divisional trains. Chabenac, I shall accompany 2nd Squadron forward to the divisional screen. Reveille at three o'clock. March at four o'clock. In location before dawn. Questions?'

In the ochre light, Jobert, Chabenac and Voreille knelt in marsh reeds and observed the activity on top of the tall dike.

'It would appear the kaiserliks seek the pre-dawn advantage as well,' said Jobert.

With their movement restricted to the dike's causeway, both advancing bodies of opposing infantry had clashed with a fierce fire fight. Along the causeway shuffled battalions of Austrian fusiliers, their march slowed by the musketry ahead. Between the Austrian column and the chasseurs on the muddy paths below ran a deep drainage ditch.

'Has anyone approached along these marsh paths this morning?' asked Jobert, looking over his shoulder to the north.

'There was a patrol of hussars early this morning,' said Voreille, 'but we saw them off.'

'Do you both maintain your two teams of riflemen?' asked Jobert.

'Yes, sir,' answered both Chabenac and Voreille.

'Then, Voreille,' said Jobert, 'detach your marksmen to 2nd Company. Have 5th Company continue screening the tracks through the marsh. Chabenac, with 5th Company's marksmen and your own, have 2nd Company focus their fire on the kaiserliks on the dike. No musketoons will find their mark at this range, but the noise will generate alarm.'

'Very good, sir,' said Chabenac. 'Bredieux, guard the marksmen. Peugeot, set a flank screen along the flank of the causeway.'

Musket balls zipped far overhead.

'Where is that fire coming from?' asked Chabenac.

'Such a dense, exposed formation of Austrians is attracting flanking fire,' said Jobert. 'Most likely our troops beyond the dike on the far side of the Adige.'

Austrian soldiers scrambled down the banks of the dike as the French muskets fired into the packed ranks. The wounded and dead slid down the steep banks into the drainage channel at the base of the dike.

Sucking deeply on his pipe, Bredieux knelt beside Jobert. Bredieux cast Jobert a wary look. 'He was a good one, that Colonel Fergnes, sir. I remember us sweeping the streets of

Valence together during the armoury raid.'

Jobert regarded Bredieux with an unwavering stare. 'Should you reach deep enough into your purse to purchase an *eau de vie* that befits Fergnes' good name, I would take great pleasure toasting the merits of his character with you. Until then, might we focus on the matters at hand?'

'Those dead kaiserliks, sir ...' Bredieux exhaled a cloud, his eyes attempting to anticipate Jobert's reaction. 'Just look at those bulging satchels.'

'My thoughts exactly, Bredieux,' said Jobert. 'Lead a platoon down into the drainage ditches. Have a section cross onto the enemy dike. Drag across their dead and wounded, then strip them.'

Blue smoke lingered around Bredieux's head. 'I see they have not promoted you yet, sir. Make sure they date your pay from the affair at Caldiero.'

'Thank you, Lieutenant Bredieux,' said Jobert. 'They probably have other things on their minds at present. Get on with harvesting Austrian purses so that Fergnes' widow might afford her weeds.'

A mounted Austrian commander rode the top of the dike exhorting his men to press the attack along the causeway. 'See that general with the red trousers?' yelled Jobert to the chasseur snipers. 'Kill him.'

'Sir,' called Peugeot, 'the Austrians are bringing guns forward.'

Three cannon belched flames westwards against French fusiliers on the far bank of the Adige River. Two three-pounder guns were manhandled further forward along the dike. 'Chabenac, pour fire onto those guns.'

The Austrian crews ceased their trundling and swung their guns into action. One pointed down the causeway. One spun towards the chasseurs in the marshes.

'Moench, sound Skirmishers Out. Chabenac, prepare to receive canister at one hundred metres.'

The chasseurs threw themselves flat in the reeds and stunted thorns.

The three-pounder fired. The rip of the canister pellets lifted a lethal hail of gravel off the road surface. An artillery sergeant behind the gun gesticulated abuse at the cringing chasseurs.

'Drop that loud-mouthed prick for a start,' Jobert yelled at the marksmen. 'Quickly, as they reload.'

'Our infantry are pushing forward,' said Chabenac.

'The kaiserliks are breaking,' called Bredieux. 'Run, you bastards, run.'

'How far away are our infantry from the kaiserlik guns?' asked Jobert.

'Three hundred metres, sir,' said Bredieux.

'Inside canister range. We must capture those guns before our infantry are wiped off the causeway. Bredieux, on me. Ascend to the guns.'

Sabre in hand, Jobert slid down into the freezing sump, then clambered onto the far bank. With boots oozing water, Jobert found limited purchase on the steep, slippery slope of the dike. He laboured to balance on the near parallel sheep paths that terraced the banks, gripping onto tufted grass while clearing a trail by pulling at the arms and legs of the wounded enemy fusiliers.

As Bredieux's chasseurs clambered behind him, the three-pounder fired just above Jobert's head. The detonation made them all cringe, and the smoke robbed their heaving lungs of air.

'Their smoke cloaks our approach, lads.' Jobert coughed against the inhaled gun smoke. 'Quick! Before they reload.'

As Jobert reached the lip of the causeway along the top of the dike, the three-pounder muzzle yawned in his face. The press of retreating Austrians around the gun ignored the scrambling chasseurs.

A brown-coated gunner screamed at the swarm of Austrian fusiliers. 'Clear the muzzle, you fucking idiots!' Two gunners held either end of a ramrod, shepherding the infantry to the rear of the gun.

Jobert punched the knuckle guard of his sabre under the ear of the closest gunner, then reversing his downward swing, brought the hilt's pommel back into the face of the other man.

Two gunners stood by the trails of the gun, the firer and the ventsman. Jobert was behind the wheel of the gun. Recognising that if the gun were to fire, the recoil would crush him, Jobert cut the powder-packed firetube , with a wrist flick, flush with the top of the cannon's touch hole.

As Jobert's blade sliced, his eyes were glued to the quick-match wrapped around the wooden portfire in the Austrian firer's extended hand. The Austrian gunner retracted his arm with a scream. Jobert's slash only knocked the fizzing portfire to the ground.

'Again!' called the ventsman on the far side of the breech. 'Try again. Grab the fucking portfire.'

Jobert lunged and stomped out the burning cord. The ventsman threw a powerful right cross that caught Jobert on the jaw. The force of the punch flung Jobert back across the breech, blocking the vent.

'Get the prick clear of the touch hole,' said the firer. 'Gut him later.'

The ventsman uncurled his fists and grabbed at Jobert's cross belts.

Jobert spat blood from his mouth into the vent hole, clogging the powder-packed fire-tube with saliva.

'You prick!' The ventsman half-lifted Jobert. A shot cracked behind Jobert. The ball smacked into the ventsman's chest. As the Austrian artilleryman reeled backwards, he dragged Jobert across the gun's trail. Jobert's ribs crunched with the ammunition ready box nestled between the trail arms.

The Austrian firer dropped his portfire and ran.

Jobert rolled on the ground clutching his aching ribs, wiping his bloody lips with his glove cuff. 'Bredieux, wheel the gun about to fire on the other bastard.'

The chasseurs, with Bredieux's urging, lifted the cannon's timber trails and spun the iron-rimmed wheels, aiming the barrel at the other gun.

'Stand back,' Jobert called in German, waving the hissing quickmatch. 'Canister. Fire!'

The Austrians crewing the other gun either dived down the far embankment or ran along the causeway.

Jobert flopped against the breech. 'Now, Bredieux, secure our prize before our bloody infantry do.'

By the evening of the third day of the battle across the swamps, the intensity of opposing musketry had not abated. As Jobert joined Chabenac and Voreille on a footpad snaking north-east from Bionde, cannonades pulsed and the fires of Arcole and Albaredo throbbed within the smoke-choked eastern horizon.

'How has this flank fared?' asked Jobert.

'The exposed dikes have not allowed us to bring up our guns on this flank in anything but pairs,' said Chabenac. 'There was an attack by the kaiserliks earlier. It was half-hearted and soon beaten off.'

'Is the gunfire towards Arcole ours, sir?' asked Voreille. 'What of Arcole's third day?'

'The guns you hear are theirs,' said Jobert. 'Masséna's casualties are mounting. The causeway leading to Arcole is a slaughterhouse. Voreille, have 5th Company join 4th Company in escorting the wagons of wounded through the night. Go now, lad.'

Jobert and Chabenac watched Voreille stride off through the marshland's bobbing reed heads to gather his chasseurs.

'Is it true Masséna is now attacking Arcole frontally?' asked Chabenac. 'A scheme which has failed consistently for three days.'

'He does,' said Jobert, 'but his assaults cover Augereau's out-flanking approach to Arcole, with the remnants of his division, up the eastern side of the Alpone, from Albaredo.'

'This has not been the Piacenza-like crossing we had hoped,' said Chabenac. 'Two divisions have failed in taking a village bridge in three days. How did we achieve such with ease at Lodi in May? The kaiserliks are fighting with a ferocity that we have not seen to date.'

'Lodi was a delaying action,' said Jobert. 'The defence of Arcole is vital. Here are patriotic volunteers who desire to charge forward combined with the hardened veterans of Lodi, those who know well the extreme cost of breaking. I do not believe the kaiserliks fight to gain Mantua. I feel they fight to keep Vienna.'

'May I ask of your observations of our endurance?' asked Chabenac.

'Our endurance cannot be a question,' said Jobert. 'Endure we must. If we do not, either the Austrian columns grind us, or we break and run for Nice. The blood we have given to date has paid for Mantua in full. Bonaparte knows a debt is owed. He will not yield at this point of the negotiation.'

Jobert and Chabenac turned towards the murmurings from the skirmishers nearby.

Bredieux's pipe smoke swirled as he scanned beyond the reeds. 'The musketry has ceased, sir,' he called.

'It is five o'clock now,' said Jobert. 'I should return for Masséna's orders.'

'Sir,' Chabenac lowered his head as he lowered his voice, 'may I ask a question?'

Jobert regarded Chabenac's motley appearance in the gloom.

'What keeps you here, sir?' asked Chabenac. 'What is your need to see this through? Your motivation is deeper than duty.'

Jobert looked down at the mauve horizon. 'Is now the time to ask?'

'I am reminded of Fergnes,' said Chabenac. Jobert winced. 'When is there a better time than now?'

Jobert shuffled and regarded the splitting seams of his leather gloves. 'In spare moments, my thoughts return to Milan last summer. Eating strawberries and baked ham, watching my horses rolling in lush pastures.' Jobert gazed up at the faint glimmer of the evening's first stars. 'Seven years ago, my expectations were to be a cavalry sergeant major in a royal barracks. Following four years of war, I am nearly a colonel.' Jobert shrugged. 'Should we force peace upon the kaiserliks, I sense opportunities beckon. Why not me?'

Jobert looked for Chabenac's reaction, but it was masked by the evening's shadows.

'Lieutenant Colonel Jobert, sir?' cried a voice.

'Lieutenant Yinot, come here, sir,' called Moench.

'Sir,' said Yinot, 'Masséna and Augereau have taken Arcole. The Austrians are withdrawing north. The 24th Chasseurs are ordered to pursue.'

At the end of a four-day pursuit, Jobert and Chabenac sat on the plateau of Rivoli, sixty kilometres north-west of Arcole. Dark snow-laden clouds billowed across Mount Baldo's dominant shoulders. Tucked like chicks at Mount Baldo's feet, the Austrian rear guard stood immobile across the road north to Trento and the Alps.

'They have gone. Is it over, sir?' asked Chabenac.

'No,' said Jobert.

'When will it end?'

'We will have our rest when Mantua capitulates,' said Jobert. 'While Mantua holds, the Emperor will keep bleeding his loyal subjects to hold the wealth of Lombardy.'

'When will they return?' asked Chabenac.

'Soon. Within weeks.'

'Will not winter both extinguish Mantua and hold the Austrians beyond the Alps?' asked Chabenac. 'They fought with ferocity in this attempt. But as an army, they grow weaker. They have lost near twenty thousand men.'

'As have we,' said Jobert. 'Arcole was a very narrow victory. The Austrians have failed three times to advance into Lombardy. Each time they have been obliged to rebuild their force. The kaiserlik generals grow wiser from these severe lessons.'

Jobert noticed Chabenac's inspection of the extra stripes of a lieutenant-colonel on Jobert's sleeves and the thighs of his tight breeches. Chabenac's eyes lingered on an embossed leather cover for the cartridge belt across Jobert's chest.

'It was Fergnes',' said Jobert.

'You are not known for expensive adornments, sir,' said Chabenac. 'You look quite smart.'

Jobert snorted.

'I miss him,' said Chabenac. 'Will you be returning his effects and purse to Milan? Will it be your duty to relay his passing to …?'

Jobert stiffened as an empty dizziness struck him. Unprepared for the sudden vertigo, he scowled at the Austrian rear guard to maintain his orientation. Jobert fumbled his reins to turn Jaune away. 'See to your duties, Captain Chabenac.'

Chapter Twenty-Four
December 1796, Milan, Italy

Within the hush of Fergnes' ornate Milanese drawing room, Marguerite, Camille and Fergnes' little boy turned toward travel-stained Jobert.

'He ... is dead.' Jobert's wringing grip choked his leather gloves. It was all he could manage. Jobert had contemplated every phrase, in every combination, to express Fergnes' passing, since he had departed Rivoli.

Camille stifled a gasp, staggering back to steady herself on the furniture.

All colour drained from Marguerite's face as she sat the baby on the carpet. A deep, wavering groan broke from Marguerite's lips as she crumpled heavily on a long sofa before cascading further to the floor.

Marguerite's collapse spurred Camille forward to support her fallen cousin. Camille sagged on her knees and placed a comforting hand on Marguerite's curling tresses.

Jobert leapt forward. 'Orlande! Anissa!'

The child, stunned at his mother sprawled on the carpet, screamed at Jobert's loud voice.

Orlande and Anissa burst through a serving door.

Squeezed tight beside Camille, Jobert gathered Marguerite's slim, quivering body in his arms, and attempted to lie her on the couch.

'No! No, leave me.' Marguerite's eyes rolled towards the wailing child.

'Anissa, the young master, please,' said Orlande as he lifted Marguerite's legs onto the sofa.

With Anissa departing, all the time tut-tutting the howling infant, Orlande gathered cushions from other chairs for Madame Fergnes. Orlande glared at Jobert. 'What?'

'Fergnes is ...' Jobert's jaw trembled. He gritted his teeth.

Sadness pinched Orlande's face. He draped a blanket across Marguerite as she shivered.

With his hands on her waist, Jobert drew Camille up from her hands and knees. Camille staggered and turned within Jobert's supporting arms, folding her arms to press deep into his consoling embrace. Jobert held her while she sobbed.

Camille stopped her tears and looked up into Jobert's face, one hand extending to caress his scarred, unshaven cheek. 'You too have lost him. You too need comfort.'

Beside them on the couch, Marguerite flung back her blanket, sweeping a porcelain vase to shatter on the floor. Bent over double, Marguerite screamed and screamed and screamed.

Jobert contemplated the crackle of the fire and the gentle hiss of the large kettles in Fergnes' tiled bathroom as the heat of the water in the deep bathtub seeped through his skin and into his bones.

As he took another deep swallow of sugary *rüsümada*, Jobert's gaze swept about the room.

He saw a fire that did not blow ash in his eyes.

Instead of standing astride a washbasin and washing his arse and armpits with a rolled-up stocking, a sponge reeking of perfumed soap jiggled on the water's surface.

A neat towel waited on a stool to dry him, not the filthy shirt he had just taken off.

Nearby, lay a fully laundered and dried shirt, drawers and darned stockings ready for his rejuvenated skin.

In lieu of the stinking, patched uniform that he normally placed back on, his boots, trousers, waistcoat and tailcoat were polished, pressed and brushed.

How often do I have this? Jobert calculated how many days had passed in such comfort since he departed the 24th Chasseur's barracks in Avignon in mid-1793 to attend the Marseille uprising. *Less than ten times in the homes of friends. Double that for the bordellos. What? Two-to-three days every two-to-three months for three continuous years. Is a home a ... luxury?*

Jobert closed his eyes and poured a ladle of frothy water over his head.

He opened his eyes to find Fergnes standing at the foot of the bath.

Jobert blinked.

Fergnes regarded Jobert with a steady gaze and a slight smile on his lips.

Beside Fergnes stood Pultiere holding two of Jobert's horses, Vert and Blanc.

Around them stood Sergeant Dalmuz, Corporal-farrier Vocuse, Corporal Duflot, Chasseurs Millone, Jonn, Arbod, Saint Dizier, Faure, Billiez, Docuse and so many others. Pressed around the bathroom wall there were men of other nations in coats of white, brown, blue, grey and red. Men in civilian clothing and women also appeared scattered in the crowd.

He noticed 2nd Company's first fatality, the boy they lost at the bridge outside Aubagne in mid-1793. *What was his name?* Jobert's eyes burned as tears formed. 'What was your name, chasseur?'

A monstrous bubble of sadness expanded in his chest, crushing his heart. The pain in his chest was intense. It exploded as a blubbering sob.

He struggled upright in the slippery bath then leant forward and vomited the black bile of despair. Another sob and another and another swelled within him, wrenching tears from his eyes while his nose and mouth streamed mucous and saliva.

A clock chimed somewhere in the house. The tremors of internal anguish no longer rose from his diaphragm.

He trembled from the cramping effort, staring with stinging eyes at the surface of the steaming water, confirming the convulsions had finished. *Like pus in a boil, never totally expelled.* He scooped the soapy bathwater to his face and rubbed away the tears and mucous. Red-eyed and puffy faced, Jobert looked to the end of his bath.

They had gone. For now.

'What do you understand of the regiment's current strength?' asked Jobert.

The chief clerk of the 24th Chasseur's regimental depot gauged the new regimental second-in-command, the third man in the role this year, with caution. 'With this second draft of recruits just arrived, there appears to be two hundred and fifty sabres on the roll. Does that tally with you, sir?'

'It does, sadly,' said Jobert. 'What is your view of them?'

'Unemployment is so severe back home they were all keen to enlist,' said the chief clerk. 'Yet so fresh faced. Standing beside their pinched and lined cousins of the same age, veterans of four years with the regiment, the recruits appear to stand beside their fathers.'

'Quite so,' said Jobert. 'My immediate concern is the health and fitness of their remounts. Schooling in winter to build their strength is difficult without forage and with limited grain. The scuttlebutt speaks of Bonaparte's commissary delivering convoy after convoy. Have we received any new equipment?'

'Our stores have received saddlery, stable clogs and stable jackets,' said the chief clerk. 'Now that Italian treasure is filling the Directory's coffers, grain is purchased in gold and silver. With grain now profitable again, there is more coming through.'

'Over-breeches?' asked Jobert. 'Capes? Gloves? Canvas for tents and horse rugs?'

'Not yet, sir,' said the wagonmaster.

'Have the regimental tailors removed the sleeves of our stable jackets to patch our over-breeches?'

'Yes, sir.'

'Can we buy what we need?' asked Jobert. 'In what state are the regimental accounts?'

'Grim, sir. The purchase of the one hundred remounts for the two recruit drafts has set us in arrears, despite loans and grants.'

'Do our stores contain surplus equipment we can trade or sell?' asked Jobert.

The chief clerk winced. 'As in sell boot soles to our chasseurs, sir?'

'No, as in selling excess wagons and horseshoes to cartage companies.'

'Oh, yes, sir.' The chief clerk gave a wicked grin. 'Forgive me when I say, that is not a solution I would have expected from your predecessors.'

'They were not old sergeants like you and I,' said Jobert.

'No, sir, well, Lieutenant Colonel Raive was.'

'If resources were water,' said Jobert, 'Raive was not licking dew off dung, as we are now. When the regiment was raised, Raive was choking on a pump hose.'

The chief clerk chuckled. 'You should consider basing yourself here at the depot, sir. The regiment would benefit with you here. You will find the commissary as devious an adversary as you would meet out there.'

Jobert lowered his face. His eyes roamed over the opened books of account before him. *Is this where I belong?*

'My apologies, sir,' said the chief clerk, 'I did not mean to … ah, what are your views of this expedition to Ireland, sir? Fourteen thousand men on forty-four ships.'

Jobert snorted. 'Having crossed the Atlantic on a troopship, I am pleased it is not me.'

Jobert could see the man was eager for any broader sense of perspective. 'Very well,' said Jobert. 'The Republic's most esteemed generals are unable to march to Vienna with one hundred and forty thousand men. Our own Army of Italy is barely clinging to Lombardy with thirty-five thousand. Our Mediterranean fleet is incapable of eliminating a squadron of British frigates from blocking our sea lines of communication. Yet our Atlantic fleet is invested against the bulk of the British navy defending their homeland. My trumpeter would be offering very long odds for France's success in Ireland.'

'Then what do you envisage the regiment facing in the next short while, sir?' asked the chief clerk. 'The Paris broadsheets say the Directory seeks peace. Yet Austria will not negotiate while Mantua stands strong. We know the Mantua garrison of twelve thousand is steeped in contagion, and having devoured their horses, they are now consuming their cross belts.'

'With Moreau's and Jourdan's pathetic jaunt in September,' said Jobert, 'kaiserlik reinforcements will be streaming towards the Tyrol. Knowing full well the dire straits of the garrison, Austria must relieve Mantua before the garrison capitulates. Bonaparte continues to stall any discussion of peace until he has the fortress in hand. I suspect the next Austrian offensive may be weeks away, if not days.'

The chief clerk started to ask another question, but Jobert cut him short with a raised finger. 'Sir,' said Jobert, 'our immediate task is to march fifty recruits to join Masséna's screen around Rivoli. In the short time I do have here, let us immerse ourselves in the details of regimental manning and our accounts.'

Paris
21st December 1796

Dearest 'Uncle' André,

It is with deepest love, my darling cousin, I announce the birth of my son Herbert Yann Chauvel.

Jobert's chin drooped toward his chest.

The birth was not complicated, and little Herbert, your first cousin once removed, is happy, healthy and strong. He is definitely a Chauvel. If he had a little moustache, you would think him Didier. I too am well.

You can imagine the fuss this gorgeous little man has caused our darling Aunt Sophie. Father is caught between conventional disgrace and grandfatherly love. He shares that burden evenly. I receive the disgrace and the baby receives his love...

Jobert's eyes skimmed Michelle's script. 'What of this bastard Colbert?'

Édouard has requested my hand in marriage from father to which father has agreed. Édouard has proposed marriage to me and I have accepted. Édouard has all the makings of a wonderful father. At each of his visits he insists on viewing his son.

Your 'nephew' demands his mother, so I must attend.
More news soon ...

A floorboard groaned. Jobert's eyelids sprang open.
Soft, short, careful footsteps sounded in the corridor outside.
Alert, Jobert rolled under his blanket. His bedframe squeaked.
The footsteps paused.
Jobert watched candlelight flickering beyond the gap at the base of his bedroom door. He looked across to his sabre hanging on a peg in the wall.
The metal latch squeaked.

Who? Camille? You too have lost. You too need comfort.

The door's hinges creaked open. The soft rustle of a night-gown brought a waft of perfumed powder. A single candle illuminated the room with wavering light.

Jobert blinked. The writhing shadows and the soft yellow flame obscured the carrier's face.

Jobert raised himself on his elbow. He pushed his blankets to his waist, ready to launch.

The candle lowered.

Marguerite.

Jobert squinted. *Is she sleep-walking?*

Marguerite contemplated the long scar across his chest. She appeared earnest. Her lips were neither smiling nor quivering with nervousness. Marguerite reached down and threw back the blankets revealing Jobert's naked belly and thighs.

'Marguerite, what are you doing?' asked Jobert.

Marguerite placed the candleholder on the side table. She tugged the waist knot allowing her dressing gown to slide to the floor. The side of her slim, white body closest to the window was blue as it reflected the frozen moon. Her other side glowed golden as the light of the candle played upon her skin.

'Please, Marguerite,' said Jobert, raising his hands in anticipation, 'do not—'

Marguerite's eyes revealed neither lust nor apprehension. 'Hush now,' she said.

She reached out, balancing on Jobert's shoulders while she straddled his hips. Her cool palms gripped the base of his neck, her buttocks warmed his thighs. Marguerite reached back and swept his blankets around her shoulders.

Contemplating her flame-lit belly, her ribs and her breasts framed by the dark blankets, dark curls and dark eyes, Jobert hardened. He rolled his hips under her, adjusting to a more comfortable position to accept her weight.

He exhaled sharply, his buttocks and abdomen tensing as she took him in hand. 'Marguerite, are you—'

Her full lips parted, eyes closing as she guided him into her. 'Shh ... I am terrified.'

A soft rap announced Orlande entering Jobert's bedroom. Orlande placed a steaming jug of water by the wash basin and a small pot of ale on the side table. 'Shall I take your laundry, sir?'

Jobert stood in breeches, stockings and shirtsleeves in front of an open window and a dead hearth, staring mindlessly beyond his snow-choked windowsill. 'Ah, thank you.'

'Including the sheets, sir?' asked Orlande.

Jobert glanced at the bed. *Did I not pull the covers up?* He had. *Noise? Scent?* Jobert turned back to the scene of snow-clogged roof tiles through his window. 'Please, Orlande.'

Orlande stripped the bed and departed with laundry basket and chamber pot.

Shaved smooth and dressed snug, Jobert came down to breakfast, where he dined alone on a mushroom and herb omelette with coffee. As mistress of the household, Marguerite would breakfast in her bedchamber. He enquired after Camille.

Anissa curtsied. 'Mademoiselle Camille has taken young master to Mass this morning, sir.'

Jobert's mind swirled at the implications of the previous evening. The only sensible notion was to spend the morning at Depot Company.

Arriving back for lunch, Jobert entered the drawing room.

When Anissa announced him into their presence, Camille was seated facing away and made no attempt to look at him.

Colonel Raive sat in the centre of the room. He marvelled at the gurgling toddler demonstrating the abilities of a carved toy horse on wheels.

Taking Jobert's hands in hers, Marguerite's flashing brown eyes scanned his face with concern. 'Oh, darling Jobert, you have only just missed our beautiful boy taking his first steps. You have been working at Depot Company. You must be famished. Anissa, fetch coffee.'

Jobert searched her eyes for the answers he needed. *What of last night?* His heart pounded. *What next?*

Her face held only sisterly regard, as his cousin Michelle's face might when he came in from his grandfather's stables.

Raive gave a polite cough. 'Dearest Marguerite, Jobert and I cannot stay for lunch. Forgive my intrusion, Jobert, I have asked Orlande to prepare your portmanteau for departure and a meal on the road. I have just had word. The Austrians are braving the snow-bound passes in their fourth attempt to break us.'

Marguerite whimpered. Jobert took her sagging body in his arms, but her hands flapped him away as she sank onto a nearby chair.

Brushing away tears, Camille wedged herself between Marguerite and Jobert.

Chapter Twenty-Five
January 1797, Verona, Italy

'The Austrian garrison of Mantua is on its knees,' said Spiccard to his senior staff officers. 'Following the horse-race from Bassano in September, the entry of fresh troops has swollen the garrison to twenty thousand. Intercepted couriers inform us that contagion and starvation have reduced their ranks to ten thousand effectives. The rations for the entire city will be totally consumed by the end of this month. We are less than thirty days from victory.

'Vienna knows this, and now races troops from the Rhine, raising reserve regiments and volunteer legions for one final offensive. We are aware their army is depleted of regimental officers, artillery, tentage, wagons and other vital campaign stores.'

A dividend from Inoubli? thought Jobert.

'They are on their knees,' Spiccard continued. 'We are on our knees. One last, desperate gamble to secure Mantua exists in January before either Lombardy is ours or we are bustled back to Nice.'

Spiccard pointed a silver letter-opener at a crumpled map.

'The enemy will approach, as they did in November, along the proven roads from the east and from the north. The avenues from the north are the quickest means of cutting our lines of communication. Rivoli is the cork in that bottle. A cork the kaiserliks removed during their first offensive in July. Now in January, the northern passes are blocked with snow.

'Alternatively, the eastern approaches allow a strike to release the garrison of Mantua. Yet the flat country is intersected by the Po's tributaries. During winter the roads will be appalling.

'General Bonaparte foresees our enemy utilising a combination of both directions, as they have done before. He will wait to see where the Austrian main effort falls before he commits his reserves. General Masséna's division secures Verona, the centre of our siege's outer cordon. Focused to the east, but ready to march north. Questions?'

Spiccard slid his eyes to Jobert.

Jobert sat straighter in his seat. *Nothing ventured, nothing gained.* 'I am interested in how the regiment might meet the needs of General Masséna in the coming operation, sir. I would like to raise the issue of our regimental strength of two hundred and fifty sabres.'

Spiccard lounged in his chair, his dark eyes glassy with his affliction. 'Ah, something that cannot be pillaged from a dead enemy's satchel, eh, Jobert? Continue.'

And the purse received from the captured guns? Jobert dropped his eyes to maintain his impassive mask. 'Our parade state includes our second draft of fifty recruits. Our entire regiment is equivalent to a squadron at full strength. Would you agree, sir, our current six companies are providing less and less utility to General Masséna. We have no coverage in our screens, no endurance in our piquet and no mass in a charge. What might your intent for the 24th Chasseurs be in these circumstances?'

Spiccard tapped the letter-opener on the table. 'My intent is to disband 3rd Squadron and create four companies of sixty sabres.'

Jobert averted his look of relief by scribbling in his notebook. 'Might I suggest both 1st and 4th Companies integrate a troop each from 3rd Company, sir, and 2nd and 5th Companies absorb a troop each from 6th Company.'

'I agree,' said Spiccard. 'Further, due to our reduced numbers and the desire to maintain experienced officers at the company level, I shall not promote Geourdai as my second chief of squadron at this stage.'

'In so doing, sir,' said Jobert, 'a regimental wedding breakfast delayed. No matter. You have tasked me, sir, with juggling the maintenance of your headquarters and attending you at the front. Had you reflected further on that arrangement?'

Spiccard set his teeth. 'I know I have my good days and bad days with these interminable Italian humours, but I shall maintain my post front and centre of 1st Squadron. I need you, Jobert, to stand ready at the front of 2nd Squadron. From that location, you will have immediate insight into General Masséna's requirements of the 24th Chasseurs, should I ... should the need arise.'

Jobert sat on the edge of his cot. His mouth felt ashen. His guts churned. His skull throbbed. He blinked gummy eyes first at the bottles by his boots then to his broken garter ribbon.

In his stockings, he shuffled down the hall towards the kitchen.

'I feel Fergnes' loss, no doubt,' said Chabenac, his voice entering the billet's dark hallway through the ajar door, 'yet one does one's best in the circumstances. Have you noticed ... anyone else ... under strain?

Jobert slid his feet to a halt and peered through the crack. Orlande kneaded dough at the table.

Koschak stood by the hearth warming his fingers. 'Perhaps Lieutenant Colonel Jobert, sir.'

Chabenac stretched his boots towards the embers. 'I agree he does not seem himself but what observations have you made?'

'My concern is for the men, sir,' said Koschak. 'The men place their lives in the trust of their commander. With Colonel Spiccard unable to rid himself of ill humours, the men feel confident that Jobert will step into the breach if needed. Yet, you and I know Jobert's mind seems elsewhere since Fergnes' passing.'

Orlande glanced at the door. Jobert froze in the shadows beyond.

'What do you suggest?' asked Chabenac.

'Perhaps you might have a word, sir,' said Koschak.

'Me? You and Jobert are as thick as thieves. I am certain he would welcome your views.'

'No, not me, sir,' said Koschak. 'I ... you are better with words, sir.'

'Then leave it to me,' said Chabenac. 'I shall seek the first opportunity.'

Jobert slid backward down the hall on his stockinged feet. 'Orlande, are you in the kitchen?' Jobert opened the door holding out his frayed garter. 'Orlande, do we have ... ah, gentlemen, well met. Breakfast?'

'No, thank you, sir, duties await,' said Koschak. 'Excuse me, please.'

As Koschak clumped from the room, Orlande picked flecks

of dough from his hands onto the raw loaf. 'I have prepared a little turnip gruel and fried ammunition bread for you both. Enjoy your breakfast, gentlemen, while I fetch spare ribbon from the cart.'

Jobert winced at combining turnip gruel with his hangover. 'More coffee, Chabenac?' Jobert poured from the pot. 'You seem wrapped in your thoughts. Are you well?'

'Quite well. Thank you, sir,' said Chabenac. 'I reflect upon Colonel Spiccard's health. As his second-in-command, I value your views?'

'Masséna cannot dismiss Spiccard unless he either falls from the saddle or makes a scandalous error in the field. Spiccard remains our regimental commander and we all shall support him as he battles this insidious illness.'

'Of course, we shall,' said Chabenac. 'Should his fevers overcome him, the regiment feels confident that their destiny will be passed to steady hands. How are you preparing for such responsibility?'

'Command of two hundred and fifty sabres?' said Jobert. 'I was responsible for a similar number of men when I assumed command as a captain four years ago. I am ready enough.'

'Yes, the numbers are comparable, hence our faith in you. But we are all worn thin. The loss of Fergnes has had an understandable impact on his friends. I grieve his loss keenly.' Chabenac sipped at coffee. 'I sense that you do too.'

Jobert stooped, his elbows on his knees as he searched the floorboards. 'Why? My drinking?'

'Do you feel you are drinking more than usual?' asked Chabenac.

'Perhaps,' whispered Jobert.

'Understandable in the circumstances. More than that though. You keep to yourself. You do not exercise your horses, nor join in morning fencing. You look exhausted.'

'It is my increased responsibilities as regimental second-in-command .' asked Jobert.

'Of two hundred and fifty men?' asked Chabenac. 'Come now, sir, any company second-in-command can deal with that.'

'We all look exhausted. The lack of food in an Alpine winter.'

'Yes, we all do,' said Chabenac. 'It is the combination of many hardships. Where does solace lie?'

Jobert shook his head.

Chabenac leant forward. 'Perhaps we can share our grief in the company of dear friends?'

Orlande knocked and entered.

Chabenac stood. 'Sir, I must away. Thank you for breakfast. An evening of chess soon?'

Jobert snorted. Chabenac saluted before he departed.

Orlande took Chabenac's seat by the fire. 'No breakfast again, sir?'

'Have Tulloc and Moench eaten?' Jobert massaged his greasy scalp.

'They have, sir.' Orlande threaded a needle to repair the worn garter with a ribbon offcut. 'With your promotion, sir, what will happen to us?'

'Us?' asked Jobert.

'Us, sir,' said Orlande. 'Koschak, Moench, Tulloc and his fiancée.'

As Jobert swivelled his head to focus itchy eyes on Orlande, his neck cricked. 'You know Koschak and Moench have joined me at regimental headquarters. Koschak as acting Regimental Sergeant Major, Moench now a regimental trumpeter. Tulloc remains my groom. His fiancée will join us when her child is born, and the conquest of Lombardy resolved. Why do you ask?'

'I want to know where our friends are.' Orlande swept his red fringe from his face. 'You know we are surrounded by our friends, sir.'

Jobert's wavering gaze returned to the embers in the hearth. Orlande pushed his glasses onto his nose to focus on his stitches. 'Yes, there is a reliance on your steady leadership from the authority bestowed upon you. But more than that, sir, your company is treasured by many. Those that hold you in high regard are proud to count you as their friend and are at pains when you struggle with a personal burden.'

'Do I struggle, Orlande?' asked Jobert.

'Do you not, sir? I have had the good fortune to know you well for many years. Your friends only observe the symptoms of the disease that ails you. I know the cause.'

'Your diagnosis, doctor?'

'Confusion,' said Orlande. 'Not just the loss of Fergnes—'

'The bedding of his widow?'

'I have observed you and Madame Fergnes express genuine affection for each other. Madame must be forgiven for coming to you in her grief.'

Jobert held his head in his hands. 'As he breathed his last, I made a vow to Fergnes. When Mantua falls and Lombardy is ours … when a respectable time has passed that I might ask …'

Orlande scowled as he held out the repaired garter. 'Madame Fergnes' safety is not in doubt, sir. Let this melancholic winter pass. We will surely find clarity in the sunshine of spring. In the meantime, might we not focus on our duties and our friends?'

Jobert stood on the threshold of the barn watching the brooding clouds vacillate on a decision to snow. Jobert sought a warmth that no amount of snuggling in his cape could satisfy.

'I have never known you to be so distracted, sir,' said Chabenac. 'May I presume upon our friendship? Will you share what occupies your mind? Your demeanour has changed since your promotion. Which affects you more? The state of the regiment or the loss of Fergnes?'

Jobert searched the wisps of straw at his feet. 'I am to receive a poisoned chalice from Spiccard.'

'How so?' asked Chabenac.

'Spiccard distrusts me as his successor. He does not want me beside him in the line. His heart desires I return to Milan and unravel the issues that dog the regiment.'

'Assuredly,' said Chabenac, 'the regiment would benefit from your attention to its administration, but the men would feel better, I sense, with you front and centre, sabre drawn. Did Colonel Spiccard not request you remain in the line, ready for … any eventuality?'

'What? Assume command of a regiment at squadron strength?' Jobert bristled. 'We departed Savona ten months ago with four hundred. We can now mount two hundred and fifty sabres, and of those, one hundred recruits on unschooled remounts.'

'You have assured me you feel comfortable employing the sabres we have,' said Chabenac. 'No one doubts your ability.'

'Yet we are desperately fragile,' said Jobert. 'Fergnes confided a similar fear. In a moment of great crisis, Spiccard will collapse. I will receive an impossible task against which neither competence nor spirit can prevail. The moment will destroy us all, our bodies and our good name. In such a circumstance, I will ensure I remain on the field.'

Chabenac grimaced. 'Such a day will be resolved on more than the actions of our regiment.'

'Despite our numbers,' said Jobert, 'there is a gravity that accompanies the expectations of a regiment.'

'I am sure Koschak will put a boot in your britches should you falter. Has there been no reward with such responsibility?'

'More money?' asked Jobert. 'Hah! I cannot access it. If I could access it, I cannot spend it here. If I could spend it, what would I spend it on? There are only so many new stockings a man needs.'

'If Fergnes pondered the same concern, how might he counsel you?' asked Chabenac.

'To know my place,' said Jobert.

'Which is where?'

Jobert shrugged a shoulder as he frowned at his toes.

'And how does the loss of Fergnes stand with you?' asked Chabenac.

'Fergnes was a good man,' said Jobert, 'but he is gone.'

'Then what troubles you? Your commitment to him concerning Marguerite? The issue clearly vexes you.'

'It does.' Jobert wrapped his cape tighter around his shoulders, his eyes returning to the clouds. 'I do not know what to do.'

'Is she in peril of which the rest of us are unaware?' asked Chabenac. 'Are her current domestic arrangements quite secure?'

'All is secure,' said Jobert. 'Raive has guaranteed the lease on her apartments.'

A wry smile curved Chabenac's cheek. 'Are we not blessed with Colonel Raive's oversight? The advantages afforded by her family, and Fergnes', ensure she and the boy shall want for naught.'

Jobert scratched at mud clinging to the barn door's hinge with his toecap. 'I have the strong sense that my commitment to him ... obliges a commitment to her.'

'What?' Chabenac jerked. 'Marriage? Has she intimated an inclination toward you?'

'No!' Jobert peered away toward the far gateway.

Chabenac raised his gloved palms. 'Marguerite is blessed with numerous attractive qualities. We are all honoured by her sisterly affections. Do you have a deeper regard for her?'

'I acknowledge her beauty and her engaging wit.' Jobert's shoulders drooped as his head rocked low. 'But ought I not provide a father to an orphaned son? You spoke of the comfortable station held by her family, yet any such proposal must sit at odds with society's requirements.'

'Do you know her family?' asked Chabenac.

'No,' said Jobert, 'only the briefest introductions to the fathers of the bride and groom at the wedding breakfast.'

Chabenac nodded slowly. 'I detect neither passion for the lady, nor a yearning for social advantage. Nor have you ever been particularly taken with the child. Your obligation is to Fergnes, not to Marguerite. When she returns to her family, as she must, why would an occasional brotherly visit not suffice to demonstrate your esteem for Marguerite, and ensure the boy honours his father's memory.'

Jobert wobbled his head in consideration. 'Perhaps.'

'We agree, at the moment, she is safe,' said Chabenac. 'Is it not wise to reflect on how best to support her once the siege is concluded?'

As snow drifted over the farmyard's walls, Jobert breathed deeply. 'I admit I am weary from the unyielding onslaught of regimental administration and have become distracted with Marguerite.' Jobert gripped Chabenac's shoulder. 'Thank you for your guidance and—'

Iron-shod hooves scrambled on the slippery cobbles, as Lieutenant Yinot entered the stone enclosure at a fast trot.

'General Masséna presents his compliments, sir.' Yinot saluted. 'He wishes you to be informed that the Austrian advance closes upon us. Two enemy columns approach from the east. One approaches Mantua, the other marches for us here in Verona. General Masséna has ordered the division to stand to arms, sir. Colonel Spiccard requests that you attend him.'

'There we are, Chabenac.' Jobert drew his shoulders back. 'Duties and friends. I am called to where I belong.'

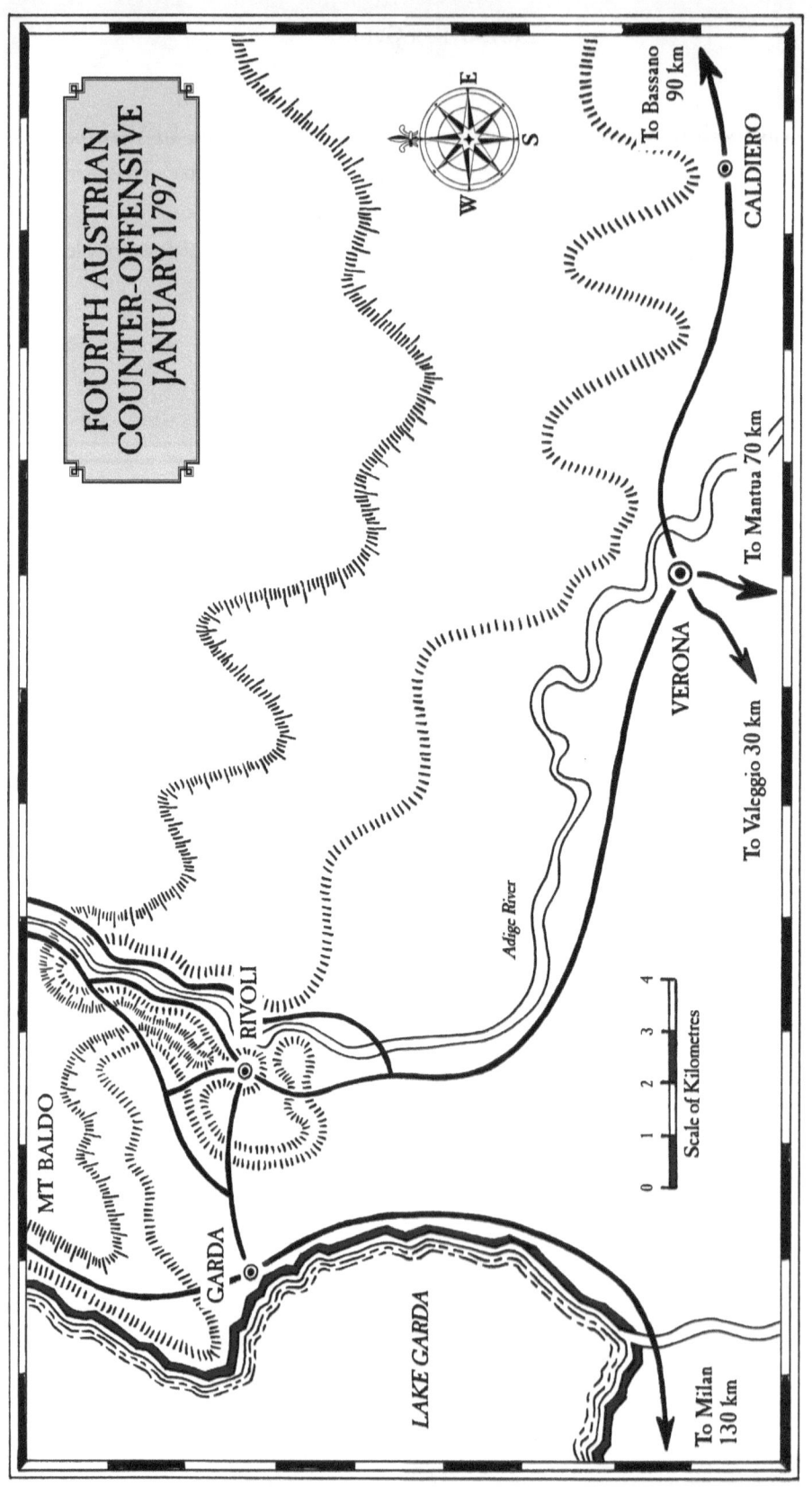

FOURTH AUSTRIAN
COUNTER-OFFENSIVE
JANUARY 1797

To Bassano 90 km

CALDIERO

To Mantua 70 km

VERONA

To Valeggio 30 km

Adige River

RIVOLI

MT BALDO

GARDA

LAKE GARDA

Scale of Kilometres

0 1 2 3 4

To Milan 130 km

Chapter Twenty-Six
January 1797, Battle of Verona, Italy

Two armies stood in snow on the plain east of Verona. Masséna formed twelve of his eighteen battalions in the French front line. Despite the French battalions being half the strength of the opponents, the front line stretched one-thousand, two-hundred metres. Three batteries of guns, calibres of all sorts, were concentrated in the centre.

Jobert and 2nd Squadron stood on Masséna's left, or northern, flank in column of troops. Looking along the front rank, Jobert noted very few horses held their heads high.

'Chabenac and Voreille, rotate your companies through rest every thirty minutes. Lead company remain mounted in the face of the enemy. Rear company stand to horse, ready to mount in an instant. Have your packhorse sections fire their kettles.'

Chabenac and Voreille saluted before departing.

Between the forces in the freezing slush the skirmishers took their post. Three hundred metres forward of the French front rank and eight hundred metres from the Austrian front line, or more importantly, beyond effective range of the Austrian six-pounders, trotted sixty pairs of chasseur skirmishers from 1st Squadron. Behind them stood the French skirmisher companies released from their parent battalions.

The Austrian line stretched nine hundred metres in the snow. Four battalions stood in the front line with two battalions in reserve. Four half-batteries of four unlimbered six-pounder guns stood ready, dispersed between the battalions. Two companies of Croatian uhlans stood on their flank, the small triangular pennants flapping on their lances.

Jobert scanned the uhlans through his telescope. All his mind registered was images of Fergnes' blue face and the rhythms of Fergnes' widow.

The Austrian guns fired a long-range bombardment, the rounds slapping into the slush, causing few casualties and wasting powder.

1st Squadron rallied at the walk to Masséna's right flank indicating that the Austrians were assaulting.

Dull enemy drumming confirmed the attack.

'Moench,' said Jobert, 'sound Assembly.' The fifth to eighth ranks of 2nd Squadron drained their bowls and mounted.

French guns responded as the Austrian line slogged forward over frozen meadows.

Closing to one hundred metres, the opposing infantry exchanged volleys of musketry.

For eight miserable hours.

With their ammunition expended, the Austrians retired east beyond the town of Caldiero.

'What was the point of today, sir?' asked Moench. 'I have served the Republic for four years now and have never seen a battle fought in a stupor. Why were all those casualties caused just to amble away?'

Jobert watched the blanket-wrapped French infantry collecting the wounded from both sides. 'The Austrian general used his brigade to tie down our division, one-quarter of the Army of Italy, for a day. Somewhere else, other than here, some other Austrian column has achieved its objectives today because we were committed. What midnight marches might General Bonaparte order to resolve the situation in our favour? Here comes our aide de camp now. What news, Lieutenant Yinot?'

'Colonel Spiccard presents his compliments, sir,' said Yinot, 'and wishes you to know that General Masséna is to retire his division behind Verona in preparation for tomorrow. 1st Squadron will maintain the screen towards Caldiero. Colonel Spiccard requests 2nd Squadron retire with the division and prepare for any eventuality.'

The next day pulsed with distant gunfire, north at Rivoli and south at Mantua. 1st Squadron reported no activity from the Austrian encampment beyond Caldiero.

While they waited in reserve and shared cups of Madame Quandalle's grappa, Jobert walked amongst the stale-smelling huddle of 2nd Squadron, those not scrounging for food, firewood or forage.

The soldiers squatted by their snoozing horses. Having been under saddle all day in the snow, the remounts' noses ran with snot, they wheezed, their glassy eyes oozed tears. Some men cleaned their remount's eyelashes of serum crust or straightened forelocks. Some slumped on their horses' shoulders, intimating a heartfelt embrace without demonstrating overt affection.

Jobert exchanged quips with the few 2nd Company chasseurs he knew, recognising too few of the remaining sixty chasseurs.

One third were recruits, one third were chasseurs from the disbanded 6th Company. Of the original seventy that had marched from Savona ten months ago, only twenty remained. Forty had been taken by battle and sickness. At least ten experienced chasseurs were posted to Bonaparte's Guides.

The soldiers' eyes flicked to any movement by their company officers, Chabenac, Bredieux and Peugeot, anticipating any indicator that impending effort was required.

Koschak prowled amongst the soldiers, peering into their smoky soup kettles, checking hooves, inspecting musketoons and saddlery. He pointed out minor tasks. Jobert knew the chasseurs resented Koschak disturbing their moment of rest, while acknowledging that Koschak's roving energy ensured their survival.

Jobert stood close beside Jaune. He had removed his gloves to both adjust Jaune's breastplate and soothe himself with the warmth of another. 'I have served in the line, young Jaune. I know how they see me.' *Another senior officer divorced from their difficulties. Demanding death or glory without bread, wine or pay.*

His chest crimped at the growing distance between him and them. *I am overcome with such ill humours. The men. Fergnes. Marguerite.* Jobert pressed his forehead to Jaune's mane. *I need to purge myself, and fast.* Jaune bent his neck so his nose might find bread or apples in Jobert's pockets. Jobert ran a gentle finger around his horse's lips. 'Accept my musings without alms, dear confessor.'

The setting sun cast a mauve shadow across icy mud, as Spiccard arrived, heavily rugged in his saddle.

'Jobert, the 24th Chasseurs march north,' said Spiccard. 'The northern defence at Rivoli is beginning to crumble. General Bonaparte has determined the enemy's main thrust is from the north. What we see to the east is the diversion. General Masséna has ordered a night march thirty kilometres to Rivoli. To arrive before dawn is critical.'

'I have no doubt as to the severity of the situation, sir,' said Jobert, 'as I have no doubt as to the regiment's ability to rise to the occasion. But thirty kilometres at night on bad roads will take us ten hours.'

'Jobert, the Austrian's northern pincers will break Rivoli tomorrow,' said Spiccard. 'Our speed now is vital to success.'

'And succeed the 24th Chasseurs shall, sir,' said Jobert. 'Moench, sound Assembly. Mount, form column of fours, walk, march!'

Eight hours later, Jobert ducked his head to enter the peasant cottage into which a party of chasseurs carried Spiccard. The bare-earth room smelt of animal manure and garlic. Disturbed livestock grunted and clucked in the shadows of the glowing embers. The peasant and his wife, in their nightclothes and gripping blankets to their shoulders, knelt and crossed themselves repeatedly. Three children peeped from a neighbouring bed.

Spiccard was lowered into the couples' slim bed. 'On his side, Laffet,' said the regimental surgeon, 'Let him vomit on the floor.' The surgeon scraped gravel from within Spiccard's collar, gathered there when Spiccard had toppled from his saddle. The regimental surgeon rolled up Spiccard sleeves. He spat *'Più fuoco! Acqua calda! Ora!'* at the peasants, while opening a glass jar of leeches.

The wife poured a bucket into the kettle. As the husband stoked the fire with split logs, he hissed a command. A girl sprang from under thin bedcovers.

'*Fermare!*' said Jobert. Corporal Laffet levelled his musketoon at the child.

'*Il prete, per favore, signore,*' said the peasant.

'They want a priest.' Jobert nodded at the girl. '*Andare!*' Laffet raised the muzzle. The girl scampered barefoot into shadows beyond a milking cow.

'Corporal Laffet,' said Jobert, 'you and your lads stay with Colonel Spiccard. Have his groom see to his horse. A guard inside and out at all times, understand? Lieutenant Yinot, send a courier to fetch the Colonel's valet from the trains.'

Once the process of bleeding was complete, Spiccard writhed within his blankets. The surgeon gave Jobert a hard look as he shrugged, before departing.

Jobert lowered his weary frame beside the rough-hewn bed's putrid covers.

Firelight blotched Spiccard's sweat-drenched face as his jaws chewed continuously. Despite convulsing, as if jabbed by devils, Spiccard rolled his dark eyes to focus on Jobert. 'Bring ... the standard.'

'Yinot, fetch the standard,' said Jobert.

As he waited, Jobert was conscious of being close enough to be in attendance but at a, hopefully, sufficient distance to avoid Spiccard's exhaled humours.

The village priest arrived as Koschak entered carrying the regiment's *tri-couleur.*

Spiccard clutched the embroidered cloth, convulsing as if it gave him pain. 'Jobert ... your regiment ... take post.' Jobert bowed his head. Tears welled in Spiccard's eyes. 'Jobert ... bring them home.'

Jobert's face tightened. 'I swear to you, sir, I shall preserve the lives of our men, and ensure the regiment's good name, while faithfully serving General Bonaparte.'

'Bonaparte ... huh!' Spiccard's characteristic sneer twisted his fevered face. 'Jobert, do not …' A paroxysm caused Spiccard to grind his teeth. Spiccard's fingers slipped from the flag, leaving it in Jobert's grip. Spiccard slumped back onto the straw mattress.

The peasant woman crossed herself before mopping Spiccard's brow. The priest intoned a soft liturgy behind her.

Jobert stood and moved to the fire, leaning the standard against his shoulder, before angling his watch face to the flames to read the time. Four o'clock. 'How far to Rivoli?'

'Our man here says seven kilometres,' said Koschak, nodding to the peasant.

'Watch over him, father,' said Jobert to the priest. 'We will return.' Jobert scratched in his waistcoat's fob and passed some coins to both the priest and the peasant. 'We had better press on, Sergeant Major.'

Koschak did not change his stance. His bulk blocked the door. The firelight burnished his scowling face and flickered in his steady green eyes. A slight inclination of his head and a raised eyebrow interrogated Jobert.

Jobert gripped the standard's staff tighter as he held Koschak's gaze. 'I have a regiment to command and an appetite for battle.' His voice was low, scratchy with fatigue. 'My chasseurs await their standard. What obstructs our march to glory?'

With a slow nod, Koschak stepped aside.

The freezing air punched Jobert as he emerged from the house holding the regimental standard aloft.

Jobert mounted Jaune. *A statement is needed.* He looked down the line of indistinct hunched figures in the gloom, the cloudless night bathing the ranks of caped chasseurs in grey moonlight. The men were silent, within their tobacco smoke haloes, pipe-bowls throbbing red. Steaming horses pawed at the thick frost. *Too dark for theatre.*

Jobert walked Jaune down the column in the rutted gutter, balancing the base of the staff on his stirruped toe.

The soldiers' heads followed him as he passed, as did their comments. 'We will do Colonel Spiccard proud this day, sir.' 'The 24th are in good shape, sir, you will not find us wanting.'

Jobert replied with 'Colonel Spiccard is too sick to continue. He will rest here under guard. Once our work is done, we will return for him.'

Behind the last file of soldiers, Jobert turned and walked up the other side, returning to the head of the column. Here he found his friends, men who were now his commanders. Their faces cast in moon shadow, their views on his assumption of command unclear.

'Moench, sound To Mess.' The trumpet's scream caused a rumble of veterans' laughter and a pulse of recruit confusion down the column.

Jobert drew in his breath to bellow his order. Bit chains tinkled as reins were gathered in anticipation. '24th Chasseurs, will form column of fours to the left, walk, march! Moench, sound Advance.'

Over the clatter of iron-shod hooves on the hard road, musketry sounded far to the north. A glow of artillery flares lit the horizon.

Jobert rode at the head of the dark column. Geourdai, Chabenac, Voreille, Bredieux and Peugeot followed. 'An hour to Rivoli,' said Jobert. 'The fighting we hear is our infantry pushing back the Austrian outposts before setting the line at dawn.'

As he rocked an exhausted Jaune to maintain the walking gait, Jobert let the officers' subdued chat wash over him.

'Why did we not strike forward at Verona when they withdrew?' asked Peugeot.

'The roads were poor and the rivers too full to allow resupply,' said Voreille. 'The Austrians suffered while we gorged on the scraps of Verona.'

'We were too poorly to attack them in the open,' said Chabenac. 'Our army is shattered. Our infantry are woefully short of officers.'

'Is that why the 33rd Ligne mutinied?' asked Peugeot. 'What were their officers doing?'

'Your fascination with mutiny is unseemly, Peugeot,' said Chabenac. 'That kerfuffle has settled. Their ringleaders have been shot.'

'And three whole companies imprisoned,' added Voreille.

'Why would they not mutiny?' said Geourdai. 'No shoes, no pay, no clothes, no hospitals, a quarter ration of bread per day.'

'How can there be no bread,' asked Bredieux, 'when Bonaparte has taken two million francs from Modena?'

'And four million francs from Livorno,' said Voreille.

'I expect the reason for the lack of bread is the lack of grain,' said Chabenac, 'despite the excess of gold.'

'But General Bonaparte has had three commissary officers executed,' said Peugeot.

'What I want to know is,' said Geourdai, 'where are the combined armies of Moreau and Jourdan and their one hundred and forty thousand men. Why are they not attempting to recross the Rhine?'

'Perhaps they are jealous of our dear Bonaparte's success,' said Chabenac.

'Piss on that,' said Bredieux. 'Our success.'

Jobert tickled Jaune's low hanging neck. 'Gentlemen, shut up. Look. Rivoli.'

In the icy still air, the broad extent of twinkling campfires of both armies was a moonlit spectacle. Above the low-hanging smoke from the multitude of enemy fires on the towering flanks of Mount Baldo, grey dawn smudged away the eastern stars.

Chapter Twenty-Seven
January 1797, Battle of Rivoli, Italy

Despite the bitter cold driving shafts of pain through their kidneys and their boot soles, General Masséna's dozen regimental commanders and senior staff officers raised their chests and chins to give an air of determination. Jobert stepped with care across the frozen mud, his knees aching from the overnight ride.

Across the half-circle, Raive frowned at Jobert's arrival before his face softened to a grim smile.

Squaring his shoulders, Jobert nodded in response.

Masséna's eyes slid across each face of his battle commanders. His eyebrows raised when he spied Jobert.

Jobert's throat tightened. 'Colonel Spiccard sends his apologies, sir. He—'

'He is indisposed, I understand.' Masséna tightened his lips as he raised his hand. 'Are you ready for the day, Jobert?'

'I am, sir.'

'Of course, you are.' Masséna opened his arms as he swept to the centre of the group. 'Gentlemen, we can see Rivoli sits on a plateau. The Adige River cuts a gorge to the east. A slight ridge curves around the plateau's rim to the west. All roads and paths onto the plateau ascend tight defiles which constrict any assault frontage and focus any defensive cannonades. We have a natural fortress at our disposal.

'The Austrians have columns ready to assault onto the plateau this morning. General Bonaparte has identified the greater threats being the enemy columns west of the Adige.

'The division which has been holding the valley for the past week has established the right of our battle-line, with entrenchments along the northern rim dominating the heads of the tight roadways. General Bonaparte expects they will receive the greater part of the enemy's focus today.

'Our division will hold the left of the line and provide reserves to General Bonaparte when called upon. It is now seven o'clock. Until I bring you forward into the line, the 32nd and 75th Ligne Regiments and the foot batteries may attend to breakfast.'

An exhalation of relief was expelled in clouds of stale steam from the assembly.

'Jobert and Suchet,' Masséna continued, 'General Bonaparte has been informed that an Austrian column is moving to our north-west along the western flanks of Mount Baldo. Suchet, march the 18th Ligne ten kilometres to Garda to block any advance towards the Mincio. Jobert, provide an escort for the 18th Ligne to Garda and locate that enemy column. Also, have the 24th Chasseurs maintain a screen beneath the plateau to the left of my line, but still maintain a reserve. With that tasking, Jobert, what will I have in my reserve?'

Jobert's chest swelled with excitement. *It begins. My first regimental deployment.* 'One company with the 18th Ligne to Garda. One company on your left flank. You will have two companies in reserve, sir, who shall piquet your resting battalions.'

The Austrian's opening bombardment roared from beyond the lip of a northern ridge five kilometres away. The morning air quivered. Small black puffs erupted as the occasional shell burst clear of the near horizon.

'Today,' said Jobert to his company commanders, 'Masséna's division will hold the left of Bonaparte's line with the 32nd and the 75th Ligne. The 18th Ligne is to secure Garda. Geourdai, 1st Company will escort Suchet's 18th Ligne to Garda … ten kilometres to the west.'

Geourdai scuffed backwards as his face tightened. The others winced as they glanced at Geourdai.

Jobert's stern gaze pierced Geourdai. 'An enemy column is suspected to the northwest. Locate that column. Take Yinot to report back on its location.' *Do you accept the task?* Jobert waited. Geourdai gave a curt nod.

'Chief of squadron Quillet,' continued Jobert, 'with Neilage's 4th Company, screen the left of the divisional line from below the plateau. Chabenac's 2nd Company and Voreille's 5th Company will be held in reserve to the left of the line. Chabenac, until the infantry and the foot batteries move forward, you are to piquet this divisional assembly area.'

Jobert looked across the smoky fire at men he had served with for four years. 'Questions? No? Then I have a question for all of you. We have fought outside Verona for the last two days. We have just pushed our horses for ten hours through a freezing night in fetlock-deep slush. Are your men tired?'

Everyone shuffled to either look away or peer intently at the ground.

Looking around the group, Jobert scowled at their hesitation.

Some looked down to give slight nods and shrugs. Koschak ground his teeth at the captains' response.

Jobert's nostrils flared in anger. 'Shit on your fatigue. Find your strength.' The young officers jerked in response. 'Mantua is about to capitulate within days. This is the fourth and final attempt to break us. The kaiserliks have played their diversion to the east. Today, if their main force breaks us at Rivoli, we will have achieved nothing these ten long months but a harsh walk back to Nice.'

Jobert stepped forward and chopped a flat, stiff hand at each face in his command group.

'Masséna holds the left of Bonaparte's line. The 24th Chasseurs hold the left of Masséna's line. Today matters. Find your strength.'

A bawl of voices jolted Jobert's aching shoulders erect. A rumble of shoes on gravel oriented his squint.

Along the Verona road jogged a broad throng of French infantry, well over two to three hundred routing bluejackets. In their midst, Masséna and two aides galloped towards 5th Company's outlying piquet.

Musket shots sounded from Voreille's chasseurs. The 5th Company trumpeter sounded To Arms.

'Chabenac, inlying piquet, stand to arms!' Jobert closed his watch cover with a snap. Nine o'clock. 'Moench, sound To Arms. Tulloc, fetch Bleu.'

Muscle-stiff horses and men groaned as 2nd Company's inlying piquet swung into their waiting saddles and formed column of fours. Masséna cantered past the camp of the 24th Chasseur's inlying piquet, shouting for his commanders. Among the resting battalions in reserve, drums beat To Arms. Masséna's three and a half thousand French infantry rose from their soup kettles, responding to their general's call with a roar.

'Who has caused the rout?' called Jobert. 'Have they come through 4th Company's screen?

Beyond the wheeling horses of Voreille's vedettes and their musketoon smoke, crouched a wide group of green-jacketed enemy infantry, distinct in their broad-brimmed, befeathered felt hats.

'Some form of jaeger, sir,' said Koschak. 'Austrian light infantry.'

'Chabenac,' called Jobert, 'form line and straight at them. Drive those kaiserlik light infantry back over the rim.'

Jobert trotted Bleu to the centre of 2nd Company's depleted battle-line. As he cocked his musketoon, Jobert looked beyond Chabenac to the company's troop lieutenants, Bredieux and Peugeot. 'Are your men ready, Bredieux?'

'2nd Company will not let you down, sir,' called Bredieux, amidst a swirl of tobacco smoke. 'We will show those idle 4th Company bastards how business is done.'

'Moench, sound Advance.'

With a cheer, the two ranks of thirty riders each surged forward over the uneven slush.

Jobert urged Bleu's trotting gait. With the cold having stiffened his body, his thrusting lower back and buttocks were gripped with pain. Working against the spasms, he watched the enemy. The Austrians sprinted from the approaching chasseurs. 'Too far from your fusiliers, boys. Moench, sound Charge!'

As Jobert lifted the musketoon's butt to his shoulder and skipped Bleu onto a right-lead canter, Bleu stumbled and broke to a trot.

'Chabenac,' called Jobert, 'drive them over the rim, then turn back.' Jobert fired his musketoon at the scampering green enemy mass. Jobert grinned as he reloaded. *Back where you should be, old friend.*

With horses huffing steam, Chabenac's chasseurs cantered past Jobert to discharge their musketoons into the backs of the fleeing light infantry.

'That is enough. We have seen them off.' Jobert swung down from the saddle. 'Moench, sound Rally.'

Jobert scraped the snow and mud from Bleu's hooves. Having checked that the shoes were still attached, and the sole of the hoof had not been pierced by a loose nail, Jobert mumbled to his horse as he itched Bleu beneath his bridle's straps.

'All well?' asked Koschak.

'I felt Bleu go lame in his near fore,' said Jobert. 'A stone-bruise, perhaps. With Jaune having marched ten hours, I intended to keep Rouge as a spare, but ...' Jobert gave a gentle stroke to Bleu's neck before placing the hoof pick back in his pistol holster. 'Did we bag any wounded? What do they have to say for themselves?'

'Yes, sir. These green jackets are volunteer jaeger legions. Gamekeepers and the like from their nobles' estates. They say they can shoot, so they sport rifles.' Koschak held out a captured weapon. 'Not all, maybe half.'

Jobert looked up from inspecting the rifle towards the muted roars of Austrian charges against the base of the plateau and the crackle of answering volleys. 'Our patriots showed their mettle at Valmy when they were told their homes were threatened. Perhaps Vienna attempts to plumb that spirit with these green jackets.'

'I do not doubt these kaiserliks' conviction,' said Koschak. 'Admittedly, those we opposed in '92 were in better condition than we are today. We may have a grim day ahead.'

Jobert straightened Bleu's forelock. Bleu dropped his great head so that Jobert scratched around the base of his ears. 'Our moment is still before us, old friend. You need to limp to keep Rouge fresh. Just a little while longer. Can you do that for me?'

Trumpets screamed from the northern ridges of the plateau. Sharp foreign calls.

Jobert shortened Bleu's reins as he scanned the gun smoke for enemy cavalry pouring towards the French reserve line. *Is this our time?* '2nd Squadron, stand to arms. Moench, sound Assembly.'

A savage explosion of guns silenced the enemy trumpets, their smoke obscuring Jobert's view. The exultant roar erupted from thousands of French throats. An intense and prolonged volley of musketry poured down the steep defiles.

'Sir,' said Moench, 'Captain Geourdai and Lieutenant Yinot approaching.'

Geourdai and Yinot slumped their lathered geldings to a halt. Both horses held their heads low and panted through blood red nostrils.

Geourdai fought to regain his own breath as he saluted Jobert. 'Sir, we found the Austrian column that approached from the north-west along the shores of Lake Garda. But we found them too late, sir. That brigade of four, perhaps five, battalions is now behind us. The enemy now blocks the Rivoli-Verona road at the southern end of the plateau.'

'Geourdai, how could you … of all people.' Jobert snatched at his watch. 'Eleven o'clock. Chabenac, take 2nd Squadron south.

Find this enemy brigade. Enclose them in a screen, 2nd Company to their south, 5th Company to their north. Geourdai, bring 1st Company into reserve. I do not care how tired your men think they are, you are now the only mounted reserve available to Masséna, probably even to Bonaparte. Geourdai, I know you have ridden fifty kilometres in eighteen hours, but do you understand the gravity of your post?'

Utterly exhausted, Geourdai blinked back tears. '1st Company stands ready, sir.'

'I do not doubt it, my friend.' Jobert twisted in the saddle to his aide de camp. 'Yinot, ride now to Masséna. Inform him of the situation and tell him I am placing a squadron screen around the enemy. That will leave him sixty sabres in his reserve. Repeat that message.'

Sucking air between clenched teeth, Yinot repeated the message, then regathered his reins.

'Lieutenant Yinot, stand fast, sir!' said Koschak swinging out of his saddle and looking to Jobert. 'This message needs a fresh horse, sir.'

As Koschak passed his reins to Yinot, Jobert nodded with grim appreciation. 'Then take your fresh Pegasus, Yinot, and fly.'

Chapter Twenty-Eight

Jobert jerked as Koschak, having sidestepped his horse into Bleu, discreetly thrust his knee into Jobert's thigh.

'Shrug off your dark humours, sir,' whispered Koschak. 'Now!'

Jobert closed his eyes and bowed his head. 'As the commander of Bonaparte's and Masséna's screen, I bear responsibility for the enemy arriving in our rear.'

Koschak's face reddened, his nostrils flared. 'That is horseshit, sir, because—'

Jobert held up a hand and looked Koschak in the eye. 'We can discuss this at our leisure later. As of this moment, I must fix this.'

Jobert scanned the ranks of the enemy infantry with his telescope.

Four fully manned battalions of white-coated Austrian fusiliers formed a three-rank fire-line extending five hundred metres either side of the Rivoli-Verona road. The enemy brigade held the defile through which the road ran before it descended south of the Rivoli plateau.

Austrian fusiliers draped in blankets, attended fires behind the rear rank, melting snow for water. They scoffed hungrily from their hands, not eating soup from bowls. Jobert identified four saddled horses, but no one mounted. A general in red trousers, but few officers in feathered bicornes moved along the line.

Jobert lowered his glass to look to farm paths ascending the flanking slopes of the four thousand Austrians. He recognised the enemy could be bypassed but were secure to any attack.

On the road in the middle of the Austrian line stood a four-gun battery. Jobert scrutinised them. Three-pounder mountain-guns , their pack mules standing behind them. *Pack mules. Limited ammunition.*

Jobert collapsed his glass. *Safe in numbers but worn thin. A decent shock will break you. But the longer you rest, your strength returns.*

Hundreds and hundreds of green- and brown-jacketed light infantry, their wide-brimmed hats turned up at the side, maintained a thick swarm of skirmishers up to one hundred metres out from the Austrian fusiliers' front rank.

Jobert remembered the grey-jacketed jaeger he experienced in Belgium. Those well-trained marksmen carried rifles with an assured range of two hundred metres. With careful observation, Jobert calculated at least ten, possibly twelve, companies of light infantry to the front of the enemy fusiliers. In essence, another two battalions to account for.

Koschak coughed a warning. Jobert turned. Yinot trotted towards them.

'General Masséna …' Yinot took a deep breath.

'Yes,' said Jobert, 'despite his outrage at our predicament, a situation he ordered me to prevent, Masséna presents his compliments. Very well, get on with it.'

Yinot grimaced. 'The reserve battalion of the 75th Ligne has orders to block any enemy advance into our rear. They march here now. General Masséna has ordered the immediate recall of the 18th Ligne from Garda.'

Jobert rubbed Bleu's neck. Until Suchet's 18th Ligne arrive, one French battalion of six hundred muskets and little more than one hundred sabres must hold four thousand Austrians in open meadows. He ground his teeth at the forbidding possibilities.

Jobert watched the 75th Ligne's reserve battalion approach as an attack column with a frontage of two companies. Each company of eighty fusiliers twenty-five men wide in three ranks. Forming a fire-line at the thrash of the drums, the front two companies in the column halted. The six companies behind, using the space between the companies in front of them, then moved left and right extending the line. Once the line set, the battalion's frontage now extended to one hundred metres. Over six hundred men in three ranks squeezed shoulder-to-shoulder, half a metre apart.

The drums ordered Skirmishers Out. Forty pairs of fusiliers scampered forward from the battalion's left flank, one hundred metres in advance of their mates in the ranks.

Extended for nearly five hundred metres, the four Austrian battalions readied themselves for the encounter.

Twelve o'clock. Jobert tucked his watch into his waistcoat fob pocket.

'Good afternoon, sir,' said the infantry battalion commander. 'The 3rd Battalion of the 75th Ligne at your service. How in the name of the Saviour have these bastards appeared behind us?'

Jobert pivoted in the saddle. 'How they came to be here is not the critical question, sir.'

The infantry major ground his teeth. 'What is your assessment of our foe, sir?'

'Four battalions of fusiliers, sir,' said Jobert. 'The brigade is well served by around ten individual companies of light infantry. You see the green- and brown-jackets, there? Some, but not all, are issued with rifles. These fellows can drop an individual target at two hundred metres. Their numbers provide two or three companies of skirmishers in front of each of their battalions. The range of their rifles pushes effective fire three hundred metres in front of their fusiliers' front rank.'

The infantry major's mouth twisted.

Jobert pointed to the pairs of mounted chasseurs. 'I have two companies of sixty sabres each screening north and south of the enemy brigade. At fifty metres, our musketoons are no match for rifles. But we restrict the limit of their skirmish line to one hundred metres from the safety of their front rank.'

Separated by over three hundred metres, both sets of opposing skirmishers minimised their exposure to one another. Voreille's 5th Company chasseurs trotted eternal muddy circles so as not to present a stationary target. The crouching Austrian jaeger remained alert to sprint to the safety of their line should the French cavalry charge.

'Perhaps, sir,' said the chief of battalion, 'if my skirmishers join your fellows, our muskets might even the terms.'

'As you wish,' said Jobert. 'You will note they have four three-pounder mountain guns in the centre of their line. They have been brought in by pack mules, so they have limited ammunition.'

'Three-pounder canister to three hundred metres.' The infantryman squinted at the intervening space. 'Effective range of three-pounder ball is six hundred metres. Here we are at eight hundred. If they advance, all my battalion can do is stand firm.'

'Are you aware Suchet's 18th Ligne marches to join us?' asked Jobert.

'Welcome news, indeed.'

Behind the 75th Ligne, the din of battle on the ridges to the north intensified. The incessant rattle of musketry, mixed with an undulating vocal roar and interspersed with the occasional ripple of cannon fire.

'What news from the front?' asked Jobert.

The infantry major grimaced. 'The regiments on the centre and the right are taking a beating. They have stood in line for eight hours now. Despite the slopes up to the plateau and the narrowness of the ascending roads, the kaiserliks press hard. Very hard.'

Multiple trumpet calls tore across the din four kilometres to their north.

'Ours, sir?' asked the infantryman.

'The Advance,' said Moench behind them.

Jobert searched the swirling gun smoke above the heads of the ranks of infantry. 'Yes, French calls. It appears our hussars and dragoons are committed. But to what?'

'Gentlemen, from General Masséna, the day is ours,' said Yinot. 'On the right, sir, less than two hundred of our dragoons have sent the kaiserlik columns reeling backwards. The enemy now stream north, pursued by our dragoons and hussars.'

Jobert, Suchet and the chief of battalion from the 75th Ligne turned their horses around to observe north. The heights which bordered the Rivoli plateau stood five kilometres away. Suchet and Jobert extended their telescopes. Many small groups moved along the slopes. On the paths in the saddles between the knolls, columns of infantry and artillery disappeared to the valley floor below.

'Very good, Yinot,' said Jobert. 'Any other messages from General Masséna?'

'Yes, sir, a battery of twelve-pounders comes to support the attack on the Austrian brigade which holds the Verona road.'

Suchet whistled. 'The kaiserliks will not like that.'

'Yinot, return to General Masséna,' said Jobert. 'Extend to him our compliments. Inform him the 18th Ligne has returned and now holds the enemy to the south.'

'Sir,' said Moench from behind the officers. Jobert twisted in the saddle to see a chasseur cantering towards them from the south.

'Yinot, stand fast,' said Jobert. 'Yes, Corporal Durand?'

'A French column approaches from the south, sir.' The soldier wheezed as he saluted. 'Captain Chabenac estimates four regiments.'

'Victor's reserve division,' said Jobert. 'Welcome news, thank you, lad. Has Captain Chabenac sent a messenger to the approaching column, informing them of the enemy holding the road?'

'Yes, sir, Lieutenant Peugeot was dispatched.'

Jobert twisted in the saddle to his aide de camp. 'Yinot, inform General Masséna that General Bonaparte's reserves are within two hours march from us. I will ride there now and liaise.'

'It is two o'clock and here are my battalions now,' said Suchet. 'I suggest, gentlemen, that the 18th Ligne form beside the esteemed 75th Ligne. We shall conceal the battery until the arrival of Victor's column from the south. Then the twelve-pounders can lay their gun-line to our front and tear the kaiserliks apart before we charge home from front and rear. Until we advance, might the 24th Chasseurs continue to restrict the proximity of the kaiserliks' volunteer rifles?'

'The services of our 5th Company restrict the jaegers' wanderings,' said Jobert. 'I shall have the company commander, Captain Voreille, attend you in my absence to the south.'

'Ah, General Victor arrives,' said Jobert.

Departing Chabenac, Jobert rode further south of 2nd Company's screen along the Verona road towards Victor and his approaching command party.

Jobert saluted Victor. 'Good afternoon ... sir.' Amongst the bicornes of Victor's commanders and staff, Jobert spotted a mirliton cap, wrapped in a capucine flame. The mirliton's owner was bowed and caped. *Spiccard!* A sneer spread across Spiccard's face as their eyes met.

'Promoted, Jobert?' said Victor. 'Congratulations. With Colonel Spiccard waylaid, the 24th Chasseurs are in good hands and Masséna well served. What do we have to our front?'

'The day is ours, sir,' said Jobert. 'General Bonaparte holds Rivoli. The enemy flees the field to the north. As to our immediate predicament, four battalions of enemy fusiliers and two battalions of light infantry stand across the Rivoli-Verona road. A battery of four mountain -guns holds the centre of their line.'

Victor looked to the cloud of gun smoke engulfing the dale through which the Rivoli-Verona road ran. 'How did they come to be here? Were our flanks not screened?' Victor shrugged off his frown. 'No matter, for here they are. What holds them firm?'

'They are positioned to block the retreat of our divisions,' said Jobert. 'With night soon falling, they stand ready to support any fresh Austrian assaults tomorrow.'

'They do not know they are lost?' asked Victor.

'The lull in the battle north of the plateau has only occurred in the last hour. They have no vision of their army routing north.'

'Who occupies them currently?' asked Victor.

'Suchet's 18th Ligne and a—'

'Suchet, eh? Again, we brothers of Toulon stand together in glory at the end.'

'Indeed, sir,' said Jobert. 'Also, a battery of twelve-pounders attends us.'

'Twelve-pounders, indeed.' Victor winced. 'This will be short work. I have a regiment at my immediate disposal. I will come straight at them with the bayonet. What is their formation?'

'They are near four thousand and remain in good order, sir,' said Jobert. 'They have changed formation as your column has approached. Two battalions face north, and two battalions face south, each face supported by a pair of three-pounders. The length of their adjusted line has reduced to under three hundred metres. They are well served by their jaeger, sir. You face around six volunteer companies armed with rifles, or two hundred and fifty pairs of skirmishers in four lines. They maintain effective fire some three hundred metres forward of the front rank of their fusiliers.'

Victor wobbled his head and tapped his fingers on his chin. 'My lead regiment will barely have one hundred pairs of skirmishers. These volunteer rifles will strip my skirmishers away and provide my assault a stiff approach before I can close on their fusiliers.'

'Suchet suggests allowing our twelve-pounders to soften the enemy line before you approach,' said Jobert. 'With the effective range of twelve-pounder canister at eight hundred metres, Suchet has ordered the gun-line to set at six hundred metres to their line. We may be blessed with a few of their pellets on our side of the enemy.'

Victor flinched. He closed his watch and twisted in the saddle to observe the progress of his dark blue infantry column.

'Three o'clock now,' said Victor. 'My lead regiment will be here by four o'clock. Then eight hundred metres to the Austrian line or eight minutes. I shall beat a tattoo to signal my intention to advance. On my tattoo, fire eight rounds of canister, on the minute, against their northern face. No ball mind you. I do not want to receive the shot into my ranks.'

'May I suggest, sir ...' Jobert's eyes flickered between Victor and Spiccard.

'Speak, Jobert,' said Spiccard, 'as you are the most conversant on the immediate topic.'

'May I suggest, gentlemen,' said Jobert, 'your drum corps' signal to the guns is reinforced with our trumpets.'

'Make it so,' said Victor. 'Now, what of these jaeger, Jobert? Can your ...' Victor turned to Spiccard. 'Can your chasseurs clear them?'

'We shall do our best, sir,' said Spiccard, 'Shall we not, Jobert?'

Sixty sabres against five hundred. Jobert's fingers tickled Bleu's shorn mane. *Here is the moment.* 'The 24th Chasseurs are ever at your service, sir.'

Jobert looked to the eastern horizon. A blanket of gun smoke obscured the surface of Lake Garda. Beyond the haze, steel-grey clouds draped over the Maritime Alps.

One hour until dusk.

'You have earned your rest, beautiful boy.' Jobert scratched Bleu's wither. 'Tulloc, fetch Rouge.'

From Victor's command group, Spiccard rode to join Jobert.

'Did the enemy evade the screens of the 24th Chasseurs?' asked Spiccard.

Jobert's heart sank and his guts churned. 'The enemy column's advance was known to General Bonaparte. General Masséna ordered Suchet's 18th Ligne to stand as flank guard. I attached Geourdai's 1st Company to Suchet to identify the column. In the intervening ten kilometres, the enemy failed to be detected.'

'Exhaustion and under-strength contributing to an unfortunately predictable outcome.' Spiccard shrugged. 'No matter. What are your views on our task, Jobert?'

Jobert's face creased with concern. 'I am unsure, sir.'

'You?' scoffed Spiccard. 'Unsure?'

Jobert lowered his face towards his pistol holsters. 'I have reflected on your counsel, sir. I seek a path of caution. As you have advised, I work to bend my impulsion to prudence.'

Spiccard searched Jobert's face. 'Then, perhaps my ... how have you disposed the regiment currently, Jobert?'

'Geourdai's 1st Company stands as General Masséna's reserve,' said Jobert, raising his face to the north, beyond the enemy brigade on the road. 'Neilage's 4th Company screens our left flank. Voreille's 5th Company screens this blocking force from the north.' Jobert turned to Spiccard. 'And, here in the south, Chabenac's 2nd Company stands at your convenience for the present task.'

'Then, there is your prudence, Jobert,' said Spiccard. 'The regiment has received an order to which you have determined only one quarter of the regiment need be committed.' Jobert frowned as he stared at a point beyond Spiccard's mount's ears. 'Jobert,

I approve your economy. Now, summon your 2nd Company brigands, release your intuition and describe your scheme.'

Returning his focus to the road running towards Verona, Jobert watched the steady plod of Victor's lead infantry regiment approaching the southern edge of the Rivoli plateau. 'Moench, sound Commanders In.'

Chabenac, Bredieux, Peugeot and Koschak gathered around Jobert and Spiccard. Their eyes shifted apprehensively between Jobert and Spiccard.

A smirk spread across Spiccard's face. 'Gentlemen, we have been tasked by General Victor to clear the enemy jaeger. Listen now to Jobert's orders.'

Jobert gave a nod to Spiccard before turning to the others. He stared hard at each man. 'The kaiserliks know they are doomed, but they will not give themselves lightly. They will shred any morsel they can reach. We are that morsel. Our time is upon us.'

The officers straightened themselves in their saddles.

'Once Victor is ready to assault,' said Jobert, 'he will signal for the twelve-pounders to come forward. On that signal, Chabenac, take Peugeot's troop to the left. I shall take Bredieux's troop to the right. Trot forward in skirmish pairs, three horse lengths apart.

'There are two companies of jaeger forward of each battalion facing us. They are packed tight. They will easily block our infantry skirmishers and tear open the front ranks of our attack, but they will run from us. Aim for the outer edge of the kaiserlik line. Push the jaeger toward the central road to confound their guns.

'I will stand firm in front of their line marking where you will peel away. On my order, sweep across the exposed front rank of their fusiliers at one hundred metres out and fire. The kaiserliks will hold their first volley for the attack column.'

Bredieux's and Peugeot's eyes flickered from Jobert's face to the enemy line. 'Questions?'

'Yes, Jobert,' said Spiccard. 'Where would you recommend my station?'

Jobert's face tightened. 'Might I suggest you take the *tri-couleur* forward with Chabenac on the left, sir? We shall all rally on you and the standard.'

The officers turned their horses to take their posts.

'Chabenac?' A tightness gripped Jobert's chest. He extended his gloved hand to Chabenac. 'Good luck.' Jobert gripped Chabenac's hand hard. 'I believe Orlande has tucked away a decent bottle for dinner this evening. You will join me, will you not?'

'The field is ours, sir,' said Chabenac, his face softening to a relaxed smile, 'and Mantua will soon yield. The 24th Chasseurs lead the last action of the day. With you, sir, at the front of 2nd Company, who can doubt success? As for dinner, why ever not? I shall see you all at the rally point.'

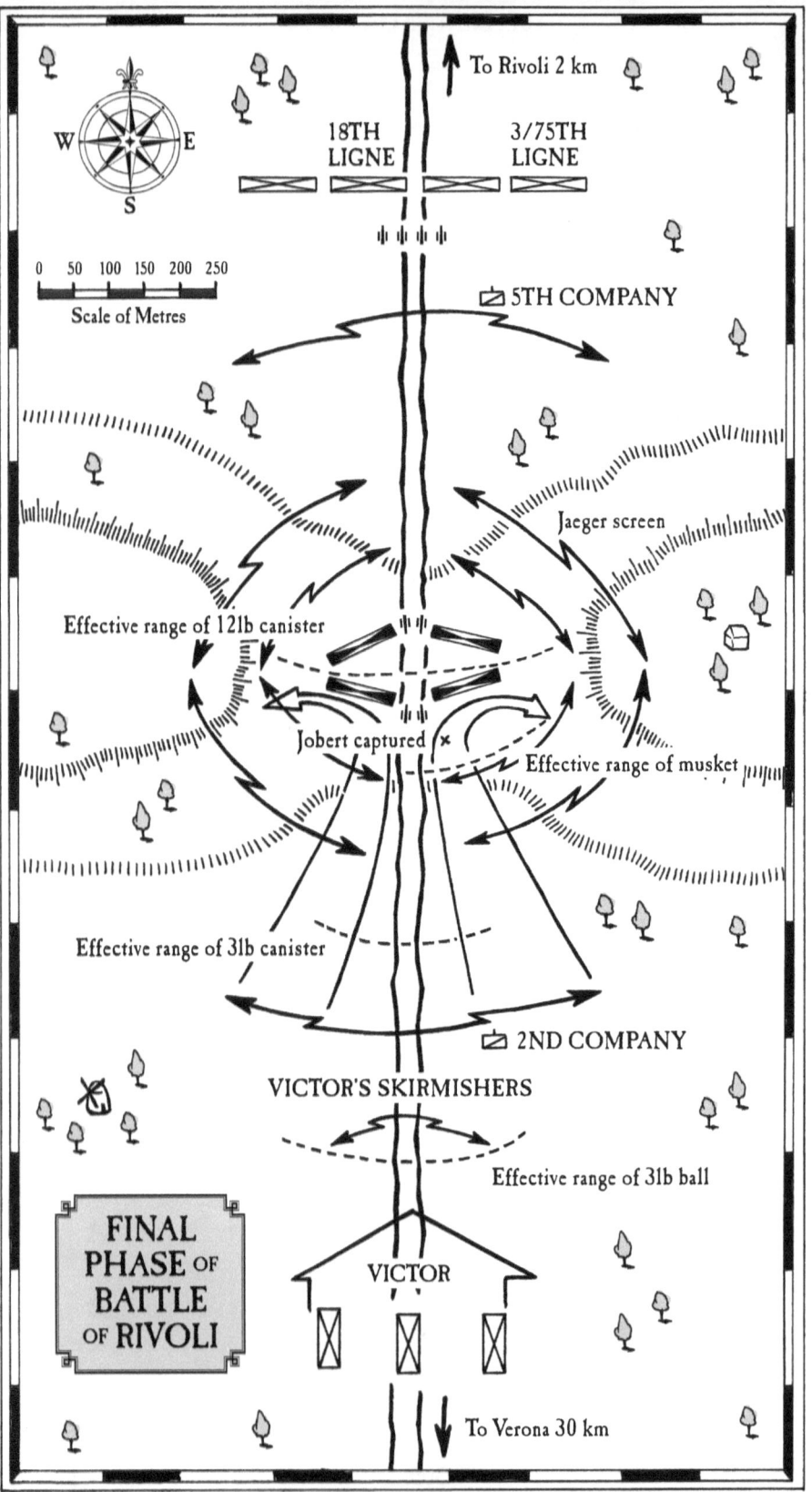

To Rivoli 2 km

18TH LIGNE

3/75TH LIGNE

5TH COMPANY

Jaeger screen

Effective range of 12lb canister

Jobert captured

Effective range of musket

Effective range of 3lb canister

2ND COMPANY

VICTOR'S SKIRMISHERS

Effective range of 3lb ball

VICTOR

FINAL PHASE OF BATTLE OF RIVOLI

To Verona 30 km

W E
S
(compass rose)

0 50 100 150 200 250
Scale of Metres

Chapter Twenty-Nine

Four hundred metres behind the chasseur screen and eight hundred metres from the Austrian three-pounders blocking the road, Jobert turned to watch Victor's leading French battalion form an attack column to the side of the road. The halted column splayed outwards from its centre. Two eighty-man companies formed three ranks either side of the centre point. The other six companies replicated the movement behind so that the battalion became fifty men wide and twelve men deep.

The next battalion in the regiment formed an identical formation on the road. The final battalion formed the same to the other side of the road. The regiment now sat ready to launch, one hundred and fifty men wide covering a frontage of seventy-five metres.

Victor, his commanders and the regimental drum corps of thirty drummers, positioned themselves front and centre on the road. 'Beat Skirmishers Out.'

One company in the rear ranks of each battalion dissolved into pairs at the rattling beat from the drum corps. Near two hundred and forty skirmishers scurried forward the rear of Jobert's chasseur screen.

Jobert cocked his musketoon. At the familiar sound, Rouge threw his head in discomfort as rein pressure was eased.

'I need your strength today, my beautiful man,' said Jobert. He tickled Rouge's wither before pulling back his shabraque and cocking the exposed pistol. 'Bring us home and I will buy you an orchard of apples.' Rouge tipped his nose and nipped at Jobert's stirrup.

Upon Victor's signal, the drum corps erupted with an air-shattering drum roll. The tattoo's undulations rose and fell. The signal to the twelve-pound battery, fifteen hundred metres away on the far side of the enemy block, that Victor was ready to assault.

Jobert shortened his reins. 'Moench, sound To Mess.' 2nd Company's trumpeter replicated the call. Beyond the Austrians on the rise, 5th Company repeated the call to indicate the signal was received.

'Do not freeze in front of the enemy, lads,' yelled Koschak. 'Keep moving your horses in small circles. Corporal Durand, you know better, put a toe in their arses.'

Jobert turned Rouge with his knee to face Bredieux's mounted skirmishers.

The fear amongst the new chasseurs was palpable. Jobert squeezed Rouge into a trot amongst the skirmishers. *No years of preparation for them.*

'Listen in, lads,' called Jobert. '2nd Company has always done well in the face of the kaiserliks. Most of you fellows here have skirmished along the front of a fire-line. They will not fire at you. They need to keep their touchholes clean for our attack columns. Lads, listen, our twelve-pounders are coming forward. We are to sweep away the jaeger and expose the kaiserliks to our infantry's assault. On Advance, trot forward with me. Sergeant Major Koschak and I will mark the point you are to sweep right. On Moench's call To Mess, sweep to your right and fire. On Moench's call, rally on Bredieux. One hour until sunset and this is all over.'

The next five minutes passed slowly before 5th Company sounded To Mess once more.

The two Austrian three-pounders, sited on the northern side of the defile, fired. 'Our twelve-pounder battery is forming line,' cried Jobert to Bredieux's thirty skirmishers around him. 'Sixty seconds to fire. 2nd Company, ready'. Grips tightened on the waists of sixty musketoons' stocks.

Jobert turned to Moench. 'Moench, sound ...' Moench's eyes flickered with fear as he gulped at the freezing air. 'Moench, look at me. Keep your eyes fixed on Rouge's arse, Moench. Just stay up with his rump. Stay with me. We all need you now. We all need you to sound Advance.'

Moench wiped his brow with his glove cuff and brought the trumpet's mouthpiece to his lips.

Jobert set his mind for the four hundred metres to the fusilier line and the muzzles of the three-pounders laid down the road. Hunting bugles called the squatting light infantry to readiness. *Sixty seconds of trotting up a gentle incline. How hard could it be?*

Jobert shortened his reins and drew his sabre. Rouge lifted his shoulders in expectation. Jobert rocked Rouge to a trot up the slope to the right of the road, staying wide of the cone of fire from the pair of Austrian cannon.

Three hundred metres from the fusilier line, bugles blew and the first rank of jaeger fired and withdrew to the safety of their fire-line.

Rifle rounds zipped by. Grunts and cries as ball thwacked into the oncoming men and horses.

Double-shotted, one three-pounder fired. The ball cracked the mud-slicked road as it bounced for the second time, three hundred metres from the gun. Along the road, the gravel hissed as the canisters' balls ripped into the road surface before leaping and clattering to a stop.

A shiver passed though Rouge. Jobert squeezed him into a longer trot stride. *Why fire? Confirming the shot's grazing bounds? Firming the fusilier's resolve?*

Bugles honked. A second line of jaeger fired before scuttling back. Balls zipped to punch chasseurs from saddles.

At two hundred metres from the fusiliers a third line of jaegers fired. With jaeger streaming back around the ends of the fusiliers', intermittent fire zipped high.

The other three-pounder fired. Bugles signalled. The remaining jaeger rose from their kneeling positions to run for the white-jacketed ranks.

At one hundred metres from the fusiliers, just beyond their effective range, Jobert lifted his reins. Rouge checked his swinging gait. *The fusiliers will save their volley for our columns. I hope.*

Beyond their ranks a distant gun fired. A ripple of cries from the far Austrian ranks facing north. Canister pellets whizzed overhead.

The two white battalions closest to Jobert, their lines extending one hundred metres away either side of the mountain-guns on the road towards the flanks of the defile, shuddered. Heads turned at the French twelve-pounder threat behind them.

A three-pounder fired. The ball thudded into the road close by Jobert before leaping toward the packed ranks of the French assault.

'Moench, sound To Mess,' called Jobert. A quick glance confirmed the French skirmishers trotting forward, still one minute away from bringing their fire against the Austrian ranks.

As chasseurs thundered forward on Moench's stuttering blast, a cacophony of musketoons cracked towards the Austrian front rank, drowning out the twelve-pounder canister fire seven hundred metres away.

Jaeger rifles fired at the horsemen swirling through their smoke cloud.

Koschak fired his musketoon into the backs of the jaeger surging between the guns and the files of patient fusiliers. 'Moench, stay focused on our last man passing Jobert.' Koschak reloaded. 'I will watch the fucking kaiser—'

A thump from a ball striking flesh.

Koschak's horse emitted a wavering grunt before staggering sideways. Koschak bellowed with pain as he kicked his feet free from his stirrups. His horse collapsed with a deep moan. Koschak screamed as his horse rolled on his lower leg, trapping his foot.

'My leg is broken,' said Koschak, as his horse quivered, its legs jerking straight as it died. 'I am trapped.'

'Moench, take my reins,' called Jobert as he sidestepped Rouge towards Moench's grey. Balls zipped as jaeger and chasseurs fired close by. As jaeger balls thumped into his neck and hindquarters, Rouge jerked to the right before crumpling.

Determined to clear sabre, musketoon and right leg from Rouge's collapse, Jobert threw himself to his left. Arm outstretched backwards, his recently mended collarbone snapped. A spasm of nausea rocked him.

Green jackets sprinted towards him, bayonets lowered, shouting in German. 'He is an officer. Take him alive.'

Jobert rolled away from Rouge's heaving. Adrenalin flooded his body. His vision narrowed. Vomit, from the pain in his shoulder and chest, scorched his throat. He lifted his left wrist to grip his collar, his useless left arm crooked across his body.

Jobert extended his musketoon in his right-hand and fired at the nearest jaeger. The man's head snapped backwards.

Jobert wrenched the agonising weight of cross belts, with

cartridge box and musketoon, from his left shoulder. The surge of relief. The need to piss. Glancing at Koschak at his feet, Jobert snatched at his sabre's grip. With a deft parry against a clumsy bayonet thrust, Jobert let the blade slide down the musket barrel.

The jaeger lost his fingers. A scream. The bayonet withdrew.

'Sir, take my stirrup,' shouted Moench.

'Moench, go,' bellowed Jobert. 'Go now! Do it! Sound Rally for Bredieux.'

Rouge groaned in an attempt to stand. His hind legs kicked out at Koschak's head and ribs. Jobert's chest shrivelled in misery at the sight of Rouge. Jobert released his sabre onto its sabre knot, then grabbed at the pistol butt in his nearside holster.

'Enemy behind. Fire!' yelled Koschak.

Jobert spun and fired.

A jaeger gasped as his butt stroke swung wide.

Rouge continued to scramble. His hind legs would not respond. His flailing hooves struck at Koschak, who shielded his face with his forearms from the heavy blows.

More jaeger circled the two downed horses.

'Where is my second fucking pistol?' Jobert clawed at his other pistol holster. 'Has Tulloc not transferred it from Bleu?'

'That fucking von Maefeld has it,' said Koschak.

'That utter bastard.' *Reload! Where is my cartridge box? Under Rouge's hooves.*

Rouge extended his neck to rise yet again.

Jobert dropped the pistol and lunged with his sabre at Rouge's outstretched throat. The blade sliced through arteries, veins, oesophagus and trachea.

Blood gushed from the wound. Rouge rolled his eyes towards Jobert. Jobert howled in anguish as he sawed upward into Rouge's vertebrae, cutting into the spinal column.

As he subsided, Rouge's eyes dulled, but never left Jobert's tear-streaked face. His sabre stuck fast in Rouge's crimped neck, Jobert was yanked off his feet as his sabre was ripped from his grasp.

'Now! Get the bastard,' said a German voice.

'Jobert, take mine.' Koschak fumbled with his sword knot trapped by his glove cuff.

A shot above. A jaeger spun away.

'Sir, take my stirrup.' Moench again. This time with Bredieux and Durand.

'Not without Koschak.' Jobert heaved one-handed on Koschak's cross belts. Koschak screamed.

More shots. Durand toppled from his saddle knocking Jobert down onto Koschak. Both men bellowed in pain. In frustration.

Jobert shrugged Durand's bulk from him. An instant mist of blood appeared from Bredieux's head and arm. Bredieux rocked backwards, his pipe fell from his teeth into the bloody mire.

'Moench, save Bredieux,' screamed Jobert. 'Do as you are told. Just fucking go!'

Somewhere in the smoke generated by the continually firing three-pounders, whistles shrieked. The remaining jaeger jerked towards the sound.

'Our skirmishers are deploying,' said Koschak, flapping at the blue-black shapes in the haze around them.

'Take them alive!' said a German voice. 'Take them both to the general.'

Jobert groped for his dagger within his left cuff. With the jacket sleeve angled across his chest to support his injured left arm, the blade's handle was elusive to his gloved fingers.

A jaeger stepped forward and delivered a butt stroke.

Its impact shattered Jobert's jaw. Flames seared his face and neck . Jobert stumbled to his knees, sobbing with pain. His mouth poured with blood and saliva down his thighs. Jobert's tongue brushed against slivers of bone in his mouth.

Rough hands heaved him to his feet.

French skirmishers fired. Flames clawed the dense smoke. Struck by a ball, a jaeger supporting Jobert leapt away. The falling man tugged on Jobert's injured left arm. His shoulder flared with pain.

Jobert jerked to a familiar trumpet call. *Rally? Are they clear?*

A three-pounder detonated close by, its heat wave slamming Jobert.

His captors shoved him past the three ranks of one Austrian battalion into an inner world of bellowing Austrian sergeants.

A dull boom through the smoke. The French twelve-pounders maintained their lethal spray. Pellets hissed overhead. Pellets ripped into bodies nearby. Muskets clattered onto the wounded. Austrian sergeants roared to close files.

Jobert was released behind the three-pounder guns in the middle of the line.

'Canister, load.' Jobert observed a brown-jacketed artillery officer at the rear of a three-pounder scrutinise his watch. *He cannot see Victor's lads, so he estimates . I guess three minutes ... three more minutes of twelve-pounder canister.*

The jaeger slumped Koschak against Jobert. As Koschak returned Jobert's gaze, his face twisted with appalled concern at Jobert's injuries. Koschak hopped to keep his balance. 'Help me stand, sir.'

'Cannot ... hold you.' Jobert mumbled through his broken jaw. Excruciating pain buckled Jobert's chest as he was unable to lower Koschak's weight to the mud.

Koschak vomited with shock. He wiped the beads of mucous from his stubbled chin. 'Here we are in our hour of glory, sir ... and we have lost our fucking mirlitons.'

Jobert loose jaw flexed at the unexpected humour, and then winced in pain at the movement.

An Austrian general approached as the three-pounder rocked back on its trails, spewing its blast. The general's white jacket was black with grime, his red trousers torn. The man's bicorne was pulled down hard onto loose locks unravelling from his powdered curls.

'How close is France to breaking?' the Austrian asked Jobert.

'Us breaking?' said Jobert. 'Day ... ours. Austria ... flees north. France pursues.'

'You lie! How dare you lie to me now on the field of honour.'

Jobert spat blood to clear his mouth. 'We ... no cavalry ... force you to square. All in pursuit. Smaller guns north. If we are ... to break,' Jobert struggled to speak against the bloody dribble, 'why bring twelve-pounders out of our line?'

The Austrian snarled as he held Jobert's eye.

Canister pellets hissed from the north. Skirmishers' musket balls zipped from the south.

Bodies were dragged into the space behind the battalions' rear ranks to be piled onto mounds of writhing fusiliers, their jackets and trousers soaking dark red. Hundreds and hundreds of silent jaeger squatted on their haunches, cringing between the outfacing white ranks, rifling through the dead and wounded for water.

'Stand up, you cowards!' roared the general at the morose jaeger. 'Even these French bastards remain standing under their own fire.' He turned and smoke swallowed him.

The mountain-guns fell silent. Their crews, having expended all their ammunition, sat on their mules' corpses and wept.

Whistles pierced the smoke.

'Their skirmishers withdraw,' shouted sergeant majors behind the rear rank of the south facing battalions. 'Now, boys, it is our fucking turn.'

Jobert watched those sergeant majors step over their wounded who were rolled onto their sides, their backs torn open by canister.

Austrian drums smacked an insistent beat. 'Battalion, present!'

Eight hundred muskets clattered off shoulders and into readiness, firelocks clacking back to fire.

French drums changed tempo.

The gun smoke thinned on the breeze.

Jobert saw Victor's lead regiment shuffle to a halt one hundred metres away. Their muskets came off their shoulders. Waving their swords, dark command figures in bicornes stood on the road in the centre of the line.

'Fire!' All along the Austrian line, disciplined blasts rippled by half-companies. Cartridge papers flitted within the gun smoke. Ramrods clattered in and out of muzzles.

The French line sizzled in a sheet of flame. A single regimental volley of two hundred balls from the front two ranks.

Jobert bowed his head to the incoming hail. Balls hissed across the abandoned mountain-guns, pinging off barrels and wheel rims.

The Austrian line staggered backwards. Bodies were thrown to the rear.

Muskets fired in spasms. Cowering jaeger screamed.

French drums pounded. French voices roared. French shoes rumbled.

The jaeger started to run.

The Austrian fusiliers stepped back or were pushed back. The rear rank broke to hop over the mounds of wounded.

Men tripped around Jobert and Koschak. Koschak roared as his broken leg was buffeted in the stampede. Jobert knelt and wrapped his right arm around Koschak.

Howling blue jackets and flashing bayonets tore amongst the scrambling green and white jackets. The frantic jaeger pushed against Jobert and Koschak in their fear.

Closing with their quarry, the French straddled the bodies

underneath. French fusiliers thrust and slashed with their bayonets. On withdrawing their bayonets, the French would follow up with a butt stroke.

Impaled by a thrust, a green-jacketed jaeger fell screaming beside Jobert. The French fusilier put his foot on the Austrian's writhing chest. He wrenched his bayonet free. His manic eyes locked on Jobert's green-jacketed chest.

'We ... French.' Jobert coughed against his dribble.

'We are French chasseurs, you dumb bastard,' called Koschak.

Jobert was only able to cover his mangled jaw with his right elbow before the Frenchman's butt smashed into his left eye.

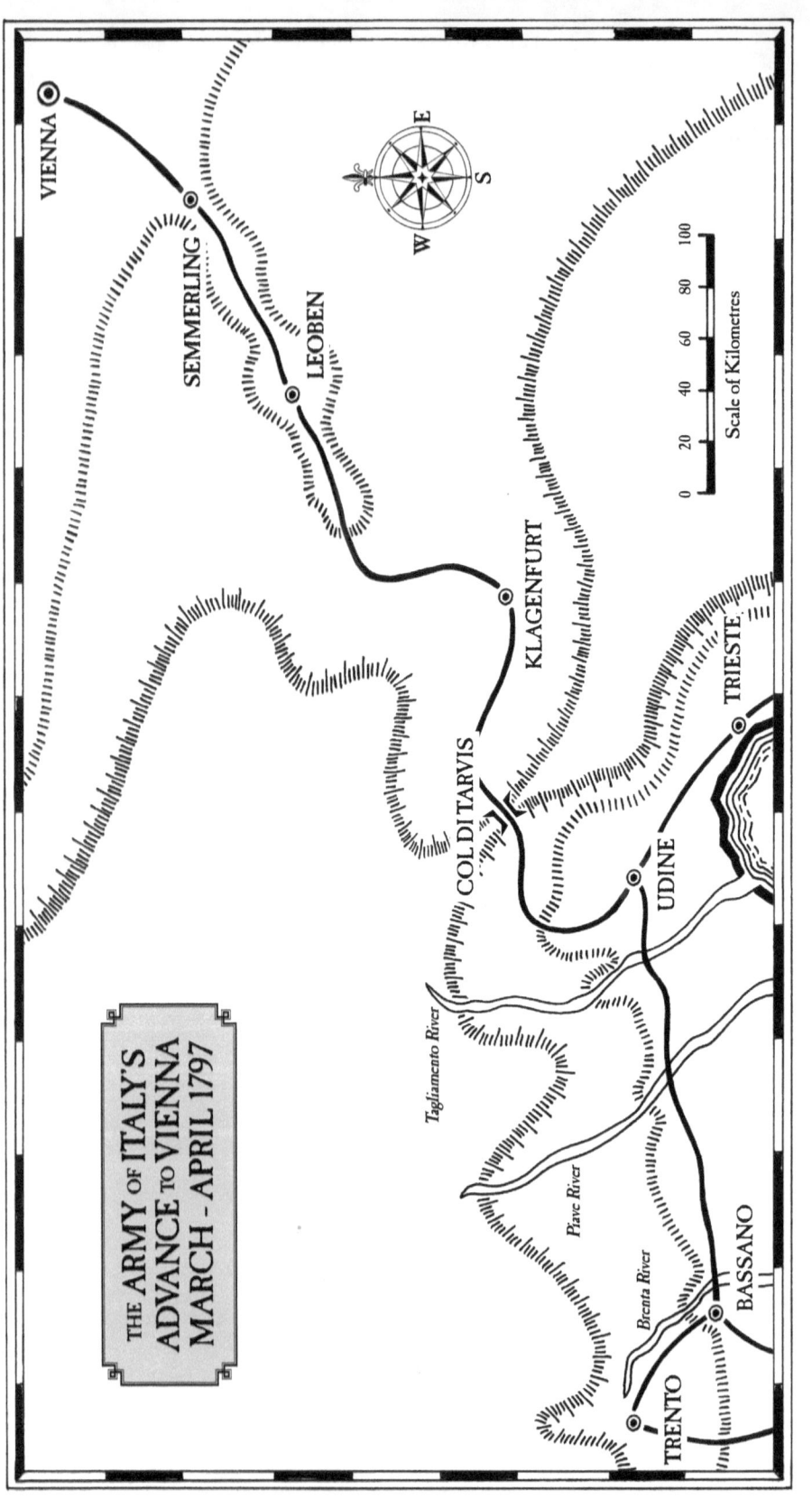

THE ARMY OF ITALY'S ADVANCE TO VIENNA MARCH - APRIL 1797

VIENNA

SEMMERLING

LEOBEN

KLAGENFURT

COL DI TARVIS

TRIESTE

UDINE

Tagliamento River

Piave River

Brenta River

TRENTO

BASSANO

Scale of Kilometres

0 20 40 60 80 100

N W E S

Chapter Thirty
March 1797, Bassano, Italy

As the four companies of the regiment marched past in review, Jobert, standing rear of the reviewing party, saw tremors run the length of Spiccard's sabre.

The reviewing officer, General Masséna, noticed them too. 'What say you, Spiccard?' asked Masséna. 'One last advance?'

Spiccard wheezed as he lowered and raised his blade in salute. 'Just the one, sir? Why? Are your infantry unable to maintain the resolute pace of the 24th Chasseurs?'

Jobert breathed through his headache – his fractured eye socket still gave him pain – as he reflected on the eight weeks since Rivoli.

Bonaparte's army had conquered Lombardy. With the failure of the fourth Austrian attempt to break through to Mantua at Rivoli, the emaciated, diseased garrison of the great fortress had capitulated in early February.

France's latest ally, the newly created Cisalpine Republic centred on Milan, now controlled the bountiful Lombardian plain. Initiated by Bonaparte, this invention of the French Republic drove the Emperor of Austria with greater urgency to the negotiation table.

Bulletins from Bonaparte's headquarters described how his Army of Italy posed a direct threat to Vienna, and considerable numbers of Austrian units were being transferred from the Rhine. To counter these fresh troops, Bonaparte ordered an advance into Austria to hasten the peace process.

Now the 24th Chasseurs departed Bassano for Vienna.

Jobert rolled his tongue within his tender jaws and felt the smooth gumline which had lost three teeth. He looked forward to purchasing a fine set of Viennese dentures.

Jobert gave a grim smile to Chabenac as 2nd Company passed the senior officers. While the regiment passed in review, Jobert ran his eye over the regimental remounts stumbling past, hooves scarcely skimming the icy mud. Despite the attentive brushing, thick, scruffy coats softened the press of ribs and hips through gaunt skin. With manes hogged short, the horses held their heads low, their listless tails flicking.

Jaune twitched his ears as Jobert tickled his wither. Standing rock steady with head relaxed, now a veteran warhorse, Jaune was not inclined to expend any unnecessary energy.

Campfire scuttlebutt agreed the advance into the snow-clad peaks of Tyrol was a desperate gamble. Jobert studied the faces of the chasseurs as they passed in review. Either jaws clenched in bloody determination or eyes dull, faces impassive at the relentless demand to march. The strength of the emaciated 24th Chasseurs was two hundred sabres. Four companies of fifty men, captains commanding troops, sergeants leading sections.

Jobert raised his gaze northeast, towards the tattered remnants of the Austrian army across the Tagliamento River. Raive had whispered that Austrian ranks were swollen by untrained schoolboy conscripts raced from Vienna. The shadow of Inoubli slid beneath such information.

The last troop of the regiment passed.

'Back from Milan, Jobert?' asked Masséna. 'I have not seen you since Rivoli. The 24ᵗʰ Chasseurs performed admirably there. Thank you for that.'

Jobert bobbed his head. Masséna took his leave.

Spiccard grinned without humour over his shoulder at Jobert. 'Did you find Milan pleasant this time of year?'

'I visited both Depot Company and the hospitals, sir.'

'Koschak and Bredieux?' asked Spiccard.

'They both avoided the surgeon's saw and convalesce well,' said Jobert. 'Koschak reports his delight in being issued a replacement mirliton.'

'Hah! And did you pay the regiment's respects to the widow Fergnes?' asked Spiccard.

Jobert adjusted his weight in the saddle. 'My duties restricted me to impose briefly on the ladies for morning coffee. I can report the household quite well, sir.'

Spiccard regathered his reins. 'No musketoon at the ready, Virginian?'

Jobert forced a smile. His healing left shoulder could not have borne the weight since. 'My forearm aches from wielding my quill these last weeks, sir, that I no longer have the strength to lift a musketoon.'

'Pah! Are you fit enough to advance to the Col di Tarvis, the gateway to the Austrian heartland?'

Three weeks later, freezing gusts buffeted the sides of the marquee to the rear of Jobert's cart.

With ascendency to regimental second-in-command, his cart became the location of the regimental headquarters while the 24th Chasseurs were on the march. Tucked in close to the cart's hissing firebox, Jobert cringed at his desk, flexing his frozen fingers around his quill. Horseshoes, upturned bowls and even one of Orlande's ladles served as paperweights for the reports and returns that lay across his folding camp table.

Yinot snorted a runny nose as he entered the marquee. 'From General Masséna's headquarters, sir.'

Jobert placed two envelopes addressed to himself into his tailcoat pocket, before he broke the divisional order's wax seal and read. 'Now we are to march from Klagenfurt to Leoben.' Jobert unrolled a chart of the area.

The 24th Chasseurs had led Masséna's infantry three hundred and twenty kilometres from Bassano to Klagenfurt in the last seventeen days. Now another order to march even further into Austria. A one-hundred-and-forty-kilometre stab deeper into the guts of the vast Holy Roman Empire.

'At headquarters, did you hear any further talk of peace?' asked Jobert.

'I did hear discussion of a ceasefire once the Austrian delegation returns,' said Yinot.

'Any news from the Rhine?'

'I asked, sir, but nothing has been heard of General Moreau returning to the Danube.'

Jobert clenched his lips to stop himself swearing.

'There is no further news of our invasion of Wales either, sir,' said Yinot.

Jobert looked up incredulous at the distraction. 'Returning momentarily to our own invasion, Lieutenant, General Masséna directs the 24th Chasseurs to lead the division another six-days' march closer to Vienna.'

At the news, Yinot's face flushed with disappointment and

his shoulders slumped.

Jobert narrowed his eyes at Yinot's unshaven jowl, unkempt hussar braids, threadbare cape, battered scabbard, filthy, patched over-breeches, and boots with split seams. 'The people of France declared war on the Holy Roman Emperor five years ago. The army of the people are on the verge of delivering that victory. Why would we not wish to provide greater encouragement to His Imperial Majesty's desire for peace?'

Yinot drew his chest up and raised his chin.

Jobert stretched back on his camp chair. 'We started together at Avignon four years ago, Lieutenant Yinot. In all that time as a chasseur, what would you say were the four essential elements of a cavalryman?'

Yinot wobbled as he looked about the marquee, scabbard clacking on spur. 'An intuitive knowledge of sabre and horse, sir.'

'That is certainly two.' Jobert scrawled an acknowledgement on the original order from Masséna's headquarters.

Yinot squinted at Jobert before blinking at the shuddering canvas walls. 'A heart that desires only to come within blade's length of the enemy.'

Jobert's placed down his quill, passing across the folded document. 'Quite so. And?'

'And ... a mind that never ceases to seek opportunity, sir.'

'Return my acknowledgement to Masséna's headquarters. Inform all company commanders to assemble here at two o'clock. Warn them for a four o'clock reveille. For, Yinot ... opportunity awaits.'

Jobert tore open the envelope from Marguerite. A waft of her scent brushed his nostrils.

Milan
1st March 1797

Dearest Jobert,

Just a quick note to let you know that Lieutenant Bredieux and Sergeant Major Koschak have arrived and are now well settled. Young Fergnes has his first tooth ...

We all send our best wishes and prayers,
Marguerite

Jobert scanned the letter. *What of us? Nothing.*
He opened the second letter.

Paris
26th January 1797

Darling André,

Father writes that Didier is home and well. Once the weather passes, they are all to come here for Didier to select a new foot. I wish you could join ... Duque visited last ... yesterday the baby ... Édouard continues to ... your annuity grows now that your lieutenant colonel's wage ...

One line caused Jobert to pause.

You are now our family's last soldier ...

Jobert brushed away a tear. Jobert folded the lilac pages and slid them into an inner pocket. *I will savour them tomorrow.*

Over a week later, as Raive raised a flap of the marquee to enter, a bitter gust caused the firebox to flare and spit. The slender flame on his desk threatened, Jobert lunged to shield the guttering candle. With the survival of the wavering yellow light assured, Jobert struggled from his blankets to stand in the presence of the senior officer. Jobert assumed an erect stance to salute. 'Broth, sir?'

Raive waived his hand in exasperation. 'No. For this special occasion I have brought a decent Ruster Ausbruch.'

Jobert poured the dregs of his tepid soup into the dirt. He rummaged for a spare cup in a box on the back of the cart which provided the back wall of the marquee. Dark lumps under the cart's axles snored.

'Where is Colonel Spiccard?' asked Raive.

'His fevers have sent him to bed, sir. If you have march orders, I shall fetch him.'

'Yes, I have march orders, but no, let him rest. Sit, man, before we both fall over.' Raive drew up a folding camp stool to the edge of Jobert's table and poured two cups of the fragrant liquor. 'How are you?'

'My headaches persist, sir,' said Jobert. 'The stiffness in my shoulder and jaw softens. My gum has healed with the loss of the teeth, but Orlande maintains my regimen of soup.'

Raive's face tightened. 'Do you take laudanum for the pain?'

'No.'

'Good,' said Raive. 'You were fortunate Victor's physician provided such swift attention at Rivoli. To our business. Word from Bonaparte's headquarters. His Imperial Majesty's pleni-potentiaries are to arrive here in Leoben within the next few days. Masséna's forward outposts are to press forward to the Semmering Pass, reinforcing to the Austrians how close we are to Vienna.'

Jobert took a deep breath and rearranged his documents to reveal a map of the area. Illuminated by a candle, his finger searched the chart, stopping when it found the Semmering Pass. 'Sixty kilometres. A march of three days to be ... one hundred kilometres from Vienna.'

Raive passed another mug of dessert wine across the desk. 'As it was for Turin, the peace negotiations will preclude us from entering Vienna. No Sacher torte with our schokolade.'

Jobert sagged. 'Nor dentures for my ammunition bread.' Jobert masked his sullen stare with a sip from his cup.

Raive smirked. 'And no immediate opportunity to arrange the return of your pistol.'

An image of Rouge's dying eyes engulfed Jobert's vision. He lowered his face. *Soon, von Maefeld.* 'Peace, you say, sir. What then?'

'Milan,' said Raive. 'Having been whittled down to two hundred sabres, the 24th Chasseurs are to be withdrawn from the line. The regiment is to refit in Milan.'

'Two hundred.' Jobert shook his head slowly. 'Three years ago, we marched into Nice with six hundred.'

'Absent brothers,' Raive toasted.

Jobert raised his cup. 'Absent brothers.'

'Speaking of brothers, any news from Didier?' asked Raive.

'I am aware that he arrived home safely, sir,' said Jobert.

'Then take leave, Jobert, return to your family. It would be over three years since you have been home, no?'

Jobert raised his chin to look Raive in the eye. 'That would be most pleasant, sir, but my family will have to wait. Colonel Spiccard's convalescence is the greater priority.'

Raive grimaced as he tapped his cup on the folding table. 'It has been a long year since leaving Savona. Bonaparte has marched the Army of Italy one thousand, three hundred kilometres, defeating an army of fifty thousand and forcing peace upon the greatest empire in Europe. All within twelve months.' Raive raised his cup. 'General Bonaparte.'

Jobert snorted. 'The Army of Italy, sir.'

'Army of Italy, indeed,' said Raive. 'You are no longer a sergeant, Jobert. I foresee your talents being used elsewhere than re-raising the regiment. I have a sense there will be a fresh beginning for you once we get back. As for our special occasion ...' Raive lifted his wine once more. 'Happy thirty-second birthday, Jobert.'

Jobert's adventures, from 1798 to 1800, continue in
Neither Up Nor Down.

Visit **www.jobert.site**
to learn more of Jobert's adventures.

Author's Note

This story is a work of fiction set within historical events. Those events referred to within the story are included in a chronology, an appendix to this book.

May I share with you, using one example, of how much fun these stories are to create?

I chose for Jobert to participate in the battle of Castiglione. On page 401 of my primary reference, Martin Boycott-Brown's *The Road to Rivoli* (Cassell & Co, 2001), I am gifted this opportunity to descend into imagination.

'... when the castle of Solferino was captured, putting the Austrian right in peril of being cut off. Indeed, Massena tried to outflank them, but was resisted by Schübirz and Mittrovsky, who had the good fortune to receive timely assistance from Weidenfeld. The latter appeared in the nick of time with his whole force of four battalions and one squadron, and subjected Massena to such an emphatic attack in the left flank, that he was obliged to discontinue his advance.'

I tease out Boycott-Brown's passage from a tactician's perspective. The requirements of the outflanking French and the counter-attacking Austrian commanders are clear.

What intrigues me are their orders to subordinate commanders to achieve what is described in the passage. How much space would the infantry formations absorb on the steep terrain on the eastern flanks of Solferino? How long would it take for them to change formation? As each element interacts, what would have been the reactions of the different commanders and their men?

How would the conflicting infantry commanders make use of the small units of cavalry available (the squadron of Austrian cavalry Boycott-Brown reports that was present and my fictitious insertion of Jobert's 2nd Squadron)? How would those cavalrymen and their horses react in turn?

To describe these actions and counteractions is not sufficient to the art of storytelling. More than the chapter remaining an account of sports-like interaction, how does it contribute to the tale? To move from tactical exposé to narrative structure, how does Jobert's involvement in the battle build tension towards the story's climax? What unexpected event causes a critical choice by Jobert which reveals aspects of his character?

It is a conundrum I, as a spinner of yarns, find immensely enjoyable, for which I thank historian Martin Boycott-Brown for the opportunity. For the example above, my solution is Chapter Seventeen.

I would welcome your thoughts on the matter, via **www. jobert.site**.

Rob McLaren
Veresdale, Queensland
February 2022

Bibliography

Bourgeot, V., *Les Tresors de l'Emperi*, Paris, 2009.

Boycott-Brown, M., *The Road to Rivoli*, London, 2001.

Bucquoy, E., *Les Uniformes Du Premier Empire*, La Cavalerie Légère, Paris, 1980.

Bukhari, E., *Napoleon's Cavalry*, London, 1979.

Calvert, M., Young, P., *A Dictionary of Battles, 1715-1815*, New York, 1979.

Chandler, D.G., *Napoleon's Marshals*, London, 1987.

Chartrand, R., *Napoleon's Guns 1792-1815*, Oxford, 2003.

Chandler, D.G., *The Campaigns of Napoleon*, New York, 1966.

Dodge, T.A., *Warfare in the Age of Napoleon*, Vol. 1, 2011.

Doisy de Villargennes, Chuquet, A., *Soldiers of Napoleon, The Experiences of the Men of the First French Empire*, 2008.

Dupuy, R.E., Dupuy T.N., *The Encyclopaedia of Military History*, London, 1970.

Devereux, F.L., *The Cavalry Manual of Horse Management*, Cranbury, NJ, 1979.

Elting, J.R., *Swords Around A Throne*, London, 1988.

Erkmann, E., Chatrian, A., *The History of a Conscript of 1813*, London, 1946.

Fremont-Barnes, G., *The French Revolutionary Wars*, London, 2001.

Haythornthwaite, P., *Austrian Specialist Troops of the Napoleonic Wars*, London, 1990.

Haythornthwaite, P., *Napoleonic Light Cavalry Tactics,* London, 2013.

Haythornthwaite, P., *Uniforms of the French Revolutionary Wars 1789-1802,* Poole, 1981.

Letrun, L., Mongin, J., *Chasseurs à Cheval, 1779-1815,* Vol. 1-3, Paris, 2013.

Maughan, S.E., *Napoleon's Line Cavalry – Recreated in Colour Photographs,* London, 1997.

Muir, R., *Tactics and the Experience of Battle in the Age of Napoleon,* Bury St Edmunds, 1998.

Napier, C.J., *Lights and Shades of Military Life. The Memoirs of Captain Elzear Blaze,* London, 1850.

Petard-Rigo, M., *La Cavalerie Légère du Premier Empire,* 1993.

Smith, D., *Napoleon's Regiments, Battle Histories of the Regiments of the French Army, 1792-1815,* London, 2000.

Tranié, J., Carmigniaini, J.C., *Napoléon Bonaparte 1ère campagne d'Italie,* Paris, 1990.

Walter, J., *The Diary of a Napoleonic Foot Soldier,* London, 1991.

Wise, T., *Artillery Equipments of the Napoleonic Wars,* London, 1979.

I also acknowledge the insights and detail provided by the Wikipedia, Google Maps and YouTube websites.

Chronology of Events

The following chronology lists the historical events that
are referred to within the story.

1796

2 Mar   General Napoleon Bonaparte assigned to
command the Army of Italy.

26 Mar   General Napoleon Bonaparte arrives at the
headquarters of the Army of Italy in Nice.

8 Apr   Austrian offensive begins with a coastal
advance towards Savona.

10-12 Apr Battle of Montenotte. Austrian launch attacks
along ridgelines above Savona resulting in a
French victory.

13-16 Apr Battles of Cosseria, Dego and Ceva. French
victories which divide the Austrian and
Piedmontese forces.

19-21 Apr Battle of Mondovi. French victory over
the Piedmontese.

27 Apr   Armistice with Piedmont. Under Bonaparte,
French forces defeat Piedmont within
fourteen days.

28 Apr– French forces advance into Lombardy to
10 May   cross the Po River at Piacenza and secure
victory at the Battle of Lodi.

14 May   French forces enter Milan.
Napoleon establishes the Cisalpine Republic.

23-26   Civilian insurrections in Milan, Binasco
May   and Pavia crushed by French forces.

29 May– Battle of Borghetto. French cross the
2 Jun   Mincio River and begin the siege of Mantua.

5 Jun	Napoleon signs armistice with Naples.
15-26 Jun	Bonaparte's military expedition against the Papal States ends with a signed armistice and British fleet evicted from Livorno.
29 Jul– 6 Aug	First Austrian counter-offensive raises the siege of Mantua. Battles of Lonato and Castiglione. With a French victory, the siege is re-established.
4 Jun– 16 Sep	Moreau and Jourdan advance across the Rhine River and down the Danube River. Jourdan is defeated at the battles of Amberg and Würzburg. Moreau withdraws west of the Rhine.
1-15 Sep	Second Austrian counter-offensive. Battles of Rovereto, Trento, Bassano and San Giorgio. The siege of Mantua is raised. With a French victory, the siege is re-established.
21 Oct– 23 Nov	Third Austrian counter-offensive. Battles of Fontaniva and Caldiero before the French victory at Arcole.
15 Dec– 13 Jan	French invasion of Ireland fails.

1797

7-16 Jan	Fourth Austrian counter-offensive. Decisive French victory at the Battle of Rivoli.
2 Feb	Fortress of Mantua capitulates. France controls Lombardy.
22-24 Feb	French invasion of Wales fails.
15 Mar– 15 Apr	French advance to Klagenfurt and Leoben.
18 Apr	Napoleon forces the Peace of Leoben on Austria.

Ready Reference – Military Organisations

A quick and simple overview of military organisations:

Squad/File/Patrol – Cavalry soldiers were grouped together in threes or fours to patrol, cook and sleep together as well as ride together in larger formations.

Section – Twelve men, when at full-strength, or three squads/files, commanded by a corporal.

Platoon – Two sections, twenty-four men at full-strength, commanded by a sergeant.

Troop – Two platoons, fifty men at full strength, commanded by a second lieutenant.

Company – Two troops, one hundred men at full strength, commanded by a captain.

Squadron – Two companies, commanded by the senior captain of the two companies.

Regiment – Three or more squadrons of cavalry or battalions of infantry commanded by a colonel. A cavalry regimental commander had two chiefs of squadron (major) who assisted him by commanding squadrons on independent tasks.

Brigade – Two or more regiments of infantry or cavalry, with supporting artillery, engineers and logistic support, commanded by a brigadier (a rank of general).

Division – Two or more brigades, with associated support, commanded by a major general.

Corps – Two or more divisions, capable of significant independent operations, commanded by a lieutenant general.

Army, or Army Wing – Two or more corps, commanded by a general.

Ready Reference – Measurement Conversion

An approximate conversion of metric measurements:

One inch is approximately two and a half centimetres.

One metre is approximately one yard, or three feet.

One thousand metres, or one kilometre, is approximately two-thirds of a mile (five-eighths).

One mile is approximately one and a half kilometres.

One kilogram is approximately two pounds.

One litre, or one kilogram of water, is approximately two pints.

Dramatis Personae

This story is a work of fiction within a historical setting.
In the list below, those characters with their names underlined
existed, otherwise the character is an author's creation.

Army of Italy
(Napoleonic ranks in brackets)

Bonaparte   Commander of the Army of Italy
(général de division). Future Napoleon I,
Emperor of France.

Berthier   General Bonaparte's chief of staff. Future
Marshal of France under Emperor Napoleon.

Murat   Bonaparte's senior aide. Future Marshal
of the Empire and King of Naples under
Emperor Napoleon.

Clemusat   A senior officer from the 24th Chasseurs
who becomes an aide on General
Bonaparte's headquarters.

Bessières   Commander of Bonaparte's mounted Guides.
Future commander of the Imperial Guard.

Augereau,   Divisional commanders within
Laharpe   the Army of Italy.
and **Sérurier**

Masséna   Divisional commander (général de division)
within the Army of Italy. Future Marshal of
France under Emperor Napoleon.

Raive	A staff officer on General Masséna's headquarters.

The 24th Regiment of Chasseurs à Cheval
(Napoleonic ranks in brackets)

Spiccard	Commanding officer (chef de brigade).
Fergnes	Lieutenant colonel (major), second-in-command.
Huin	Lieutenant, regimental aide de camp.
André Jobert	One of two chiefs of squadron (chef d'escadron) assisting the regimental commander of the 24th Chasseurs.
Koschak	Jobert's squadron sergeant major (adjutant major).
Moench	Jobert's trumpeter.
Orlande	Jobert's valet.
Tulloc	Jobert's groom and marksman.
Geourdai	Captain, commander of 1st Company, 1st Squadron.
Neilage	Captain, commander of 4th Company, 1st Squadron.

2nd Squadron, 24th Chasseurs à Cheval
(Napoleonic ranks in brackets)

Chabenac	Captain, commander of 2nd Company, 2nd Squadron.
Peugeot and Bredieux	Second-lieutenant (sous lieutenant) troop commanders in 2nd Company.
Voreille	Captain, commander of 5th Company, 2nd Squadron.
Yinot	Second-lieutenant troop commander in 5th Company. Promoted to lieutenant aide de camp.
Duval and Durand	Chasseurs within 2nd Squadron.
Madame Quandalle	Cantiniere of 2nd Squadron.

Others

Didier Jobert -Chauvel	Jobert's brother. Chief of squadron in the 1st Hussars.
Yann Chauvel	Jobert's uncle. Ex-sergeant-veterinarian. Manages the family farm in the high country of the Auvergne.
Michelle Chauvel	Jobert's cousin, daughter of Yann. Seamstress. Lives in Paris with her great aunt Sophie, Madame de Chabenac and Valmai de Chabenac, mother and sister of Captain Chabenac.

Marguerite and Camille   Marguerite is the wife of Fergnes. Camille, Marguerite's cousin and companion, has a relationship with Geourdai.

Inoubli   A pair of identical twins revealed to be Austrian spies, now turned to work for the French Republic.

Anissa   An Avignon prostitute who had previously worked with the spy Inoubli.

Valentin and Wolff von Maefeld   Austrian hussar officers linked to Jobert's past.

The Jobert Series

www.ingramcontent.com/pod-product-compliance
Lightning Source LLC
Chambersburg PA
CBHW030403030726
47497CB00002B/458